DIANE JEFFREY is a *USA Today* bestselling author. She grew up in North Devon, in the United Kingdom. She now lives in Lyon, France, with her husband and their three children, Labrador and cat. *The Other Couple* is her sixth book.

Diane is an English teacher. When she's not working or writing, she likes swimming, running and reading. She loves chocolate, beer and holidays. Above all, she enjoys spending time with her family and friends.

Readers can follow Diane on Twitter, Instagram, or on Facebook and find out more about her books on her website.

Also by Diane Jeffrey

Those Who Lie
He Will Find You
The Guilty Mother
The Silent Friend
The Couple at Causeway Cottage

The Other Couple

DIANE JEFFREY

ONE PLACE. MANY STORIES

HQ
An imprint of HarperCollins*Publishers* Ltd
1 London Bridge Street
London SE1 9GF

www.harpercollins.co.uk

HarperCollins*Publishers*
Macken House, 39/40 Mayor Street Upper,
Dublin 1 D01 C9W8

This paperback edition 2023

2

First published in Great Britain by
HQ, an imprint of HarperCollins*Publishers* Ltd 2023

ISBN: 9780008547974

MIX
Paper | Supporting
responsible forestry
FSC
www.fsc.org   FSC™ C007454

This book is produced from independently certified FSC™ paper
to ensure responsible forest management.

For more information visit: www.harpercollins.co.uk/green

Printed and bound in the UK using 100% Renewable Electricity
by CPI Group (UK) Ltd, Croydon, CRO 4YY

For my Number-One Fan, Barry.
This one's for you, Unc, with my love
and gratitude for your support.
xxx

PART ONE

Chapter 1

Kirsten

They have to leave that afternoon, and she's dreading going back to London, back to reality. The long weekend has been incredible – almost three days and three whole nights together, without life getting in the way for once. The perfect break from the hustle and bustle of the Big Smoke; a brief escape to the seaside.

Lazing for a few minutes more between the brushed cotton sheets, she sniffs the salty air as it drifts into the bedroom through the open window, making the curtains billow and whipping up dust motes that eddy in a shaft of sunlight.

She strains to make out the song Nick's singing in the shower, but the running water drowns out the words and melody. Nick sang at the top of his lungs on the drive down, too, streaming Eighties hits from the music app on his phone through the car speakers. He's not much of a singer, but knowing he's happy and that she has contributed to his happiness brings a smile to her face. For a few seconds, she manages to mute the voice in her head that is spewing out pessimistic clichés such as *all good things must come to an end* and *nothing lasts forever*.

She has woken up with her stomach contracting and her throat constricting, unable to shake the impression that they're careering towards some inevitable disaster from which they won't recover. She has no idea where that presentiment has come from and can't quash it, even though she finds it completely irrational. Is it something Nick said? She racks her brains, replays snippets of the previous day's conversations, but she can't think of anything. Is it some subtle change in his body language she has picked up on subconsciously? She dismisses that notion. He has been nothing but loving and they've never been so close.

She wouldn't classify herself as insecure, and yet minutes earlier she clung to Nick like a limpet to a rock. Clingy Kirsten, he'd called her, jokingly, physically extracting himself from her grasp to get out of bed. She's being paranoid, another adjective she wouldn't normally use to describe herself. Their circumstances make it difficult for either of them to have faith in their future. No, she's feeling this way simply because there are only a few hours left before they have to head home. It's the weekend that's coming to an end, not their relationship.

Nick materialises in the doorway, a towel wrapped around his waist, and the sight of him banishes those thoughts from her head. Water drips from his thick salt and pepper hair onto his broad shoulders. He's quite toned. For his age. A cloud of *Gentleman Givenchy* wafts into the room with him. He comes over to the bed and pulls the covers off her naked body. She raises her eyebrows at him suggestively and tries to pull him to her.

'We've spent more than enough time in bed these past couple of days,' he says with a chuckle. 'Get a shower and we can go for one last walk along the beach before lunch.'

Feigning resignation, she gets out of bed. When she comes out of the en-suite bathroom a few minutes later, Nick is sitting on the bed, still enveloped in his towel, talking in a low voice on the phone. He peers up at her, through long eyelashes, and hastily ends the call.

4

'Work,' he says with a tight smile, tossing his mobile onto the bed.

She highly doubts that, even though he is a workaholic, but she knows better than to challenge him. There aren't many taboos between them, but if she probes into this particular aspect of Nick's life, she'd break an unspoken rule.

She gets dressed, painstakingly applies her make-up and blow-dries her long, fine, strawberry blond hair in front of the mirror. During this time, Nick reads the news or emails on his phone, looking up every now and again as if to check on her progress. When she's ready, she assesses her reflection.

'That will have to do,' she says, fishing for a compliment.

'You look perfect. As ever.' Nick always says the right things. 'I love the new hair colour. It looks very natural.'

They pack their bags into the car and take the coastal road around the headland.

Nick stops at the home of the holiday let owners. They'd been flexible about the checkout time, so Nick offered to drop off the keys – it was on their way. Kirsten takes in their small, chocolate-box cottage with its thatched roof and well-tended garden. It's not far from Croyde Bay, but it doesn't have sea views, unlike the one-bed flat they've just vacated a few miles away in Woolacombe.

'Stop scoping out their house,' Nick says, squeezing her knee. 'Anyone would think you want to burgle it.'

'Can't help it. Goes with the job.'

She's an estate agent. That's how she met Nick. She sold him his house. She often appraises other people's houses, mentally calculating how much they're worth and imagining what renovations she'd have done if she lived there. She isn't house-hunting, though. She has lived in her forever home since she was born. A large, spectacular end-of-terrace Edwardian residence in Muswell Hill, a short walk from Alexandra Park. She inherited the property from her father who had inherited it from his parents. She has had it completely renovated and modernised. It's worth an absolute fortune now – at least two million pounds – but she has no

5

intention of ever selling it. She can't see herself living anywhere else. Ever. Kirsten and Nick have often discussed selling his place, eventually, and living together in hers.

Despite the sunny start, it's drizzling now. Nick stays in the car and keeps it running while Kirsten gets out to hand over the keys. A black-haired, petite waif of a woman with a wide, white smile opens the front door before Kirsten knocks. She's wearing a sleeveless T-shirt, revealing a small tattoo on her shoulder. Kirsten inspects it. An ocean wave. Kirsten can't understand how people would deface their bodies by getting inked, however discreet the tat.

'Was everything OK for you, Mrs Taylor? Did you enjoy your stay?' the woman asks as Kirsten hands her the keys.

Kirsten didn't see her on Friday. The woman's husband was the one who met them at the flat to demonstrate how everything worked and give them the keys and the Wi-Fi password. 'Everything was wonderful. Thank you.' Kirsten tries – and fails – to remember the couple's surname. It will probably come to her later, when it's too late.

'Oh, that's good to know.'

There's no porch and Kirsten has to stand around, getting wet, while the woman tells her how much she'd appreciate a good review online. The woman is wearing flip-flops, and although she's elevated by the doorstep, Kirsten towers over her in her heeled boots.

'I'll do that as soon as I get home,' Kirsten assures her. 'No problem.' She has no intention whatsoever of honouring her promise. Leaving a review would be tantamount to leaving a trace. And she can't risk that. Not even if she uses the fake name Nick gave for their booking.

As Nick drives away, Kirsten turns around in the passenger seat to see the woman waving them off from the doorway of her little cottage. There's no way Kirsten could live in a poky house like that. The windows are too small and the trees too tall. There wouldn't be enough natural light inside. And she's a city girl. Always has been. She'd love to stay in North Devon and suspend real life a little longer – prolong the weekend and postpone going back to work – but she wouldn't want to live in the countryside indefinitely. Not even with Nick.

By now, the rain is falling heavily and the wind is getting up, so they jettison Nick's idea of a romantic stroll on the beach. Just as well, really. Kirsten isn't wearing appropriate footwear – she's not short, but Nick's very tall and she'd feel dwarfed next to him without heels or platforms. She would have had to ditch her impractical ankle boots and walk barefoot, and she hates getting sand between her toes. Nick pulls into a car park in Croyde, leaving the engine idling and the windscreen wipers and heating on. From the safety and warmth of his Audi A8, they watch some hardcore surfers catching waves.

Nick suggests an aperitif before lunch. Kirsten is concerned about how much he has been drinking lately, but she goes along with it and they arrive early at The Thatch, where Nick has booked a table for two in the name of – or perhaps, more accurately *under* the name of – Taylor. They'll pay in cash, of course, as they did for the flat. No paper trail. Another unspoken rule between them.

There are hardly any other vehicles in this car park, either. Kirsten wonders if the pub is open yet. But the lights are on inside.

'Nice and quiet,' Nick says. 'That's one advantage of coming here during the off-season.'

Kirsten looks at the clock on the touch-screen display on the dashboard. It's not quite midday, which seems a more plausible explanation for the lack of diners, and she points this out to Nick.

As Kirsten had feared, Nick downs a pint before they order their meals, another pint while they're waiting for their meals and then washes down his scampi and chips with three glasses of wine. She studies him over the top of her glass of sparkling water with ice and lemon. He can hold his drink and doesn't seem inebriated, but he must be well over the limit and it's a long drive back to London.

They've talked about his alcohol intake on a few occasions. It's a subject Kirsten can broach more easily when he's sober. Nick readily

7

admits he drinks too much, but he sees it as a predilection rather than a problem or an addiction. Kirsten's not so sure. Nick says he likes to relax when he's in her company, but she has no way of knowing whether he drinks as much when he's not with her. She's partial to wine herself, which makes her feel hypocritical for suggesting he might have a problem, but she wouldn't normally drink so much so early in the day.

She can hazard a guess at what's driving him to drink – his job is highly stressful – and right now she's worried about him driving after drinking. She wants to bring up both matters and doesn't usually shy away from confrontation, but she's afraid it will ruin the jovial mood and the intimacy between them. She'll see what state he's in when they leave, but she knows from experience that if she says anything, he'll insist he's OK to drive and if she offers to take the wheel, he'll say she's not insured for his car. She suppresses a sigh of defeat.

She orders dessert and coffees to delay their departure as much as possible, not only to allow more time for the alcohol to wear off, but also to grant them a few minutes more together. This is their last meal before heading home.

When they finally leave the pub, Nick retrieves his umbrella from the stand by the door. They stand outside, protected by the eaves of the building, entranced by the sheer force of the rain lashing down. Nick is about to put up the umbrella, but Kirsten loops her hand into his arm and restrains him, stalling for a moment before they make a dash for the car.

They take a wrong turning coming out of the village. Kirsten spots a sign for Putsborough and she's sure that's the wrong direction. Nick punches his home address into the satnav. They'll head for her place first, but his own address is one of the saved destinations. The satnav promptly instructs them to do a U-turn.

8

The dog comes from nowhere as they round a bend. Nick swears; the car brakes squeal. Kirsten is propelled forwards, then thrown backwards, but they're not going fast and the car slides rather than crashes into the hedge – one of those incredibly tall, thick hedges that line the roadsides in Devon, making the lanes appear even narrower.

It's all over in a heartbeat.

'We missed the dog.' Kirsten's sentence comes out with the emphasis on the word 'dog'. It must be the shock talking. They haven't hit the *dog*. Her mind is already trying to eclipse the dull thud of the body hitting the windscreen, the horrific sight of it rolling off the side of the bonnet and dropping onto the tarmac, although she's aware that what they've just witnessed can never be unheard and unseen.

For a split second, neither of them moves. Then they both leap out of the car. Bowing her head as the rain lashes her, Kirsten looks at the dog owner as he lies on the ground, face downwards and immobile. Her hands fly to her mouth, muffling her scream. Nick crouches at the man's side and rolls him over gently. She kneels opposite Nick. Instantly, the legs of her linen trousers are soaked. Taking her cue from Nick, who is pressing his fingers to the man's wrist, she fumbles frantically for a pulse in his neck. She remembers fragments of what she has learnt on first aid training courses, years ago at school and more recently at work. Radial. Carotid. Those words come to her, in this moment, as Nick looks at her and shakes his head.

'Should we try to . . . resuscitate him?' she asks, hearing the quaver in her voice.

She pulls the man's chin down, tilts his head back. There's blood in his mouth. Nick attempts chest compressions while Kirsten tries with hesitant, clumsy hands to clear the airway, but she knows it's a token effort on both their parts.

'I need a towel or a handkerchief or something,' she says. 'I can't blow into his mouth . . . like this.' She doesn't add what she's

9

thinking, that she could end up contaminated or infected. AIDS, Hepatitis B or C, Covid-19. At the same time, it seems selfish not to take the risk. How great is the risk? On the other hand, how high are his chances of pulling through if she tries to resuscitate him? Infinitesimal, in both cases, probably.

Despondent, she sits back on her heels. With the wet sleeves of her cardigan, she swipes ineffectually at the rivulets coursing down her cheeks. She forces herself to look at the dead man. The *victim*. He stares back at her, unblinking, through clear blue eyes, making her shudder. Only then does she realise she knows him. She glances at Nick, searching for a sign of recognition from him, too, but his expression is one of sheer panic. He doesn't seem to have placed him at all. To be fair, the man's nose and lips are bruised from the impact, his mouth and eyes wide open, all of which make him harder to identify. Kirsten closes his eyelids, first one then the other. She shuts his mouth.

'We should call 999,' Nick says, almost inaudibly. His shirt is drenched and has stuck to his torso. 'We need to call an ambulance.'

Have they really killed someone? They weren't going that fast. The collision didn't seem violent. There's no broken glass. And yet this man has no pulse. He's dead. What will happen to them? Kirsten is shivering irrepressibly. Unbidden, an image of Lily flashes before her – wearing her *Frozen* pyjamas, demanding a bedtime story, her white-blond hair spilling out of its plaits at the end of a school day.

'Is there any point?' she asks, unable to meet Nick's eyes. It doesn't sound like her voice. It doesn't sound like *her* – this can't be her own thoughts she's saying out loud.

'What?'

More images spool through Kirsten's mind, one after the other, in rapid succession. Her daughter. Her husband. Her home. Her career. Her *life*. Portraits of what's important to her, the things she has worked so hard to build up. 'Will they be able to save him?' she whispers. 'The paramedics, I mean.'

Nick doesn't answer immediately, but Kirsten can tell from the look he throws her that he has heard her over the rain. She knows he's weighing up their options, as she is. This man has lost his life. Nothing they can do now will do him any good. But they could do themselves a lot of harm. If they fetch their mobiles from the car and dial 999, their lives will change irrevocably. They'll be found out. They'll lose everything.

'Probably not, no,' he says softly. She feels a rush of relief. Nick is on the same wavelength. But then his tone changes and becomes harsh. 'You . . . you should have . . .' Out of the corner of her eye, she sees him pointing an accusatory finger at her.

She turns to him, rounds on him. '*You* are drunk,' she says. 'This is all your fault. If you hadn't been drunk . . .' Her voice trails away.

The silence that ensues is broken by the dog whining. She'd forgotten all about the dog. It looks like a yellow Labrador, but its coat is a golden-red colour, although that might be because it's soggy. It pushes its muzzle into her hand, its nose wet and cold. She strokes its ears, although the gesture doesn't calm her. It doesn't seem to be working for the dog, either.

Nick gets to his feet, a determined air about him. 'Help me get his body off the road, Kirsten,' he says. 'Quickly, before anyone comes along.'

Chapter 2

Kirsten

'Help me, Kirsten,' Nick repeats when she doesn't move. His tone is more forceful this time.

She's still kneeling on the wet ground, the dog beside her. She stands up, bends over at the waist and takes hold of the man's ankles with hands that are shaking – from the shock or the cold or both, she's not sure. Then she lets go and straightens up. Nick has wound his arms around the man's chest and hoisted him to a sitting position.

'We can't do this, Nick.' She sounds unconvincing, even to herself.

'It was your idea,' he growls.

'We have to call an ambulance. And the police.'

'We have too much to lose,' he argues. 'If we do call the police, both of us will lose everything.'

This had been her thinking, just seconds ago, but now she's oscillating. 'Not if I take the blame. I'll say it was me.' Would she get a prison sentence? How long? Nick's a lawyer. He'll know. It was an accident. But driving away would be a crime. A hit-and-run.

Nick seems to consider this. Then he shakes his head. 'Kirsten, we can't save this man now. But we can save ourselves.'

She can tell he's making an effort to speak softly, cajoling her. 'Think of Lily,' he adds. 'You can't do this to her.'

She *is* thinking of Lily. Her daughter, who she once thought of as her Mini-Me, but who at the age of just seven is already very much her own person. Kirsten wants to be a good mother, someone her daughter will grow up to admire, an example, a role model. Someone Little Lil will aspire to become. And yet, here she is, in a place she shouldn't be, with a man she shouldn't be with, contemplating hiding a body. It's surreal.

'This has to stay between you and me, Kirsten. Think of all the hurt we'll cause our loved ones otherwise.' That makes her cringe. 'Come on! Hurry up! Someone could come along at any moment.'

She bends over and picks up the man's legs again. She assumes Nick means for them to roll the body into the ditch at the side of the road, but he leads the way, shuffling backwards, to behind the car. Holding onto the man with one arm and propping him against his legs, Nick opens the boot. Her eyes widen in terror.

They can't remove the body! They have to leave it here. She wants to protest. But nothing comes out.

'Listen, Kirsten, this is the only way,' he says, apparently sensing her alarm. 'No body, no crime. Hurry up!'

They've come away with one small bag each. Nick throws them over the parcel shelf into the back seat. Somehow, they get the man into the boot. Kirsten takes one last glance at him. His left hand is wrapped around his body and she can't help noticing his wedding band. His head is turned to one side, his legs buckled with his knees pointing the other way. He looks so uncomfortable with his body contorted like that. Instinctively she wants to cover him with a blanket, not to conceal him, but to keep him warm.

Nick slams the boot shut on her incongruous thoughts just as a car hares round the bend towards them, skidding to a halt two or three feet from Nick's Audi. An old Volkswagen Polo, second generation. Kirsten's very first car was the same make and model. She's surprised clapped-out heaps of junk like this are still allowed on the road. They must be really harmful for the environment and his brakes are obviously worn out. This car belongs in a museum. Or a scrapyard.

As the driver winds down his window, the dog whines pitifully. Kirsten yanks open the passenger door and pushes the dog into the footwell discreetly, folding in its tail with her foot before closing the door as noiselessly as possible. She's confident the driver didn't notice. Nick was hiding her from his view.

'I nearly drove into the back of your car, mate,' the driver remarks unnecessarily. 'What are you doing, stopped on a bend?' His rhotic pronunciation and drawn-out vowels are unmistakably West Country. A local.

'I'm sorry,' Nick says, not sounding in the least contrite. 'We've had a bit of an accident, swerved to avoid a . . . sheep and ended up in the hedge.'

'You're both drenched.' Another redundant observation.

'We had to change a tyre. I've just put the triangle back in the boot, otherwise you would have had warning before the corner.'

Nick has had to think on his feet. It's a credible lie, delivered so persuasively that Kirsten almost believes it herself. She comes to join Nick. The driver has edged his car forwards, so that it's alongside Nick's Audi. He's leaning out of his window despite the rain, assessing the damage to the car. Is it her imagination or does his inquisitive gaze fix on the boot when Nick mentions putting the triangle away?

'You're not injured?'

'No, no. We're both fine.'

Kirsten's heart stops as she sees a wallet on the road. It must have fallen out of the dog owner's pocket. No, it probably flew out rather than fell out, at the moment of impact.

She thinks she hears the sound of a seatbelt being detached. She hopes the nosy driver isn't going to get out of his car. She takes two steps towards his vehicle and stands on the wallet, scanning the ground for anything else they might have missed. Is there blood on the road? If he notices, can it be explained away? Too much for a nose bleed? But if there was any blood, it appears to have been washed away.

'Your car all right to drive?'

'I think so,' Nick replies. 'There doesn't seem to be much damage. The airbags didn't even inflate.'

'I'll wait and see you off, if you like,' he offers.

'That's very kind of you,' Nick says through gritted teeth.

Kirsten goes down on one knee. She has no laces, so she pretends to do up the zipper on her boots. She doesn't look up to see if the driver is watching her but retrieves the wallet as quickly and inconspicuously as she can, thrusting it into her back pocket as she stands up.

Nick gets in behind the wheel. Avoiding eye contact and any verbal exchange, Kirsten nods her thanks to the driver of the other vehicle.

'Bloody grockles,' she hears him mutter as she turns away.

She walks round to the passenger side of Nick's car. She has to put the seat back to make room for her legs next to the dog. Nick adjusts his seat, too, and his hand is steady as he angles the rear-view mirror. She's anxious to get away, but Nick appears to be taking his time, composing himself, doing all the checks. The words 'stable', 'door' and 'horse' spring to mind, but she bites her tongue as he puts on his seatbelt as if in slow motion.

She holds her breath as Nick pushes the start ignition button, but the car roars to life immediately. When she breathes again, a damp doggy smell pervades her nostrils. The dog puts its head on her knee and looks up at her with doleful, dark eyes. She pats it.

'We'll stop off somewhere and change into some dry clothes,' Nick says as he reverses out of the hedge and finally drives off.

They're still going the wrong way. Nick takes the next two right turnings, following the satnav's directions, to get back on course. Kirsten twists around in her seat, half-expecting the driver to be following, but there's no one behind them.

'Do you think he suspected anything?' she says.

'The driver? No, of course not. If he'd arrived a minute earlier . . .' Nick's voice tails off. 'It doesn't bear thinking about.'

Kirsten feels numb and nauseous. They've killed someone. They're on the point of covering that up. This man has a wife. He might have children. His loved ones will never find out what happened to him. It will torture them for the rest of their lives. As for Nick and her, they'll be running from this – and from their victim's family – for the rest of their lives. Or until the day they're caught.

'What are we going to do with that bloody dog?' Nick asks suddenly.

She whips her head round to look at him. Is he seriously worrying about what to do with the dog when they have its owner in the boot? What are they going to do with his body?

His words from earlier come back to her. *No body, no crime.* Kirsten remembers reading about an English serial killer who had dissolved the bodies of his victims in sulphuric acid, mistakenly assuming he couldn't be convicted of murder in the absence of a corpse. She shudders at her morbid thoughts. As a criminal defence barrister, Nick would know you don't need a body to be convicted of a crime.

'No body, no crime,' Kirsten says aloud. 'What did you mean when you said that?'

'*Corpus delicti*,' Nick says. 'It refers to the body of evidence rather than the physical body of a victim. But without an actual body, it makes it harder to put together a body of evidentiary items to prove a crime has been committed.'

Kirsten is astounded at the detached way Nick explains this, as if he's talking about a general concept instead of the crime they're in the process of committing.

'In a case like this, the police will open a missing persons investigation,' Nick continues. 'But even if they did suspect foul play, the body of evidence would be largely circumstantial.'

She wonders what evidence they have left, both at the scene of the crime and on the body itself. Have they left any of their DNA on his body or in the road? A fingerprint? A hair? Or did the rain wash everything away? There will be fibres from the boot on his clothes now. They'll have to find a way of getting rid of the body that will destroy all that evidence. And are there traces of the dead man on them? Traces of his blood on their clothes? His saliva or skin cells on their hands? They'll need to wash themselves and everything they're wearing. Now she's shocked at herself more than at Nick. She's starting to think like a criminal, the criminal that she is.

She starts to cry again and in seconds she's sobbing uncontrollably. Keeping one hand on the steering wheel, Nick pulls her to him and she cries into his shoulder for a while. He utters some words of comfort, platitudes no doubt, but she can't make out what he says and it wouldn't be soothing anyway. He leans into the back seat to get her jacket, which he wraps around her. He turns up the heating. But she can't stop trembling.

The dog licks her hands and she untangles herself from Nick's embrace. She finds a metal tag on its collar. A mobile number is engraved on one side, the dog's name on the other. Rusty. That's when the name of the dog owner comes to her.

Kirsten doesn't know how much time has passed before Nick stops at a petrol station. It has almost stopped raining. While Nick fills up the car with petrol, she changes into dry clothes in the toilet. As she takes off her trousers, she feels the weight of the wallet in her back pocket and pulls it out. She gets back into the car, still holding the wallet in her hands. While Nick is getting changed, she turns it over and over and finally opens it. She slides a photocard licence out of the wallet. The dead man's face stares back at her. She checks the name and address. There's no mistake. She feels the colour drain from her face and her head spins. She opens the car door, leans over and throws up on the ground.

They're on the M5 before she mentions it to Nick, not that

she has taken the wallet, but that she knows who the man is. Who the *dead* man *was*. She sees Nick's knuckles whiten as he grips the wheel.

'Yes,' he says at length, keeping his eyes on the road. 'I recognised him, too.'

Chapter 3

Amy

A wave of nausea surges inside me and I take a few deep breaths, hoping I won't throw up again. The sickness is worse this morning, aggravated no doubt by last night's celebrations. It was low-key, only my parents-in-law and us, at their house. I didn't drink any alcohol, but we didn't get to bed until gone three and the lack of sleep seems to have taken its toll. The smell wafting from the oven, where a leg of lamb is cooking, isn't helping.

Everything's ready, so I turn down the temperature of the oven, drain the vegetables and wash up the saucepans. I can always heat up the veg in the microwave when Greg gets home – any second now. I'll feel better when I've had something to eat. I cradle my rumbling tummy, gently rubbing my tiny bump, which is just about visible if I arch my back when I'm naked or wearing a tight top.

'You make me so happy and also rather queasy,' I say, looking down at my stomach, 'but you're well worth it.'

I set the table and potter about, wiping down the worktop and wiping up the pans, killing time. But thirty minutes later, Greg's still not home. I try his mobile, but he doesn't answer.

It was spitting when he went out, but the rain is hammering down now. Typical weather for a May bank holiday weekend in North Devon. Maybe Greg has taken shelter somewhere until the worst of the downpour is over. Or, more likely, he has bumped into a friend of ours, stopped to chat and lost track of the time.

Greg's always late. He set the precedent for this on our very first date. He said he'd pick me up at seven and he arrived at eight. I thought he'd stood me up. When we got to the restaurant, the table he'd reserved had been given to another couple. Greg's tardiness is probably the main thing about him that irritates me. Perhaps even the only thing. He doesn't have many flaws.

The lamb will be dried out by the time Greg gets round to carving it. I turn off the oven altogether, take out the lamb and wrap it in tin foil. Then I start to pace the ground floor of the house, from the kitchen to the living room and back. As I'm stomping around, I catch sight of the card on the mantelpiece. Greg gave it to me yesterday – and showered me with gifts, too – for our tenth wedding anniversary. That's what we were celebrating last night, our anniversary. A wedding in the springtime. It just worked out that way. The local vicar, Rob, had a cancellation, and as Rob's a friend of Greg's, he knew Greg had proposed and I'd accepted, so he asked if we wanted to get married on that date. I pick up the card and reread the message inside.

Thank you for the past fifteen years you've spent by my side.
I love you more than ever.
Greg
X

My simmering irritation subsides and my face breaks into a smile in reminiscence.

Fifteen years ago. We met on the beach. Greg was eighteen, a year and a half older than me. He was working as a lifeguard that summer at Croyde Bay before going to university. I had a holiday job selling ice cream from a van parked above the high tide mark at the top of the beach. Greg came by at least twice a day, usually wearing little more than a pair of red swimming trunks, to buy a Mr Whippy. I lost count of the number of ninety-nines I sold him over the course of the next two weeks before he finally plucked up the courage to ask me out. I sometimes joke that I'd known Greg for a fortnight before I saw him with his clothes on – the evening he rocked up at my place an hour late. A fond memory and an anecdote that has been repeated several times over the years.

Because punctuality is not Greg's strong point and I'm used to it, it's an hour before I get really annoyed. I try his mobile again, but there's still no answer. I leave a message this time. A short, snappy one. He said he was just going up the road. Why isn't he back yet?

But my anger is short-lived. Fear jostles its way to the surface instead. What if something has happened to him? He might have had a heart attack or something. He's young and fit, but it happens, doesn't it? Or perhaps he's been involved in an accident.

I consider phoning my parents-in-law. They live about a mile away, in the neighbouring village, Georgeham. Maybe Greg popped in to help them clear up after last night's dinner. But I don't want to alarm them. They've already lost one son – Greg's older brother – five years ago now. It has made them ultra-protective of Greg and me, and more than a little paranoid about our well-being and safety. Plus, they were so excited when we announced we were having a baby. I'd only burst their bubble if I rang them.

I ring everyone else I can think of, though – most of our surfing mates who live locally – probably interrupting them as they eat lunch with their families. No one has seen Greg today. Between them, they propose a number of hypotheses, none of which are particularly helpful. Matt: Perhaps he went for a swift pint down the pub. Sharky: Surf's up! Maybe he couldn't resist. Tom: Could he have gone into work for a bit, do you think?

By the time I ring Liz, my best friend and colleague, I'm almost in tears.

21

'What was he doing out in this weather?' she asks. It sounds as if she's talking with her mouth full. She's certainly got her hands full – I can hear at least two of her four kids screaming in the background.

'He took the dog out for a pee—' I glance at the clock on the living room wall. I've never noticed before how loudly it ticks. '—an hour and a half ago.'

'Oh.' Pragmatic as ever, Liz comes up with a plausible suggestion. 'Didn't Greg have a dodgy knee?' she says. 'Complaints like that are always worse in wet weather. He might be limping home as we speak.'

'Yeah, but that doesn't explain why he isn't answering his phone.'

'His mobile might be on silent mode in the house somewhere,' Liz says. 'Would he take it with him if he was walking the dog?'

'I'll drive around and see if I can find him,' I say, grabbing hold of her theory as if I'm drowning and someone has thrown me a lifeline. He's gone out, without his phone, and his knee has given way. That must be it!

I turn down Liz's offer to come with me and leave her to her family. I know she'll call or text me later to check Greg has turned up. Before setting off, I have a quick look round for Greg's mobile. I check the usual places – on the bedside table, on the arm of the sofa, down the back of the sofa, next to the Bluetooth speaker. But I'm wasting time. I need to get going. Greg could be in pain. He'll be drenched. And hungry. I check I've got my own mobile, pull on a sweater over my T-shirt, push my feet into my trainers and grab my car keys.

I drive around for a while, scanning fields and lanes leading off from the road I'm on. The rain has eased to a light drizzle, but the visibility is poor and I wish I'd thought to bring binoculars. But I don't need them. There's no one on the beach, no Greg or anyone else. There aren't even many cars.

In the end, I head for Georgeham and pull into the driveway of my parents-in-law's house. Pam, my mother-in-law, bundles me into the house out of the damp before I can tell her why I've come. It smells of food in the hallway, but I can see into the dining room and the table has already been cleared. They've finished eating. It's way past lunchtime now. My father-in-law joins us.

I don't know how to break it to them gently, so I just come out and say it. 'Have you seen Greg at all today?'

'No, no. I haven't. Well, not since you both left early this morning after our little party. At about three, wasn't it? Hugh, what about you?'

My father-in-law shakes his head. 'Was he coming over to see us?'

'No. He took Rusty out for a quick walk before lunch. That must have been at a quarter to twelve.' I can see the worry etched on their faces and it's an effort to keep the panic out of my own voice. 'He hasn't come back. Yet.' The last word sounds like an afterthought and I wince.

Hugh looks at his watch. 'It's half past two now,' he says. 'How long have you been out looking for him?'

'Quite a while,' I say. 'He's probably home by now and we've crossed paths.'

Pam and Hugh both nod in unison, but they're probably thinking what I'm thinking. Greg would have called me if he'd got home and I wasn't there. He could have used the landline if he'd lost his mobile while he was out.

'I'll head home now,' I say.

'You'll let us know, Amy, won't you?' Pam says.

Before I back out of their drive, I check my mobile. But I've got the volume right up and I haven't missed any calls or text messages.

My ringtone blares out from my jeans pocket as I'm opening my front door. Finally! I nearly drop the phone in my haste to answer it. But it turns out to be Pam.

'Are you home? Is Greg there?'

'No, he's not back. No sign of him or the dog,' I say. 'I wonder if I should call the police.'

I don't realise I've voiced my thoughts aloud until Pam says,

23

'Don't you have to wait for twenty-four hours before you can report someone missing? An adult, I mean?'

Missing. Is Greg a missing person?

'No, I think that's a common misconception, Pam,' I say. I don't add that I doubt the police will take me seriously if I report my husband missing when he's only been gone for about three hours. It has seemed a long time to me, but it sounds short. 'Perhaps I'll just ring the police station and ask if they know of any . . . incident around Croyde that might explain why Greg has . . . been out for so long. Maybe he went to help someone in trouble in the water.'

'Good idea,' Pam says. 'Hugh and I are on our way. We'll stay with you until we find out where Greg has got to.'

I google the police station in Braunton, five miles away, but fail to find the number. It's our local police station, but it has suffered such drastic cuts in recent years that there's only a handful of officers providing a minimal police presence. Perhaps I should call the station in Barnstaple instead, but that's ten miles away. I'm hopeful Greg's absence will turn out to be due to some minor incident, so I'm reluctant to dial 999. In the end, I punch in 101 for a non-emergency and press call.

'Hello. My name is Amy Wood. I live in Croyde. Er . . . I'm ringing because my husband has gone . . . well, he's missing,' I say.

'OK, Amy.' A pleasant female voice. 'When was the last time you saw him?'

'Earlier today,' I say. 'About three and a half hours ago.' It doesn't sound long and I feel faintly ridiculous. I hope this turns out to be a false alarm, though.

'OK. Can you start by telling me your husband's name, please?'

'His name is Gregory Wood,' I say.

Chapter 4

Kirsten

'His name was Gregory Wood,' Kirsten says, putting the dead man's driving licence back into his wallet.

Mr and Mrs Wood. The owners of the holiday rental they'd stayed in. Kirsten pictures his wife standing on the doorstep of their thatched cottage a few hours ago – short, slim, dark hair scraped into a knot, ocean wave tattoo on her shoulder. She closes her eyes to shut out the woman's image, but it's as if it has been branded on the insides of Kirsten's eyelids. She can't blink her away. Kirsten couldn't remember the woman's surname earlier when she was talking to her, but now it reverberates through her head.

'What is that? His wallet? You have to get rid of that, Kirsten.' Nick's voice is authoritative, a tone she hasn't heard before that she imagines he uses in court.

She locks eyes with him, briefly, before his concentration turns back to the road. Studying him, she takes in the determined set of his jaw and the almost imperceptible vein pulsing in his temple. The lips that kissed her hungrily this morning are now pursed together. She knows every inch of his body, from the tuft of hair that stubbornly sticks out, no matter how much gel he uses, right down to the scar on his ticklish feet from where he cut himself on broken glass as a child. She can usually interpret his body language and work out what he's thinking. His thoughts are often synced with her own. She can tell he's rattled by what has happened, but he's lost in his reflections, lost to her, and for once she has no idea what's going through his mind. He's no longer simply her partner; he has become her partner in crime.

She suddenly finds him unfamiliar, a stranger sitting next to her and it unsettles her. Or does it seem that way because they're plunging into icy, uncharted waters?

'Promise me you'll dispose of that wallet,' he repeats when she doesn't respond.

Dispose.

'I promise,' she says solemnly. She intends to keep it – the wallet, that is, not the promise – although she's not sure why she wants to. She'll hide it somewhere safe so that no one will ever stumble across it. 'How are we going to dispose of the body?' It sounds even worse when she uses that word. You dispose of waste. Or an asset. There should be a more euphemistic word for disposing of someone's remains.

Various scenarios shoot through her mind, all of them gruesome. Should they dissolve the body in sulphuric acid like that serial killer did to his victims' corpses? Burn it? Bury it in woodland somewhere?

'Leave that to me,' Nick says. 'I know people.'

Of course he does. Nick has often boasted that many of his clients have literally got away with murder thanks to him. There must be people who owe him, from whom he can call in a favour. She's better off not knowing what they do with Gregory Wood's body. Nick will take care of it. She relaxes slightly.

'Listen, Kirsten, it might be a good idea if we don't see each other for a while,' Nick says without looking at her. 'No contact at all, in fact.'

26

Her heart clenches and she tenses up again. She wants this to bring them closer together, somehow, not push them apart. Surely, they are inextricably linked to each other now, bound together with strangulating ties like garrottes. Kirsten doesn't like to admit it to herself and certainly isn't going to admit it to Nick, but she needs him. She won't be able to keep up the pretence or cope with the enormity of it all without him.

'No. Don't do that,' she implores. She must sound pathetic and desperate to Nick.

'Don't worry. Just until it all blows over,' he says. 'It'll probably be in the news, at least locally, in Devon. We should wait until we're absolutely sure they've got nothing on us before we risk being seen together again, even by people who don't know us.'

'What could they possibly have on us?'

'I don't know. Probably nothing. But let's make sure it stays that way. I'll have to sort out a couple of things. First and foremost, the body, and, after that, the bodywork on my Audi. It's dented at the front and it needs a new bumper.'

She's shocked that Nick can enumerate in the same breath 'body' and 'bodywork' on the to-do list he has compiled mentally. But she nods. 'What do you want me to do?'

'Nothing. Carry on as if none of this ever happened. Act normal. Oh, and Kirsten? One more thing.'

'What?'

'Take that bloody dog to the pound.'

They don't talk for the rest of the journey. Nick drives too fast and Kirsten worries he'll get flashed by a speed camera. But she doesn't ask him to slow down. She has an overriding urge to get as far away and as fast away as possible from the scene of the accident.

The scene of the *crime*.

Nick must feel the same as she does. It's as if they're on the run. Fugitives. She remembers this morning not wanting their weekend to end. Now she can't wait for it to be over. She's anxious to get home.

Finally, Nick drops her off at the end of her road. She walks briskly to the front gate of her house, the dog at her heels. The lights are on in the living room and the curtains are drawn. The porch light comes on automatically as she walks up the short driveway. Everything is as it should be, but for a few seconds, Kirsten gets the uncanny sensation she isn't at the right house. She has lived here nearly her whole life, and yet it no longer seems like home.

It's not the house that is outlandish. It's Kirsten herself. As she opens the front door and steps into her home, she feels as if she has dragged her body into someone else's life. Wincing at the image her clumsy choice of words has conjured up, she drops her duffle bag and handbag in the hall. The dog sits and waits while she takes off her boots and hangs up her jacket.

She peeps through the open door of the living room. Jamie is watching the television, Lily's blond head on his lap. He puts his finger to his lips. As she hovers on the threshold, she feels strangely disembodied, as if she's watching herself from above.

'Lily waited up, but she fell asleep,' he whispers. 'Was it ghastly?'

She flinches, then realises he's referring to the cover story she spun him about a conference and exhibition weekend in Cardiff. She nods, not trusting herself to answer.

'Are you hungry?'

She shakes her head. She has the impression she's on stage, playing a part, but she isn't quite in character and she has forgotten her lines. 'No.' It comes out hoarse and she clears her throat. 'Big lunch.'

Jamie laughs and Kirsten can't imagine what's so funny, but he points at the dog, sitting by her side in the doorway.

'My colleague, Sarah, took ill while we were in Wales.' Her words flow more fluidly now she's telling a lie. 'I offered to look after her dog for a few days.'

'Lily will love that!'

'That's why I'm so late. I had to go and fetch it. On the Tube.' Kirsten isn't sure if the TfL network is dog-friendly, but she has seen pets in underground trains. She hopes she won't be caught

28

in a lie. She was supposed to have taken the train to London and then the Tube home.

'I hope she'll be OK.'

'I think it's a he, actually.'

'I meant your colleague. Didn't you say Sarah?'

'Oh. Yes.'

Lily is roused by their voices. 'Mummy!' she calls, her voice thick with sleep, stretching her arms out towards Kirsten.

'Ah. Speak of the devil,' Jamie says good-humouredly.

'Hello, Little Lil,' Kirsten says. She tries to affix a smile to her face, but she thinks it must look more like a rictus. 'Have you been a good girl for Daddy?'

Accompanied by the dog, she walks over to her family, gives Jamie a perfunctory peck on the lips and kneels beside the sofa to hug Lily, burying her face in her daughter's hair. She's transported back to the moment when she knelt on the wet ground beside Gregory Wood's lifeless body. She shudders and holds Lily more tightly.

'A dog! A doggie!'

Kirsten repeats her lie for the benefit of her daughter, who leans around Kirsten to stroke the dog.

'Is it a boy or a girl?'

'A boy.'

'What's his name?'

What was his name again? She read it on the metal tag on his collar. Rusty. That's it. 'Rusty,' she says. Lily pulls away from her mother and flings her arms around the dog.

'Can we keep him?'

When she doesn't answer, Jamie steps in. 'Your mum's just looking after him for a while. You can help her.'

'Come on. Let's put you to bed,' Kirsten says.

'Ooohhh.' Lily pouts. Kirsten seems to disappoint her daughter a lot.

'You can play with the dog when you get home from school tomorrow.' Kirsten scoops up the seven-year-old. 'Wow, you're getting heavy.' Kirsten's own voice sounds foreign to her, but Lily doesn't seem to notice. Putting her thumb in her mouth, she rests her head on her mother's shoulder as Kirsten carries her upstairs.

It's an effort to go through the motions. Tucking her daughter in, kissing her and Teddy goodnight. Act normal, that's what Nick said she had to do. Kirsten tells herself she can do this. She says it over and over in her head like a mantra. *You can do this. You can do this.* She has to do this. For Lily's sake as well as for her own.

Hi,

I've written to you several times, but so far I've scrunched up and thrown out every attempt. It's important to me to get the wording right, even though I know you'll never read this letter – I probably wouldn't send it, even if I thought you would.

As you can see, I'm writing to you from His Majesty's Prison Sevenhams Park. It's a newish prison, a modern one. It comprises both a Category-A men's unit and a top-security female unit for restricted-status prisoners, although, obviously, the two sections are kept separate.

My first hearing took place last week at the Magistrates' Court. It was over so quickly – in just a few minutes – it hardly seemed worthwhile making me attend. My case has been sent to the Crown Court as I'm accused of committing an indictable-only offence, or, as my solicitor explained to me in layman's terms (as if I didn't already know!), a serious crime for which I'll be tried by a jury. My solicitor has warned me there's no chance of me being released on bail. After my hearing, I was brought here, to HMP Sevenhams Park, in a prison van, and I'll be held here on remand pending trial.

I intend to plead not guilty. I told my solicitor I'm innocent, but I could tell from her expression that she didn't believe me. I'm glad she won't be the one defending me in court because if she doesn't believe me, how could she convince twelve jurors to believe her?

You would believe me. You're the only person who knows the whole truth. You were there when the crime was committed.

Chapter 5

Amy

By the time I hear the tyres of the police car crunching outside on the driveway, Greg has been missing for almost five hours. I open the front door as the two uniformed officers are getting out of the car. It has taken them a long time to get here, although I did call 101 instead of 999, I suppose. They must have come out from Barnstaple. Pam is glued to my side as they walk towards us.

'I'm Sergeant Lucy Harris,' says a sinewy woman with an uneven fringe cut into her mousy hair and a dour expression pasted onto her face. She looks to be in her mid-thirties, maybe four or five years older than me. She holds out her hand, first to me, then to my mother-in-law, then uses it to gesture at her colleague, a younger, rotund man.

'I'm Constable Owen Wright,' he says, taking his cue. He lifts his arms to take off his peaked cap, a gesture that puts his shirt buttons under considerable strain and reveals small patches of sweat under his armpits.

Moments later, we're all sitting in the living room. I'm sandwiched between my parents-in-law on the sofa. The officers have taken the armchairs. Pam has made mugs of tea for everyone, but I feel too sick to drink any of mine.

Constable Wright starts by asking me much the same questions as the woman I spoke to on the phone when I rang the police station: *What's your husband's full name? What's his date of birth? At what time did he go out?* Neither officer seems perturbed by how long Greg has been gone, which reassures me and angers me at the same time.

Wright then asks me about Greg's favourite haunts and his friends. I tell him I've rung his close friends who live locally. The constable nods and jots down notes with a Biro as I give my answers. This strikes me as outdated. I would have thought police officers used tablets, electronic notebooks or their smartphones nowadays, not that I've had any experience with the police. I tell Constable Wright I've rung Greg several times and have no idea if he has his mobile on him or not. I ask if they can trace his phone and find him that way.

'It's feasible,' he says. 'If it comes to that.'

I want to ask what he means by that, but before I can do so, the constable turns to my mother-in-law. 'What about relatives other than you and your husband? Does Gregory have any other family members who live around here?'

I feel Pam stiffen next to me and know she's thinking of her older son, Greg's brother. She was the one who found him, dead, in his home in Braunton. 'No,' she says.

Sergeant Harris clears her throat to signal she will take over. She has a bored expression, as if this is beneath her or an inconvenience to her. Maybe there was no one else available on a bank holiday Monday. I'm a little surprised at someone of her rank coming out for a man who has been missing for only a few hours. I would have expected two PCs. But, again, I don't know anything about policing. Harris looks familiar, but I can't place her. She has prominent cheekbones and a long, thin nose. She keeps her beady, brown eyes trained on me while she talks. Her penetrating gaze unnerves me, but her tone is kind, at odds with her sharp features.

33

'Mrs Wood – can I call you Amy?' She doesn't wait for an answer. 'Amy, can you think of any reason why your husband might have wanted to have some time to himself?'

I frown. 'No.'

'Why would he want time to himself?' Hugh's voice is unusually brusque. I can tell he's worried.

'Well, maybe he needed to blow off steam or think something over,' Harris suggests gently.

'We didn't have an argument, if that's what you mean,' I say. My mouth feels dry and I go to pick up my mug of tea from the coffee table to take a few sips after all, but then realise my hands are shaking. I clasp them together on my lap. Wright's concentrating on his notebook. I hope Harris hasn't noticed, either. I'm in my own home, but I feel ill at ease and self-conscious. I wonder what the officers think of me. I'm anxious not to appear guilty. Of what, I don't know.

Pam takes my hand and squeezes it. She says to me, 'Do you think Gregory was having difficulty digesting . . .?' She breaks off.

Harris turns from me to Pam. 'What were you going to say, Mrs Wood? What do you think your son was having difficulty with?'

Pam pulls an apologetic face at me. 'My daughter-in-law is pregnant,' she says. 'They found out not long ago. I wondered if . . . perhaps . . .'

She doesn't need to finish her sentence this time. Everyone has understood the implication. Greg has freaked out at the news he's going to be a father and run away. Now Pam has provided the police officers with a plausible reason for why Greg might have taken off, they won't take his disappearance seriously. An expression of mild irritation creeps across my face, but I quickly hide it. The constable is furiously scribbling notes.

'Oh, now, Pam. Gregory was over the moon when he told us the news last night,' Hugh says at the same time as Sergeant Harris asks me a question. I have to ask her to repeat it.

'Does Greg have any medical conditions?'

34

'No. He's in good health,' I say. Greg doesn't smoke; he does a lot of sport. He hardly ever goes to the doctor's. I don't mention his knee injury.

Harris and Wright then take it in turns to ask me questions, a quickfire round. My head rotates from one to the other as if I'm watching a tennis match. Greg's social media accounts, his frame of mind, his personality, our marriage, all sorts of questions.

Finally, Harris says, 'OK. I'll need a recent photo.'

'I took some last night,' Hugh offers.

He brings them up on his mobile and the sergeant gets up and goes to inspect them. She selects a couple of pictures that she asks my father-in-law to send to her by email and hands him a business card. I'm still trying to work out if I know her from somewhere.

'I think we've covered nearly everything,' Sergeant Harris says.

'One last thing.' Constable Wright gets to his feet. I'd almost forgotten he was here. 'Would you mind if we had a look round before we go?'

'The house?' I assume they want to look for Greg's phone. 'No. Go ahead.'

'Most people who go missing return of their own accord or are found within forty-eight hours,' Harris says. 'More likely than not, Greg will show up before tomorrow, but if not, Amy, would you come to the station and give a statement?'

'Yes.'

'That reminds me, speaking of statements. Can you access Gregory's bank statements online?'

'Yes. We have only joint accounts. Apart from his business one, which I also have access to.'

'In that case, while we're having a look round, it would be helpful if you could check them for any unusual transactions.'

'I'm sorry,' Pam whispers to me as soon as they've left the room. 'I've made them think Greg has just wandered off, haven't I?'

Pam means well. Right now, her only concern is to find her son alive and well. 'Don't worry about it,' I say. 'If that does turn

35

out to be the reason he's disappeared, we'll all be relieved when he comes home.'

'That Harris woman, she went to the same school as Greg,' Pam says.

Did she insist on coming because she knew Greg? Is that how I know her? But surely she's a little older than Greg.

As if reading my thoughts, Pam adds, 'She was in the same year at school as William. She came out when we found William . . .'

Now I've got it. 'She came out to see us, too,' I say. Not in a professional capacity. She simply wanted to offer her condolences. Remembering her kindness, I warm to her a little.

I can hear Harris and Wright, traipsing about upstairs in their heavy boots while I open the banking app on my phone and scroll through the latest transactions. Our balance is low. Almost in the red. Money is tight at the moment. Greg owns a shop in the village that sells surf clothes, wetsuits and surfing accessories. His business suffered during the pandemic. I hope the police don't find that out. Like Pam, I'm convinced they think Greg has deliberately gone AWOL. I don't want to give them more information that they can twist to support their theory.

There's nothing unexpected in our bank statements. No sudden withdrawals or transfers. I tell Sergeant Harris this when she comes back downstairs, hoping she won't ask me to print out our statements.

But she seems to have her mind set on a different approach. She stands over me, waving a bottle of prescription tablets in my face. 'Can you tell me what this is for?' she says.

'I have no idea.' I take the bottle from her hands and examine it. It's in Greg's name. He hasn't taken many of the pills, by the look of it. Then I register the date on the label. This was prescribed five years ago. Sergeant Harris must have found it at the back of our medicine cupboard in the bathroom. I lower my voice, although my parents-in-law will still hear me. 'Greg struggled a little after his brother, Will, committed suicide. He was prescribed a course of antidepressants by his GP.' Out of the corner of my eye, I see Pam's hand covering her mouth. 'He didn't take many of the tablets in the end, as you can see. He wanted to get through it without medication.'

'Would you say your husband has a history of depression, Mrs Wood?' Constable Wright interjects.

'No. Definitely not.'

'Because sometimes it runs in the family.'

Pam gasps at his brutal tactlessness. I catch the look Sergeant Harris throws him, but the constable doesn't. Hugh leaps to his feet and walks round to Pam's side of the sofa. He sits on the armrest and puts his arm around his wife's shoulder.

Whirling round to face the constable, he says, 'I don't know what you're suggesting, but—'

'Mr Wood, we're examining every possible angle to find clues pertaining to your son's whereabouts. It could be that Gregory is not missing to himself. Only to those he left behind.' My father-in-law's eyes widen. 'In the case of men in their thirties, forties and fifties, they often intentionally disappear due to marital breakdown, mental health issues or financial problems,' the constable continues.

Sergeant Harris edges towards Wright and places her hand on his arm.

'You're barking up the wrong tree, Constable,' Hugh spits.

Barking. The word spurs me to change the subject. 'The dog hasn't come back,' I remind them. 'He's a fox-red Labrador called Rusty.'

Constable Wright nods pensively, but he doesn't share what he's thinking this time.

'Fox-red?' Harris queries.

'Yes. A yellow Lab, really, but with a coat that's a deeper red.'

'Would you say it's a rare breed?'

'They're becoming more popular, but there are far fewer fox-red Labs than black, yellow or chocolate, that's for sure.'

'That might be helpful. Anyone who saw Greg walking the dog is more likely to remember an unusual dog.'

Sergeant Harris is talking about potential witnesses. I feel a surge

37

of hope, but then my heart sinks. It was raining earlier, although it has stopped now. There won't have been many people out walking in that weather and I feel certain there won't have been much traffic on a rainy bank holiday Monday, especially around lunchtime. Plus, Rusty's fur would have been damp, making him less distinctive.

My phone pings with a text notification, causing another spike of false hope. It's Liz, asking if Greg has turned up yet. I put my mobile back in my pocket. I'll get back to her later.

Thankfully, Harris and Wright seem to have finished with us for now. I can't wait to see the back of the pair of them. I feel as if I've been interrogated. I walk them to the door.

Sergeant Harris stops in the hall. 'Does Greg have a computer in the house?' she asks.

'No,' I say. 'The only laptop here is mine. I use it for work. I'm a primary school teacher.' I'm going into way too much detail. I shut up before I can add that Greg has a computer in the little office at the back of his shop and that he often uses my laptop when he's at home. I have nothing to hide and neither does Greg, but that's the point. They'll be wasting their time looking through snippets of irrelevant information instead of getting out there and looking for my husband, or at least looking for clues that will reveal what has happened to him.

But later that evening when my parents-in-law have also left, I boot up my laptop and check the browser history. Just in case. It hasn't been deleted recently and I'm the one who has visited most of the web pages that come up. There's nothing here that can lead me to Greg.

I close the lid of my laptop and fetch my phone to send a text to Liz. I type out a message, telling her Greg hasn't come home yet and I'm not up to coming into school tomorrow. I decide to ring Greg again. I don't expect him to answer. I just want to hear his voice on the recorded message greeting.

I'm about to tap on the call icon when something on the screen catches my eye. I hardly dare to breathe, let alone hope, even as I promise aloud, 'I will find you, Greg.'

Chapter 6

Amy

For a moment, I stare at the screen of my phone, my finger hovering over the icon. *Find My.* We share our locations with each other, both on our phones and on my laptop, so that if one of us ever loses our mobile, we'll have a chance of finding it, or if it's stolen, so we can erase the data from a distance, which might save us having to change all our passwords and cancel our bank cards. We've never used it and until now I'd forgotten all about it.

When Greg set up the tracking app on our devices, I joked about it because he's always losing his phone and we invariably find it behind a cushion on the sofa or next to the bathroom washbasin or in one of his pockets or something. We don't need a tracking app to locate it and I doubt the application is that precise, anyway. I imagine it gives an approximate location – an area or a street. Maybe you can narrow it down to a particular house, but certainly not a room in that house.

My heart pounds, in my ribcage and my ears. I try not to build up hope in case it turns out to be false hope again. If Greg's mobile is switched off or if it's out of juice, I don't know if this will work.

If Greg is somewhere where there's no signal, I won't be able to find him. That seems like an awful lot of ifs. With trembling hands and without much conviction, I open the *Find My* icon. I tap on devices, then on Greg's phone. A map comes up. My eyes widen in disbelief. Less than a mile away! He must be on his way home! Adrenaline courses through me, but I mustn't get carried away. This doesn't mean Greg is nearby, only his phone.

The rain has started up again with a vengeance, coming down sideways in the wind and battering the windowpanes. Daylight is fading fast. I pull on a waterproof jacket and before setting off, I fetch a torch from the garage. It will give out much more light than the flashlight on my mobile. It feels strange to be out late in the evening without Rusty. As I bring up the directions on my mobile, I try ineffectually to protect the screen from the rain.

I soon realise where Greg was going earlier. It's one of the shorter walks we take Rusty on when the weather is bad or when we're busy. After half a mile or so of walking along the narrow main road we can let the dog off the lead along the South West Coast Path and follow it towards the headland. But judging from the map, Greg didn't make it as far as the footpath. Either that or he was on his way back and almost home when something stopped him.

Pulling my hood low over my forehead and hunching into the wind, I set off. As I approach the point shown on the map, I check my phone, trying to shield it from the rain. *Oh, no!* A moan escapes my lips and is drowned out by the wind. I've lost the connection. The 4G coverage around here is notoriously sketchy, the 5G coverage practically non-existent, and the weather can't be helping. I walk a few steps further. Still nothing. I must be almost at the spot Greg's phone should be when one bar tentatively appears on my phone.

It's dark now and there's no one else around. A tiny sliver of moonlight peeping through the clouds projects a huge shadow of me on the ground. It's quite creepy, but I'm not scared. At least, not for myself. My only fear is for Greg.

Greg's mobile isn't a particularly recent model, but it is water-resistant with a battery that lasts several hours, even days. It must be switched on because it didn't go straight to voicemail when I phoned him earlier. And it must be working, despite the rain, because its location has come up on this app. I call him again but if his phone rings, I don't hear it. The battery on my own mobile is low and I wish I'd charged it up. I pace several feet up and down the road, around the bend and back again, using the torch to check the ground.

I don't know how many minutes go by before something glitters in the light of my torch. It's at the side of the road in the long grass. I bend to examine it, my heart plummeting when I see it's not the mobile. It's a piece of orangey-yellow plastic. It looks like it's from a bicycle reflector. A blend of disappointment and frustration surges inside me as I pluck it out of the grass. I throw it down on the road and stamp on it, shattering the small fragment of plastic into even smaller fragments. But the gesture doesn't make me feel any better.

In the end, I have to admit defeat. I have little chance of finding Greg's mobile in these conditions. I decide to go home. Maybe Greg wasn't walking along the road at all. Perhaps he was in the fields behind the hedge and that's where his phone is. It seems unlikely – the fields belong to farmers and landowners and the public footpath is further up the road, but it's possible.

I'll come back first thing tomorrow morning, at daybreak, before going to the police station to make my statement. Even if Greg's phone battery is dead by then, I know it's around here somewhere. I'll comb every inch of this place until I locate it, although I no longer hold out hope that finding Greg's mobile will help me find Greg himself.

I'm about to put my own phone into my pocket out of the rain when I spot an option on the app. *Play sound*. I tried ringing Greg a few minutes ago and that didn't work, but this might make his phone emit a loud alert even if it's on silent mode. My battery is down to five per cent, but I tap on the option on the screen to give it a go.

It's barely audible above the roaring of the wind through the trees and the smacking of the rain on the tarmac. At first, I think I'm hearing things, but there's definitely a chiming sound. It's close to me. Very close. Then I see a light. Not from the moon or my torch. From the smashed screen of a phone lying in the ditch at the roadside. I scramble into the ditch and grab Greg's mobile, which I clasp to my chest.

The next morning, I arrive at the police station in Barnstaple a few minutes before opening time at nine o'clock. Last time I came – years ago, having lost my purse somewhere in Green Lanes shopping centre – the station was still in North Walk. I know from the local news that it had to be urgently relocated because of a deteriorating roof. The new, temporary station is housed in what used to be Barum Autoparts on the Seven Brethren estate. The building looks a bit like a warehouse, but it beats the dump in North Walk.

I wait impatiently for the doors to open and then wait again while the officer at the front desk informs Constable Wright that I've arrived. Inside, the station is spacious and clean. It smells of fresh paint. Wright takes his time coming to get me. I hear his footsteps before I see him. As I stand up, I get a whiff of his cologne. It fails to mask an underlying smell of sweat. The mixture of paint and perspiration makes me feel a little sick.

'Good morning, Mrs Wood.' The constable doesn't look pleased to see me. 'I was hoping your husband would have come home by now. Follow me this way, please.'

I wave Greg's phone in Constable Wright's face as we walk along a corridor. 'I found this. It's Greg's.'

He seems unimpressed, which irritates me. If he and Sergeant

Harris had taken Greg's disappearance more seriously, they'd have located Greg's phone and checked the data in it themselves. The constable leads me to a small office to make my statement.

'Where did you find it?' he asks. 'In the house?'

'No. Along the roadside. Less than a mile from our house. I used a tracking app. Is Sergeant Harris working today?' I ask, thinking I'd much rather talk to her than him.

'She is, but she's been called out on another matter. I don't suppose you know the passcode to your husband's phone, Mrs Wood?' He slides into a worn office chair behind a desk and wiggles the mouse of his computer.

'Yes, I do. Greg and I have no secrets from each other.'

He nods, turning from the computer screen to look at me. 'In my experience, all married couples keep secrets from one another,' he says.

I notice he isn't wearing a wedding ring.

Greg and I have always confided in each other. Right from the start. Greg had had a couple of girlfriends and had even slept with a woman who was a lot older than him when we started dating. He told me all that shortly after we first met. He was my first. My one and only. I've shared everything with him since I've known him. I like to think that because we've known each other since we were teenagers, we've built our marriage on solid foundations and have a strong bond. Like me, Greg has nothing to hide.

'Not Greg and me,' I say.

Wright shrugs.

'I've been through the phone. There are no strange emails or calls, incoming or outgoing, and no photos of people or places I don't recognise. The fact the phone was lying in a ditch by the roadside shows that either Greg didn't get as far as the footpath or he didn't make it back home.'

Wright nods. He seems to do that a lot, even when he doesn't agree. 'We'll take a look at the place where you discovered the phone, Mrs Wood, check out the area.'

'Can you call in forensics?' I ask hopefully.

He doesn't answer straight away, as if he's weighing up his words. I can tell from his expression that the answer is no. A missing man certainly doesn't warrant the expense and police resources that a missing woman or child would.

'Given the heavy rain that day, I think it's unlikely we'll find much in the way of evidence now. But we will take a look at the place where you found your husband's phone.'

'OK. Thank you.'

'If your husband knew you could track his phone, he may have thrown it away on purpose,' Constable Wright surmises. A spark of annoyance flares inside me, like a match catching. 'Can you be absolutely sure, Mrs Wood, that Greg didn't keep another phone? One you didn't know about?'

'What on earth for?' I sound indignant and the constable holds up his hand, a signal for me not to take offence. I tell myself he's just examining all the possibilities. He doesn't know my husband. He knows virtually nothing about our marriage.

'In my experience—' he begins.

The constable seems to like that expression, but he's younger than I am. Really, how much experience can he have had?

'—and as my colleague told you yesterday, missing adults, especially men, usually show up within forty-eight hours. And as I told you, of those who don't, not all of them want to be found. Is it possible your husband planned to disappear deliberately? He might have had a second phone to make arrangements – one you didn't know about. One you couldn't track. He may have thrown away this mobile on purpose.'

My face flames. I want to get up and storm out, but that won't help Greg. I'm filled with dislike for this police officer, who I find insensitive and blunt. Wright is getting this all wrong.

He must sense that he has upset me because his tone softens. 'Look, I wouldn't be doing my job if I didn't consider every eventuality. I don't know your husband, Mrs Wood—'

44

'Sergeant Harris does,' I say, thinking perhaps I could come back when she's here.

'Yes, I know. I'll bring her up to speed as soon as she gets in. Do you feel up to making a statement? It will be more or less an official version of everything you told us yesterday. Details about your husband, his description, the last time you saw him, his job and pastimes, where he likes to hang out and so on.'

'Yes, of course.' I sound calmer than I feel.

'We can add the information about Greg's phone and the exact location you found it in. That could be useful to our investigation.'

The word 'investigation' should reassure me. At least the police are going to look into this; they're going to look for Greg. But I think they've already drawn their conclusions. Constable Wright seems to believe Greg was suffering from depression and had planned to disappear and start a new life somewhere else. He didn't want to be found, so he got rid of his phone.

'What investigation?' I scoff. I'm being rude, but I don't care. 'What are you actually doing to find my husband?'

'Well, for one thing, we're checking footage from the security webcams in the village to see if your husband went that way.'

I don't need to ask if they've found anything. The phone proves he was heading the other way.

'We've also sent out a search and rescue team,' Constable Wright continues. 'A helicopter has come out from St Athan.'

This is news to me. I saw a red and white helicopter earlier. It's a common sight along the coast. I didn't realise it was there for Greg.

'They've been scouring the headland and beaches since first light this morning,' the constable adds.

The implication is clear. The police have come up with another theory. In the bad weather, Greg has slipped over or got blown over the cliff edge. Or jumped. Or got pulled over by Rusty if he was on the lead. That would explain why neither of them came home. But I know Greg had no intention of going that far.

45

'Believe me, if your husband wants to be found, there's every chance we will find him,' Constable Wright says as I stand up to leave.

I have no idea where Greg is. Or our dog, for that matter. But I know my husband. He wouldn't have left me like this without explanation. He would never have left me, full stop.

Which means someone else must have been involved. Someone somewhere knows the truth. Someone somewhere knows where Greg is and why he hasn't come home.

Chapter 7

Kirsten

Kirsten is trying to follow Nick's instructions and carry on as if nothing has happened, but she's failing abysmally. How is it possible to act normal when she's feeling so abnormal? How can she and Nick get on with their lives when they have ended Gregory Wood's life and upended Amy Wood's life?

Kirsten doesn't regret not calling the police. It was an accident, after all. A terrible, tragic accident. Of course, she and Nick were willing to suffer the consequences, but if they'd called the police, their respective families would have suffered, too. Jamie and Lily – and Nick's wife – have nothing to do with any of this. No, not informing the police was definitely the right decision.

What she regrets is not leaving the body where it lay. It would be easier for Gregory Wood's wife – his *widow* – if she knew for sure what had befallen her husband. It must be killing her – Kirsten rephrases that in her head – it must be *torture*, having no idea where he is and why he has vanished. Knowing the truth would shatter the poor woman's hopes, but at least it would allow her to grieve.

More importantly, Kirsten feels the decision to remove the body might have repercussions for Nick and her further down the line. Killing someone accidentally is one thing. It can't be helped. But by deliberately loading the dead man's body into the boot of the car, she and Nick have transformed the scene of an accident into the scene of a crime. If the police do manage to trace the incident to Nick and her, the legal ramifications will be far greater now.

She hopes that Nick has taken care of any evidence that could incriminate them, including Gregory Wood's body – *especially* Gregory Wood's body – but the only time Nick has replied to any of her text messages, it was to tell her not to send any more, he would ring her soon. He didn't say when. It has been four days and apart from that single text message, Kirsten hasn't heard from him. It's not unusual for her not to hear from him for days on end – he goes quiet every now and then, ostensibly whenever his workload is particularly heavy. But his radio silence when she needs him most is distressing.

She can't remember when she last took time off work, but since she got home on Monday night, she hasn't even left the house, much less gone to the office. She's the branch manager of a high-end London estate agency and she prides herself on running a tight ship. She imagines her colleagues will be having a field day – or more precisely, a field *week* – in her absence.

She hasn't taken a shower for a couple of days, either. She'll have to get washed and dressed and go out today, though. For a start, she needs another packet of cigarettes and some more alcohol. And the dog keeps whining. It doesn't go upstairs – it must have been trained not to – but it follows her around downstairs, looking longingly towards the front door from time to time. She should take it somewhere. Out for a walk, maybe, or better still, to the animal rescue centre at Battersea.

Standing under the power shower jet, she turns up the temperature until the water almost scalds her. She scrubs her body and lathers her head with shampoo until the foam runs into her eyes, but she feels no cleaner when she gets out.

48

She pulls on tracksuit trousers, a hoodie she'd forgotten she had and trainers – an outfit so far removed from her usual weekday smart suit and high heels that she can almost kid herself she's someone else. She uses one of Jamie's leather belts as a makeshift lead for the dog. Stepping outside, she is blinded by the sun, so she takes her sunglasses out of her handbag, puts them on, then heads for the corner shop.

Kirsten is a non-smoker, really. She keeps a packet in the house for dinner parties and one in her handbag. She only ever smokes and drinks when she's with friends. She has never smoked in front of Nick. His wife smokes and Kirsten knows Nick finds it a filthy habit. This week, however, she has puffed her way through both packets of cigarettes and consumed more bottles of wine from Jamie's wine rack than she'd care to count. The empties are in bags in the garage. She'll take them to the bottle bank before Jamie notices. He doesn't know that every day this week she has spent most of the morning drunk and the whole afternoon trying to sober herself up before he and Lily arrived home.

She buys a packet of Marlboro Gold and a lighter at the corner shop and goes to the park. Dogs are only allowed in here on leads, but at this time of day, there's no one else around, so she sits on a bench, dumping her handbag beside her, unbuckles the belt from the dog's collar and lets it loose. If it doesn't come back, she doesn't care. It will save her the drive to Battersea later. Then she remembers the dog tag on its collar. It has both the dog's name and a mobile number engraved on it.

Her hands are unsteady when she lights up. What if the dog doesn't come back when she calls it? It will no doubt be found near here – eventually – and lead whoever finds it straight to the Woods. Well, to Mrs Wood. Kirsten exhales smoke and calls the dog. It has bounded down the slope to the duck pond and is about to jump in.

'Rusty! Here, Rusty!'

Rusty turns and looks at her, as if he's hesitating, then he jumps into the water.

'Shit!' she says aloud, leaping to her feet. She grabs her handbag and runs to the pond. 'Bad dog,' she shouts. 'Come here!' She expects it to swim away from her, after the ducks, who appear as agitated about the dog as Kirsten feels. She imagines the dog getting out of the water on the other side. She sees herself chasing it, but knows she has no chance of catching the damn mutt. How can she have been so stupid? Less than an hour ago, she'd been hoping Nick would get rid of anything that could link them to the accident or to Gregory Wood, and now here she is, releasing their victim's dog with its name and a contact phone number on its collar, a couple of blocks away from where she lives.

But to her surprise, the dog clambers out of the pond and saunters towards her, its head down and its tail between its legs, as if it knows it has been naughty. Kirsten is so relieved she squats down to pat it and it almost knocks her over as it licks her face. She laughs for the first time since last weekend, which only serves to encourage the dog. It bounces around her, bumping into her and causing her to lose her balance. She shoots out one hand to break her tumble onto the grass and holds the other hand aloft, still clasping the cigarette.

Nick's words come back to Kirsten. *Take that bloody dog to the pound.* She'd intended to do that today. It only dawns on her now that even if she removes the collar, the blasted mongrel is probably microchipped. Taking it to an animal shelter is not an option. She gets to her feet, pulls the strap of her bag up to her shoulder and stubs out her cigarette against a tree trunk. She puts the butt back in the packet and picks up a stick, which she throws into the pond for Rusty to fetch.

'Good boy,' she says, when he comes back out of the water, the stick in his mouth. He drops it at her feet and shakes the water off his fur, spraying her and making her squeal. 'Come on, I think we'd better get you some proper dog food instead of feeding you our leftovers,' she says. 'And a new collar and a lead.'

Because she'd planned to drive to Battersea, she hasn't drunk any

50

wine yet this morning. She drives to the pet shop instead, leaving Rusty in the house. They could walk there – it's not far, and she'd rather not take the car, but the dog food will be heavy. She hasn't been in a car since the accident and she drives so slowly that in the short distance to the shop, she gets hooted at three times. When she gets back, Rusty greets her as if she has been gone for several hours. She unloads her supplies in the kitchen. It's only when she's replacing Rusty's collar with the new one that her thoughts return to the mobile number on the dog tag. She wonders if it's Gregory Wood's number or his wife's.

Another thought occurs to her and she freezes, her hands around the dog's neck. Did Gregory Wood have his phone on him when they mowed him down? If so, it would still have been on him when they put him in the boot of Nick's car. Have she and Nick inadvertently laid a trail of breadcrumbs that will lead the police straight to them?

Kirsten's heart races as she fetches her own mobile phone from her handbag. She types 'track movements' and 'smartphone' into the search bar. *Your mobile will connect to the nearest phone mast,* Kirsten reads, *even if you don't make a call or send a message from it. Information from the base stations can then be used to triangulate your location.*

Kirsten's palms are sweaty and the mobile slips through them onto the floor. She bends down to retrieve it. Her breathing has become erratic and she forces herself to inhale deeply, reasoning with herself. Is there a chance he didn't have his mobile on him? If he was out walking the dog, as Kirsten has assumed, is it possible he left his phone at home? She clutches at this idea, but realises she's clutching at straws. She had her mobile on her in the park this morning. And Gregory Wood had his wallet on him. If he took his wallet, it seems likely he would have taken his phone, too.

Her mouth is dry and it hurts to swallow. She could do with a drink. She pours herself a glass of red wine and takes several gulps

51

from the glass. Then she calls Nick. He doesn't answer. She doesn't know if he's busy or ignoring her. She leaves a message, imploring him to call her back urgently. She's halfway through typing a text message saying the same thing when her ringtone blares out, making her jump, even though she's holding the phone in her hands.

'What's up, Kirsten?' He sounds grumpy.

'Gregory Wood's mobile phone.' She's out of breath and can't get the rest out.

There's a moment's pause, then Nick says, 'Please tell me you didn't take his phone as well as his wallet.'

'No. Did he . . . did he . . .?' The walls seem to be moving towards her and the floor is pitching. She's still struggling to catch her breath. She sinks to the tiled floor, her back against the kitchen island. 'Where is it?' she manages.

'Don't worry,' he says. His voice is more tender now. 'He didn't have it on him. I checked before we got him into the car.' As calculating as she finds that, Kirsten's glad he had the foresight to do it. 'He must have gone out without it,' Nick continues. 'If he even has a phone. Not everyone does, you know.'

He gives a little chuckle, so familiar to Kirsten that she aches for him. She wishes he were holding her. She desperately wants to feel connected to him again. She grips the mobile tighter against her ear and her breathing slows. 'And the body?' she asks.

'Don't worry,' he repeats. 'It's all taken care of. Have you thrown out the wallet?'

'Yes.'

'What about the dog?'

Kirsten looks at Rusty. He's lying on the floor beside her, his head on her thigh, looking up at her as if he has sensed something's wrong. She echoes Nick's words back at him. 'All taken care of.'

'Good. How are you doing?'

'Not great, but better for talking to you. How've you been?'

'I've been so busy preparing a case for court that I haven't had much time to think.'

Kirsten wants to complain that he hasn't had time for her, either, but Nick hates it when she whinges. 'When can I see you?' she asks instead.

'I'll get back to you at the end of next week,' he promises. 'We'll arrange something then. In the meantime, don't draw unnecessary attention to yourself and be careful what you write in text messages and emails. Oh, and Kirsten?' He doesn't wait for her to respond. 'Don't look up anything on the Internet.'

Nick ends the call before she can ask him why. Has something happened that she should know about? Are the police onto them? Already? Or is Nick simply warning her to be careful about what her browsing history might reveal in the unlikely event they're investigated at some point?

She goes into the study and boots up her laptop. She types Gregory Wood's name and the word 'missing'. She finds what she's looking for immediately in the form of a short, online article in *The North Devon Gazette*. She reads the headline. POLICE ARE APPEALING FOR INFORMATION ABOUT MISSING MAN FROM CROYDE BAY. The piece itself says little more than that, adding only that he was last seen on Monday morning when he took out his dog – a fox-red Labrador – for a quick walk before lunch. There's a brief description of Gregory Wood and of the clothes he was wearing.

The journalist has quoted Gregory Wood's wife, Amy Wood. *My husband would not simply disappear like this,* Kirsten reads. *We're very concerned that something might have happened to him and beg anyone who knows anything or has seen anything to speak to the police.*

Kirsten wonders if the police think Gregory Wood has intentionally left his wife while Mrs Wood – Amy – obviously suspects something untoward has happened to her husband. Kirsten deletes her browsing history and closes the lid of her laptop. She drums her fingers on the lid for a few seconds before fetching Gregory Wood's wallet from where she has hidden it in the sock drawer of her walk-in wardrobe. Rusty waits for her at the bottom of the stairs and follows her into the living room when she comes back down. She looks through the wallet to see if there's anything in there with Gregory Wood's mobile number on it. She wants to know if the number on the dog's collar is his or his wife's. She can't say why, but it's important. A gut feeling, some sort of survival instinct, perhaps, similar to the one that made her keep the wallet instead of throwing it away.

She pulls out everything. Money, stamps, bank card, driving licence, a supermarket loyalty card, business cards. In a small zip-up compartment, Kirsten stumbles on a Post-it that has been folded in two. It has a four-digit number written on it by hand. Could this be the PIN code to Gregory Wood's bank card? She picks up a business card. Gregory Wood, *Swell Surf Clothing & Wetsuits*, Croyde Bay. There's an email address, a shop address, a landline number and a mobile number, which she compares with the mobile number on the dog's collar. It's not the same. Either Gregory Wood has a separate mobile number for work, which is certainly possible, or the mobile number on the collar is for his wife's phone.

Kirsten puts everything back into the wallet. She's none the wiser, but as an idea gradually takes shape in a dark corner of her mind, she hopes this is Amy's number. Holding the wallet in one upturned hand, she slowly strokes the leather with her thumb and stares ahead blankly, as if she were handling worry beads or prayer beads.

After several minutes, she leaps up and runs upstairs again. She kneels on the thick-carpeted floor, pulls out a large suitcase from under the bed, hoists it onto the mattress and opens it. Then she gets to her feet, selects some clothes from her wardrobe and starts to pack.

Chapter 8

Amy

There's so much blood. Too much blood. My heart plummets. At first, I thought I'd woken up marinating in my own sweat, then I wondered if I'd wet the bed, but now I've switched on the light, I can see it's not sweat and it's not urine; it's blood. I howl in pain, not from the stomach cramp, although that's excruciating enough, but because I know what this means. I'm having a miscarriage.

Slowly, I get out of bed, but I'm dizzy and my legs are wobbly. I whimper, like a child. I want Greg. Failing that, I want my mum. It's times like these I still need her. I thought she and I were reasonably close, as mothers and daughters go. We got on most of the time as I was growing up. But as soon as I became a primary school teacher, in my early twenties, she emigrated to Australia with her boyfriend at the time, a divorced cardiologist from Melbourne. He has since become her husband. I never knew my father. I'm not sure my mother did, either. Hugh is the only father figure I've ever known and Pam has loved me like the daughter she never had from the moment Greg introduced me to his family.

I manage to get out of bed. I take a shower. The cramps in my

55

stomach get stronger, so wrapped in my damp towel and sobbing, I sit on the toilet for what seems like hours, but is probably more like half an hour. More blood and some other stuff come out of me. I don't dare to peer into the toilet bowl. Eventually the pain subsides enough for me to stand up again. I'm shivering. It's an effort to pull on a pair of pants with a sanitary pad and a clean pair of pyjamas. I don't feel up to putting clean sheets on the bed. I won't be able to get back to sleep anyway.

It's the middle of the night and I'm not sure what to do. I want to take some painkillers, but I don't know what to take – paracetamol or ibuprofen? Do I need to go to hospital? Should I call an ambulance or can I drive?

I call my parents-in-law. This will devastate them, but it's not something I'll be able to keep from them for long. They're bound to keep their mobiles switched on and next to the bed at the moment, as I do, and I'm sure that like me, they must jump in anticipation every time they get an incoming call, hoping it's good news about Greg.

Pam and Hugh arrive so quickly, you'd think they were camping in the garden. They probably weren't asleep when I rang. I haven't slept much lately, either. Pam's nightshirt is poking out from under her woolly pullover and Hugh sports a bushy bedhead that would make me laugh in different circumstances. Pam wraps my dressing gown around me and stays by my side while Hugh finds some Nurofen in the bathroom cupboard and hands me a tablet and a glass of water. They're both so efficient. Then Hugh bundles me outside and into the passenger seat of their car.

They take me to the A&E at the North Devon District Hospital in Barnstaple, half an hour's drive away. Hugh drives at least ten miles per hour below the speed limit, even in the thirty zone, but, from the back seat, Pam repeatedly asks him to slow down. She asks me if I'm in pain. Her own pain is perceptible in her voice. She leans forwards and squeezes my shoulder from time to time.

It's the middle of the night and, thankfully, there's no waiting around once we arrive at the hospital. I need to see a consultant, though, and there won't be anyone until the morning. My tummy cramps are so severe that I'm kept in overnight for observation. My parents-in-law are sent home, but they promise to come back first thing in the morning, which means in just a few hours' time.

The rest of the night goes by in a daze. I vaguely remember a nurse coming to draw some blood for testing, but I have no idea what time it is. The nurse gives me another painkiller. The ward is silent except for the footsteps of health professionals in the corridor and the snoring of the patient in the bed next to mine. I drift in and out of sleep.

The following morning, I'm taken in the lift to the Early Pregnancy Assessment Clinic on Level 2 for an ultrasound. The nurse asks if I need a wheelchair, but I insist on walking. It's still a little early for visiting hours, but Pam and Hugh have already arrived at the hospital and Pam accompanies the nurse and me to the unit, although she stays in the waiting area when I go in for the scan.

The consultant is a middle-aged woman with large, black-rimmed glasses and long, grey hair fraying out of a loose bun. I keep my eyes fixed on her face as she concentrates. She frowns and I already know what she will say.

'I'm afraid there's no heartbeat,' she confirms. 'It does look like you've miscarried.' I nod. I don't trust myself to speak past the lump in my throat. 'We can confirm this with another blood test to check your hormone levels in a day or two,' she adds.

She goes on to explain, clearly and gently, that as I'm bleeding, there's a good chance the tissue will pass out of my body naturally and that no further treatment will be required. 'You'll need to come back in just over a week's time so we can check there's no pregnancy tissue left.'

I nod again. I already have an appointment at this very hospital a week next Tuesday – for my twelve-week scan.

'Miscarriage isn't uncommon in the first weeks of pregnancy,' the consultant continues, 'but most women go on to have another pregnancy, a successful one, and a healthy baby, so there's no reason not to try again, if you want to, when you feel physically and emotionally ready.'

She knows nothing about my situation. How could she? I've said little, limiting myself to monosyllabic responses to her questions – yes or no. She hands me a leaflet and says something about counselling, but I don't take it in.

'Do you have any questions?' She looks at me expectantly.

'No,' I say, but then I change my mind. There is something I need to know. 'Was this caused by stress?' I ask. 'I've been under a lot of stress the past few days. Is that why I've miscarried?'

'No,' she says. 'It's natural to want to find a cause, but it's not linked to the mother's emotional state. In other words, it's not caused by stress. It's natural to want to blame yourself, but you mustn't. It's not your fault.'

'OK. Thank you,' I say. I'm not convinced.

By mid-afternoon, I'm discharged. Pam and Hugh take me back to their house. I sit on the sofa, legs tucked up. Hugh makes me a cup of tea and Pam makes me a hot water bottle. I pretend to doze for a while, to stop them fussing. I don't mean to eavesdrop on their conversation, but I find myself straining to make out what they're saying as they whisper to each other in the adjoining kitchen.

'Sergeant Harris called earlier while you were at the Early Pregnancy Clinic with Amy,' Hugh says.

'Oh. What did she want?'

'They want to do a short, televised appeal for information about Greg's disappearance. On the local news. ITV West Country.'

'Do they want us to read out a statement or something?'

'No, I don't think so. Sergeant Harris said she would be making the appeal herself. She wants another photo – a good, recent one, preferably with Gregory wearing the same clothes as the day he went missing.'

There's a pause, then Pam says, 'You'd think if there were any witnesses, they'd have come forward by now,' she says. She's obviously trying not to get her hopes up.

'Until now, it has only been briefly mentioned in the local papers. This should get a bit more coverage. It was a bank holiday weekend. Maybe there were tourists down for the weekend who saw Greg, but who are unaware he's gone missing.'

'It's a shame they can't broadcast it on national television, then.'

I think either Hugh or Pam must close the door, because their voices become louder, but muffled, and I can't follow the rest of the conversation.

Something Hugh said strikes me as potentially important, but my mind is slow; I'm a little groggy from the painkillers or whatever they gave me before I left the hospital. What was it he said? Something about holidaymakers spending the bank holiday weekend in North Devon.

I sit bolt upright. I've got it. We had a couple renting the flat that weekend. Maybe they saw something. The Taylors. That was their name. Mr Taylor made the booking over the phone, instead of online, which is irregular, but he wanted to pay in cash. I wrote down his number and I remember asking him for his email address. I could get in touch with him and ask if they saw Greg. They saw him on the Friday evening when they arrived. If they saw him again on the Monday, they would certainly have recognised him.

I get a sinking feeling as I realise the timeline isn't right. The couple came round with the keys to the flat before midday. They were on their way home. I don't know where they live – I didn't take down an address with the booking, which was an oversight on my part, but they would have been heading for the link road and then the motorway. Greg was in the house when they swung by, prepping the veg for the roast dinner. He set out later, about an hour later. And he was walking in the opposite direction.

Pam and Hugh offer to make up the bed in Greg's old bedroom, but I would rather sleep in my own bed. They encourage me to eat a little dinner before they take me home. The dinner – pork chops with apple sauce and boiled potatoes – smells delicious, but I have no appetite. I can tell my parents-in-law are forcing themselves to swallow some of it, too.

Hugh drives me home while Pam clears away the dinner dishes. He carries my bag upstairs for me. I wait in the living room, unable to tear my eyes away from an acrylic print we had made from a photo Greg took while we were on our summer holiday in the Lake District last year. We rented a cottage for a fortnight and hiked in the hills and swam in the lakes every day with Rusty. The weather was glorious nearly the whole time we were there. The photo was taken from Friar's Crag in Keswick. It captures the breathtaking view of Derwentwater we enjoyed on one of our walks. It was here that we decided to start a family. I resist the urge to take down the picture. I want to throw it to the floor and smash it. The image no longer represents a happy memory; it serves only as a painful reminder.

When Hugh has gone, it's eerily quiet. There was always music on in this house. Greg and I would make playlists together and stream them through the Bluetooth speaker, but I haven't listened to a single song since he's been gone.

A memory charges at me: Greg in the kitchen, singing at the top of his voice one evening as we prepared dinner. He grabbed the ketchup bottle and used it as a microphone, prancing around like a rock star. Rusty bounded around him excitedly, barking. A deafening duet. I laughed at them until I cried. I can't remember now which song Greg was singing along to or even which band we were listening to. I swipe at the tears cascading down my face.

I unpack my overnight bag from the hospital, throwing everything into the washing basket. I clean my teeth and crawl into bed. The sheets are clean. Pam must have changed them while I was in hospital. These sheets don't smell of Greg, so I get up and rummage through the clothes in Greg's side of the chest of drawers until I find a T-shirt that still carries his smell. I put it on and get

60

back into bed, pulling the covers up to my chin and the neck of the T-shirt over my nose.

I feel empty and exhausted; distraught and depressed. But there's something else simmering beneath all of that, a feeling it takes me a few seconds to identify. Anger. According to the consultant at the hospital, miscarriages aren't caused by emotional stress. She also said I mustn't blame myself. I only partly agree. I firmly believe that stress was a factor. To my mind, there's a definite connection, of cause and consequence, between losing my husband and losing my baby. But I don't blame myself. I think someone else is to blame.

And I think they should pay for what they've done.

Chapter 9

Kirsten

'Where are you going? What's going on? Are you . . . you're not . . .?'

Kirsten hadn't heard Jamie and Lily come in. Her daughter rushes to her and wraps herself around Kirsten's legs. Hearing the quaver in Jamie's voice, Kirsten turns round. He looks dismayed. She pictures the scene through his eyes. His wife has been behaving out of character all week – she hasn't been to work and has neglected her personal hygiene and he has just found her in their bedroom, packing a suitcase. He probably assumes she's leaving him.

'*We* are going to Folkestone,' she replies. 'The three of us.'

Jamie's eyes narrow. They have a second home in Folkestone. It belonged to Jamie's mother and father before they died of cancer and old age, respectively. Jamie bought out his sister, Claire, so it's all theirs. They hardly ever go there. In fact, Claire goes more than they do, even though she lives much further away. Kirsten hates it, mainly because she's not a fan of the beach, and prefers to stay in London at weekends. It has long been a source of contention between Jamie and her.

'I thought it would do us good to get away for the weekend,' she says.

'You went away last weekend.' As if afraid she'll change her mind, Jamie adds hastily, 'Are you sure? Are you feeling better?'

'Yes, much better, thank you.' Kirsten had contracted a fake tummy bug to account for this week's listlessness and absenteeism from work. She extricates herself from Lily's grasp and zips up the suitcase. 'I think I've got everything—' she looks pointedly at Lily '—including Teddy.' Once, Kirsten forgot the tatty bear and Lily threw such a tantrum that Jamie offered to drive all the way back and fetch him. Kirsten overruled that suggestion. Lily was five at the time, for fuck's sake. She could spend – and in the end *did* spend – two nights without a smelly stuffed toy with a missing ear.

Kirsten has probably forgotten something. But she has double-checked she has packed the two most important things. Firstly, Gregory Wood's wallet. She wonders if she has known subconsciously all along why she felt she should keep it. Secondly, her burner phone, which she has charged up. Nick gave her the prepaid mobile five years ago at the beginning of their affair, but Kirsten saw little point in using it. Jamie has always had a trusting, guileless nature and even if he suspected she was being deceitful or unfaithful, she's certain he would never go through her things. He doesn't know her passcodes and passwords, not that they would be hard to find if he looked. But Kirsten's sure he won't. Anyway, no one really uses burner phones anymore – she doesn't think they did back when Nick gave it to her – but now it will come in handy.

Jamie hoists the suitcase into the boot of their Ford Mondeo. The nondescript hatchback – Jamie's choice – is too big for the three of them and nowhere near as comfortable as Nick's luxury saloon. Jamie doesn't think they need a car. Both of them use public transport to go to work and they could easily buy their shopping online and take the train for their rare weekend breaks, but Kirsten maintains that having a vehicle is essential when you have a kid, if only for emergencies. She also insisted on an automatic. Jamie bought the dark blue Ford Mondeo second-hand. It lacked that clean smell that still radiates from the upholstery in Nick's car.

As Rusty jumps into the boot and lies down next to the suit-case, Kirsten remembers travelling back from Devon with the dog wedged into the footwell against her legs. Jamie closes the boot and Kirsten shudders as she pictures Gregory Wood's lifeless body in Nick's boot. This image is imprinted on her brain now.

Jamie fetches some snacks for the journey and they set off. Apart from the short trip earlier today to the pet shop, which was just round the corner, she hasn't been in a car since the accident. She's jumpy and has to resist the urge to ask Jamie, who is keeping more or less to the speed limit, to slow down. Lily soon falls asleep in the back. To Kirsten's annoyance, Jamie yawns noisily from time to time. He works hard, as a copywriter, and even though last Monday was a bank holiday, he has had a long week, making up for the lost day at work as well as looking after Lily and making the meals in the evenings. She should offer to take the wheel for a bit and let Jamie sleep, but she hates driving. And Jamie does only work part-time.

She turns up the music to deter any conversation. She needs to collect her thoughts. When she came up with her idea earlier, it seemed like a brainwave, but since then doubt has tiptoed into her mind. She's no longer sure it would be wise to carry out what she'd planned to do. She needs to think it all through before they get to Folkestone.

She brings up the article she read online about Gregory Wood's disappearance on her smartphone and rereads it. Then she types similar keywords into the search bar to see if there's any more information. The only other online article she finds, from another local paper, contains fewer details. But it has a slightly different quote from Amy Wood. *My husband would not have upped and left of his own accord,* she is reported to have said. *His parents and I feel certain that someone out there knows something that could help us find out what has happened to him.*

This confirms what Kirsten thought. Amy Wood believes that someone has had a hand in her husband's disappearance. Kirsten will have to put her plan into action. Something has to be done to change the widow's mind. She closes her eyes. It makes her less jittery about being in a car and if she pretends to sleep, Jamie won't disturb her while she thinks this through. She can't afford to slip up.

Kirsten feigns a headache the next morning. Lily actually cries when Kirsten says she isn't going out with them this morning, which tugs a little at Kirsten's hardened heart. Jamie is concerned about Kirsten's health and fusses around her. She's never ill, and yet this week she has had both a tummy bug and a headache. Should he take her to get a blood test? Does she need him to go to the chemist? Kirsten just needs him to get out of the house and take Lily with him, although she's careful to phrase this a little less bluntly when she says it out loud.

Jamie has fetched her a cold, damp flannel and Kirsten lies in bed with it draped across her forehead, waiting impatiently. Lily has recovered quickly from her disappointment – her excited chatter drifts to Kirsten from the breakfast table downstairs. Kirsten listens to her husband and daughter's conversation. Jamie promises to take Lily to Sunny Sands Beach and make sandcastles with her. Lily wants to take Rusty but Jamie checks on the Internet and dogs aren't allowed on the beach between May and October.

Their little cottage is a mere stone's throw from the harbour and beach, so they can go there by foot, which means Kirsten can take the car. So far, so good. Kirsten feels a small pang of guilt that she won't be spending the morning with her husband and daughter. She'll make it up to both of them when she gets back.

The dull thud of the front door finally closing galvanises Kirsten into action. She gets out of bed and races downstairs. On the console table in the entrance hall, she finds a pad of paper. She hunts in the drawer of the console for a pen, but doesn't find one. She hunts through her handbag for one instead. She scribbles a note for Jamie, saying her headache has gone and she has popped out to buy some food for their lunch. Hopefully, she'll be back before Jamie and Lily, but she'd better leave a note in case.

She checks the burner phone is in her handbag. It's turned off for the moment. She'll leave her own phone upstairs. She also checks she has both her wallet and Gregory Wood's. And sunglasses and a sunhat. Rusty wags his tail as she pulls on her shoes. She promises him that someone will take him out later. When she can't find the car keys, she panics and swears. She and Jamie usually leave the keys on the console table, but they're not there. Jamie must have them on him. She rummages around in the drawer where she looked for a pen a minute or so ago. No keys. She swears again. She's going to have to abort her mission.

She spots Jamie's jacket on one of the wooden hooks. It's sunny today. He has gone out without it. She thrusts her hand into one of the jacket pockets. Relief floods through her as her fingers close around the car keys.

She steps outside and locks the door behind her. After checking there's no one around, Kirsten lifts the lid of the ceramic ashtray on the garden table and leaves the front door key inside, as they always do. Seconds later she's in the car, on her way to Dover. She follows the road signs to avoid using the satnav, but she knows it's a twenty-minute drive.

She heads for the ferry terminal and pulls into a supermarket car park close to the port. She parks as far away from the super-market entrance as possible, checking for CCTV cameras. She doubts anyone will ever check them, but she doesn't want to take any unnecessary risks. She pulls on the sunhat, tucking her hair inside, and gets out of the car. She has almost reached the sliding doors of the supermarket before it occurs to her that she has forgotten a shopping bag. She returns to the car and fetches one from the boot.

Kirsten notices there's an ATM outside the supermarket. She has memorised the four digits on the Post-it, convinced that they are Gregory Wood's PIN, but if she buys a few groceries, she won't need it, as she'll be expected to make a contactless payment. She considers making a cash withdrawal. It would appear more authentic if she made a transaction using his PIN. There's no security camera above the ATM. Kirsten flounders. Is this a good idea? What if the cash machine has a built-in camera? And maybe the number isn't his PIN, or it is the PIN, but he deliberately wrote it backwards. Would the police know someone tried to use Gregory Wood's card and entered the wrong code? No, better stick to the original plan. Safer that way.

Kirsten enters the supermarket and picks up some fresh bread, cheese, pâté, coleslaw, lettuce and cherry tomatoes and some of those kids' yoghurt drinks that Lily loves. That will do nicely for their lunch. She also grabs a couple of bottles of Pinot Grigio. She'll need some alcohol after this to calm herself down. At the checkout, she pulls out Gregory Wood's debit card. What if the card has been cancelled? Sweat prickles under her arms and beads on her forehead under the hat as she holds the chip to the card reader.

She can hardly believe it when the payment is confirmed and the girl hands her the receipt. It has worked! Kirsten picks up her shopping bag and mumbles her thanks. Keeping her head down, she scurries out of the supermarket. For a minute or two, she sits in the car, trying to slow down her breathing and her heart rate before carrying out the second part of her plan.

Once she has composed herself, she drives around, looking for a suitable spot. It has to be near the ferry port, but not in a lay-by along the road. She contemplates going to the train station, but in the end, she parks in Marine Parade.

She switches on her burner phone, checks her caller number is hidden and makes the call from the car. She still doesn't know whose mobile number is engraved on Rusty's collar, but if Gregory Wood left his phone at home that day, as Nick assumes, there's a good chance Amy Wood will answer the call either way. She may think it's her husband calling, which is what Kirsten's hoping, even if the incoming call is to his phone. After all, Kirsten doesn't know Jamie's or Nick's mobile numbers by heart; only her own.

Kirsten hears the ringtone. Given the circumstances, if it is Amy's phone, she'll probably have it right next to her, wherever she is, even if she's in the shower or on the toilet. The volume will be turned right up so she can't possibly miss an incoming call. How long before Amy will stop thinking that it's news about her husband every time her mobile goes? A month? Six months? A year?

As Kirsten had anticipated, Amy answers immediately. Kirsten remains silent, although her heart is beating so loudly in her own ears that she's sure Amy must hear it.

'Hello?' Amy repeats.

Still Kirsten says nothing.

Then: 'Greg? Greg, is that you?'

Kirsten has achieved what she set out to do. Her mouth curls upwards as she ends the call, but it's more of a rueful grimace than a triumphant smile. She's not proud of what she has just done, but needs must. This is about protecting her family. And herself.

She turns off the burner phone, gets out of the car and walks to the railings along the esplanade. She checks no one is watching her and lobs the phone as far as she can into the sea.

Chapter 10

Amy

I receive the phone call the day after coming home from hospital, five days after Greg's disappearance. It takes me another two days before I feel up to going to the police station to report it. Greg has been missing for a week. It's the longest we've ever been apart.

I'm shown to the same office in which I gave my statement to Constable Wright, but this time, to my relief, I'm sitting opposite his colleague. Sergeant Harris's mousy hair is scraped back into a ponytail, with clips holding back her fringe, making her face appear even more angular.

'I was going to call you. Tomorrow I'm filming the appeal our media office set up with ITV West Country,' she says before I can tell her why I've come in. 'Did your father-in-law mention it? I rang him when I couldn't get hold of you. He said you were resting?' I nod. 'It will probably only last one or two minutes, but hopefully it will jog someone's memory and we may get some useful leads into your husband's disappearance.' She gives me a smile, but it looks as if she's baring her teeth. I don't smile back. 'Mr Wood – your father-in-law – gave me a photo of Gregory I can use for the appeal. I wanted to ask you for a decent photo of your dog,' she gushes. 'Have you got one?'

I bring up some photos of Rusty on my phone and she selects two of them. She gives me her email address and I send them to her.

'That's perfect,' she says, as we hear the swoosh of the email sending from my phone followed by the ping of it arriving on her desk computer. 'With the weather being so bad, if anyone did see Gregory, they might not have got a good look at his face, but they may remember the dog.' Without stopping to take a breath, she asks, 'So, what brought you in today?'

I tell her about the phone call with the long silence from the blocked number.

'What makes you think it might have been your husband?' she says when I've finished.

I want to believe it was Greg and that he's alive somewhere, being kept against his will for some reason, but deep down, I don't buy that. It's wishful thinking. I'm just not ready to consider the alternative scenarios. I didn't tell Harris I thought it was Greg. What I said was that I thought it may have something to do with Greg, but I don't correct her.

Instead, I answer her question with one of my own. 'Can you trace the call?'

She sighs and my heart sinks. She's no better than Constable Wright. She doesn't seem to think there's anything to investigate, either. 'It's poss—'

'Can the police trace an incoming call from a blocked number?' I insist.

'Theoretically, yes. The fact the number's blocked makes no difference. It would be possible to retrieve the number of that phone and the approximate location where the call was made.'

She launches into a lengthy explanation of how they can trace a call, but I only take in isolated words and phrases. *Single point of contact . . . grid reference . . . mast . . . azimuth.* My brain fixes

70

on what she said before that. *Theoretically.* Does that mean they could but they won't?

I'm about to put this to Sergeant Harris, but she gets in her next question first. 'You said the call lasted several seconds? Did you hear any background noise during that time? Traffic, music, voices, the television, something like that?'

'No. Nothing.'

'And you couldn't tell if the caller was a man or a woman?'

'No.'

'Are you sure Gregory knows your number off by heart?'

'What?'

'You've got his mobile phone in your possession. So, if he was the one who rang you, he'll have punched in your number from memory. Does he definitely know it?'

I have no idea if Greg knows my number or not. I don't know his number by heart. Only my own. He's not great with numbers – he forgets important dates and has trouble remembering his PIN when he needs to withdraw money. I shake my head.

'The thing is, Amy, there could be any number of explanations for that call. A wrong number. Telemarketing. A long-distance call that didn't connect.'

She pauses and I wonder if she's aware my mum lives in Oz.

'I've already thought of all these possibilities,' I say, 'but I still think it's worth a try.'

'Most silent calls are made by automated systems in call centres,' she continues as if I haven't spoken. 'It takes a few seconds to connect you to a call centre agent once you answer your phone.'

'I realise that. But what if this phone call *is* related to what happened to Greg?'

Another sigh. 'Amy, your husband went missing a week ago. We need something to warrant . . . We have no reason to believe he didn't leave home because he wanted to.'

I get what she's saying. A grown man who has disappeared

71

without a trace is not a priority for them. I've told them myself he's not suicidal. Greg is my priority, though.

'You have no reason to think he did leave because he wanted to!' I counter. 'What if someone has taken him and this is the call from his . . . his kidnapper?'

'Amy, we need to be reasonable and not make wild assumptions. Your theory doesn't hold water for two reasons. Firstly, why would anyone kidnap Greg? We've looked into your husband's business. To say it's not doing well would be putting it mildly. There's no money to pay a ransom. Why else would someone kidnap an adult male?'

I say nothing. She's right. It doesn't make sense. There would be more obvious motives, albeit unthinkable ones, if a woman or a child had been abducted, but for a man in his thirties, it's a different story. I wait for the other reason.

'Secondly, let me ask you this,' Harris continues, leaning forwards, putting her elbows on the table and resting her chin on her hands. 'Where is your dog? If someone had taken Gregory, wouldn't your dog have come home by itself? It knows the way, right?'

This has troubled me, too. I've rung all the local dog pounds and walked miles looking for Greg and calling for Rusty. If someone has found Rusty, my mobile number is on his collar, but no one has rung. Unless . . . I don't tell Sergeant Harris what I'm thinking. It would only provide her with another hypothesis for this strange silent call. She'll think someone has found the dog, but couldn't get through. Plus, even if the call was made by someone who has found Rusty, they might know something about Greg's disappearance. I can't be sure this call is important, but I want Harris to check it out.

'Amy, why didn't you report this before now?' Harris asks. 'You got this phone call the day before yesterday.'

'I wasn't well. I'd just come home from the hospital.'

'Oh? Nothing serious, I hope?' She sounds genuinely concerned.

Tears prick my eyes and I lower my head. I notice I'm playing with my wedding ring, turning it round and round. It brings back a memory. Greg and I bought matching wedding rings. In Argos, of all places. They cost less than a hundred quid each. They were supposed to be temporary, to tide us over until we could splash out on an exotic, belated honeymoon, renew our vows on a white sandy beach somewhere and replace our rings with better quality, higher karat gold ones. Every now and then when the plain gold band pinches my finger too much, I have to take it to the jeweller's to be teased back into shape. Greg and I never did get to go on that honeymoon, but I'm glad I still have this ring. It may be cheap, but to me it's invaluable.

'Sorry. None of my business.' Sergeant Harris's voice jolts me out of my reverie.

'I had a miscarriage,' I say softly.

'Oh God. I'm so sorry.' I can tell from her expression that she means it.

I look up and lock my eyes onto hers. 'Sergeant Harris, will you or won't you trace the call?'

'It may not turn out to have anything to do with Gregory's disappearance and I can't promise we'll get the results quickly – it can take several days or even weeks,' she says, 'but, yes, I'll apply for the incoming call data to your mobile number.'

Chapter 11

Amy

When I get home from the police station, there's a car in front of the entrance to the cottage. Standing next to it, waiting for me, is a scruffy, lanky man with light brown hair that flops messily over his forehead. I haven't seen him for a while, but I recognise him immediately. Simon Tucker. He has sent me several text messages since he read about Greg's disappearance in *The North Devon Gazette* and I replied, succinctly but politely, to a couple of them. I didn't expect him to come round, though. I was at school with Simon and I think he developed a crush on me. According to Greg, he still fancies me. He's harmless, but I've always found him a bit creepy, a bit too intense.

'Hi, Amy,' he says as I get out of the car. 'Any news about Greg?'

'No, not yet.' He follows me to the front door and we stand there awkwardly. He's standing so close to me that I can smell his minty breath. I take a step away from him, my back now against the door. I feel bad about not inviting him in, but I don't really want to be alone with him. Or anyone else, for that matter. I would rather be by myself for a while, at least until Pam and Hugh come

74

round this evening. 'I'm sorry, Simon,' I say. 'I'm not up to having company right now.'

'That's fine,' he says, although I can tell from his voice that I've hurt his feelings. 'I just wanted to stop by and let you know I'm here if you need anything.'

'That's good of you. Thank you.'

'Have the police got any leads?' he asks.

'No. They seem to think Greg planned to leave and that he doesn't want to be found.'

'I see. And what do you think happened?'

I'm fiddling with my keys and drop them on the ground. I bend down to retrieve them, but Simon beats me to it.

'I don't know,' I say. 'I think something happened to him. Maybe he was involved in an accident. Or perhaps he was abducted, although I can't even begin to imagine why.'

'And you've had no news whatsoever?'

'No,' I say, mildly annoyed. He has already asked me that. 'I got a phone call the other day, but the caller didn't say anything, so I don't know if it has something to do with Greg or not.' I'm not sure why I'm telling Simon all this. I'm holding out my hand for the keys, but Simon doesn't seem to have noticed.

'Was it from Greg's mobile?' he asks.

'No. The number was blocked. Greg doesn't have his mobile. I do. I found it the night he disappeared, in the ditch at the side of the road less than a mile away from here.'

A stitch appears in the small gap between Simon's eyebrows. 'He went missing last Monday, is that right?' He enunciates slowly.

'Yes. A week ago today.' At this time of day, in fact. I don't say that out loud. 'He popped out to walk the dog before lunch.'

He nods, looking pensive. His eyes bore into me, making me feel uncomfortable. 'Which road?' he asks.

I'm not sure what difference it makes, but I answer the question. 'Moor Lane. Near the end where the South West Coast Path passes.'

Simon's face is a ghoulish white. His mouth is wide open, as if he's in shock or gasping for air. I decide I'd better invite him in, after all.

'Simon, would you like a cup of tea or something?' He's still holding my keys, so I seize them from his hand. 'You've gone awfully white.'

He shakes his head. 'Can you show me?' he says.

'Show you what? The phone?'

'No, where you found it. The exact spot.'

'Why?' I've already shown the police where I found Greg's phone and they didn't find anything else.

'Just show me.' I'm about to protest and demand to know why, but he adds, 'Please. I'll drive.'

'Do you mind if we walk?' I say.

Simon looks miffed and I realise I must sound ungrateful or snobbish. For years, he has been driving around in the same old rusty car. I must have given him the impression his wheels aren't good enough for me, but that's not it. I've walked all the way out to Baggy Point and back a couple of times since Greg has disappeared, although I feel certain Greg wouldn't have gone anywhere near as far that day. Each time, I hope to see something I've missed. A clue. A sign. Anything that might indicate where he went. I explain this to Simon. I don't tell him that I'm supposed to be taking it easy, because although I'm feeling low, I don't feel physically weak and I think the fresh air and light exercise will do me good.

'Of course I don't mind,' he says. 'Let's go.'

I unlock the front door and change my shoes. I take my mobile out of my handbag and slide it into the back pocket of my jeans so I don't have to take my bag with me. Then we set off.

As we walk, I try again to draw Simon out, but he won't say why he wants to see for himself where I found Greg's phone. I tell myself he wants to check the area in case I've missed something and his mysteriousness is just to avoid giving me false hopes.

The conversation between us starts off stilted before drying up altogether. The short walk seems long, especially without Rusty by my side. When we reach the spot, I stop and point.

'That's where I found the phone,' I say. 'In that ditch. Its screen was smashed, as if Greg had dropped it.'

It's only as I tell Simon this, that I remember Greg's phone has a screen protector. We spent ages one evening trying to follow a YouTube tutorial to install it correctly without air bubbles. Even if Greg had dropped it on the tarmac, the screen shouldn't have cracked, and it certainly wouldn't have smashed like that. If the phone had fallen into the ditch, onto the grass and brambles, it wouldn't have been damaged at all, except maybe by the rain. I didn't think to mention this to Constable Wright. It didn't occur to me until now, but this might be important.

'I thought as much,' Simon muses, nodding his head vigorously. I suddenly find him infuriating.

'Tell me what's going on!' I didn't mean to shout. 'Please tell me what's going on,' I repeat, more quietly this time.

'OK. I'm sorry. I just wanted to make sure. On the day Greg went missing, around lunchtime, I came round that there bend in my car—' he points behind him '—and almost drove into the back of another car that was stopped on the corner.'

His North Devon inflections are really pronounced and I remember him being mocked for it at school. I always felt sorry for him. It's not like the other kids at the local comprehensive had plummy accents. We all spoke with varying degrees of Devonian burr.

'Go on,' I say, trying to keep the impatience out of my voice.

'It was pissing down. There were two people in the car. I'm pretty sure they were grockles, not locals. A man and a woman. Actually, they weren't *in* the car. He said they'd just changed a tyre. His missus was standing next to the car. They were both drenched.'

'I don't understand what this has to do with Greg's mobile.'

'They were acting really suspicious, you know. At first, I thought it was because he'd been drinking.'

77

'What do you mean?'

'I wound down my window to see if they needed help and when the bloke stooped to talk to me, I could smell alcohol on his breath. He'd driven into the hedge, you see. The front of the car was dented.' He pauses, maybe to let this sink in before he hits me with the next part. 'It's a hell of a coincidence. Don't you think?' Simon continues. 'The same place. On the same day.'

'You think they hit Greg. Could Greg have been in the car? In the back seat? Were they taking him to hospital?'

'Maybe, but I stopped my car more or less alongside theirs, well, as close to it as I could, and I leaned out of my window to get a look at the damage and all. If someone had been in the back seat, even lying down, I think I'd have seen them. Or heard them. If Greg was injured, he'd probably have been screaming in pain.'

'So, what do you think happened?'

'The bloke was closing the boot as I rounded the bend. He said he'd just put the warning triangle back into the car. He sounded convincing, but he wouldn't look me in the eye. I didn't believe him.'

Finally, I grasp what's going through Simon's mind. I feel as if someone has tipped a bucket of icy water over me. The blood drains from my face. Simon grabs my elbow as I sway. 'You think he ran over Greg and shut him in the boot.'

'I'm trying not to think that, to be honest, any of it,' Simon says, 'but it adds up, doesn't it?'

Simon's words have winded me, as if he has punched me. The pain is unbearable. I double over, my hands on my knees, and try to breathe in through my nose and out through my mouth. Simon rubs my back. I don't want him to touch me, but I don't resist.

As I'm bending over, staring at the tarmac, I see myself the night I found Greg's phone, stamping on that piece of coloured plastic. It was right here, in this very spot. I look around, but there's not even a tiny fragment of plastic here now. At the time, I thought it might be part of a bicycle reflector. But what if it was a piece

78

of broken indicator from a car? The car that hit Greg? Oh, God. I may have destroyed a vital piece of evidence.

'Perhaps we're jumping to conclusions,' Simon says. 'It doesn't explain why both Greg and the dog have gone missing.'

He's backtracking, hoping there's another scenario, one we haven't considered. But now I've pictured Greg, bloodied and bruised, lying lifeless in the ditch, I can't get that image out of my head. Is he dead? Did he die straight away, on impact? Or did he suffer? A sob rises from deep inside me and erupts from my mouth. I sound like a wounded animal. I'm still hunched over, my eyes fixed on the ground. I feel sick and it's all I can do not to throw up.

When I've caught my breath, Simon says, 'Do you want me to fetch the car? I can jog back to get it and come and pick you up,' he offers. 'Then we can go to the police station, if you like.'

The thought of facing Sergeant Harris again today fills me with dread. Or worse still, having to talk to Constable Wright. 'I want to go home. I need to tell my parents-in-law.'

'OK. I'll go to the police station once I've taken you home.'

I tell Simon about the piece of plastic and ask him to tell the police. But I'm not hopeful. I couldn't see any trace of it just now and the police have already searched the spot where I found the phone. They can't have found anything, either, or they would have said.

Simon puts his arm around my waist and leads me a little further along the road, towards the footpath. He stops at a grass verge. 'Sit here,' he says. 'I'll be as quick as I can.'

I sit on the grass and pull my knees to my chest. The same words go through my head, over and over again. *Hit-and-run. Hit-and-run.* Then, a question. *Is there any chance Greg is still alive?* I want to believe he is, but if the couple put him in the boot of their car, he can't be. They must have run him over. They must have killed him.

A dog walker stops to ask if I'm OK. I've seen her several times before when I've been out with Rusty. My answer doesn't sound coherent to me, but she sits down on the grass next to me and puts her free arm – the one not holding the lead – around my shoulders. She and her dog wait with me until Simon gets back.

Simon is the one who thanks her. I can hardly speak. As I get into his VW Polo, a thought springs to mind, but it's not until Simon pulls into the driveway of my cottage that I'm able to express it. I'm wondering if the boot of the car was big enough for both Greg and Rusty, if they were both killed by the motorist.

'Si . . . Simon? Did you recognise the car? The make and model, I mean? How big was the boot?'

'It was an Audi. Not sure about the model,' he says. 'I'd recognise it if I looked it up on the Internet. Grey. Yeah, a fairly big boot, I'd say.' I realise Simon has followed my train of thought when he adds, 'Big enough.'

But my thoughts have already moved on.

Simon gets out of the car and walks round to the passenger side to open the door for me. He takes my arm, but I don't move.

'What's wrong?' he says. When I don't reply, he says, 'I'm sorry. That was a really stupid—'

'Simon,' I say. 'I think I'd better come to the police station with you.'

'OK, if you're—'

I interrupt him. 'I know who was driving that car. I know who's responsible for what happened to Greg.' I don't dare to say out loud the words that are going through my head.

I know who killed my husband.

Chapter 12

Kirsten

Nick has booked a day room in their usual hotel. When Kirsten's estate agency has a convenient upmarket furnished flat to let, they sometimes meet up there for a change, but otherwise they come here. The hotel is situated in Notting Hill, less than a ten-minute Tube ride from Kirsten's office in Kensington. It takes Nick – or rather his chauffeur, since Nick doesn't use his own car for work – about half an hour to drive there from his chambers in Blackfriars. It's sufficiently far away from both places of work for them not to risk bumping into someone they know.

The first time they came here, about three months into their affair, Kirsten was nervous and embarrassed. Until then, they'd met up only in the evenings, in hotels with renowned restaurants. But Lily was young and Kirsten found it hard to get away and could rarely spend the night in the hotel room. After a while, so they could see each other more often, Nick suggested a daytime hotel. It carried sordid connotations for Kirsten, akin to renting a room by the hour. Nick assured her that all sorts of people used day rooms – foreign businessmen and -women who came to London for conferences and required somewhere quiet to work and freshen up, pilots and flight attendants with long layovers or jetlagged travellers who needed a nap before the next leg of their journey.

But Kirsten is convinced that, like them, the majority of this luxury hotel's clients are lovers who come here during their lunch breaks for an extramarital shag and a postcoital shower. The receptionist must know it and certainly recognises the two of them by now, but she maintains a perfectly expressionless face and a strictly professional tone when taking their cash and handing them their key card.

As Nick lies in her arms, still inside her, she wonders, not for the first time, what he's doing with her. He's the one who pursued her – with dogged determination – when they met five years ago, and to this day she's surprised that he set his sights on her. She has seen his wife – once in real life, but she regularly checks out the other woman's social media accounts – and she's absolutely stunning. Nick refers to his wife as Edie, an anglicised form of her real, Nigerian name – Ediye, meaning beautiful. Every time she stalks Ediye online, Kirsten is reminded of that pretty Kenyan actress in *Black Panther*. Lupita Something – Kirsten never can remember her surname. With her perfect skin and white teeth, Ediye could be a supermodel. And judging from the photos she posts on Instagram in which she's standing next to Nick, she's a lot taller than Kirsten as well as a lot more attractive.

Kirsten likes to think Ediye is shallow and stupid – they would have gorgeous-looking kids, Ediye and Nick, and would be better off with his brains than hers. But Nick has told Kirsten that they are childless by choice. Kirsten doesn't know whose choice it is – Nick's, Ediye's or a mutual decision – but according to the story Kirsten tells herself, vain Ediye doesn't want to ruin her hourglass figure by getting pregnant.

When Kirsten wonders what Nick is doing with her, she has to remind herself to turn that question around. What is she doing with Nick? On paper, Kirsten has everything: a loving and loyal husband, an adorable daughter, her forever home. To all intents and purposes, she is happily married. Jamie might not have as prestigious a job as Nick or drive such a nice car, but he's just as intelligent and a lot more empathetic. She wishes she loved Jamie more and Nick less.

Sexually, her husband satisfies her, in some ways better than Nick does. Disappointingly, Nick is not that well-endowed. Jamie is. Seriously, only men claim that size doesn't matter. Every woman knows it does. But Nick can bring Kirsten to the brink of orgasm by merely kissing her. He's such a good kisser. She finds the illicitness of it all, paired with the danger, so exciting. It's not just about the sex, though. She loves the way they share things, just the two of them, that no one else knows about. And when she's with Nick, she feels like a woman, not a mother. She can have adult conversations that don't revolve around nits, Disney princesses and the pet gerbil at school. Kirsten knows she's far from perfect, but when she's with Nick she doesn't feel like a complete failure.

But her relationship with Nick can be challenging. He sometimes ignores her. He says he's busy, and with his high-flying career, he must be, but she suspects he plays on that, using his workload as an excuse to fob her off when he has something better to do. She struggles to keep time with the unpredictable rhythm he sets. He bombards her with affection and attention, and she gets used to her phone pinging or ringing several times a day, whenever he has a free moment. Then she doesn't hear from him for days. When he does resurface, he lavishes her with compliments, gifts and praise. One minute, he makes her feel like she's at the bottom of his to-do list and the next, he makes her feel like she's the most important person, not only in his life, but in the world. That's part of what keeps her coming back for more. It's cyclical. It's sickening going round and round, up and down, but she's addicted to him and constantly craves the next high. He has a hold over her that sometimes resembles a stranglehold. She has tried to give him up, she really has, but he has become a fixture in her life. They're made for each other, cut from the same cloth.

With their own bodies still entwined, Kirsten asks Nick what he has done with Gregory Wood's body. He rolls off her and lies on his back on the starched sheets, fingers interlaced behind his head.

'I thought we agreed not to bring that up again,' he says. She doesn't recall that conversation. 'The less you know, the better.'

She slits her eyes at him. She doesn't fully trust Nick. Never has. He's too good at lying. It's part of his job. He lies at work as well as at home, to his wife. He has never lied to Kirsten, as far as she knows. But there's no doubt in her mind he would pin everything on her, if it came to it. He'd throw her to the wolves to save his own skin and come out of it all with his beautiful wife on his arm and without a blemish on his reputation.

'You don't need to worry about it. I told you that.'

She is worried, of course she is. She's terrified they might get caught.

'He had a wife, Nick. I can't imagine what—'

Nick cuts her off. 'Look, Kirsten. It was an accident. Nothing we could have done. Don't dwell on it. Don't beat yourself up about it too much.'

Kirsten has been trying not to beat herself up about it; she's been trying not to think about it. But the fact remains, they're responsible for a man's death and for covering up his death. Kirsten feels for the widow, she really does, but despite that, she doesn't feel the need to assuage her guilt as much as she thinks she should. She blames Nick more than she blames herself. This is all his fault. If only he hadn't drunk so much.

She has considered denouncing him to the police. It would put an end to this limbo, get rid of the sword of Damocles that she senses above her head when she wonders if Gregory Wood's disappearance can be connected to Nick and her. She could tell the police Nick was drink-driving and say she didn't come forward sooner out of misplaced loyalty and fear of what he would do to her if she did.

But she can't do it. She might lose Jamie and Lily as well as Nick, and she won't take that risk. And Nick knows how to twist the truth, not only to make her doubt herself or comply with his wishes, but also to manipulate the jury. He gets most of his clients off, even when they're accused of murder. He certainly won't go down for it himself. No matter what happens, he'll sail through all this with impunity.

He reaches for his made-to-measure jacket and extracts one of his mobiles – he has at least two in addition to the burner phone – from an inside pocket. His brow furrows as he focuses on the screen, typing something into the phone with his thumbs.

Kirsten knows what will get his attention. 'I used Gregory Wood's bank card to pay for some shopping the other day,' she says, feigning nonchalance.

A storm cloud passes over his face. 'What the fuck, Kirsten?' He throws his mobile onto the bed and sits up, pulling the sheets over his bare legs. 'What the hell were you thinking? You told me you'd got rid of his wallet.'

Maybe using the dead man's card wasn't such a good idea after all. 'I thought it might throw the police off the scent a bit,' Kirsten mutters.

'What scent? There was no scent! Nothing to connect him to us.' Nick is apoplectic. Kirsten inches away from him. 'Now the police will know he ended up in London!'

'London? Who said anything about London? I used the card in Dover.'

Nick gets out of bed and harrumphs loudly, which, despite herself, Kirsten finds comical. Luckily, he stomps off to the bathroom without a glance behind him and doesn't see her trying to suppress a smile.

They always take a shower together before leaving the hotel, but Kirsten thinks it would be wise on this occasion to wait her turn. What the hell was she thinking? Nick's question is a good one. Why did she tell him? Did she expect him to congratulate her for taking her own initiative for once? It's odd – she's the one who wears the trousers at home and she knows she's got a reputation for being

85

a bossy bitch at work, but until now, she has liked the fact that, of the two of them, Nick's the one who calls the shots. It's really only since the accident that this has started to bother her. It used to give her the impression he was taking care of her and she liked that. Only now does it feel as if he's controlling her.

When Kirsten has also taken a shower and emerges from the bathroom in a haze of steam, Nick's sitting on the bed, propped up against the pillows, dressed except for his shoes and jacket. Before he even speaks, she can sense that the mood has changed. He's no longer angry with her. He looks slightly flustered, although Kirsten has no idea why. She hovers in the doorway, observing him.

His tie is dangling around his neck. She always knots it for him before they leave the hotel room. He's a renowned criminal defence barrister, an incredibly clever guy, but even though he wears a tie to work every day and must have worn one to school, as she did, he's still hopeless at knotting it himself. Kirsten finds this endearing, but resents the thought that his wife must do the honours in the mornings before he leaves the house.

'Come and see this, Kirsten.' Nick pats the mattress to indicate she should sit next to him. 'This is the latest,' he says, 'from North Devon.'

She's about to remind him that he said she wasn't to look up things online so why is he doing it, but she swallows down her retort. Wrapped in her white hotel towel, she does as she's told. He puts one arm around her shoulders and angles his phone towards her to show her a YouTube video. *ITV News – West Country* is written as a caption underneath, along with yesterday's date.

A police officer wearing uniform appears on the screen. Her name comes up across the bottom of it. *Sergeant Lucy Harris, Devon & Cornwall Police.* Kirsten's vision blurs as she realises it's an appeal for information in connection with the disappearance of Gregory Wood. She blinks to bring the woman back into focus.

To begin with, it's along much the same lines as the succinct online newspaper articles she has read. The officer gives a description of what the missing man was wearing. The time and date on which he was last seen. The camera cuts to a picture of Gregory Wood, wearing similar clothes to the outfit being described. He's smiling at whoever took this photo – his wife, probably. Kirsten will be haunted now by this picture of Gregory Wood, immortalised with a happy, unsuspecting expression on his face. At least it beats the image she has had scored into her brain until now, of him staring at her through unblinking, unseeing eyes as he lay on the tarmac. Shivering, Kirsten tries to wrap the damp towel round her more tightly and wishes she'd put on the fluffy hotel bathrobe.

The photograph of Gregory Wood is no longer on the screen, thankfully. The camera is once again on the stony-faced police officer.

'At the present time, there's no suspicion of foul play,' she's saying in her rather monotonous voice, 'but Gregory Wood's family and the police are concerned for his welfare, particularly as it would be out of character for him to have disappeared of his own volition.'

No suspicion of foul play. Kirsten's shoulders relax a little.

But then there's a shot of the road she and Nick were driving along. It looks completely different in the sunlight, but Kirsten recognises it. It's the scene of the accident. The exact place where they ran over Gregory Wood. Her heart skips a beat. And then another. She fails to grasp a scrap of information. Something about a mobile phone. Kirsten's brain fills in the gaps. She makes an effort to concentrate on the news bulletin and catches the next bit. The couple's fox-red Labrador hasn't come home, either. A photo of Rusty fills Nick's mobile screen.

The police officer is still speaking. Suddenly Kirsten's whole body stiffens. 'Play that back a bit,' she says. Nick does as she asks. He looked a little bemused before, but now he seems unperturbed.

'If you were driving in the area, please check your dashcam footage in case you captured something that could help us with our investigation,' the police officer is saying. It's the next bit that Kirsten thinks she must have misheard. She grips Nick's arm. 'Police are

87

also keen to speak to the owner of a silver Audi A8,' she says. 'The car was sighted in the vicinity . . . the driver to come forward . . .'

Kirsten doesn't take in the rest. She feels as if she's drowning and the sergeant is above the surface talking to her, but refusing to reach out to her, as she goes down. She can hear the police officer's words, but she can't decipher any meaning from them.

The report is over. It must have lasted less than two minutes, but time seems to have stopped for Kirsten. Nick puts his phone on the bedside table and holds Kirsten tightly to him with both arms, rocking her until her breathing slows. She can't speak. *What scent? There was no scent!* Nick's words are on a grating loop in her head. There's a scent now. A strong stench. They have the colour, make and model of Nick's car. Someone must have seen them. Presumably that brainless moron in his unroadworthy old banger who almost crashed into the back of Nick's Audi. How did they put two and two together? How is Nick so unruffled?

'The car! Someone saw your car! If they find your Audi—'

'They won't. New reg plates, new owner. I've ordered another car. Different colour, different make. A Range Rover Velar. It was time for a change, anyway.'

She feels her pulse slow to a more normal rate. Nick has got rid of the body and the car. He's taken care of all the evidence against them.

'You did good, baby,' he says, planting a kiss on the top of her head. He hasn't called her that for a while. 'Looks like your idea of using his bank card was a good one. You've laid a false trail. When did you make the transaction?'

'Last weekend.'

'Why Dover? That's an excellent red herring. With a bit of luck, they'll assume he got on the ferry to France!'

'That's what I was hoping. We went to our cottage in Folkestone. I drove to Dover.'

Nick doesn't usually like it when she makes references, even oblique ones, to her family or anything connected with her husband

and daughter, which includes Jamie's holiday home, but he shows not a hint of his customary jealousy. She tells him about making the phone call from the burner phone, too.

'Well done, baby!'

And just like that, she's back in his good books and she feels her heart lift as she basks in his praise.

'What do we do next?' she asks.

Chapter 13

Amy

I'm on edge in the days following Sergeant Harris's appeal. Pam, Hugh and I watched it on the news together the evening it was broadcast, sitting on my sofa, my parents-in-law clinging to each other. Now we're waiting to see if someone can provide the police with a useful lead. The wait is long.

'No news is good news,' Pam says. She repeats this like a mantra. It's not, but I don't contradict her. I know she's trying to find the right balance between staying positive, but not hoping too much. Unlike Pam, I'm not holding out much hope that Greg will be found alive, but like them, I badly need answers.

'They should have asked us to participate in the appeal,' Hugh comments for at least the third time since it was aired. 'It would have had more impact.'

I wince at his choice of words. With every day that passes, I'm more and more convinced Greg is the victim of a hit-and-run.

'The police don't think there's any foul play,' Pam reminds Hugh patiently. 'It's an appeal for witnesses to come forward with information, not for someone to confess to a crime.'

'But what about the car? That driver crashed into the hedge on the bend where Amy found Greg's phone. Surely that proves foul play.'

'It doesn't prove anything,' Pam says, although she has admitted she's also leaning towards this sequence of events. 'Constable Wright said the police found nothing at the scene. No clues at all. You know that.'

That makes me wince, too. I may have destroyed the only piece of evidence the couple left behind if, as I now suspect, the piece of plastic I stamped on was from their car. When I told Sergeant Harris about it, she promised to send someone to check, but, as I feared, nothing came of it. I'm not sure how hard the police looked, or if they looked at all. Despite the appeal, I get the impression that even Harris has more or less written off any hope of finding Greg, or of finding out what happened to him.

There's no lead on the Taylors, either. Like Greg, they've disappeared without a trace. I've tried the mobile number I had for Mr Taylor a few times, but the calls didn't go through. I got a delivery error message when I sent an email to the address he gave me when he made the booking over the phone. I must have written it down wrong. Or perhaps he deliberately gave me a fake mobile number and a fake email address, for some reason – to avoid getting spam or something. Despite her promise, Mrs Taylor hasn't left an online review for the flat, so I can't contact her that way, either.

As Constable Wright pointed out when I relayed all this to him and Sergeant Harris, Taylor is a common surname and I have no idea where they live, so we don't have anything to go on. They've got away; I've reached a dead end. I never even saw Mr Taylor. Greg went to greet the couple when they arrived and Mr Taylor stayed in the car, behind the wheel, while Mrs Taylor got out and dropped off the keys. I wouldn't recognise him if our paths crossed again.

My parents-in-law come round every day. They need to feel useful and I find their presence comforting, even when they bicker. Pam cooks, so I force myself to eat, even though I have no appetite whatsoever. I'm sure they don't, either. Right now, Hugh is pacing, as he often does, in the living room. My mother-in-law is keeping herself busy in the kitchen, cleaning or cooking, I'm not sure which.

By being here, they're helping to keep me sane. I've lost my husband, my baby and even my dog. I've lost my life as I lived and loved it. The depth of my loss hits me several times a day and each time it does, I feel as if I'm drowning. It's all I can do to stay afloat. It's an effort to breathe. The pain is almost unbearable. Pam and Hugh are all I have. I may well be all they've got left now, too. The only other thing that keeps me going is the anger. I hold on to it, let it build up and store it. I may need it.

My own mother was supportive, in her own way, when I rang her a few days ago, at around midday for her and in the middle of the night for me. I couldn't sleep and I wanted to hear her voice. But her voice didn't sound familiar, an Aussie twang having swallowed up all hint of a Devonian accent. The geographical distance has lengthened the emotional distance between us over the years. I've only seen her twice since she emigrated. She was sympathetic on the phone, but she's so far away and there's not much she can do. When I rang her, I just wanted to talk to someone – someone I could feel close to and who, contrary to Pam and Hugh, wasn't so close to Greg. I can't rely on my parents-in-law to patch me up when they're falling apart themselves.

My mum clearly felt helpless. I hadn't told her I was pregnant, so I didn't tell her about the miscarriage. It would only have upset her more. I did make the mistake of telling her that the police thought Greg might have done a runner because of marital problems, mental health problems or financial problems with his business. My mum's response was to transfer some money to my bank account. We didn't have much money when I was growing up. My mum worked, but as a single mum, she had to work around me. It must have been hard for her. After I left home, though, she landed on her feet. Jayden, my stepfather, is loaded.

I protested when Mum promised to send money, but she insisted. She suggested I should use it to find out what has happened to Greg, perhaps by offering a reward or hiring a private investigator. My phone is on the coffee table in front of me. I grab it to check if the money shows up on my account yet. If it does, I need to let my mum know I've received it and thank her. If I'm honest, I'm also a little curious to see how much of my stepfather's money my mother has sent me.

I gape at the amount. There must be an extra zero. Or maybe this is the amount in Australian dollars. I have no idea what the exchange rate is. Unless I'm mistaken, my mother has transferred almost thirty thousand pounds into my bank account. She and my stepfather must be absolutely rolling in it. I suppose as a cardiologist, he earns a good living. My mother keeps busy and does a lot of volunteer work, but as far as I know, she hasn't had paid employment since she moved to Melbourne.

Before I can check the amount, another transaction grabs my attention. A much smaller amount – £49.50 – but just as shocking. My heart beats hard against my chest and in my ears. This can't be right. I check the date. It's for the Saturday after Greg went missing. The payment was made from our joint account with Greg's debit card at a supermarket in Dover. *Dover?* That's all the information I have. The amount, the place, the date. My online statement doesn't show the time the transaction was made. It can't be Greg. Is this a mistake? Has Greg's card been stolen or cloned?

I'm about to discuss this with Pam and Hugh, but the doorbell rings. The sound makes all three of us jump, even though we're expecting Sergeant Harris and Constable Wright and they're bang on time. They said they'd drop in with an update. They do this regularly and usually have nothing to report, so this doesn't mean they've got any new leads. But the appeal was three days ago, so maybe today they'll have something to share with us.

I open the front door while Pam calls out from the kitchen that she's put the kettle on. She knows by now how the officers take their tea. A paragon of British hospitality, Pam wouldn't dream of having people in her home – or mine – without serving them a mug of tea.

Once we're all seated in the living room, mugs steaming on the coffee table, Sergeant Harris begins. 'Someone has come forward,' she says. 'A witness.' Pam, who is sitting next to me on the sofa, leans towards Harris. 'A waiter from The Thatch saw a couple leave in a silver Audi A8 after lunch,' the sergeant continues. 'He couldn't say at exactly what time, but he did remember the couple were their first customers that day, so it seems highly likely that this puts them in the relevant time frame for Gregory's disappearance.'

'There's a security camera and we're in the process of checking the footage from it,' Constable Wright says, 'but given the weather and where the waiter says they were parked, we're not optimistic about making out the registration plate.'

'We'll keep you posted, though,' Sergeant Harris adds with a tight smile.

'So, it *was* a hit-and-run.' I don't mean to say it out loud.

'Not necessarily,' Wright says. 'That's not the line of inquiry we're pursuing at the moment.'

'We're keeping our minds open,' the sergeant says, looking pointedly at the constable.

'But the smashed phone, the driver closing the boot. It all . . .' Sensing Pam tense up beside me, I don't finish my sentence. She doesn't want to rule out the possibility that her son might still be alive, whereas my reasoning is that if he were alive, he would have found his way back to me by now.

'We think there's a strong possibility that Gregory was in the car, but not in the boot?' Harris makes it sound like a question.

'We think he might have been hitchhiking and the couple stopped to pick him up,' Wright says. 'Your husband and your dog.'

'Before or after they drove into the hedge?' Hugh says, his voice laced with incredulity. This is the first thing he has said since the officers arrived. He can't stand Constable Wright and has referred to him as 'that cocky copper' when talking to Pam and me.

'Simon didn't see anyone in the back of the car,' I point out.

'There could be a couple of reasons your friend didn't see anyone

94

in the back seat.' Constable Wright chooses to respond to me rather than my father-in-law. 'The windows on the Audi were probably tinted. And your friend's Polo . . . he didn't get out of his car and he wouldn't really have been in a position to see into the Audi.'

'What do you mean?' Pam asks.

'Well, Mr Tucker's car . . . there's a far lower ground clearance.'

Out of the corner of my eye, I see Pam frown.

'The ride height,' the constable clarifies for her benefit. 'Basically, the Audi would have been far higher off the ground. Mr Tucker probably wouldn't have been able to see into the back seat, not clearly, anyway, no matter how close the two cars were.'

'Or he might not have seen anyone in the back seat because there was no one in the back seat.' Hugh isn't buying Wright's theory.

Sergeant Harris takes over, scrutinising me through eyes the colour of mud. 'Amy, do you or your husband have friends or relatives on the continent?'

The complete change of subject throws me. 'The continent? You mean Europe?'

'France, perhaps?' This from Wright.

'No! Why do you ask that?'

Instead of answering my question, Sergeant Harris poses another one. 'Does Gregory have a passport?'

'Yes.'

'Could you fetch it for us, please?'

I get up too quickly, making my head spin. My legs feel wobbly as I walk through the kitchen to the small room leading off from it. It was once a pantry, but it seemed too big and too square to be used for that purpose, so Greg and I made it into an office, although it's too small, really, to serve that function.

I fumble around in the top drawer of my desk, but can't find either of our passports. They must be in here somewhere. My mind is racing. France? Passport? I should probably feel reassured that the police don't seem to think Greg is dead. If he's alive, things might eventually go back to normal. *Damn!* The passports aren't in the second drawer, either. I close it with a bang. But I know my husband. I know they're wrong.

I find both our passports in the third drawer.

'They're no longer valid,' Sergeant Harris says, flicking through them when I hand her the passports. 'The expiry date on both of them was six months ago.'

I shrug. 'We weren't able to travel during the pandemic. We didn't have any immediate travel plans.' I don't add that we don't have the budget at the moment to travel, anyway.

'Sergeant Harris, would you please tell us what's going on.' It's not a question or a request, but a demand. Hugh has clearly had more than enough of this. 'This is all rather cryptic and I think an explanation would be in order, don't you?'

'Yes, Mr Wood. Of course.' Harris doesn't apologise or sound contrite. 'We traced the incoming call to Amy's phone. The call with the blocked number?' She pauses, expecting us to urge her on, perhaps. 'It was made from a burner phone,' Harris continues. 'And we managed to—'

'Was it made from Dover?'

'Yes!' Harris turns to me, her eyebrows disappearing into her fringe.

'How did you know that?' Constable Wright asks.

I can't answer straight away. Based on that one phone call, that Harris warned might not even be relevant to their investigation, they've now concocted a story in which Greg has left me of his own volition, hitchhiked to Dover and, from there, fled to France. It's such a ridiculous idea. The longer Harris and Wright veer off course, following false leads, the further we'll stray from the truth. I'm aware that what I'm about to tell them about the debit card transaction will only support their far-fetched theory, but I can't keep the information from them.

I stare vacantly at the coffee table, avoiding the gaze of the police officers. It's only when I blink and the table swims back into focus that I realise tears are welling up in my eyes, threatening to spill down my cheeks. As I clear my throat to speak, I notice no one has touched their tea.

Hi,

I appeared in the crown court today for my plea and preparation hearing. I felt like an extra in a TV courtroom drama. The preposterous wigs and extravagant gowns were merely props and costumes; the legal jargon badly scripted lines. But it turned out I didn't have a walk-on part; I had the starring role. The grave faces looking my way and the accusing eyes fixed on me were all too real.

A date has been set for the trial. It is to start in just over six months' time. I'm terrified. I'm going to be tried for murder. Me! Can you believe it? It's all so ironic. There's a lot of evidence against me. Some of it is circumstantial, but most of it is conclusive. Damning. If I'm found guilty, I'll be sentenced to life imprisonment. Perhaps I should say, when, not if. A guilty verdict seems to be practically a foregone conclusion.

I want to proclaim my innocence at the top of my voice. I'M INNOCENT!!! But there's no point. I'm only innocent until proven guilty. I've always thought that phrase should be 'innocent unless proven guilty'. With 'until', it doesn't sound like a presumption of innocence; it sounds more like a question of time.

I wish you could visit me. I'd love to know what you think about this, what you would do in my shoes. But even if the circumstances were different, I probably wouldn't dare to ask you. There's nothing you could tell me that I don't already know, and nothing you or anyone else could say that would make me believe I have a fighting chance of getting out of this mess.

Chapter 14

Amy

He doesn't have a face, and yet he haunts me day and night. It troubles me that I don't know what he looks like. Does he have dark hair? Fair hair? Is he good-looking? Average? Is he tall? Short? Skinny or stout? People sometimes say they can't put a name to the face. For me, it's the other way round. I know his name. I need to put a face to the name so I can visualise the person I'm directing all my anger and hatred at, the man who I'm convinced drove out of my driveway that day in his Audi A8, and then later that same day drove his car into my husband.

Greg has been missing for over a month now and I haven't seen either Constable Wright or Sergeant Harris for a week. Harris has phoned me a couple of times, ostensibly to keep me in the loop, although she doesn't seem to have anything new to share. Apparently, the police were inundated with calls after her television appeal, but none of those calls resulted in any concrete leads.

One motorist did come forward with dashcam footage. He passed Greg on Moor Lane, the road where I found his mobile phone. The police showed me the video so I could confirm it was my husband. Despite the weather, the images were surprisingly clear. There was no doubt it was Greg, with Rusty on the lead, pulling him along. Rusty never minded the rain. Greg must already have been soaked as the motorist drove by, but the driver slowed, as if careful not to splash him. Greg waved at him just before he drove past. That image has seared my brain.

The motorist was probably the last person to see Greg alive. Apart from the Taylors, that is. But other than confirming that Greg was indeed walking along the road where I found his phone and providing a more precise time frame for his disappearance, ultimately the dashcam footage isn't of any use.

Similarly, as Constable Wright had predicted, the police weren't able to get the Audi's number plate in the footage from the surveillance camera in the car park of The Thatch. Without a registration number, Sergeant Harris explained, the police can't get any vehicle location data for the Taylors' car from ANPR cameras. Nor were they able to get a decent image of the Taylors themselves, since they entered and left the restaurant with their faces and bodies concealed by an umbrella.

Sergeant Harris and Constable Wright haven't said as much, but I sense that the investigation, such as it is, is grinding to a halt. They have nothing to go on. Constable Wright still wholeheartedly believes that Greg left me willingly, hitching a ride with the Taylors to get away. They seem to have put the phone call from Dover down to an aborted attempt from my husband to say goodbye. As for the contactless payment from a Dover supermarket, which turned out to have been made just before midday, Constable Wright suggested that this was Greg buying lunch and possibly clothes and forgetting to use cash before embarking on a ferry to Calais. According to Sergeant Harris, they didn't find anything helpful on the CCTV footage.

All of this runs through my head as I lie in bed, trying desperately to get back to sleep. Sleep has become sporadic and I no longer take it for granted. I want to be proactive and do something to find out what has happened to my husband, but I've no idea where to start. This thought preys on me every night, as images of Greg come to me in succession, as if I'm scrolling through the photos on my phone in the dark. Greg in his red swimming trunks the day I met him on the beach, Greg standing behind the counter of his shop the day he opened it, Greg crying with joy the morning we found out I was pregnant, Greg clinking his glass of sparkling wine against my glass of sparkling water the evening we celebrated our anniversary at his parents' house, Greg lying lifeless in a ditch. It always ends with this last image, the only one not based on something I've seen with my own eyes.

In the end, I get up. Despite the hopelessness I'm feeling, I need to be strong. Today I'm going back to work. I'll go mad if I continue to stay at home doing nothing. Liz said it was too soon, but I insisted, so she has organised a phased return for me to take off the pressure. For the moment, she's keeping on the supply teacher who has replaced me and I'm to give him a hand.

I can't help feeling nervous about my first day back. It hasn't helped with the insomnia. I've woken up way too early, so I decide to go for a walk before making myself eat at least a little breakfast. Instead of going along Moor Lane towards Baggy Point, as I'm used to doing with Greg and Rusty, I deliberately go the other way and head for the village.

Croyde is a beautiful seaside village. In the off-season, it's a bit of a ghost town, but when the tourist shops and cafés start to open up again, from Easter onwards, there's a vibrant vibe to the place. The village appears quaint and old world, but it attracts younger-age visitors who rock up in their droves to surf. Annual music, food and surfing festivals also enhance the vitality and atmosphere of the place.

When Greg went missing at the beginning of May, many of the local businesses had recently reopened for the summer season, or at the very least were opening their doors at weekends. Greg had also opened for business on the Saturday and Sunday, but when he saw the forecast, he decided it wasn't worth it for the Monday. He said no one would be interested in buying surf shorts and T-shirts or hiring wetsuits. He thought it unlikely any tourists who had come to North Devon for the bank holiday weekend would hang around in the pouring rain.

Greg's disappearance is surrounded by if onlys and what ifs. If only the weather had been good for the May Day weekend. If only Greg had been at work. He wouldn't have gone missing; he would be here. What if I hadn't rented out the flat to that couple? What if I'd refused to take a booking over the phone or a cash payment? Perhaps, then, they would have gone somewhere else or even stayed at home, or maybe now I'd be able to locate them.

It's only as I pass The Thatch that I realise there is something I can do. I want to talk to the waiter myself in case he remembers a detail he didn't think of when he was talking to the police. Perhaps he overheard a snippet of the Taylors' conversation during their meal or maybe he noticed something that might indicate where they were heading when they left the restaurant. I resolve to come back when the pub is open. I can ask the server to describe Mr Taylor to me as well. Then I'll know what he looks like.

I pass a shop on the corner with its name painted in bright colours on a signboard above the door. *Swell Surf Clothing & Wetsuits*. Greg's shop. I'd resolved not to look at it, but I can't help myself. In the window, a mannequin sports an improbable combination of boardshorts, flip-flops, a thick waterproof jacket and a woollen beanie. I spot a sign through the glass of the door. *Sorry. We're closed.* Most businesses have similar signs up, but they'll be open from ten a.m. Greg's won't.

That's not the only difference. Of all the shops and businesses along St Mary's Road and in Hobb's Hill, *Swell Surf Clothing & Wetsuits* is the only one not displaying a poster in its window. I see it everywhere. I see *him* everywhere. The village shop and post office, the ice cream parlour, the gift shop, the bistro, even the rival surf clothing shops. I've deliberately come this way on my walk so

101

as not to be reminded of Greg, but he's all around me, peering at me through the windows, from the photo underneath the capital letters: HAVE YOU SEEN THIS MAN?

I've lived in Croyde all my life. Among the locals, everyone knows everyone else's business. I've been avoiding people. I couldn't bear to see the sympathy in their eyes or answer the same question over and over again. *Any news?* I still receive several text messages a day with those exact words. I haven't come into the centre of the village since Greg disappeared. I've driven through it a few times, on my way to the police station in Barnstaple or the supermarket, but I didn't notice the posters. Liz told me she'd designed a poster and run off some colour photocopies at school. But I had no idea that every single shopkeeper had put one up.

I'm overwhelmed by the support and the sense of community, and tears cascade down my cheeks. I remember Sandra, Tom's wife, telling me shortly after Greg went missing that Tom, Sharky and Matt, our surfing buddies, had organised their own search. Apparently, there was a huge turnout of locals, who scoured the beaches and dunes alongside volunteer coastguards. No one has given up on Greg and it both buoys me up and pushes me under because I've been telling myself he's dead. I can't see another explanation for him not coming home and I don't want to cling to false hope. Am I wrong not to consider he might still be alive? I'm sobbing uncontrollably now and in Greg's shop window, I catch sight of my reflection, my body hunched over into a question mark.

A horn hoots from the other side of the road, making me jump. I try to get a grip and swipe at my tears. The car has stopped. I recognise it. Simon winds down the window of his old Volkswagen and sticks out his head.

'Need a lift?' he shouts.

'No, thank you, Simon. I came out to get some fresh air.'

He looks crestfallen. 'I'll pop in later.'

'I'm going back to work today.'

'Well, I'll come round in a few days' time, then.'

'OK,' I call back. 'Thank you,' I add, hoping it doesn't sound too much like a postscript.

I could ask Simon to describe the driver of the Audi to me, but although I'm desperate to know what this man looks like, it's a question I'd rather ask the waiter at The Thatch. Simon is keen to help in any way he can. But he's too keen. I don't want to encourage him. I tell myself he means well and I try to smile as I wave him off. But as I turn to walk home, I shudder involuntarily. I've always found Simon a bit insistent and invasive. I can't put my finger on what it is exactly, but something about him makes me feel uncomfortable.

Chapter 15

Kirsten

He's late. Over half an hour late. Nick can't stand tardiness in others and is always on time himself. Kirsten is trying not to get annoyed, but what little patience she has grows thinner. Has he stood her up? She got the impression he only suggested having dinner together to mollify her because he hasn't had much time for her lately. Nick has always kept her on her toes. She has never taken his love for granted. But since the weekend in North Devon, she feels more insecure than ever. She has no idea where she stands with him anymore.

Sitting at the bar in The Ivy in Covent Garden, she takes a gulp of her second glass of Condrieu. She could do with a cigarette, but she makes it a point of honour never to smoke around Nick, especially as he's always whingeing about his wife smoking. Besides, Kirsten doesn't want her breath to stink when she's with Nick. She doesn't realise she has been staring at one of the bartenders, mesmerised by the way the light bounces off his bald head, until he catches her gaze. She looks away, towards the door. Someone enters the restaurant, but it's not Nick. How long before she should consider his lateness a no-show?

This isn't like Nick. He hasn't even sent a text. She checks her phone again, just to make sure. Still no messages. No missed calls, either. Should she be worried? Has something prevented him from coming? Surely nothing has happened to him. Her heart thumps with a few erratic beats.

Without warning, her thoughts wander to Gregory Wood's widow. How long did Amy Wood wait for her husband to come home before she realised something was wrong? Did her feelings also swing like a pendulum from anger to concern and back again?

She wonders if Amy Wood was happily married or if she had a lover. She knows from the online newspapers that Amy is a primary school teacher. Did she want children of her own? In the minute or two Kirsten talked to her when she dropped off the keys, Amy came over as laid-back and scruffy whereas Kirsten is rather highly strung and likes to dress smartly. Does she have anything in common with Amy Wood?

She opens the Instagram app on her phone and searches for Amy Wood. She has already checked out Gregory Wood – she looked him up the day after the accident – but he kept a surprisingly low online profile, barely using Facebook, and using Instagram and Twitter for his business. He didn't have a TikTok account at all, as far as Kirsten could see.

Amy Wood must be a common name worldwide, so she searches for the right one among Gregory's followers. Amy herself has fewer than thirty followers and, to Kirsten's disappointment, her grid consists of only a handful of photos. Kirsten shares pictures to her Instagram feed several times a week, although she hasn't posted anything since her weekend away with Nick. She probably should. Her sudden silence on social media could appear suspicious.

She scrolls down to the bottom photo, the first one chronologically, and works her way up. She's struck by a shot in which Amy is walking on the beach, away from the sea and towards the photographer, smiling at the camera. She's wearing a short-sleeved wetsuit and carrying a surfboard under one of her suntanned arms.

Her hair wet and scraggly, she has obviously just got out of the water. So, she's a surfer. That explains her tacky ocean wave tattoo.

There are a couple of photos of Amy's dog. Well, Kirsten's dog now. At least for the time being, until she works out what to do with him. Kirsten examines another photo of Amy, wearing pink Crocs, a pleated cotton skirt that makes her look frumpy and a tank top that was probably once white, but must have been washed with the darks. A wide, colourful headband holds back her hair. Kirsten, who prides herself on her elegant sense of dress, smirks at this sartorial disaster, but she has to admit that Amy's pretty, albeit in an understated way.

None of the photos have more than five or six likes and few of them have any comments. Except for the most recent photo. In it, Amy is beaming at her husband, who is holding a glass of champagne or prosecco and looking into her eyes. It's the photo that has the most likes – over three hundred, far more than the number of Amy's followers. And of Kirsten's followers, for that matter. Kirsten furrows her brow. Why has this photo attracted so much attention? It's not a good photo by any means. Both Amy and her husband are out of focus, for a start, and the lighting is poor. She reads the caption below the photo, *Happy anniversary to my husband, my rock, my soulmate.* It's so romantic it's almost nauseating.

Kirsten checks the date on this post and that's when it dawns on her. The photo was taken the evening before the accident. There are close to eighty comments, which Kirsten skims. They all seem to be from complete strangers who have looked up Amy Wood's profile after watching the news. Some people need to get a life. Most comments are from well-wishers, hoping Amy's husband comes home soon. Some are praying for his safe return; others are praying for Amy herself. A staunch atheist, Kirsten scoffs at this. A couple of the messages are rather malicious, accusing Amy of killing her husband and wasting police time.

The fact that the photo was taken just hours before the smile was wiped clean off Amy's face is gnawing at Kirsten's conscience.

She's not sure what to make of this post, but she can't look at it any longer.

As she closes the app, she notices the time on her mobile screen. Nick's now nearly an hour late. She has a sudden need to get out of this place as quickly as possible. After checking the ringtone volume is on max, Kirsten puts her mobile in her handbag and takes out her purse. Then she knocks back what's left of her wine and signals to the bald barman that she'd like to pay.

'My husband has had a problem and isn't going to be able to make it,' she explains, reluctantly handing over a fifty-pound note. If she'd known Nick wouldn't be paying, she'd have chosen a cheaper wine. 'I'm afraid we'll have to cancel our dinner reservation for this evening.'

'Table for two, was it?' he says. 'In what name?'

'Taylor.' The name slips off her tongue automatically before she remembers Nick has changed their fake name. He said they couldn't go by the name of Taylor anymore – it connected them to North Devon. They used that name to book the holiday let. And the restaurant. Kirsten can't recall what Nick changed their pseudo to, though. Another common English surname.

Luckily for her, the barman hasn't heard her blunder and asks her to repeat it.

'Baker,' Kirsten says, as the new name comes back to her.

'No problem, Mrs Baker. I'll take care of that.'

'Thank you.'

Kirsten would like nothing more at this point than to go home, give her daughter a kiss goodnight and curl up with her husband on the sofa, but it's too early. She's supposed to be out for a meal with her colleagues. That's the story she fed Jamie. He has no idea how much her colleagues hate her – not that she cares what they think – but the idea that they would accept to socialise with her is almost comical.

Passing a Nando's, she realises she's ravenous. She'll have to eat before she goes home, but she wouldn't be seen dead in Nando's. Not even with Lily. She fumbles in her handbag for her packet of

Marlboro and lights up. She drags on her cigarette, relishing the heady rush of the nicotine hit, and walks away from the crowds at Covent Garden. A few minutes and another cigarette later, she ends up on the Strand.

As she passes the Royal Courts of Justice, she sees the most recent photo on Amy Wood's Instagram feed before her eyes, as clearly as if she has brought it up again on her phone. Even as Kirsten tries to blink away the vision, Amy Wood's blurred face sharpens stubbornly into focus and turns towards her, staring at her with reproving eyes as her smile inverts to a frown. A pang of guilt stabs Kirsten. This woman was happy before she and Nick mowed down her husband. Her remorse is mixed with fear. Fear they will somehow be tracked down and caught. And fear she will lose Nick. They were fine before the accident, she and Nick. Amy and Gregory Wood, too. If only she could turn back time.

Walking along the Victoria Embankment, Kirsten realises she's not far from the chambers of Bell, Jackson and Hunter. She walked past the Grade II listed building in Temple Avenue once, months ago, but she was terrified Nick would step out of his chauffeur-driven car or look out the window of his office, and see her peering through the wrought-iron bars of the front gate. She didn't dare go there again. She wonders if Nick's there this evening, working late. Perhaps there has been a last-minute development on a case. But that doesn't explain why he didn't fire off a quick text message to warn her. Kirsten can't quell her growing unease.

She finds a little Italian restaurant in a side road near Temple Bar that looks decent enough and has a small table free. She orders pesto tagliatelle and a glass of Vermentino. She would usually steer clear of the most garlicky meals when she's out with Nick, just as she resists the temptation to smoke. But it won't matter if her breath stinks this evening. The pasta is delicious, but although she's hungry, she's too jittery to enjoy her food. As she pushes it round her plate, she tries to ring Nick again, but it goes straight to voicemail. Next she texts Jamie.

Bored out of my head.
I'll think up an excuse to get
away and come home asap.

Kirsten pays – with her credit card this time, she could feasibly have eaten here with her colleagues, after all – and leaves. She heads for Holborn Underground Station. From here, the Tube is direct to Wood Green on the Piccadilly Line and then it's a ten-minute walk. The whole journey takes her less than half an hour, but it seems interminable.

Kirsten checks her phone one last time as she stands on the doorstep of her house. Still no news from Nick. She drops the mobile into her handbag and rummages around for her keys. She's now frantic with worry as well as tipsy and has difficulty inserting her front door key in the lock. She opens the door and bends down to undo the buckles on her strappy, heeled sandals. They're new, bought from Jimmy Choo on New Bond Street specially for her date with Nick, and after traipsing all over London in them, she has a blister. Just as she curses Nick for this under her breath, her mobile pings. She fishes it back out of her handbag. It's Nick! Finally! She reads his message.

Something came up.
Will explain.
N x

She's relieved that Nick is safe and nothing has happened to him. But he doesn't seem at all contrite about letting her down this evening. She wants to hammer out a reply, demanding an explanation immediately, or at the very least an apology, but she resists the urge and decides to ignore him instead. She opens the mirrored door to the cupboard under the stairs and tidies her sandals onto the shoe rack. Then she goes into the living room.

Jamie has waited up for her, watching the news as usual, and Rusty immediately leaps up to slobber all over her. She welcomes the affection, for once not even concerned that the dog will wreck her silk top.

'How's your colleague?' Jamie enquires, as she plops down on the sofa next to him. 'I take it she didn't come this evening?'

It takes Kirsten a couple of seconds to work out who he's referring to. What did she christen her imaginary colleague? Susie? Sharon? She racks her brains. She must be careful not to slip up. Jamie remembers things like this; he listens attentively when she talks.

Kirsten has it on the tip of her tongue to say her colleague has died. Perhaps killing off her fictional co-worker would give her a sense of satisfaction. But she remembers Amy's fuzzy, happy face from the Instagram post and feels bad for entertaining that thought, albeit briefly.

'No, she's still in a bad way—'

'Oh dear. Poor Sarah!'

Sarah! That was it! 'But she's going to be all right,' Kirsten says, patting the dog on the head. 'She's got a long recovery in front of her, though. She'll be off work for a while and she won't be able to look after the dog for the foreseeable future.'

'Well, we can do that, but it might be an idea to look for a dog walker at some point. Rusty can't stand being left alone in the house all day.'

'How do you know that?'

'I mean, today he tore apart a couple of cushions,' Jamie says.

Kirsten, who by her own admission is obsessively house-proud, would normally take this sort of thing badly. 'Oh well, they're only from John Lewis,' she says with a shrug.

'And he seems to have mistaken the coffee table for a chew toy.'

Kirsten peers under the table. The wooden legs look as if they have been attacked by beavers. Damn! She bought that table at Chaplins. It cost a fortune. But it's not affecting her. She caresses the dog's velvety ears. 'It must be separation anxiety or something,' she says. 'I've heard about that on TV, on one of Lily's animal programmes. You're right. We should definitely look into getting a dog walker. And some chew toys.'

Rusty lies down alongside the sofa with a contented yawn. There's no way Kirsten can get rid of him now. Lily would be heartbroken, for a start, and Kirsten is growing quite fond of the hound, herself.

She snuggles into Jamie and closes her eyes. But they snap back open again. 'What was that?' She realises she sounds alarmed and tries to dial it down a notch. 'Sorry. It's just . . . I . . . er . . . I was near there today. For a viewing.' She was in the office all day, but it sounds feasible. She points at the television screen. 'Turn it up!'

But by the time Jamie has located the remote control behind one of the cushions Rusty didn't destroy, Kirsten has missed the news bulletin. Her heart and mind are racing. She tries to calm herself down before Jamie notices. She only caught a few words. She replays the images in her head, but they didn't show much.

Really, there was nothing to suggest it had anything to do with her, Nick or Gregory Wood.

Chapter 16

Amy

I'm doing my best to be strong. I haven't broken down in front of my parents-in-law. I've tried to keep going. And I insisted on coming back to work, even though Liz and Pam both warned me it was way too soon. By morning break, though, I have to admit they're right.

Liz and I are standing side by side in the playground, nursing mugs of coffee as we keep an eye on the kids. A wayward strand of my unruly, dark hair has escaped from my ponytail and tickles my face. I tuck it behind my ear.

I've known Liz for years. She's my kind of person. She's very different from me in many ways, but we hit it off from the start. She went to a private school while I went to the local comp. We met at gym club when we were nine or ten – we were both really bad at gym, but we had a lot of fun, giggling together all the time. Liz seems to sail effortlessly through life, and yet she is modest and self-deprecating. She adores kids – her own and her pupils – and she's a great mother and a great teacher. She suggested I should apply for a job at her school when it came up five years ago and prepped me for the interview.

Our primary school is situated at a bend in the road, above the seaside resort of Woolacombe, which sprawls out below us. From the playground, there's a terrific panoramic view of the long, golden beach and the Atlantic Ocean. There's a light offshore wind, a glassy sea and perfect barrelling waves, about six foot. Usually on a day like this, I'd be itching to finish work so I could go home, grab my surfboard and get into the water. Today, I just want to go home.

'If that's enough, leave it there,' Liz says softly, as if she has read my mind.

She turns towards me, but I keep my gaze fixed ahead. I can't take the concern I read in everyone's eyes and the sympathy I hear in their voices. I'm trying not to crumble, but people's pity serves as a reminder that my whole world has turned upside down. Sometimes, I see something mixed with the compassion in their expressions. Relief. This could have happened to anyone, to any couple, but it has happened to Greg and me, and not to them.

'No point in rushing this. Come back tomorrow,' Liz suggests. 'Do half-days for a while.'

'I don't think I can come back,' I say.

'What do you mean?'

I try to word my answer in my head.

'Amy?'

'I don't think I can do this anymore. This job. I can't stand being around other people's children.'

'Oh, I see.'

She doesn't. How can she? I didn't tell her I was pregnant. She's my best friend, but I haven't confided in her. Now is not really the time or place. But I owe Liz an explanation. As the head teacher, she's also my boss. 'I had a miscarriage, Liz. Shortly after Greg went missing.'

'Oh no. I'm so sorry, Amy.'

I continue to avoid eye contact.

'We break up in a few weeks. Why don't you stay off work until then?' Liz suggests. It's actually six weeks until schools are out at the end of July. 'That way, you won't need to make any rash decisions until September,' Liz continues. 'Hopefully, things will look better by then.' Holding her mug in one hand, she places the other hand on my arm.

I want to scream. *How will things look better? I've lost my husband; I've lost my baby. None of that will have changed by the start of the new school year.* But none of my anger is directed at Liz, so I choke back my outburst. 'OK,' I say.

I don't even wait for break to end. I take my mug inside and leave it by the sink in the staffroom. I go to my classroom to grab my denim jacket and bag. Primary schools have a distinct smell – a mixture of wax crayons, kids' glue, school dinners and the pupils' body odour. Usually, I wouldn't notice it, but today it makes my stomach heave. The supply teacher is there, getting everything ready for the maths lesson after break. I mumble an apology to him for leaving him in the lurch and make a hasty exit.

I don't look back as I close the wooden gate. But as I drive away, I watch the school building shrink in my rear-view mirror until it's out of sight.

Perhaps Liz is right after all. Maybe I'll change my mind by September. I love working with children and I don't know what I would do for a living if I gave up teaching. Right now, though, all I want to do is curl up for a while on my sofa or in my bed and shut out the world until I can face it again.

But there's something I've been meaning to do and I decide to do it now, before I go home. At the bottom of the hill, I pass The Red Barn, trying to erase a recent memory of a seafood dinner here with Greg before it can fully take shape in my head.

I park on Bay View Road, above the Esplanade, in front of a building that used to be a large house and was converted a few years ago into four flats. One of them is our holiday let. We bought it as an investment, although it stretched our finances to the absolute limit, even before the pandemic. I've got the key on my keyring with my own front door and car keys. I haven't rented out the flat since the weekend the Taylors were here. I pay someone to do the housework after each letting and so the flat was cleaned before I realised the Taylors might have had something to do with Greg's disappearance. But there's a chance there's still a clue, some forgotten object that might lead me to them. If they've left anything behind, I will find it. As long as it hasn't already been destroyed like that piece of plastic I found in the road.

I check everywhere. Under the bed, in all the drawers, on the shelves, on the floor. I even empty out the vacuum cleaner I keep in the cupboard and sift through the dirt and dust.

I don't know what I'm hoping to find, but there's nothing. They were here, but now they've gone and they've left nothing behind, no proof that they were ever here, no clue that can lead me to them.

I sit on my heels after checking under the bed, knowing they have left a trace. It's just I can't see it. Their DNA must be here, in this room with me, somewhere, perhaps even their fingerprints. Along with those of several other guests, no doubt, as Constable Wright pointed out when I asked early in the police investigation if they could send a forensic team to the flat. What he actually said, with his usual brusqueness, was that it would be 'a waste of money as well as a waste of time'.

A growl escapes me and becomes a sob. I want to do something to uncover the truth, but I don't know what. And then I remember the waiter at The Thatch. I'd intended to talk to him myself and find out if there was anything he hadn't mentioned to the police, any detail that might turn out to be significant.

I lock up the flat and drive around the coast to Croyde. I drive past the turning to my cottage and head into the village. I park in the restaurant car park. This is where the Taylors also parked that day. If I'm right, they drove into my husband minutes after they left. It was raining heavily on the bank holiday Monday. Today is also a Monday, but it's warm and sunny. I shrug out of my jacket and throw it onto the passenger seat, then get out of the car.

The restaurant owner rushes to greet me as soon as I step

through the door. We used to come here a lot, Greg and I, just the two of us, sometimes, on other occasions with our friends. It's our local pub. There are several of Liz's posters on display inside and the sight of Greg's face takes my breath away.

'Amy! How are you? Any news? What can I do for you?'

I shake my head. 'I'd like to speak to the waiter. The one who served that couple the day Greg went missing.'

'He's taken a few days off, I'm afraid. His mother's ill. She lives up north somewhere. Perhaps you could come back towards the end of next week? Or I can give him your mobile number if you like?'

I don't really want to bother the server if he's off work to look after his ailing mother and, realistically, if he did know something, he would already have told the police. But what if he noticed something seemingly insignificant that turns out to be important? 'Yes please,' I say.

'Leave it with me. Let me know, Amy, if there's anything else I can do. Anything at all.'

I sit in the car, I don't know for how long, trying to subdue my frustration. I'm trying to retrace the Taylors' movements, but it feels as if I'm several steps behind them and will never catch up. A sense of helplessness encompasses me as I realise I don't know what to do next. I turn on the ignition and open the window. Eventually, I start up the car and head home.

Another car is parked in my driveway. A police car. Sergeant Harris and Constable Wright are both standing next to it. I haven't seen either of them for at least a fortnight now, although Harris has checked in with me a few times by phone. She never has any news and I no longer get hopeful when I see her caller ID on my screen.

Even though I know that in all likelihood Greg's dead, my heart lifts briefly when I clock Harris and Wright. I throw off my seatbelt, ready to leap out of the car and race towards them. But it doesn't take long for my brain to boot up. They have come out together from Barnstaple. Unannounced. This can't be good news.

116

I get out of the car, slowly, my legs threatening to give way. Both officers are giving off a funereal vibe, Sergeant Harris wearing a sombre expression on her face and Constable Wright holding his cap in front of him, his head lowered. Questions chase each other through my mind: *What are you doing here? What's happened? Have you found Greg?* But nothing comes out of my mouth. I have a strong urge to get back into the car, reverse out of the driveway and take off, so that I don't have to listen to what they've come to tell me. I sense they're about to drop a bombshell and destroy my world.

It's Sergeant Harris who speaks first. 'Can we go inside, Amy? We need to ask you a few questions?' Her grave, business-like tone gives nothing away.

I wobble and lean against my car for support. Sergeant Harris takes my arm and holds me up. The blood drains from my face as I try to process her words. But they only raise more questions. Why do they need to question me? Am I a suspect? I don't know why I have this thought. I have nothing to reproach myself with. But when a woman goes missing, everyone automatically suspects the husband, so surely it's the same the other way round. Plus, I've always felt as if I'm under scrutiny when Harris and Wright come round – under investigation, almost.

'There's been a possible development in our inquiry,' Sergeant Harris adds, making me wonder if I've voiced my questions aloud.

'Wh . . . what's—?'

'Let's go into the house, Amy,' she says. 'We'll talk inside.'

Chapter 17

Amy

I open the front door. Sergeant Harris and Constable Wright follow me inside. I lead the way into the living room. Harris asks Wright to fetch three glasses of water, although I'm not thirsty.

Sergeant Harris and I wait in silence. I hear Constable Wright fumbling around in the kitchen, opening cupboards to locate the glasses. Gesturing at the sergeant to sit on the sofa, I sink into what used to be my favourite armchair. I find it uncomfortable now. I scan the room, but I barely recognise it. It's as if I've never seen the pictures on the wall, and yet Greg and I chose most of them together. The trinkets and ornaments once meant a lot to me. Some of them were expensive, but they've all become worthless.

My guitar leans against the wall. I often played it at weekends and Greg would sing while I strummed. When we were younger, we used to sing and play the guitar in the evenings on the beach around a campfire. I've played the guitar since I was little. But I haven't touched it since the day Greg left to walk the dog and neither of them came back. This is my house. Everything in it is familiar. But it no longer feels like home. It doesn't smell or sound like home, either.

'What's this about?' I ask. 'Should I ring someone?' I'm wondering if I need a lawyer. Am I about to be accused of something? Arrested?

'Let's talk first?' Sergeant Harris says. I've noticed before that even when she's not asking a question, her intonations often rise as if she is. 'Then before we go, it might be a good idea for you to have someone here, someone you're close to. Your parents-in-law, for example? But perhaps for the moment, we don't need to alarm them unnecessarily.'

Her words alarm me, although it doesn't sound as if she intends to bundle me into the police car and take me away in handcuffs.

Constable Wright materialises in the doorway at this moment, carrying three glasses of water rather precariously in his hands. He nods his agreement. He hasn't spoken since he set foot in the house. I don't think he even said hello before we came in. He looks awkward, and not just because his body is squashed into a shirt that's too tight. He sets the glasses on the coffee table and takes a seat, his eyes fixed on the door to the hallway, as if he's considering legging it out of here.

'We need to ask you a couple of questions, Amy,' Harris continues, 'to help with our investigation.'

'OK.' Just now she said there might be a development in their case and part of me wishes she'd just come out with it. Another part of me doesn't want to prompt her. I'm not sure I want to know what they think they've found out.

'I know we've asked you this before, Amy, but it's important.' She takes a deep breath. 'Can you tell me if Greg has any distinguishing marks on his body?'

At first, I don't understand. At the beginning of the investigation, Harris or Wright – I can't remember which – did ask me if Greg had any marks on his body – a birthmark, a mole or a scar – particularly on his face, or if he had any unusual traits. At the time, something out of the ordinary might have helped them locate Greg if it could jog a potential witness's memory.

Now, though, we're past that. We must be. The police aren't going to find my husband thanks to an unusual scar or a mole. And then it hits me. If they're asking this question again now, it can only be to identify him.

'Oh God.' I look from Wright to Harris. I feel as if there are icy hands around my neck, strangling me. I gasp for air. 'You've found . . . Have you found . . .?' I still can't breathe. I'm wearing a T-shirt, having left my jacket in the car. I pull up the sleeve and show them the tattoo on my shoulder. 'Greg has the same one. On his right shoulder.' I didn't think to tell them about the tattoo before. It didn't seem important – it was on his arm, not his face, so it wouldn't have been visible when Greg was out walking Rusty.

They exchange a glance. It feels as if the temperature in the room has plummeted and I wrap my arms around myself.

'Amy, I'm so sorry to have to tell you, but a man's body has been found in the Thames. We have reason to believe it might be Gregory.' She pauses, perhaps to allow me to digest this.

Constable Wright seems to take the silence as his cue to speak. 'The National Crime Agency has a Missing Persons Unit. Thanks to their central database, we can cross-match outstanding missing persons with unidentified body cases,' he explains.

I hear Wright's words, but I can't take in their meaning. It's as if he's speaking a foreign language. I'm still trying to get my head round what Sergeant Harris said. I hold up my hand, a signal to stop while I sift through my thoughts. I remember from geography lessons years ago that the Thames is the longest river in England and flows through the south of England, practically across the entire length of the country. I'm trying to remember where its source is. Gloucestershire? Wiltshire? Definitely nowhere near the county of Devon. This doesn't make sense. It can't be Greg. A tiny spark of hope flickers briefly inside me. But it fails to ignite. I frown at Sergeant Harris. 'The Thames?'

'The Met's Marine Support Unit recovered the body near Embankment, Westminster,' Sergeant Harris says.

'London?' What was Greg doing in London? I look from Sergeant Harris to Constable Wright and back to Harris. 'I don't understand.'

Constable Wright pushes a glass of water into my hands. I try to take a few sips. Neither officer speaks.

'Greg didn't drown. He was rammed by a car. I'm sure of it. He can swim. He used to work as a lifeguard. He wouldn't have drowned. He wouldn't have gone to London. He hates big cities. There's been a mistake.' My voice sounds strangled and I'm surprised I can get out any words at all, but it all gushes out in one breath.

'I didn't say the man had drowned, Amy,' Harris says gently. 'Only that his body was recovered from the Thames.'

'The death is being treated as unexplained,' Wright interjects.

'The coroner ordered a post-mortem to try to determine the cause of death,' Sergeant Harris says gently. 'I believe it's being carried out today. There will no doubt also be an inquest.'

If this is Greg, and he was hit by a car, his body must have been dumped in the Thames. This man, this body, this could be Greg. The walls of the cottage seem to close in on me, the floor pitching as if I'm on a raft, adrift in the middle of a choppy ocean. I gasp for air.

'What makes you think . . .? Are you sure it's . . .?'

'The age and race correspond,' Constable Wright says.

'And this man . . . there's a tattoo on his body?'

'I'm afraid so, Amy. Yes.' Sergeant Harris leans across the coffee table and places her hand on my arm. It reminds me of Liz's gesture earlier when we were standing in the playground. I don't want Harris to touch me and I flinch involuntarily. She removes her hand.

'A tattoo of an ocean wave,' Constable Wright adds.

'Obviously, the victim will need to be formally identified before we can be one hundred per cent sure,' the sergeant says. 'But I think we need to resign ourselves to—'

A loud noise fills the room, something like a bellow. Out of the corner of my eye, I notice both officers start in surprise and

I realise it's me who is wailing. Greg is dead. I've known this all along, and yet it rips me apart hearing it.

'Call her parents-in-law and ask them to come round,' Sergeant Harris instructs Constable Wright. I'm not sure if this is for me, because I'm losing it, or for my parents-in-law. Now I've confirmed Greg had an ocean wave tattoo, Pam and Hugh also need to be informed about the body that's been recovered from the Thames. Greg's body.

Constable Wright leaves the room and Sergeant Harris gets up and comes over to me, perching on the arm of my chair. This time when she touches me, I don't pull away. I turn towards her and sob into her chest.

I don't know how long we stay like that but when I finally pull myself together, there's a wet patch on Sergeant Harris's blouse from my tears. She hands me a tissue and goes back to her place on the sofa. I hear the crunch of gravel as my parents-in-law pull into the driveway. Constable Wright must have opened the front door for them.

'Amy, I've asked you once before if you'd like us to assign you a family liaison officer,' Sergeant Harris says.

I told her on that occasion I didn't want a stranger in my home. I imagined someone who would make endless mugs of tea with far too much sugar, someone who would spy on me to check I had nothing to hide and nothing to do with my husband's disappearance.

'Perhaps you'd like to reconsider it?' she continues. 'Family liaison officers are experienced and it would be useful for you to have a direct link with the investigation team from now on, someone who can keep you in the loop about any progress they make.'

'The investigation team?'

'Major Crime Investigation Team.'

'Can't *you* . . .? Why can't you . . .?'

I look up, over Sergeant Harris's head to see Pam and Hugh standing in the doorway. Sergeant Harris is facing me, her back towards the door, and she clearly hasn't seen or heard them arrive.

My mother-in-law's face is deathly pale, even before Sergeant Harris answers my incomplete question.

'Amy, obviously we need to wait for the results of the post-mortem, but it seems likely that if the body recovered from the Thames is confirmed as Greg's, this will no longer be a misper – a missing persons investigation,' she says. 'It will be a murder inquiry.'

Chapter 18

Kirsten

Kirsten sleeps fitfully, although she is careful not to toss and turn too much in case she wakes Jamie. She doesn't want him to realise there's something wrong. Lying in the dark, staring blindly at the ceiling, she convinces herself she only caught snippets from the TV news bulletin. If that. More like isolated words, out of context. It was merely a coincidence. It doesn't have anything to do with Gregory Wood.

After what seems like hours, she starts to nod off. But the presenter's words echo in her head. She tells herself she has recollected them incorrectly. It's her sleep-deprived brain playing tricks on her. Then she sits bolt upright in the bed. She's wide awake now. There's no way she'll be able to get back to sleep. She can't deny it, can't delude herself. The newscaster definitely said something about the body of a Devon man.

She slips out of bed, pushes her feet into her slippers and pads downstairs. In the kitchen, she makes herself a mug of herbal tea, which she takes through to the living room. Sitting on the sofa, the dog at her feet, she switches on her mobile. She types

'Devon man body' into the search bar, but this throws up results for Plymouth, Exeter and Dartmoor. Kirsten immediately realises her keywords are too vague. Not only that, but it's not the right location. The image in the news bulletin was an establishing shot of Westminster Bridge spanning the Thames.

Kirsten googles 'body Devon man Westminster'. This time, she finds what she's looking for in a succinct online piece in the *Evening Standard*. She skims the article, then rereads it more slowly, mouthing the words as she does so.

Body recovered from Thames
thought to be missing Devon man

A body found in the Thames three days ago is thought to be that of a Devon man who went missing in May. Officers from the Met's Marine Support Unit recovered the body near Embankment, Westminster, after being alerted by the RNLI at 10.23 on Tuesday. The man's death is being treated as unexplained and a report is being compiled for the coroner. Formal identification is underway and inquiries are ongoing.

Kirsten's hands are clammy and the phone slips through them onto her lap. So, Nick's cronies dumped the body of Gregory Wood in the Thames. They obviously didn't weight it down, at least not enough. Unless Nick meant for the body to be found. Perhaps he thought it would give Amy Wood some sense of closure. Kirsten discards that idea. Nick often exhibits a shocking lack of empathy for others and a blatant disregard for people's feelings, including hers. Ruthlessness seems to be a prerequisite of his job. He would not have spared a thought for their victim's widow. In addition, the fact that Gregory's body has washed up at Westminster now connects him to London, if not directly to Nick and her. This was definitely not part of Nick's plan.

Kirsten needs to let all this sink in. She grimaces at the phrasing in her head. Gregory Wood didn't *sink*. Well, not for long. That's the problem. She gets to her feet and fetches the dog's lead. Rusty is ecstatic at the prospect of being taken for walkies, even at this unearthly hour, whipping Kirsten's leg repeatedly with his tail.

Kirsten puts on her long parka over her pyjamas, pockets her phone and steps outside. The temperatures have been unseasonably low recently and the crisp, cold air hits her like a slap in the face. As Rusty pulls her around the block, she tries to unjumble the thoughts racing around and colliding with each other in her head.

There's no doubt in her mind that the body recovered from the Thames is Gregory Wood's, but what does that mean for Nick and her? She remembers what Nick said about the body of evidence. Without a physical body, the evidence would be largely circumstantial. But now there is a body. There will be a post-mortem. A pathologist will attempt to determine the cause of death. Will that be possible? Kirsten's no expert, but it will certainly be evident that Gregory Wood was dead before he was immersed in water. Will it also be possible to ascertain how he died? That he was hit by a car?

Kirsten tries to reassure herself. It's been over a month. Gregory Wood's body must be quite badly decomposed at this stage. Perhaps it will prevent the pathologist from establishing a cause of death. But a voice in Kirsten's head counters her arguments. His body wasn't that badly decomposed if the police were able to work out whose body it was.

There's a green space on the road parallel to Kirsten's. Too small to be called a park, it's little more than a square of grass with a tree and a bench. The locals use it as a communal dog toilet. Kirsten lets Rusty off the lead and sits on the bench. She takes out her phone and looks at the text Nick sent earlier.

> Something came up.
> Will explain.
> N x

She stares at the screen for a while. She ignored the message when she received it because although she was relieved that Nick was all right, she was still mad at him for standing her up. Now she wonders if the reason for his no-show in the restaurant is linked to Gregory Wood's body . . . resurfacing, for want of a better word.

She's no longer angry. Or relieved, for that matter. She'd like to call Nick, to hear his voice, to have him comfort her. After all, they're in this together. But even if his phone is switched on in the middle of the night, he may not take her call and she might wake up both Nick and his wife. She decides to reply to his message instead. Perhaps if he's awake, he'll write back. She knows to be careful. Nick has warned her not to use Gregory Wood's name or to refer to the accident in writing – text or email. She has to phrase her text so that Nick understands she knows about the body from the Thames without typing anything that could ever be used against them.

Something or someone?

She scowls as she sends it, but it's the best she can do at this time of night. A few seconds later, to her surprise, her mobile rings. It's Nick. She stabs her finger at her phone screen and slides to answer, but it doesn't work on the first two attempts and she thinks she's going to miss the call. She takes a deep breath and forces herself to slow down. Then she slides her finger across the screen again, pressing hard.

'Kirsten, are you OK?' The sound of his concerned voice lifts a little of the tension from her shoulders.

'It was on the news,' Kirsten says, getting straight to the point. 'It's him, isn't it?' she asks, not that there can be any doubt. 'Did you dump his body in the Thames?'

'Not personally, but, yes, it's him. The body hasn't been officially identified, yet, but that's just a formality. And a question of time – a day or two, at most.'

'Are we in trouble? Can this be traced to us? Can he give us away?'

'Kirsten, Gregory Wood is dead. Dead bodies don't tell tales. Don't worry. Everything will be fine.'

'But how much will they – the pathologists or the coroner or whoever – be able to tell from his dead body? That's what I mean. They've identified him, so his body can't be that . . . that . . . decomposed, can it?'

Nick pauses a beat too long. Kirsten wonders if he's considering how much to tell her or if he's about to lie.

'Nick?'

'Yes, I'm still here. I'm surprised he was identified so quickly. He was only pulled out of the water three or four days ago. In fact, I'm surprised he was identified at all. His body was immersed in cold water. The Thames must have been around eight or nine degrees Celsius at the time and it can't have risen much since then. Bodies decompose more slowly in cold water. But it's been – what? Five weeks?'

'Five weeks, yes.'

'So despite the immersion in cold water, the corpse must be in a fairly advanced state of decay by now. His skin will have sloughed off, which would prevent fingerprint identification, even if he did have a criminal record. And I'd have thought his teeth would have fallen out by now, in which case dental records won't have been much use. Not to mention animal predation.'

'Yuck! How do you know all this?' Kirsten asks. Nick can reel off all this without batting an eyelid whereas the morbidity of this conversation is making her stomach roil.

'You learn this sort of thing over the years in my line of work.'

Kirsten shudders to think what kind of people Nick has crossed paths with – or rubbed shoulders with, how many murderers he has successfully defended. 'So, how did they identify him?'

'I don't know. DNA, maybe, although that would usually take longer than three days. Anyway, the point is, they might have identified the body, but it'll be extremely difficult, or even impossible with a bit of luck, for a cause and manner of death to be established with any degree of certitude.'

'Nick, I'm . . .' Kirsten doesn't want to admit she's scared.

But Nick seems to read her thoughts. 'Don't worry. Everything will be fine.'

He said the same thing a minute or two ago. Is this his own mantra he's repeating? Underneath Nick's complacency, Kirsten detects a note of fear, and this makes her panic even more.

'Can you do lunch today?' Nick asks. 'Usual place?'

Kirsten's a little taken aback, not only by the abrupt change of subject, but also because Nick's not inviting her to a restaurant at midday. He's asking her to skip lunch and meet him at their hotel. How can he think of sex at a time like this? But right now, she wants nothing more than for Nick to hold her until this all dies down.

Kirsten and Nick's relationship has always been volatile, but the accident seems to have shoved a huge wedge between them, and Kirsten is desperate to close the gap and get things back to the way they were. Perhaps Nick's thinking along the same lines.

'Yes,' she says. She has a viewing scheduled for half twelve, but she'll rearrange it. 'See you later.'

'And Kirsten? Trust me. They've got nothing on us. Everything has been taken care of. This will all blow over before you know it.'

Kirsten ends the call. She repeats Nick's words in her head. *Don't worry. Everything will be fine. This will all blow over.* But she is worried. In fact, she's terrified. Nick's pretending the situation is under control, but Kirsten gets the presentiment that, rather than blow over, it's about to blow up in their faces.

Chapter 19

Amy

Only a few hours after Sergeant Harris and Constable Wright have dropped their bombshell, we're assigned a family liaison officer called Lorna. She must be in her early fifties. I thought I'd resent having a stranger in my house, but I take an instant liking to her. She has curly black hair, tied back with a clip; she's taller than me, although most women are; she takes off her sensible shoes in the house, wears no make-up and has rosy cheeks. She smiles a lot, but without coming over as too cheerful, and she doesn't throw me pitying looks.

The next day, Hugh drives to Barnstaple, where he, Pam and I board the train to Exeter, then change for London, where we have to formally identify Greg's body. There's no doubt it's Greg's body that has been recovered from the Thames. This is really just part of the official procedure. Perhaps it will also be the first step in the grief process for Pam, Hugh and me.

According to Lorna, it will be a deeply traumatic event for us, but not a dramatic one. She assures us everything will be done to cause us as little distress as possible. Even so, my imagination conjures up images of Greg's body lying on a stretcher in a cold morgue, a white sheet over him. We peer through a large, rectangular window into a metallic room, where the coroner uncovers a man's face and right arm, causing Pam to faint. But it's not Greg. It's someone else.

This is what I see as I look out of the dirty window of the train. I try to focus on what's actually there, get a grip on the real world, but the countryside and villages hurtle by too fast and I'm struggling to face my reality.

We take the Circle Line from Paddington to Westminster. The mortuary is an imposing, red-brick building on Horseferry Road. We're shown into a small, bright room. I sit between Pam and Hugh along one side of the table and the coroner's liaison officer sits opposite us. She introduces herself as Mary Murphy. She's a little plump and very pretty – short brown hair and dark brown eyes. I notice she has lipstick on her front teeth. She says that she's not a medical professional, but she exudes a calm proficiency that somehow slows down the butterflies hurtling around in my tummy. In a soft voice with an Irish lilt, she explains things to us as gently as possible.

'The pathologist estimates that Gregory died around four to five weeks ago. It's difficult to be more precise than that. Given the time that has elapsed between Gregory's death and the discovery of his body, the remains are in poor condition,' she says. 'The best way for us to confirm his identity is to look at photographs of the tattoo on his right shoulder.'

I wonder if I have the right to see Greg, even if his body is badly deformed and decomposed. But I don't ask. I want to keep the last image I have of him, waving as he skipped out of the door into the rain with Rusty. I want to focus on his deep voice, the sound of his laughter, the citrusy scent of his eau de cologne, his toned body spooning my body and his warm hand holding mine. That's how I want to remember my husband.

'Even when the outer layer of skin – the epidermis – has perished, tattoos remain visible on the dermis – the layer beneath,' Mary Murphy says. 'Don't expect the colours to be the same as the original tattoo. Concentrate on the design rather than the shades.'

She opens a folder and takes out two photographs, which she slides across the table. The photos are facedown so we can take our time and look at them when we feel ready.

I glance first at Pam, then at Hugh. I wait for them to nod before turning over the photos. The ocean wave is purple and black instead of blue, but it's clearly recognisable. It's my turn to nod, at the officer. I don't think I can speak. Pam is dabbing discreetly at her cheeks with a tissue and Hugh averts his gaze, but my eyes linger on the photos a little longer, reminiscing about the day we went to the tattoo parlour.

Greg and I had been thinking about it for about six months when we finally decided to get inked. We couldn't have had it done much earlier anyway, as I wasn't quite eighteen when we'd first discussed it. It had been my idea to get matching tattoos. The ocean wave was Greg's idea and he drew the design. Greg went first and I held his hand. He barely flinched and smiled the whole time. Afterwards, I realised this was for my benefit, so I wouldn't be put off, because when it was my turn, it hurt like hell.

As I hand back the photos to the coroner's liaison officer, I realise that from now on, I'll cling to snapshots of my life with Greg, like this one. I choke up as I wonder how I can ever let go of our plans for the future, all of which have been cut down along with Greg himself.

'Now, as I believe you know, the post-mortem has already been carried out.'

Sergeant Harris and Lorna have both told us this. I nod. It's all I seem to be capable of doing. I must look like one of those bobblehead dog ornaments on car dashboards or parcel shelves. I try to get a grip, for Pam's and Hugh's sakes.

'Doesn't the family have to give their consent beforehand?' Hugh asks.

'In normal circumstances, yes,' Mary says gently. 'But when a death is unexplained or suspicious, the coroner requests a post-mortem and, in that case, no permission from the family is required. The post-mortem can go ahead before the body is formally identified.'

'I see,' Hugh says. He hates the idea of Greg's body being 'carved up and taken apart'. I overheard him say so to Pam. I'm trying not to think about it, not to visualise it, anyway.

'I can share the preliminary results with you now,' Mary continues, 'and then Gregory's GP will receive a full written report. That can take a few days, or even a few weeks, but you can request a copy of the report once it has been compiled.'

Mary opens her folder again. She puts the photos back into the folder and extracts a page of typewritten notes. She then proceeds to outline the findings, more or less in layman's terms. 'According to the pathologist, given the absence of froth and fluid in the airways and lungs, drowning was ruled out as the cause of death.'

'What does that mean?' Pam breathes beside me.

'It means that your son didn't inhale any water, Mrs Wood. It also means the scene of recovery wasn't the scene of death,' Mary explains. 'In other words, your son died – on land – before the submersion of his body in the river.'

She's wording this euphemistically. What she really means is that Gregory was killed on dry land and then his body was dumped in the Thames.

'So, what *was* the cause of death?' Hugh asks when Mary pauses.

'That has been hard to establish,' Mary replies.

Out of the corner of my eye, I see Hugh gape at her and realise my own jaw has dropped open, too. I close my mouth and swallow with difficulty, my throat dry.

'Firstly, Gregory sustained several injuries, but because the body was recovered from an aquatic environment, it was difficult to determine if some of those injuries were caused before or after his death.'

'How could he be injured *after* . . .?' Hugh's voice trails away.

'Currents can cause the body to, um, drift over rocks or scrape against branches in the river. This can cause abrasions and bruises.'

'I see,' Hugh repeats.

'Secondly, because the body has been in the water for several weeks, the pathologist's examination of Gregory's internal organs hasn't been as conclusive as one might hope,' Mary continues. 'The cause of death might be due to one of . . .'

I tune out, unsure how much more I can hear without losing it. I just about refrain from bursting into tears. A whimper emerges instead. I'd hoped for more. I wanted the post-mortem to somehow prove unequivocally that Greg had died because he was run over by a car. I'd googled this. I was expecting to be told that he'd sustained fatal injuries consistent with a vehicular collision – internal bleeding and a ruptured spleen from the impact, and a fracture to his skull as his head hit the tarmac.

It's Hugh who pushes Mary for more information. 'Has the pathologist found any evidence that my son was hit by a car?'

'As I said before, I'm not a medical professional,' she says. 'But I don't believe so, no. Nothing conclusive, anyway.' She looks from Hugh to me, and from me to Pam. She must read disappointment or desperation in our expressions for she adds hastily, 'But there will be an inquest. And a police investigation is already underway, as you're aware.'

'How long will this all take?' Pam asks. Her voice is barely audible.

'I can't speak for the police investigation, obviously, but an inquest often takes six to nine months,' Mary replies. 'But now that the post-mortem has been performed, we can release Gregory's body within a week or so and issue you with an interim death certificate to enable you to arrange a funeral.'

I think this is meant to placate my mother-in-law, but I hear a sharp intake of breath to my left. She's as surprised as I am. Until yesterday, she was still hoping Greg would be found alive. Now she has to get her head round the fact we're going to bury him.

I notice I'm fiddling with my wedding ring, turning it round and round my finger. It reminds me Greg had a matching ring. Our temporary rings from Argos that became permanent. Perhaps I could wear Greg's on a gold chain around my neck.

'Can I have my husband's wedding ring?' I ask Mary.

'I'm afraid it wasn't recovered. Your husband had no personal effects on him whatsoever.'

'What happened to his ring?'

'I honestly don't know,' Mary says, sounding apologetic. 'It could have come off in the water, I suppose.'

But as she says this, I realise it's more likely that Greg's wedding ring was deliberately removed before his body was dumped in the water, not because it's worth anything – even to someone who knows nothing about jewellery, that much would be clear, but to hamper identification.

Before we leave, we are offered leaflets and advice about finding grief counselling. Pam folds the leaflets and stuffs them into her handbag. She thanks the coroner's liaison officer, but if I know my mother-in-law, she has no intention of seeking counselling. She belongs to a generation and a class where she would be expected to maintain a stiff upper lip and suffer in silence. I have no immediate desire to see a counsellor or therapist, but I won't rule out that possibility. Everyone has to find their own way to cope with grief.

Pam, Hugh and I have lunch before we take the train back home, but none of us has any appetite. I observe my parents-in-law as they eat, chewing slowly, their eyes down. Greg went missing over five weeks ago and, in that time, they've aged a decade. Between us, we've lost several pounds in weight, too.

Over the next few days, we keep busy organising Greg's funeral. The three of us prop each other up, holding it together by a gossamer-thin thread and conscious that if one of us unravels, we'll all come apart at the seams. Pam wouldn't dream of going to pieces in front of Lorna, and so she remains stoic, sometimes biting on her wobbling lip to keep her emotions in check. As for Lorna, she seems to know instinctively when to stay out of the way and when to take over. I dread the moment the funeral is over and the phone calls stop, when everything will come crashing down around us.

I know the written report from the coroner's office won't be any more conclusive than the results Mary Murphy gave us. It will no doubt contain more detail and more medical jargon, but nothing to prove that Greg was hit by a car. I have a vision on an ineffaceable loop in my head of what I believe really happened. Greg turning as the Audi A8 careens round the bend, the car ramming into Greg. Greg bouncing off the bonnet and falling to the ground. I hope he didn't suffer. I hope he died on impact.

Lorna tells us the investigation team are pursuing this line of inquiry. A fatal hit-and-run with the body moved from the scene. This offers some relief after feeling that we weren't being taken seriously enough before, particularly by Constable Wright.

But although this is now a murder inquiry, it seems doubtful that the person responsible for killing Greg will ever be accused of murder. Even if the police do manage to locate him. Other than a couple of deficient witness accounts, there's no evidence against him.

When I discuss this with Lorna, she points out that there could be DNA evidence in the car if Greg's body was taken away in the boot. I ask her what the Taylors would be charged with if there was enough evidence against them.

'Best-case scenario, the driver would end up on trial for involuntary manslaughter,' she says. 'They'd probably also both face charges of conspiracy to pervert the course of justice or preventing a lawful burial because they removed your husband's body from the scene of the accident.'

The scene of the accident. That says it all. Not *the scene of the crime.*

It's ironic. This started out as a missing persons inquiry. The police were looking for Greg. But Greg has been found and the missing person in all this is no longer the victim but the suspect. The culprit. The man who killed my husband: Mr Taylor. He had a slightly posh, authoritative voice, I remember from when he made the booking for the flat. But I'm not sure I would recognise his voice if I heard it again. I certainly wouldn't recognise him if I passed him in the street. I've never seen him. I have a sinking feeling in my stomach, as though I've come to a standstill, even as I silently vow to Greg that the man who killed him will be brought to justice.

Chapter 20

Amy

July the first is the hottest day of the year so far and the worst day of my life. There's a huge turnout of friends, family and mourners at Greg's funeral, all wearing black and looking uncomfortable as well as unhappy. The weather seems inappropriate for such a sad day. It should be cold and wet. Had it been sunny on that May bank holiday, instead of wet and windy, Greg wouldn't be in that casket. The pallbearers sweat visibly as they carry the coffin – Greg's surfing buddies, Sharky, Tom and Matt; my father-in-law; Liz's husband, Mike; Hugh's brother, who lives in Scotland.

Pam looks how I feel. Shellshocked and devastated; unable to process what's happening. Once he has finished his pallbearing duties, Hugh takes her hand and keeps hold of it, as if afraid that if he lets go, she will crumple. They come to church regularly – to this church – but I've never been a churchgoer and Greg once told me he stopped going to Sunday school when he was about nine. On two occasions, Pam, Hugh, Greg and I were in this church together. The first time was for Greg's and my wedding. Everything – the place I'm in and the people who have come today – reminds me of that day, the happiest day of my life. A series of images unfolds before my eyes, like a slideshow. These memories will be tinged with sadness from now on and taste at best bittersweet.

The second and last time the four of us were here together was for Will's funeral. Only yesterday I overheard Hugh say something to Pam and it comes back to me now. *No parents should ever have to bury their children.* They've been through this before, with their elder son. They've been forced to deal with the premature deaths of both their sons. I don't think either of them can comprehend how it is that lightning has struck them twice.

The celebrant at Greg's funeral is an old schoolmate of his called Rob. He was also the officiant at our wedding. We all call him Reverend Rob now. Rob was so wayward at school, apparently, that he was suspended several times and almost got expelled. He was notorious for forging sick notes to get classmates off PE, stealing clothes and other possessions that didn't belong to him from the lost property trunk and operating a profitable black-market service, selling Wham bars, Double Dips and Opal Fruits that he somehow managed to nick from the school tuck shop. He even forged convincing fake IDs for sixteen- and seventeen-year-olds who wanted to fuel their beach parties with alcohol or get into The Marisco, the nightclub in Woolacombe.

No one could believe it when Rob became a vicar. Greg said he probably chose that vocation to spite the school careers adviser, who had labelled Rob 'a dishonest waste of space' and predicted he'd end up either on the dole or behind bars. Reverend Rob refused to take any money for officiating today.

'Absolutely not,' he said when Pam and I talked to him. Then he turned to me. 'I want you to remember something, Amy,' he said. 'Greg was a good friend to me and if there's anything I can do – and I mean *anything* at all – to help you with your grief or to help bring that bastard to justice, don't hesitate to let me know.'

Pam looked surprised to hear a vicar swear.

It's cooler and darker inside the church. Sitting next to me on the front pew, Pam shivers and pulls on her cardigan. I'm neither hot nor cold, but slightly numb. I feel devastated, frightened and lost, but at the same time slightly detached, as if I'm watching all of this from outside of my body. I'm paying my last respects to the deceased rather than burying my husband. I'm an observer, not the widow. I keep my head down, trying not to take it all in. Perhaps that way, there will be fewer memories of this day to come back and haunt me afterwards. A temporary coping strategy that I will pay for later, no doubt, when the reality of all this blindsides me, but which for now, at least, enables me to get through this without collapsing.

Rob's memorial service is eloquent and touching. Afterwards, Pam, Hugh and I stand outside the door to the little church as everyone files past. Most of the mourners pause to offer words of comfort or an affectionate gesture. Sergeant Harris, who I noticed inside the church, touches my arm. Her eyes are wet and her voice choked as she expresses her condolences.

'Thank you for coming, Sergeant Harris,' I say.

'Please call me Lucy,' she says. 'Owen is sorry he couldn't come.' My brain is sluggish and I don't understand she's referring to Constable Wright, until she adds, 'We couldn't both get the day off.'

Simon has also attended the service. Although there were dozens of people present who Greg and I were much closer to than Simon ever was, he managed to sit on the pew behind mine in the church. In fact, every time I turn around, he's right behind me. If I wasn't flanked by my parents-in-law, he'd be standing at my side, I'm sure of it. I'm irked by his proximity, but I tell myself he's trying to be supportive and I should be more grateful.

My mother is conspicuous by her absence and I would have loved her to come, but she said it was impossible for Jayden to get away at such short notice. I don't see why she couldn't have come alone, but I didn't say that. She has rung me several times and promised they will come over soon. It might be better for my mother-in-law this way. I want my mum, but Pam has essentially been carrying out that role for years and she needs me right now.

Sharky, Tom and Matt lead a group of our friends down to the beach, where they've prepared stones to build into a cairn. I decide to go and take a photo of their memorial to Greg later and stay with Pam and Hugh. We make our way to The Thatch, where the restaurant owner insisted on 'rustling up some food for the wake'. That's how he put it. Like Rob, he refused to take any payment.

Everyone else follows me, more or less in single file and without speaking, to me or to each other. I enter The Thatch at the front of the procession, holding open the door for Pam and Hugh. I'm greeted by a welcome noise of cutlery on plates, conversation and laughter, but it dies the second I step inside. Most of the diners are locals and they know me, not well enough to attend the funeral, but they recognise me. Their eyes bore into me briefly before they look away. The silence is awkward rather than respectful. All the villagers have heard the news. A few of them have children in my class at school. It has no doubt given them something to talk about, but they want to keep their distance. It's as if my misfortune could be contagious, as if by coming into contact with me, they could be infected with my bad luck.

The landlord materialises beside me and ushers us to an area he has reserved for us, apart from the other customers. As I walk through the main dining area, I notice that the posters Liz designed have been taken down. The noise gradually starts up again behind us, but everyone is speaking in low voices now, as if the volume has been turned down.

A buffet has been laid out for us. A great spread, my mum would have said. As I have that thought, I feel another stab of longing for her. How I wish she were here today. I look around for Pam and Hugh and see them talking to their neighbours. I decide to slip outside for a while, to get some air, to be alone.

There are smokers in front of the restaurant. The man standing next to me offers me a cigarette. I shake my head and thank him without turning to look at him.

'Mrs Wood, I'm David,' he says, speaking out of the corner of his mouth as he lights his own cigarette.

'David?' I turn to look at him. I'm not sure I actually know a David, even though it's hardly an unusual name. How does he know me? I think I've seen him before, but although I'm usually good with names and faces, it's not coming to me. He's younger than me – in his twenties – with dark, curly hair and dark brown eyes.

My bewilderment must show because he adds, 'David Jacob. I work here. You came by to see me? I'm so sorry. I should have called you, but my mum's sick.'

It clicks into place. Of course. He's the waiter I wanted to see, the one who gave a statement to the police about the Taylors. I don't think I knew his name, but I don't know why I didn't recognise him. It's not like I couldn't place him out of context. We're at his place of work and I've seen him here before – many times. My brain is slow today and I have a headache coming on. 'I'm so sorry to hear about your mum,' I say. 'I hope she's better?'

'No. Afraid not. I'm just filling in here until they find someone else, then I'm going to move back home to Manchester and take care of her. Anyway, I heard you wanted to ask me a few questions?'

With the formal identification of Greg's body, the murder inquiry and the funeral, any intention I'd had of coming back to this restaurant to talk to the server had slipped my mind. I'm not sure I'm up to asking David questions right now, but I owe it to Greg to do everything I can to help bring Mr Taylor to justice. Even if the bastard only gets a few years in jail for what he did.

'I was wondering about the man who was here the day my husband disappeared,' I say. 'Mr Taylor? I met his wife, but I don't know what *he* looks like. And I . . . well, I need to.'

'OK,' he draws out that word, then takes a pensive drag on his cigarette. 'He had dark hair that was greying.'

'Go on.'

'I'm not good at guessing ages, but I think he must have been in his late forties to mid-fifties. He looked like he was in good shape, you know, worked out or something. I suppose he was quite good-looking. Very tall. Wealthy.'

'Wealthy?'

'Yes. He just looked well-off, oozed money, you know what I mean? I noticed he was wearing a flashy watch. Don't know if it was a Rolex or what, but I don't think it was fake.' David stubs out his cigarette in an ashtray on an empty picnic table in front of us. 'That said, he didn't leave a tip, the stingy git.'

An image starts to take shape in my mind. It's not exactly a photofit picture, but it's tangible enough to summon up in my head next time I feel the need, as if by visualising the man who killed my husband, I can practise some kind of mental voodoo to vent my anger and hatred.

'The police haven't found the couple yet,' I say. 'I was wondering if you heard them say anything at all that might help with that.'

'I don't think so. They asked me the same thing.'

'Who did?'

'A chubby copper. A sweaty individual.'

'Constable Wright.' The waiter shrugs. 'Is there anything else you can tell me?' I ask.

'Well, this Mr Taylor was a right pain in the arse, between you and me. He complained about how long he had to wait for me to take his order, then he sent his food back to be heated up. Oh, and he made me check stuff with the chef at least three times.

'What stuff?'

'If he'd washed the kitchen equipment – bowls and so on. What he'd used in the salad dressing and in the pie crust, that sort of thing.'

'Why?'

'Tree nut allergy, apparently.'

'Peanut?'

'No. Tree nut. I'd never heard of that before. We get customers with seafood allergies occasionally – you wonder why they come to a restaurant near the ocean, right? But tree nut? To tell you the truth, he did my head in. Gave me a huge list of things to check his food couldn't possibly have been "contaminated" with.' David

142

emphasises the word and does air quotes with his fingers. 'He made me write them all down. Pecans, almonds, cashew nuts . . . the list went on, but I can't remember any more.'

None of this seems particularly relevant. I try to think what I should be asking David. Then something jumps into my mind. Simon said he reeked of alcohol. 'Did he drink with his meal? Alcohol, I mean.'

'Yes, before his meal, with his meal. The guy drank way too much. They argued about it outside after, him and the missus. They were here, next to me, right where you are now, arguing while I was taking a cigarette break.'

I shudder. When they were standing here, in the spot I'm standing, Greg was still alive, oblivious to the fact that he only had a few minutes left to live.

'She didn't want him to drive, he said she wasn't insured to drive his car, you get the picture,' David continues.

I heard on the news recently that prison sentences have been toughened in the UK for drivers who cause death while driving recklessly. A driver can be given life imprisonment for killing a pedestrian while under the influence of alcohol. If Mr Taylor had stopped and called the police, perhaps he would have been breathalysed. But it's too late for that. Will Simon's and David's statements be enough to prove Taylor was drink-driving? Or will he get away with a much lighter sentence? I sigh heavily. Taylor will get off scot-free unless we can find him.

'Do you know where they were going?' I ask David.

'No idea. He had a posh accent. Public schoolboy. She was quite up herself, too. Don't think they were locals. I heard they found your husband's body in London? I guess they could have been from there. But they didn't have Cockney accents or anything.'

I ask David a few more questions, if he heard them use each other's first names, if he saw any of the numbers or letters on the registration plate.

'I'm afraid not. The policeman already asked me all that, too.'

143

I haven't got my phone on me, but David already has my number – his boss passed it on as he'd promised me he would – and he sends me a text with his name so that I have his.

'I'm fairly sure I didn't notice anything useful,' he says. 'I've been through this with the police twice and in my own head loads of times. But don't hesitate to get in touch if there's anything else you want to ask,' he says. 'I'd like to help if I can.'

I thank him and turn to go back inside. David might be doubtful he can help, but I get the impression he knows something. I have a gut feeling he could provide a vital clue as to who Mr Taylor is and how to find him. He's not keeping it from me, not deliberately. But I haven't asked him the right question.

Hi,

My trial began four days ago. It's being held in Central Criminal Court 13. Fortunately, I'm not superstitious, as you know. Court 13 is more modern than I'd imagined, but it's still intimidating. The public gallery is packed to the hilt, although admittedly, it's not that large – a few rows of benches. Sitting each day on a raised platform in the dock for the jurors and journos to gawk at, I'm on display as well as on trial. I feel like an animal at the zoo.

Today marked the end of the prosecution case. There's no more evidence to be called against me. I get the impression from studying the faces of the spectators and jurors every day that they all believe everything they've seen and heard, even though most of it is completely untrue.

My barrister seems unperturbed, which gives me a little hope. I can't work out if he's confident or complacent. I've decided to go with the former. He has an impressive track record and a reputation for twisting every technicality and locating every loophole. It's said that thanks to him, people literally get away with murder. You may have heard of him. He's quite famous. He's supposedly one of the most successful defence barristers in the country. He certainly looks the part, dressed smartly in a three-piece suit under his silk gown, although his wig looks like it has seen better days, but perhaps that attests to his experience.

I'm up next. My barrister wants to put me in the witness box. He says I'll look guilty if I don't give evidence and he thinks I'll hold up well enough under cross-examination. He says the burden of proof is on the prosecution and that their role is to tell a story the jury will believe. All the defence has to do is show that there are holes in that story. Gaping plot holes. But all along I've been thinking that this isn't the story they should be telling. And I realise now I should have told the truth from the start.

Chapter 21

Amy

The next few weeks streak by, and yet as I live through them, it all seems like a never-ending nightmare from which I can't wake up. Sergeant Harris – Lucy – continues to call me every now and then, although she's no longer ringing in an official capacity. I'm the one bringing her up to speed. Most of the time, I simply repeat to her what Lorna tells me. I've had nothing new to tell Lucy for a while. Her calls get less and less frequent. As the days go by, our hopes of a breakthrough in the inquiry dwindle. Before long, I sense that the investigation itself is being scaled down. Even Lorna isn't around much anymore. There are no new leads and the trail, if there ever was one, has gone cold.

I walk every day with my parents-in-law. By unspoken agreement, we avoid Croyde Bay and Baggy Point. For them, as for me, these places bring back too many memories of Greg. Instead, we drive further around the coast and walk along the beach from Putsborough to Woolacombe and back, or along the paths that lead through the sand dunes at Braunton Burrows.

Throughout August, I help out Sharky with his surf school.

He and Matt, both secondary school teachers, set up their non-profit organisation, *Smile and Wave*, for kids with special needs and challenges about five years ago. When Matt fell and broke his wrist while rollerblading with his son at the end of July, Sharky begged me to fill in. They have other volunteers and I suspect Sharky has asked me for my help in order to help me, really, but I allow myself to be persuaded.

The free surfing camps take place at Saunton Sands, where there are fewer dangerous rip currents and where the waves tend to suit beginners better than at Croyde Bay. I'm relieved not to be at Croyde, where Greg and I used to surf together. It's also the beach where I met him all those years ago. It's paradoxical. I avoid places that might trigger memories of Greg and me, and yet, at the same time, I treasure those memories, replaying them often in my mind when I'm alone for fear that I might, over time, forget even one small detail.

Sharky and I, and the other volunteers, surf in tandem with some of the children; others, depending on their disability, are more autonomous. I find the whole experience rewarding, but difficult at the same time. Not difficult because the kids are difficult. They're not. They laugh all the time, which puts a genuine smile on my face for the first time since Greg disappeared. But it's hard being around someone else's kids after losing my own. This is what has prompted my decision not to go back to work in September.

One evening about a week before schools go back, I have dinner with Liz and her family at their place. When we've finished eating, Liz's husband, Mike, insists on clearing up and putting the kids to bed. Liz and I stay sitting at the dining room table.

I come straight out with it. 'Liz, I'm afraid I've been thinking about it all over the school holidays and I've decided to resign,' I tell her.

Liz doesn't get mad at me, even though this is really short notice and I'm letting her down. Instead, she's silent for a while. Then she suggests going part-time. 'That might be a good compromise.

Especially as the money your mum gave you means you won't have any financial worries for this school year,' she suggests. 'I think you need to concentrate on yourself right now and having a couple of days off a week will enable you to do that.'

It would also give me time to spend with my parents-in-law and time to grieve. But my mind is made up. I'll stay off work altogether for a while until Greg's killer is found. I have the money my mum gave me to tide me over. When I'm ready to go back to work, it won't be teaching. Perhaps I'll take over Greg's shop, which has been closed all this time. In the meantime, I can't just sit around, waiting for something to happen. I'd like to be proactive, but I don't know where to begin looking for Mr Taylor myself. I tell all this to Liz.

'You must do whatever you think is best for you,' she says, reaching across the dinner table to squeeze my hand. 'I'll be devastated to lose you as a colleague, but I'll still have you as my best friend.'

I'm not tired when I get home, even though it's gone ten. In fact, I'm quite wired. I put on my pyjamas and brush my teeth, then go back downstairs to fetch my book so I can read in bed for a while. Lately, that has helped me get to sleep. I pour myself a glass of water from the tap in the kitchen and look up sharply as something catches my eye. A shadow has just passed by the window. There's someone outside. Could it be my imagination? Perhaps it was some trick of the light.

I should open the front door and check, put my mind at rest, but I'm frozen to the spot. I wouldn't hesitate if Rusty were here. He made me feel safe, even though he was pretty useless as a guard dog. If strangers came to the house, he tended to welcome them with slobbery kisses and before long he would roll on his back to have his tummy rubbed. Without my dog, I'm a scaredy-cat.

I grab a knife and tiptoe to the front door. But before I can open it, someone bangs on it, from the other side, making me jump. I tighten my grip on the knife, berating myself for leaving my mobile upstairs in my bedroom.

'Amy? Are you there?'

I recognise the voice and groan inwardly. 'Yes, hang on,' I call. I go to the kitchen and put the knife back in the block before opening the front door.

'It's late, Simon. What are you—?'

'I've seen him,' Simon says. I only opened the door a crack, but he pushes it open wider and barges into my cottage. I'm alone with Simon, in my nightwear, which makes me feel more edgy than self-conscious. 'I've just seen him,' he repeats.

'Who?'

Simon's face is white, and I remember how pale he went when I told him where I found Greg's phone. I almost expect him to say he has seen a ghost. I certainly don't expect the answer he does give me. 'Mr Taylor.'

'What? Here? In Croyde?' My heart beats furiously.

'No. On TV. Only he's not Mr Taylor.' Simon is out of breath and bends over, his hands on his thighs, panting.

'What do you mean? Simon, what do you mean?'

Simon holds up a hand. 'Sorry. I ran here . . . Car wouldn't start . . . Just a second.'

I wait impatiently while he catches his breath.

'I recognised him on the news,' Simon says after what seems like minutes, but was probably only a few seconds. 'His name's not Taylor. It's Hunter.'

'Are you sure it was him?'

'Absolutely certain. He made a statement to the press as he came out of the Old Bailey. Same pompous bastard, same posh voice.'

'We need to ring the police,' I say, remembering my mobile is upstairs. I close the door behind Simon and head for the living room to grab the landline receiver. 'If you're sure it's him, surely that will be enough to get him arrested!'

Simon scoffs. 'Good luck with that,' he says ominously.

I stop and turn to face him. He fixes me with crazed eyes. Instinctively, I take a step back, away from him. 'What do you mean?'

149

'He's a renowned lawyer. Nicholas Hunter QC. One of the top criminal defence barristers in the country, apparently. That's why he was on television. A high-profile case. His client – I forget his name, but he already had a criminal record – was indicted for two counts of murder. His wife and her lover. Allegedly stabbed them. Several times each.' I shudder. 'Didn't take in all the details,' Simon continues, 'but basically, both victims' blood all over the defendant's clothes and his fingerprints on the murder weapon – a boning knife. Bottom line: thanks to Nicholas Hunter, he was acquitted today. Everyone said the bloke was as guilty as sin. The verdict should have been a foregone conclusion. But he walked. Correction: he *waltzed* out of the main entrance of the Old Bailey, giving the journalists the finger. I've just seen it. On the news.'

I stare, open-mouthed, at Simon. The implication of this dawns on me, and I don't need Simon to spell it out any more clearly. If Nicholas Hunter gets his clients off scot-free, people who've been accused of murder, he must be pretty good at manipulating the legal system. He probably considers himself above the law. The law won't be able to touch him.

I walk over to the sofa and drop onto it, defeated. 'Did you record the news, by any chance?' I want to see what my husband's killer looks like. 'Or film it with your phone? What channel was it on? Was it on Sky News?' If so, I'll be able to watch it – the news will be repeated.

''Fraid not. It was the ITV news at ten. Perhaps you can watch it on catch up.' Simon seems to know what I'm after. 'But there's bound to be videos of him on YouTube. The guy's famous in his field. Hey, maybe that's why he was travelling incognito.'

'Hmm,' I respond noncommittally. Nicholas Hunter might be well known in London in the circles he moves in, but surely no one would know him all the way out here in the sticks in Devon. It's not like he'd have had to give his title if he'd used his real name. But I can't think of another reason why he would give me a fake name. Simon's probably right.

Simon sits next to me on the sofa, his thigh against mine. I inch away from him so we're not touching. He takes his phone out of his pocket, opens the YouTube app and types in 'Nicholas Hunter QC'.

Taking a deep breath, I stare at the cracked screen of Simon's mobile. Simon plays a video that dates from almost a year ago, titled 'Top Barrister Gets Harassment Acquittal for MP'. I vaguely remember the case. The wife of a Tory MP had a one-night stand with her boss, then her husband found out and went after his wife's boss online. I watch the video. The wife's boss called it persecution; her husband's barrister claimed it was freedom of speech. So far, they've shown pictures of the entrance to the law courts, social media logos – Twitter and Instagram – and the defendant hand in hand with his wife.

And then, finally, I see him. Nicholas Hunter QC. I sit up straight, rage bubbling inside me, like hot lava, threatening to erupt. Because of this man, I've lost everything. My life as I knew it, my husband, my baby, even my dog.

'This wasn't some gratuitous attack on an innocent person.' He's giving a statement on the steps of the law courts, wearing a smart three-piece suit and a victorious grin. 'My client responded to the behaviour of an individual and he didn't say – or post online – anything that wasn't true . . .'

I tune out and mentally zoom in on his face. The face of Nicholas Hunter QC. Immaculately dressed. Tidy, greying hair, gelled back, apart from one strand that's sticking up. His clothes exude money and his posture exudes confidence, maybe even arrogance. He's just like David described him. Now I can see with my own eyes what he looks like. The man who took my husband's life and ruined mine. I take the phone from Simon's hands and stare at the barrister's face until the image disintegrates into pixels.

He might be considered in legal circles as one of the UK's best criminal defence barristers, but to me, he's no more than a criminal. On the other side of the law. The wrong side. He has taken a man's life. He took my husband's life. He destroyed mine.

He can't be allowed to just get on with his own life and his high-flying career with impunity. But it will be impossible to bring this man – this *murderer* – to justice. Which means there's only one way to resolve his crime.

Silently, I make a promise to Greg. *I'll bring him down, Greg. One way or another. If Nicholas Hunter QC thinks he's above the law, then I'll take the law into my own hands.*

If I can't get justice, I will get revenge.

PART TWO

Chapter 22

Amy

I lie to my parents-in-law. I feel awful about it, but what choice do I have? If I tell them I know who killed their son but the chances of him ever paying for what he did are slim, it will break them all over again. So I've sworn Simon to secrecy. For now. Until I work out what to do next. I wish I didn't have to share a secret with Simon – I don't want him to have a hold over me – but I'm grateful he has found out Mr Taylor's true identity.

That's not the only thing I'm keeping from Pam and Hugh. I haven't mentioned I've given up my job, either. I tell myself it's because my final decision to resign is recent and I simply haven't got round to sharing this news with them. But really, it's because they'll be concerned and I don't want to add to their worries.

I superimpose the two falsehoods. I pretend I'm going back to work, but instead of driving to the primary school in Woolacombe, I head in the opposite direction, for the train station in Barnstaple. I'll ring Pam this evening and say I'm at Liz's house. And, as I plan to be away for at least two days, I'll come up with something else tomorrow. But I'll come clean as soon as I can, as soon as I get

155

back. I don't like being dishonest and they don't deserve to be left in the dark.

Before this summer, I hadn't been to London for years, but I'm on the train, heading for Paddington Station, for the second time in three months. Time seems to drag on this journey and I can't wait to get to my destination. Last time, I was with my parents-in-law; this time I'm on my own. Simon wanted to come, he was quite insistent, actually, but I turned down his offer. I don't regret that, although I'm feeling lonelier than ever.

To calm my nerves, I earwig on the conversation of the woman in the seat next to me, as she chatters excitedly on the mobile to her mother. I watch the couple at the table across the aisle as they keep their three young children occupied with colouring-in and a card game. Anything to take my mind off this visit and the last one, when I came with Pam and Hugh to formally identify Greg's body. It's a memory that is painfully raw and recent. I force myself to concentrate on more pleasant memories, more distant ones, from a time before I met Greg.

I used to come to London with my grandmother. She'd take me once a year, usually at Christmas time, to see a show – a musical, a ballet or a play. It was her treat, her Christmas present to me. I saw *Evita*, *Cats*, *The Phantom of the Opera*, *The Sound of Music*, *The Nutcracker* and *The Mousetrap* . . . Just my gran and me – the theatre wasn't my mum's thing and my grandfather died when I was a baby. Gran and I would stay in a hotel near the West End. Although I was a country girl at heart, I loved the bright lights of the city and relished what my gran called 'our annual escapades'.

After she died, I thought I'd continue the tradition with my own children one day. Like all my goals and plans for the future, that idea has been shattered, reduced to a pipe dream. I sigh. Even when I manage to think about something else, my mind always comes back to the present.

I type 'Nicholas Hunter QC' into the search bar of my mobile. I've done this several times over the last week since Simon's visit.

I already know what I will find. Top result: his website. It has an enquiry form for potential clients. You can browse all his five-star Google reviews. I've already done this more times than I can count. Most of the reviewers are unidentifiable; only their initials are given. Thanks to Hunter, people have been acquitted of charges of murder, fraud, firearms and manslaughter, according to his reviews. They're all the same. Or at least, very similar. They could have been written by the same person. Perhaps they were. If his website is to be believed, Nicholas Hunter QC was awarded UK Defence Barrister of the Year in 2021 and 2022 and Best Criminal Barrister in the UK in 2019.

There are lots of media links from his website to YouTube videos. Hunter has appeared on Sky News, the BBC *Nine O' Clock News* and the ITV *News at Ten* as well as on *The Politics Show*. I've already watched all the videos, but I take my earphones out of my handbag and plug them into the jack of my mobile to rewatch a few of them.

There are lots of other search results and Hunter has a Wikipedia page. I've read everything I can find. Several times. I know his typical fees range from £500 to £10,000 for a single hearing, depending on the case and the client. I know he has around twenty-five years' experience and took silk at an impressively young age. I know his chambers are located in Blackfriars. I know he was fined £500 by the Lord Chief Justice in 2018 for his patronising behaviour towards a fellow QC and a further £1,000 for professional misconduct relating to 'boastful and misleading' claims on his website.

I've also checked him out on social media. But although he is active on some platforms, I haven't managed to glean any information about him that could be useful to me. He has a Facebook account, but his privacy settings prevent me from seeing any of his posts and he doesn't appear to have a TikTok account. He uses Twitter in a professional capacity, retweeting newspaper articles, criticising Tory and Labour politicians alike and giving tips on public speaking and law courses. There's no mention at all of his job in his Instagram posts, but although he has over one thousand posts, they reveal little about him. He mainly posts photos of his meals in expensive restaurants, usually with a glass of champagne or similar next to the dish itself, and of his holidays on tropical islands. He's in a lot of these pictures – many of them are selfies. I scroll through some of these posts again now, in case I've missed something, but I find nothing of interest.

I sigh loudly, causing the passenger sitting next to me, who has finished her phone call, to frown at me. I frown, too, but not at her. I feel frustrated. Despite trawling through the Internet for hours, I still know nothing about Hunter's personal life. I have no idea where he lives. And although there are lots of photos of him, particularly in news items and Instagram posts, there's no mention of his wife anywhere and no photo of her.

To my mind, she's also partly to blame for what happened to Greg. She may have tried to talk her husband out of taking the wheel when they came out of the pub. But she can't have put up much of a fight when he suggested removing my husband's body. She's not blameless, even if Nicholas Hunter put pressure on her to go along with his idea. At the very least, she's an accessory to the crime. For all I know, it could even have been her call to cover it up.

For the moment, though, my focus is on him. It's him I see. Everywhere. On my mobile screen, behind my eyelids, in the face of every stranger I pass. He's handsome, I can see that, but my imagination twists and contorts his features until he becomes ugly. Just like he twists and contorts the truth into lies.

My thoughts are interrupted by the loud voice of an announcement coming over the Tannoy. We're arriving at Paddington Station. I grab my rucksack – I'm travelling light with only clean undies and a few toiletries. I've studied the London Tube map, but as I step out of the train, I'm swamped in the throng of passengers spilling onto the platform with me. I see signs towards the underground and allow myself to be swept along in that direction, striding purposefully, blending into the crowd, trying to kid myself, if no one else, that I know what I'm doing.

The chambers of Nicholas Hunter QC are located in Hamilton House, a Grade II listed building in Temple Avenue on the Victoria Embankment. This is my starting point. I negotiate the Tube easily enough, taking the Circle Line and getting off at Blackfriars. I navigate the rest of the way using the Google Maps app on my phone.

Hamilton House is imposing and beautiful, set back from the pavement, with steps leading up to double doors burrowed in an ornate stone archway. As I peer up at the five-storey building through the black bars of the front gates, I get a sinking feeling. I'm hopelessly out of my depth. There's an ongoing murder inquiry into the circumstances surrounding Greg's death. I should probably have rung the police when Simon recognised Nicholas Hunter QC on TV. I tell myself I can still go to the police. But first, I want to see him with my own eyes. In the flesh. This is also what I told Simon. Even though I'm sure I'm not fooling him any more than I'm fooling myself. I'll only go to the police as a last resort.

This isn't only about seeing the man in person. This is a field trip to find out as much as I can about him, on the ground rather than online. But I'm under no illusion. I'm no private investigator. This whole trip is a shot in the dark and it could turn out to be a total waste of time.

What I'm really aiming to do is come up with a watertight plan. Because right now, unlike Nicholas Hunter QC, I'm not prepared. I have no strategy, no idea what I'm doing. But deep down, I want to elaborate a scheme to exact revenge for what that bastard did to Greg. And for what he has done to me. I want to make him pay. I want blood. I want Nicholas Hunter's head on a platter. I want to hurt Hunter. Badly. So badly that he screams for his mother or his wife with his dying breath.

All of this scares me. I'm frightened of the rage that consumes me; I'm scared of what I might be capable of. I don't recognise myself. I'm not a pushover; I stand up for what I believe in. But on the whole, I'm a calm person, usually, definitely neither vindictive nor violent, and it's as if thoughts like these, thoughts of revenge, aren't mine, as if someone has planted ideas in my head. I don't know if I'll have the guts to go through with any plan I come up with. But what's the worst that can happen? Because of Hunter, the worst has already happened. I have nothing left to lose. I've already lost everything.

I look around me. This is a quiet street and I feel self-conscious, conspicuous. I can't loiter here all day, staking out the entrance to this set of chambers. Not with my rucksack on my back. Not without a car to hide inside. I have no idea what time Hunter is due to knock off work today, or even if he's in his chambers. He could be in court or on holiday. And even if he is at Hamilton House, he might use another exit and disappear into the gardens, which, I know from my Internet searches, are laid out at the back.

Perhaps I should have tried to make an appointment to see him, masquerading as a potential client. He doesn't know me. He wouldn't recognise me. It's not like my face has appeared on the national news. Unlike his. At best, when he and his wife dropped off the keys, he might have glimpsed me in the rear-view mirror as the rain coursed down the back window of his car. The car he then rammed into Greg.

But even if I'd blundered my way through a volley of questions on his website or on the phone and concocted a convincing cover story without raising anyone's suspicions, I doubt I would have been able to see Nicholas Hunter QC that easily or that quickly. There must be legal secretaries or other solicitors I'd have to meet before making my way up to Hunter himself.

It's way past lunchtime and I decide to get something to eat, check in to my hotel and come back tomorrow. I'm about to turn away when the entrance door opens and an elegantly dressed man steps outside, clutching a briefcase in one hand and pressing a mobile phone to his ear with the other. It's him. I'm standing only a few metres away, just outside the gates that he's strolling towards, peering at him through the wrought-iron bars. He looks in my direction. My heart starts racing out of control and I freeze.

I grabble for an excuse in case I need one, in case he asks me why I'm lurking around in front of Hamilton House. I wish I had Rusty with me. I could be out walking my dog. If only I'd thought to buy a packet of cigarettes or something. I could pretend I was having a fag. I should run. I can't let him see me. But my feet are stubbornly rooted to the ground.

The gates swing open and this spurs me into action. I spring backwards, crouch behind the gatepost and shuffle off my rucksack. Stepping out onto the street, he turns the other way and I don't think he even clocks me as I pretend to rummage for something in my bag, using my hair to curtain my face.

I glance upwards to see a man in a dark suit standing by a large, black car. A Mercedes, I think. Judging from his clothes, the man is a chauffeur. A few feet from him, a woman is smoking. She is tall and beautiful, elegant and black-skinned. As Hunter approaches, she drops her cigarette to the ground and crushes it under a stilettoed shoe. I don't know when the car pulled up. I could have sworn it wasn't there a few minutes ago. I'm clearly not cut out for sleuthing. I've got zero observation and undercover skills.

'You're late,' the woman says to Hunter.

He ends his phone call and slides the phone into an inside pocket. 'I'm sorry, darling. Busy day so far. I'll be home late tonight as well, I'm afraid.' He plants a kiss on her pouting lips. 'Shall we go? Are you hungry?' he asks.

I don't hear her answer as she folds herself into the back seat of the car, followed by Hunter. The driver closes the door and gets in behind the wheel. I've abandoned all pretence at searching for an item in my bag – no one seems to have noticed me anyway. I straighten up and gape after the car as it drives away.

I replay the short conversation I've just overheard in my head, as if that will untangle my confusion. He called her darling. He said he'd be home late.

But if this woman is Nicholas Hunter's wife, who is Mrs Taylor?

Chapter 23

Kirsten

Something is wrong. She can feel it. Her stomach and mind are both churning as she shows the Iranian couple around the two-bedroomed apartment a stone's throw from Kensington High Street and a short walk to Holland Park. She tries to get a grip, get into the zone, as she calls it. She should be concentrating on the job in hand – doing her job – but she can't stop thinking about Nick's text message.

They've been appointed sole agents for this property, thanks to a word-of-mouth recommendation from a satisfied buyer to whom Kirsten sold a luxury studio flat twelve or thirteen years ago and with whom she had a one-night stand two or three weeks after completion of the sale – in the studio itself.

With floor-to-ceiling windows in the reception room and both bedrooms, this apartment is bright and airy; it's also spacious and overlooks landscaped gardens. There's barely room to swing a cat around the patch of lawn, really, and you need to stick your head out of the window and crane your neck to spot it, but it's a good selling point all the same. The property is on the market for just under six million – rather overpriced if you ask Kirsten. But the guy is flush – Kirsten has seen proof of funds – and she stands to make a good commission on this sale if she can pull it off.

But instead of slipping into her estate agent mode and talking up the features of the property with a smile plastered to her face, Kirsten is subdued.

'I'll let you look around for yourselves, shall I?' she says.

She waits until they disappear into the larger of the two bedrooms before delving in her handbag for her mobile. She reads his text again, even though she knows what it says.

> Meet me at 1pm.
> White Mulberries.
> Hay's Galleria.

For a brief moment, Kirsten wonders if the text could have been written by someone else. Perhaps it's a trap. Nick always signs off with his initial, a capital 'N' followed by an affectionate, lowercase 'x'. And that's not the only thing that's odd. It's not unusual for Kirsten and Nick to meet up at lunchtime on a weekday. But they invariably meet at their hotel and often do without lunch altogether. They do dine together, frequently, but at restaurants in the evening. Not in coffee shops in the middle of the day. And he has never taken her to this place before. She looks it up on TripAdvisor and Google Maps. It looks fine and has good reviews, but Nick would never select this kind of eatery as a venue for a date with her.

But it sounds like Nick. An order rather than an invitation, as if he assumes she's automatically available at whatever time suits him. It's a fair assumption to make. She has always dropped everything and come running. She's at his beck and call, and she hates that, but he's like a magnet, drawing him towards her.

The Iranian couple seem enchanted with the apartment despite Kirsten's lack of enthusiasm and input. Mr Jafari – she has to glance at the documents to remind herself of his name – promises to give her a ring within the next few days. Once she has got rid of them, she makes her way to White Mulberries. Given the location, Nick must be at the Crown Court at Southwark. She gets there ridiculously early. Has Nick reserved a table? Or is this a walk-in diner? It still has several free tables – inside and out – so it won't be a problem if he hasn't booked. As it turns out, the hostess has a booking for a corner table for two in the name of Baker, their new pseudo.

She waits impatiently, even though Nick's not late. Why does he want to see her? Does it have something to do with the accident? She can't seem to muzzle the voice in her head, repeating an unhelpful saying over and over. *The truth will out. The truth will out.* Gregory Wood has been buried, along with the truth. Their victim has effectively taken their secret to his grave. Only Kirsten and Nick know what really happened. And as long as neither of them reveals the facts, no one else will ever find out.

Wiping her sweaty palms on the napkin, Kirsten spots Nick as he enters the bistro. The hostess shows him to the table where Kirsten's sitting. She notices he doesn't smile at her as he approaches. He takes off his jacket and looks around him, perhaps for somewhere to hang it. Then he puts it carefully around the back of the chair and sits down.

'Would you like a coffee or something?' he asks. Is he not even going to buy her lunch? He must notice her bewildered expression, for he adds, 'Or a bite to eat? I'm not hungry myself and can't stay long, I'm afraid.'

She orders the burrata and prosciutto 'topless' and a Coke – she needs a caffeine boost. Nick orders a flat white.

As soon as the waiter is out of earshot, Kirsten says, 'Is this about the Woods?'

'You could say that,' Nick replies. 'Listen, Kirsten.' He pauses. He often begins his sentences this way. 'Look, Kirsten' or 'Listen, Kirsten'. How has she never found this patronising before? 'We can't see each other anymore.'

She reels from the blow his words have delivered. She must

have misheard. Last time they met up, in their usual day hotel, everything had been perfect. She was reassured that they'd got back on track. 'You're not . . . are you splitting up with me?'

He doesn't answer. He can't seem to look her in the eye. So that's why he wanted to meet up here. She did not see this coming. At least he's telling her in person. One of Kirsten's colleagues was bawling her eyes out the other day because her boyfriend had dumped her with an insultingly concise text message. She'd met him on Tinder. Then he met someone else on Tinder. Kirsten bets she wishes she could go back in time and swipe left instead.

'Well? Are you?'

'Oh, Kirsten, I don't want to, believe me. I just can't see any other way.'

'What's going on?' Kirsten asks Nick, the lump in her throat puncturing her voice.

'The thing is, Edie knows.'

She wonders what he means. Does his wife know about them? Or about Gregory Wood? Oh God, if she knows about Gregory Wood, they're doomed. Either way, they're doomed.

'What does she know?' It comes out as a whisper.

'Everything.' Nick puts his elbows on the table and cradles his head in his hands. 'She found out everything.'

'But how?' It's not what she wants to ask. He hasn't answered her previous question. She still doesn't know if he's referring to the affair or the accident. Or both.

'I came clean. I couldn't keep it to myself.' Nick's looking at the table, avoiding her watery gaze.

Kirsten knows Nick better than that. He's not the kind of person who feels so guilt-ridden that he has to unburden himself by fessing up. He keeps his conscience, if he has one, out of sight and under control. He wouldn't have simply told his wife. About Kirsten or about Gregory Wood.

Kirsten arches her perfectly plucked eyebrows at him. 'What exactly has she found out?'

'About us,' Nick says, picking up the knife and running his hand along the blunt blade. 'About you and me.'

Even though Kirsten's heart is breaking, she feels a wave of relief wash over her. Ediye doesn't know they've killed someone.

'How did she really find out?'

He exhales noisily. 'I got careless; she got suspicious,' Nick says. That sounds more like it. 'She put a GPS tracker on the car.'

'The new one?'

'What? Oh, no, the Audi, not the Range Rover.'

Kirsten's heart thuds against her chest. 'Shit!' she mutters under her breath.

'She knows I went to Devon when I was supposed to be spending the weekend at the home of a wealthy client in Nottingham,' Nick continues. 'If I'd just told her he lived in Devon . . . or if we'd gone to Nottingham . . .' He gives a dry laugh, smacking his forehead with the palm of his hand dramatically. 'I'm not a good liar.'

Kirsten doesn't contradict him. Nick can lie through his teeth convincingly, but that's inconsequential right now. 'Did you sell the car with the tracker still on it?'

'Probably.' The expression on his face tells Kirsten he hadn't thought of that. 'That won't matter, though.'

'Maybe not, but Nick, you know what this means, don't you?'

Nick looks at her blankly. He's the most intelligent person Kirsten knows. He's brilliant. It's one of the things she loves about him; she finds it sexy. But he's being slow in this particular instance, focusing on the wrong thing entirely. He's concerned about his marriage.

Kirsten spells it out for him. 'This is evidence we were there. This places us at the scene of the accident. Ediye can put us away with this.'

Nick scowls. The waiter arrives with their orders. Neither Nick nor Kirsten speaks until he has gone.

Nick looks up, finally making eye contact. 'I'll get Edie to delete the app and erase any data she has saved on her laptop or mobile,' Nick says. 'And I'll get the tracker back.'

'This is serious, Nick.'

'I know. I know it is.' He reaches across the table for Kirsten's hands. 'Leave it with me.'

'And are you serious about breaking up with me?' She glances down at his hands, still wrapped around hers, and feels a glimmer of hope. She's sure he must hear her heart thumping while she waits for his verdict.

'Look, Kirsten, I don't want to. But Edie is sniffing about right now and we have to lie low. I think we should take a break, stay away from each other. At least, for the foreseeable.'

It's a wishy-washy answer. It will keep Kirsten dangling, hoping, she can see that. She's trying hard not to cry in front of him.

He lets go of her hands and looks at his watch. It's an expensive one. A Patek Philippe. A twenty-fifth anniversary present from Ediye, no doubt purchased with his money.

'I'm sorry,' he says. 'I have to go.'

As he walks away from her, she realises he hasn't paid the bill or touched his coffee. A single tear rolls down her cheek and plops onto her lunch before her sadness is superseded by intense fear. Ediye is no fool. Kirsten likes to think she's all beauty and no brains, a trophy wife, but Nick has told Kirsten enough about his wife over the years for her to know that Ediye is in fact shrewd and smart. By his own admission, Nick has been careless and Ediye has obviously been snooping. She might have watched that YouTube video of the local news in North Devon over his shoulder, or overheard the newscaster as he viewed it in her presence.

What if Nick's wife knows a North Devon man went missing that weekend and his body washed up in the Thames? What if she's suspicious about Nick getting rid of his car so hastily and factors that into the same equation? She might just put two and two together and figure out what really happened.

Chapter 24

Amy

The rest of my stay in London is uneventful and unproductive. I don't so much as catch sight of Nicholas Hunter QC again, let alone find out where he lives. I've garnered no useful information at all with this trip. It's a failed mission. By the time I take the train home, I feel despondent and drained.

The barrister's wife is definitely not the woman who handed in the keys to the flat that day. She wasn't in the car with the man who ran over Greg. How am I going to find 'Mrs Taylor'? Who is she? Could she be Hunter's lover? If he was having an affair and wanted to keep it a secret from his wife, would that explain why Hunter gave me a false name when he made the booking for the holiday rental? Is that why they paid cash?

I ponder this, but there's another possibility and it seems more likely to me. Simon must have made a mistake. Hunter and Taylor can't be the same man after all. Maybe Hunter just looks like Taylor. If Simon was wrong, I'm back to square one. No lead whatsoever. Another dead end. I'll be glad I didn't tell Pam and Hugh about my trip to London in that case. I'd have got their hopes up only to shatter them once more.

The more I mull it over, the more convinced I am that Simon mistook Hunter for Taylor. There is a way I can check. I'll ask David Jacob. He'll know if Simon's right or wrong. I so desperately want Simon to have been right. Despite the fact Hunter is this bigwig lawyer and seemingly untouchable, I would rather know the identity of my husband's killer. I'd rather feel helpless than clueless.

All I want to do is go to bed, but when I get back to Croyde, I dump my stuff at home and go straight round to my parents-in-law's house in Georgeham. I feel bad about being deceitful and I need to clear my guilty conscience. I have nothing to show for my covert trip to London and nothing new to bring to the table, so I could get away with keeping the whole episode with Simon and Hunter from them. But they deserve to know the truth.

Hugh answers the door. He's dressed smartly, as usual, in a long-sleeved shirt, despite the warm day, and trousers with precisely pressed creases down the middle. The wrinkles whittled into his face have multiplied and deepened since Greg's disappearance and death, and his eyes, once a striking azure like Greg's, have faded to a watery blue. He's not normally tactile, but he takes me in his arms and hugs me, calling over his shoulder for Pam.

I follow Hugh into the living room, where Pam jumps up from the sofa, offering to fetch drinks and biscuits. Both Hugh and I decline. Pam sits down again and I perch next to her on the worn, two-seater sofa. Hugh remains standing, his hands thrust deep into his pockets.

I haven't worked out what I want to say, but I decide to start at the beginning. 'I haven't been honest with you,' I say. I tell them that I've decided to take a break from teaching indefinitely and that I didn't start the school year as I pretended.

Hugh paces the room.

'I haven't officially resigned,' I say, 'but I can't imagine ever . . . wanting to work with young children again. Not after . . .' I wring my hands in my lap.

Pam places her hand on mine. 'That's understandable,' she says.

169

'There's something else I've been keeping from you,' I continue before one of my parents-in-law can ask me what I'll do instead of teaching. 'Something concerning Greg's death.'

Hugh stops pacing and turns towards me. 'Go on,' he says gently.

'Last week Simon thought he recognised Mr Taylor on the television. There was a news bulletin about a court case and the defence barrister got an acquittal for his client, who had been accused of murder. The barrister gave a statement on the steps of the court building. Simon was adamant this lawyer was the man who drove his car into the hedge on Moor Lane that day. His name—'

This time Pam intervenes. 'You mean the man who ran over Greg?' Her nails dig into my hand. She has as much hatred bottled up inside her as I do.

'Yes, but . . . well, I went to London to try to find out more about him, especially where he lives and where he works. And I saw the barrister's wife. She's definitely not the woman who gave me back the keys to the flat that bank holiday Monday.'

'Are you sure?' asks Hugh.

'Yes. Not the same skin colour for a start.'

'Oh,' says Pam.

'Maybe the woman Taylor brought to Devon is his mistress,' Hugh says. 'That might explain why they went under an assumed name.'

'Yes. I've considered that,' I say. 'I can only come up with two explanations. Either this "Mr Taylor" was with someone he shouldn't have been with that weekend or—'

'Or the barrister's not Mr Taylor,' Hugh finishes for me.

'Exactly.'

Pam lets go of my hand and shifts her position on the sofa so that she's facing me. 'Shouldn't we go to the police? Call the Major Crime Investigation Team? Lorna?'

'I don't know,' I say. 'The reason I didn't go to the police before is that this barrister – Nicholas Hunter QC, he's called – has an impressive track record for getting his clients acquitted. And some of them are pretty shady. I'm worried we won't win if we go up against him.'

'No, no no,' says Hugh. 'We can't go to the police yet. We have to find out if it's the same man first.'

'But how can we know for sure if it's him?' Pam asks.

'There's one person who can confirm if Taylor and Hunter are the same person,' Hugh says.

Pam nods, grasping the next step without needing us to fill her in.

'Yes, I was planning to pop in and see him later. Leave it with me,' I say. I get up to leave. 'I'll come round again tomorrow and if it really is him, we can decide what to do then.'

When I get home, I ring Liz and arrange to meet her for a pub dinner this evening. She's delighted when I suggest it.

'Squee! A night out without the kids,' she enthuses. 'Let's see how Mike copes for once with all four of them on his own!'

I walk to The Thatch, arriving early, and sit at the table for two I've reserved. I feel sick. Perhaps it's because the last time I was here was for the wake. Memories of Greg's funeral now come rushing back to me. Or it might be due to the smell of food taunting my empty stomach. Maybe it's a mixture of the two. Liz's excitement and energy as she bursts through the doors only serves to add a dash of guilt to my nausea. She's gone to the trouble of getting dressed up and made-up. I've brought her here on false pretences.

Despite her carefully applied make-up, Liz looks tired from the stress of going back to school after the summer holidays. I tell her this and she retorts that I look drawn and thin. She's right. I've always been slim, but since I've lost Greg – and our baby – I've had no appetite and my clothes now hang off me.

'I'm worried about you,' she says.

I can't respond; a lump is blocking my throat. These days, I'm never far from tears and anything can set me off – a kind remark, a commiserative look, or even someone hooting their horn at me for driving too slowly.

'Are you getting help? It's a lot to process, you know, what happened to Greg and what happened to you.'

'I have all the help I need,' I manage. 'I have Pam, Hugh and you. The only thing that will really help me is for the man who did this to be found and punished.' I don't add what I really mean, that I'm out for revenge rather than justice.

I decide not to tell Liz about my trip to London. She's my best friend and I can share anything – everything – with her. But it's precisely because she's my best friend that I have to keep her out of the loop. If I ever get near Greg's killer – whoever he is – I may end up breaking the law. And I don't want to bring anyone down with me. I don't want Liz to be an accessory to any crime I might commit.

Instead, I change the subject and ask Liz about her first week back at school. I try to smile, concentrate on what she tells me and laugh in the right places at her anecdotes. From time to time, I steal glances at the waiter. He's the real reason I'm here this evening: David Jacob. He's the only person who can confirm if Hunter is the man I'm looking for or not. He saw the Taylors that weekend. He was able to give me – and the police – a detailed description of the man who got behind the wheel of the Audi. Inebriated. I should have come to see David before going to London, instead of taking Simon's word for it, but the fewer people who know about this, the better.

David comes over to take our orders and politely enquires how I am.

'I'm doing OK,' I say.

Liz raises her eyebrows at me from across the table, her way of saying she begs to differ.

'I'm doing my best,' I amend. 'How's your mum?'

'Much the same,' he answers. 'I'm moving back to Manchester – did I mention that? – to be on hand. My last shift here is the day after tomorrow.'

'I'm so sorry she's no better.'

'Thanks for asking, anyway,' David says. 'Are you ready to order?'

I order a big meal – the food is delicious in this place – and force myself to eat it all. Liz is pleased to see me polish off every last chip. I keep an eye on David. A few customers pay and leave. Eventually, I spot him slip out for a cigarette break.

'I'm just going to the loo,' I say to Liz. I don't want to lie to Liz, so I do pop into the ladies' and go for a quick pee before heading outside to talk to David.

'Hi again,' he says as I emerge through the doors and stand next to him. He offers me a cigarette, which I turn down.

'I was wondering if I could talk to you,' I begin.

'Of course. Is this to do with—?'

'Yes. A friend of mine thought he recognised Mr Taylor, you know, the man who—'

'Did he come back here? To North Devon?' David sounds indignant on my behalf.

'No. My friend was sure he saw him on TV. But I think he might have been mistaken. Perhaps this guy just looks like Mr Taylor. Can I show you a video of him? Then you can tell me if you think it's the same man or not.'

'Of course,' David repeats.

I take my phone out of my handbag, bring up the YouTube video I watched with Simon on my sofa and angle my mobile so David can see. He stubs out his cigarette and leans in. He views the whole video without saying anything. Simon was wrong. He must have been. If David recognised this man, he'd tell me immediately, wouldn't he?

'That's him,' David says calmly. I get him to repeat it, thinking I've misheard. 'No doubt about it. That guy – that lawyer – it's definitely Taylor.'

'You're absolutely sure?'

'One hundred per cent certain. Appearance, voice, even the wristwatch. It's the same bloke.'

I'm so stunned I don't know how to respond to that. I gawp at David.

'I don't understand why you're so fixated on him, though,' he says, lighting another cigarette.

Fixated? A spike of anger jabs at me, but I reply calmly. 'Because he killed my husband.' Doesn't David know this?

'Well, technically, he didn't.'

'What?' My brow furrows.

'Technically, it wasn't him.'

'I don't get it.' But as I say that, it dawns on me.

'Did you think it was him driving? It wasn't. He was wasted. His wife insisted on taking the wheel. She hadn't drunk a drop of alcohol. They argued. Right here.' He gestures to where we're standing. 'I heard it all, like I told you before. But in the end, she was the one who got in the driver's seat. I saw her drive away.'

I'm staggered. 'Did you tell the police this?' I manage.

'Of course.'

Did this never come up? With Sergeant Harris and Constable Wright, even with Lorna, we discussed finding the couple and tracing the car. We never spoke specifically about the actual driver. They knew it was her; I was under the impression it was him. His wife got into the passenger seat after giving me the keys. I didn't see him – he didn't get out of the car and it was raining – but he was the one who drove away from my place. I'd assumed he was the one who drove into Greg.

'I need to get back.' David thumbs over his shoulder. I nod. 'I'm around later. Or tomorrow. After that, you can call me if there's anything I can do.'

I nod again. David's bombshell has rendered me speechless and I can't catch my breath. I stay outside after he goes back in, leaning against the wall as my legs threaten to give way. I rack my brains, trying to recall the conversation with Simon the day we walked out to Moor Lane, to the spot where I found the phone and David saw the couple with the Audi.

174

I can't remember Simon's exact words, but I remember the account he gave me clearly. Simon almost ran into the back of the Audi as he came round the corner in his Volkswagen. The front of the Audi was in the hedge. Both the woman and the man were standing beside the vehicle in the pouring rain. The man claimed they'd just changed a tyre after driving into the hedge. Simon saw him close the boot, supposedly after putting away the warning triangle. Was it because the man spoke and not the woman that Simon – and I – assumed he was the driver rather than her? No, there was more. Simon said he could smell alcohol on the man's breath and thought he'd lost control of his vehicle because he'd had too much to drink. Simon definitely said, *he'd* driven into the hedge. I'm sure of it.

I take a few deep breaths, scroll through my phone to Simon's number and call him. He answers on the second ring.

'Hi, Simon.' I try to sound as normal as possible.

'Hi, Amy. How are you? How did your trip to London go? I was hoping you'd call and bring me up to speed,' he gushes.

'Simon, I'm with Liz. I don't have much time, but I have something important to ask you.'

'Fire away.' Simon sounds disappointed.

'Who was driving the Audi?'

'What?'

'Who was driving? Him or her?'

'Him.' There's a pause. 'Well, he was the one who drove away. I only arrived on the scene after the accident. But now I think of it . . . why do you ask?'

'Is it possible *she* drove the car into the hedge?' Simon will grasp the subtext. It's in bold capital letters. Is it possible she was the one who killed Greg? 'What do you mean, now you think of it?'

'Well, Taylor-slash-Hunter adjusted the seat and the rear-view mirror. I thought he was making a big show of it for my benefit. You know, I'm a careful driver, I swerved to avoid a sheep, I was going so slowly the airbags didn't even inflate, I'm not drunk, et cetera.'

'You didn't tell me he adjusted the seat and mirror before he drove off!'

'I didn't think it was important.'

'Simon, it was vital.' It comes out as a whisper.

He drove off. But *she* drove into the hedge – and into Greg. He's very tall and has long legs. She's taller than me, but a lot shorter than him. He had to adjust the driver's seat and reangle the mirror because she'd set them for her when she got behind the wheel at The Thatch.

'Do you think . . .? Do you want me to come round?'

'No, Simon, thank you.' I'm brushing him off and he'll take it badly. I try to soften the blow. 'You've been very helpful, but I'm not at home. I really have to go now. I'll get back to you in a day or two, OK?'

'OK,' he says sullenly. 'Shall I ring the police and tell them?'

'No! No, thank you. They already know. I'll handle this, Simon.' I end the call.

I'm reeling. I've been directing my hate against Mr Taylor all this time and *she* was the one who ran over Greg. She wasn't pressured into going along with her husband's story and helping him cover up his crime as I'd imagined; she drove her lover's car round the corner and into Greg, taking his life. And effectively taking mine, too.

David has confirmed that Hunter is Taylor, but he has presented me with another hurdle, one that seems unsurmountable: Who is Mrs Taylor? And how can I find her?

Hi,

Ten days. My trial lasted merely ten days. It doesn't seem much when my freedom is at stake. I've been told that, on average, a murder trial lasts around two weeks. Is it a bad sign that mine has been so short? Or am I being paranoid?

I should never have been on trial for murder. I was simply in the wrong place at the wrong time. But who's going to believe that? The prosecution has established a convincing motive and presented what they claim is 'incontrovertible proof'. And I have no alibi. I was there. At the scene of the murder – or fatal accident, depending on your perspective.

Both the barrister for the prosecution and my own barrister have made their closing speeches. There's nothing more to be done. Yesterday was the last day of my trial and the judge's turn. The Common Serjeant of London, no less. You could tell he loved the sound of his own voice. He reviewed the whole procedure in great detail, reminding the jurors of everything they'd seen and heard in the courtroom. Finally, he instructed them to reach a unanimous verdict, although I know how this works. If they can't agree, he'll eventually accept a majority verdict. How many of the jurors believe I'm innocent? Surely they can't all think I'm guilty. Not all twelve of them.

And now it's Saturday. I'm in my cell, writing this to you. And waiting. The jury won't even start deliberating until Monday. How long will it take them to reach a verdict? A few hours? Several days? Either way, it will be an agonising wait.

Chapter 25

Amy

Pam and Hugh's car is parked next to mine in the driveway when Liz drops me off at my place on her way home from the pub. Pam is sitting on the doorstep, the top of her grey head illuminated by the spotlight I switched on just before I went out, and Hugh is standing next to one of two large pots, on either side of the front door, which would usually still showcase hydrangea at this time of year. Greg was green-fingered, I'm not, and our garden is now overgrown, the plants and flowers wilted or dead.

'How long have you been here? Why didn't you let yourself into the house?'

'Not long,' Pam says. She refuses to meet my eye. I wouldn't be surprised if they've been here the whole time I was out.

'We didn't want to invade your privacy,' Hugh says.

'You have a key. We gave you a key. You wouldn't be intruding if you used it,' I say, a light undertone of reproach in my voice. I don't add what I'm thinking, that they would have waited inside if Greg were still alive.

There has been an almost imperceptible shift in my relationship with my parents-in-law since we found out Greg's dead. It's so subtle that at times I think I might be imagining it. But a curtain has come down between us, albeit a see-through one, and we tiptoe around, less familiar and more formal with each other. Do Pam and Hugh look at me and think of what they've lost: their remaining son and his baby, their grandchild? Or is it because we've all lost the one official relation that wove us into a family?

'Come in,' I say, opening the door. I lead the way into the living room.

It was a warm day, but the air has got considerably cooler, so I offer to make them some tea to warm them up. But they shake their heads. I know why they're here, so I won't keep them in suspense. I gesture at the sofa and armchair.

'The server at The Thatch confirmed that the barrister, Nicholas Hunter, is the same man as Mr Taylor,' I begin as we all sit down. 'He identified him categorically.'

I pause to allow Pam and Hugh to take this in, realising I haven't computed the information I've learnt this evening myself. Pam exhales loudly.

'So we know who killed Greg.' Hugh sounds both relieved and incredulous.

'No,' I say. 'It wasn't him.'

Opposite me, Hugh visibly stiffens in the armchair, his back suddenly ramrod straight. 'What do you mean?'

'It was her.'

I summarise what David told me, looking from Hugh to Pam and back again. Pam gawps at me, her mouth and eyes open wide, and Hugh's eyebrows knit together.

'What do we do now?' Pam asks when I've finished.

'Well, we could go to the police,' I say, although my voice gives me away. It's not a suggestion. There's an unspoken 'but' at the end of my sentence.

'But you don't want to,' Hugh says.

I look down at my hands. My nails, which I used to keep

neatly filed, are bitten to the quick. 'I'm a bit confused,' I admit. 'I was convinced Hunter ran over Greg and I thought it would be impossible to bring him to justice because he has a reputation for manipulating the law.' I hesitate before telling them the full truth, but I don't want to keep any more secrets from them. 'I'd been . . . fantasising about getting revenge rather than getting justice.' I look up and study them, but their faces are impassive. 'Not that I'd managed to come up with a plan or anything,' I add quickly. 'Now it turns out *she* was the one driving and I haven't wrapped my head around that yet.'

'If she's his lover, I don't suppose there's any more chance of her going down for what she did to Greg than Hunter himself. Presumably, he'll cover for her and lie for her. He'll defend her. Legally, I mean,' Hugh says. Pam looks as if she's about to burst into tears. 'Shall we wait for a day or two?' Hugh continues. 'Give ourselves time to absorb this new information first, see if we can find out something about her – her real identity, for a start.'

'I don't know,' Pam says. 'I still think we should call the police. Or Lorna.'

Hugh leans across his armchair towards Pam, who is sitting on the sofa, and places his hand on her knee. 'We need to find out as much about this woman as we can,' he says. 'Then we can decide what to do next.'

As soon as they've left, I'm on it. I bring up images associated with Nicholas Hunter QC on the screen of my phone and swipe through them, hoping to spot the woman who came to Devon with him. I soon realise that discovering Mrs Taylor's real identity will be easier said than done. It may even be impossible. After an hour or so, my eyelids are too heavy to keep going. It's two in the morning and I'm going to have to call it a day.

I sleep fitfully for a few hours and get up early. I pull on my dressing gown and push my feet into my slippers, then pad downstairs to the kitchen, to make myself a cup of coffee and a slice of toast. I take the plate and mug into the tiny room Greg and I converted from a pantry to a study and, sitting at the desk, I boot up my laptop.

There must be something I've overlooked. There must be a clue somewhere, hidden in one of Hunter's numerous Instagram posts. He may have around one thousand posts, but he has fewer than two hundred followers. He follows only thirty-five accounts, so I start with those. But they are mainly celebrities and bands who have had trouble with the law – Johnny Depp, Snoop Dog, Martha Stewart and Mike Tyson, for example.

Next, I go through his followers. I find his wife almost immediately – his real wife, that is, not Mrs Taylor. Her Instagram handle is @Ediye_Adekoya, which explains why I didn't notice her when I scrolled through his followers before. She doesn't use her married name, at least not on Instagram. She does post photos of her spouse, but without tagging him. Like me, she doesn't appear to have a large social media presence – she only follows twenty people, she has only twelve followers and she hardly ever posts on Instagram.

Other than Hunter's wife, I don't recognise any names or faces among his followers. Of course, if Mrs Taylor is Hunter's mistress, they may well not follow each other on social media. If the two of them go as far as giving a fake name for bookings for holiday rentals and restaurants, they're probably very careful not to raise any suspicions.

I cling to the belief that there's something here somewhere, so I make a start on Hunter's posts, starting with the most recent. I read the captions he has written and also check out the people who have left comments or liked his posts. He comes over as rather pompous and narcissistic, or perhaps it just seems that way because I feel sickened at the sight of him in these photos. By lunchtime, it's clear that this task may take me several hours, or even several days. After lunch, I decide to scroll down to the oldest post and work my way up. His first post dates back to seven years ago.

I'm starting to despair when I find it. At first, I have no inkling that I've stumbled on something. It's a photo of his house, which he apparently bought in 2017. The caption reads: *My new home, where love and happiness will reside! This place might look like it cost a fortune, but really, it was a steal – you could almost accuse me of theft! Ha-ha! Just kidding! I'm keeping the exact location a secret for security reasons, obvs!!!*

It has only three likes – a man, judging by the profile pic, whose account is private; his wife, Ediye, and *Streets of London Estate Agency*, for which the profile picture is the logo – a white-columned building on a red background. According to the bio, this particular branch is situated in Kensington. Presumably, this is the estate agency that sold him the house.

I didn't pick it up last time I looked through his posts, perhaps because I was working through them the other way round. I'd started with the most recent one. I must have given up hope of finding anything useful by the time I got this far, merely scrolling through the images at this point. If I'd spotted this when I first looked through Hunter's account, perhaps I would have been one step closer to finding out where he lives, although I realise the estate agency would hardly be forthcoming with his address. But if I look up the postcodes the agency covers, perhaps I can narrow down my search for his house to a specific area. If I can find him, I'll have more chance of finding her.

This is the closest thing I've had to a lead so far, so I pursue it, typing 'Streets of London Estate Agency Kensington' into the search bar of my Internet browser. I click onto the agency's website and then onto the 'About' tab, where the branch manager beams at me from my computer screen, her name in small capital letters underneath the photo. I stare at the headshot, my heart hammering in my chest and my ears.

Is it her? Is this Mrs Taylor? It looks like her. If it is her, I have her real name. I read it aloud: 'Kirsten Bailey.' I only saw Mrs Taylor once, over three months ago, back in May. I thought I'd recognise her instantly if I saw her again, but now I'm looking at this picture, I'm not sure. She's blond in this photo. Her hair is not the same colour as I remember. Mrs Taylor had red-blond hair. Strawberry blond, that's what that colour is called. But she may dye her hair, of course, and vary the shade from time to time. David was certain that Hunter was the man he served at The Thatch that day. How did he know? I'm usually good with names and faces. Wouldn't I know for sure if it was her? Or maybe it's simply that I don't dare to believe I've found her.

I open Instagram again. There are roughly fifty accounts under the name of Kirsten Bailey, but it only takes me a few minutes to find the account I'm looking for. The profile picture is similar to her headshot on the agency website.

I start to scroll through the posts, doubt gaining more and more ground in my mind with every photo. This can't be Mrs Taylor.

Kirsten Bailey is clearly house-proud. Everything is pristine with no clutter or ornaments in sight. From the captions, I learn that her house has been renovated and revamped. She displays photos of practically every room – the bathroom with its clawfoot bath, the kitchen with its central island, the living room with its modern art paintings on the walls and magazines perfectly aligned on the coffee table, the bedroom with new Egyptian cotton sheets. Her entire home looks like a showroom.

Kirsten Bailey is married – happily, if the camera doesn't lie – to a man named Jamie, according to the captions and tags. He's good-looking: short brown hair, a rotund face with light stubble infringing on his cheeks. I'd say he's in his late thirties. Kirsten and Jamie have a young daughter. I find the girl's name in one of the captions under a gallery post with multiple photos of the little girl's seventh birthday party: Lily. Kirsten appears to be a loving wife and mother. She has even gone to the trouble of baking the birthday cake herself. It's a unicorn-themed cake, with a lot of pink icing, and it looks very professional. In the photo, Kirsten holds back her daughter's light blond hair so she can blow out the candles safely. None of this fits with the image of the monstrous woman I've concocted in my mind. But perhaps this is simply the image she wants to convey.

I click on the tag of Jamie Bailey in the birthday photo. He has even fewer followers than me and seems to post very rarely. I'm losing hope and interest now. I'm about to give up altogether and shut down my laptop when my attention is grabbed by one of Jamie's recent posts. My heart skips two or three beats in a row as I gape in disbelief at the photo. It's a recent selfie of Kirsten, Jamie and Lily, all grinning, the phone held in Jamie's outstretched arm. They're outside, perhaps in a park. I don't know how to zoom in on my computer, so I lean forwards, studying the detail that has struck me. There's no longer any doubt in my mind.

Kirsten Bailey is Mrs Taylor.

My eyes cloud with tears and, as I stare at the bottom right-hand corner of the photo, the image distorts. I swipe at my eyes and blink furiously until the photo becomes sharp again. He's sitting on the ground, next to Kirsten. The angle of the selfie means you can just see his head. But it's definitely him. His tongue is sticking out and his mouth is wide open, as if he's laughing at his photobomb. The photo would have made me laugh, too, in other circumstances.

'I've found you,' I whisper aloud. As the words pass my lips, I'm no longer sure who I mean: Kirsten Bailey, my husband's killer, or Rusty, my dog.

Chapter 26

Kirsten

Kirsten is having a nightmare of a day. She was awake most of last night, her body crying out for sleep while her brain whirred in overdrive. She looks like shit: dark, swollen bags under her eyes; blotchy cheeks from where she bawled her eyes out once Jamie had gone to bed and she was able to give up the pretence that everything was all right. She has achieved only limited damage control to her face even though she trowelled on her make-up this morning. She has a mountain of work to get through today, but it's unsurmountable. She wishes she'd rung in sick with another bogus bug. As it was, she arrived late – and dishevelled – due to someone throwing themselves into the path of a train on the Piccadilly Line and the blustery weather respectively. She's unable to focus on anything remotely work-related. She can't steer her thoughts away from Nick.

There would be some consolation in knowing that this break-up was hurting him as much as it's hurting her. But, evidently, it isn't. It's been eight days since he ended their relationship – after five years – and he hasn't so much as sent a text message to ask how she is. He can tell how she is from the innumerable text messages she has sent him. To begin with, she just asked – politely – if they could talk. In her more recent text messages, she has practically begged him to reconsider his decision, to stay with her, to agree to see her so they can work things out. She's aware she's debasing herself, but she thought she had nothing left to lose as far as Nick was concerned. Now she realises she was mistaken. She has lost her dignity and self-respect, too.

The only news she has had of him – indirectly – in all that time is the rather unoriginal photo he has posted on Instagram of his own hairy feet in the foreground of the shot as he lounges in front of his indoor pool. The caption reads: *Having a well-earned break at home today!* A day off rather than an off day. She sold him that home. Five years ago. That's how it all began. A celebratory dinner after the sale was completed.

Kirsten is bereft, barely functioning, but Nick doesn't seem to care at all. Didn't their dreams mean anything to him? Was he faking it every time they fantasised about their future? He promised her they would get married one day, move in together, grow old together. Empty promises, as it turns out. He has lied to her, and yet they swore to be honest with each other. It was Nick who said if they had to lie to other people in order to see each other, then it was important for them to be truthful with each other.

They've made so many memories. They've confided in each other, kept each other's secrets, done things together that no one else knows about. Kirsten finds that scary now. Especially this last secret. Nick knows what really happened in Devon. It's one thing to share a secret together; it's another to share it apart. She has always found Nick a little untrustworthy. How can she trust him now? She wouldn't put it past him to set her up to take the fall for Gregory Wood's death. He'd manage to wriggle his way out of it all, looking squeaky clean.

When she and Nick made the decision to cover up the accident, she thought things would get easier in time. With each day that goes by without the police knocking on her door, she should feel more confident that that day will never come. But instead, she has become more and more scared. Paranoid. As if that day is getting closer. Sometimes, she just wants it over with. There would be an element of relief if what she's dreading actually happened. She wouldn't dread it anymore.

She wonders if she should go to the police. She has a guilty conscience when she thinks about Gregory Wood or his widow, but it's not remorse that has planted this idea in her head. She has no intention of confessing. If she does go to the police, it will be to denounce Nick. Does she want to lash out at him, get back at him? Or does she fear he might turn her in and want to pre-empt his confession?

She knows she can't lay all the blame on Nick. She can pretend he was driving, but she can't denounce him without incriminating herself. If nothing else, she'd have to admit to the police that she helped him remove Gregory Wood's body. That would make her an accessory. She could downplay her role, but if the police find out that she had a hand in Gregory Wood's death, then everyone else will find out about the affair. Ediye might already have found out about it, but Jamie doesn't suspect a thing, and it needs to stay that way.

So, there's no question of Kirsten going to the police. It's a ridiculous notion, something her sleep-addled brain has come up with, and now she has thought the idea through, she bats it away. But since Nick has broken up with her, there's a feeling Kirsten can't shake off so easily: that one day it will come down to his word against hers and that everyone will believe him.

She makes herself another strong coffee – at least her fifth today. The crappy machine at work isn't a patch on the top-of-the-range espresso machine in her kitchen and the coffee tastes revolting. She downs it as soon as it's cool enough. She should be feeling wired by now, but she's exhausted and anxious, crawling up the walls rather than bouncing off them. She has snapped at her colleagues all day long and they're doing their best to avoid her, leaving a wide berth around her desk each time they pass by in the open-plan offices of the estate agency.

Kirsten rings Mr Jafari about the flat near Holland Park that he viewed with his wife just over a week ago, an hour or so before Nick discarded her like a used nappy. She'd shown other couples around the flat after the Jafaris and she had one other potential buyer for the overpriced property, but Mr Jafari, a cash buyer, made an offer that was higher than the asking price – without even requesting a second viewing – and the sellers, in the middle of a messy divorce, have just accepted it without much delay.

Mr Jafari is delighted. Kirsten should be, too. She'll make a huge commission from this sale. But she doesn't feel like celebrating and certainly not with her co-workers. She wants to go home. She has two viewings scheduled for this evening – both for the flat near Holland Park. She cancels them and knocks off early for a change.

As she steps through the automatic doors onto the street and into the gusting wind, Kirsten notices two police officers – one male, one female – to her left. They're only a few feet away and seem to have their eyes riveted on the window of the estate agency. Are they here for her? She lowers her head, her hair blowing in front of her face, hiding it, and she walks briskly in the opposite direction, the wrong direction, since the way to the nearest Tube station would mean walking past the officers.

She throws a worried glance over her shoulder, but the police officers haven't moved. They're not looking at her, let alone coming after her. Kirsten berates herself for being paranoid, even as she continues walking the other way.

She gets on the Tube at Earl's Court instead of South Kensington. She's lucky enough to get the one remaining seat, beating an older woman to it. The other woman glowers at Kirsten, but she's not elderly or infirm and Kirsten stays put. As the train pulls out of the underground station, Kirsten's hackles rise. Someone is watching her. She whips her head round, then moves it more slowly, scanning the carriage, but no one is paying her any attention. Not even the woman who made a beeline for Kirsten's seat.

She doesn't feel any easier when she gets off at Wood Green. In fact, the whole walk home from the Tube station, Kirsten is convinced someone is following her. She strains her ears for footsteps behind her, but if someone really was walking right behind her, she'd hardly hear them over the noise of the traffic. She senses a pair of eyes trained on her. Her pulse races and she keeps whirling round, checking behind her, but she sees nothing out of the ordinary and no one acting suspiciously. She gives herself a stern talking-to, deliberately walking more slowly rather than speeding up so that her heart rate decreases.

As she turns into her road, she throws one last glance over her shoulder. She stops in her tracks as she sees someone duck beside a parked car. She was right! She *is* being followed! She races towards the car, without even considering what she'll do or say, but when she reaches it, there's no one anywhere in sight.

Kirsten groans. She's seeing things. It's because she's tired. If her insomnia continues, she'll have to get some medicine to knock herself out at night. Slipping her hand into her bag as she walks away, she grasps her mobile to call Nick. It's an automatic gesture and as soon as she becomes aware of what she's doing, she stops herself. Subconsciously, she's probably looking for an excuse to contact him, but this is too flimsy. She'll come over as a weak damsel in distress. Or, worse, mad and desperate. She's used to ringing or texting him or leaving him a voicemail whenever she has a problem, or to tell him something funny or loving, or simply to tell him about her day and ask about his. She can't call him anymore when she has a problem. She can't call him anymore, full stop. This realisation hits her like a blow to the stomach and she doubles over in pain, tears springing to her eyes.

She straightens up again. She doesn't know how it has come to this, how she has allowed herself to become this dependent on Nick, but she has to pull herself together. She has everything she needs and more than she deserves. Opening the front door, she musters a smile and calls out to Jamie and Lily. As she steps inside, Rusty greets her, darting all around her, his tail wagging. Lily is as delighted to see Kirsten as the dog is and also bounds around her mother before Kirsten can even take off her shoes. Although their excitement doesn't rub off on Kirsten, she feels the tension evaporate from her shoulders. She's home.

But as she closes the door behind her, she thinks she sees movement in the street, as if someone has taken cover behind the tree right opposite her house. She locks the door, her smile upending to a scowl. Was it her imagination? Or did someone follow her home?

Chapter 27

Amy

Even though she has closed the door, I stay hidden behind the plane tree, frozen. That was close! She saw me. Twice. I nearly ruined everything. Perhaps I should have used my mum's money to pay a private investigator to do the legwork for me. I'm a useless amateur sleuth, as I already demonstrated to myself when I attempted to stake out Nicholas Hunter's chambers and stalk Nicholas Hunter himself. But I should give myself a little credit. I now know where Kirsten Bailey lives and works. I'm confident she only caught a glimpse of me. I wasn't close enough for her to recognise me, even if I hadn't been wearing a cap and sunglasses. She might not place me, anyway. After all, we met each other briefly just that once and I wasn't sure it was her when I saw her headshot on the estate agency website.

I'm reeling in shock not only from almost being caught, but also from seeing my dog. As Kirsten opened the front door and Rusty bounded to meet her, it was all I could do not to call out for him to come to me. He was pleased to see her, so she must be treating him well, although, even from this distance, I can see he has put on weight. Labradors need a lot of exercise. Until he injured his knee, Greg used to take Rusty with him when he went running. Poor dog. I bet he misses that. He must miss the beach, too. He loved rolling in the sand and jumping over the waves. He would shake all over Greg and me when he came out of the water. Pain slices through me as it hits me all over again how much I miss my husband and my dog. My life. I miss my life.

Daylight is fading now, so I take off my sunglasses. Because I'm wearing a cap, I can't push my glasses onto my head, so I hook them into the neck of my hoodie. I peep out from behind the tree and peer across the street at the impressive house – some sort of period property, I think, although I've no idea which period. It's set back slightly from the pavement, but I can still see inside, through the large sash window on the ground floor. The pavement is higher on my side of the road, which gives me a good vantage point.

A lamp goes on in the living room. I see Kirsten's little girl playing with Rusty. I watch them all as they go about their evening routine. Mesmerised, I don't move for ages – I don't know how long exactly. Dinner is a ready-made meal from the freezer that Jamie pops into the oven.

As Kirsten, Jamie and Lily sit around the high kitchen table and eat it, Rusty begs for titbits. Greg and I tried – and failed – to train him not to do that. We managed to train him not to go upstairs and not to sit on the sofa and armchairs, but when it came to keeping him away from the table while we were eating, Rusty wasn't having it. Typical, mischievous Labrador. I see Lily slip him some meat under the table when her parents aren't looking, which makes me smile.

When they've finished eating, Kirsten clears up. Jamie and Lily disappear from view. A light goes on upstairs, so presumably it's the little girl's bedtime.

I have to duck behind the tree again when a neighbour drives down the residential cul-de-sac and parks in his driveway. When it's safe for me to peep out from my hiding place, Kirsten and Jamie are sitting side by side on the sofa, watching TV. I can't see right down to the floor, but I picture Rusty lying at their feet. She has a glass of wine in her hand. They haven't drawn the curtains, but this is a quiet road and they live at the end of it. Apart from the neighbour coming home, no one has come near me. Kirsten sensed me following her earlier, but she's oblivious to the fact I'm observing her now.

They're obviously watching a comedy. At one point, Kirsten tips back her head and laughs. Although I can't hear her from here, her laughter seems to echo loudly in my ears. How can she be so carefree? She has wrecked my life, but her life goes on as though nothing has happened. She doesn't seem to realise how lucky she is; she doesn't seem to appreciate what she has. And yet, her life is everything I've ever dreamt of for myself. She has a loving husband, a beautiful child, a dog, a happy home.

The image stabs me right through the heart. At the same time, it renews my determination to seek revenge rather than justice. The idea of retribution first came to me when I thought Hunter was the one who'd run over Greg because I didn't think the law could touch him. But now I know she was the one driving, nothing has changed. If anything, I want revenge even more. She has taken everything from me. She even took the one piece of my life she could have left me: my dog.

The evening air has a bracing nip to it, so I decide to head back to the Tube station and make my way to the room I'm renting as a lodger with live-in landlords in Pimlico. It's not ideal; it's tiny, basic, noisy and expensive – almost £1,000 a month – but it's clean and I don't plan to be there for long. I hope to wrap up everything within a month. Two months tops.

For the next two days, I tail Kirsten Bailey everywhere she goes. I wait for her in the mornings at the end of her road and follow her. I'm getting better at this – she hasn't glanced over her shoulder once since that first day. I stick so closely to her now that I get the occasional whiff of her heady perfume. I've become her shadow.

On the Wednesday and Thursday, she goes into the office first. Fortunately, there's a café right opposite the estate agency, where, so far, I've managed to grab a window seat while I wait for her to re-emerge. She comes out at various times during the day to visit properties, either for viewings or valuations, I suppose. She uses public transport, which makes it relatively easy to follow her. There's little chance of her jumping into a chauffeur-driven car and giving me the slip, unless, of course, she meets up with Hunter. I expect them to see each other at some point. I want her to lead me to him, as the fact he wasn't the one at the wheel doesn't exonerate him in my eyes and the intense hatred I feel towards the man hasn't waned. I'm still curious about him, and I think Bailey and Hunter should both pay for what they did to Greg. They were in it together.

But to my disappointment, I don't so much as overhear a phone conversation between them, so I'm no nearer to finding out anything more about him. I learn nothing new about Kirsten, except that she works long hours.

On the Friday, I decide to get up a little later and wait for her to arrive at her office in Kensington. But I wake up well before the alarm, so I get up and make my way to the house in Muswell Hill, where I watch Kirsten and her family through the window as they eat breakfast, spying on them as they get ready for work and school, just as I've done on the previous two days. Above all, I gaze longingly at my dog.

But today, even though I didn't plan to, I change tack. I don't follow Kirsten when she leaves, deciding instead to wait for Jamie and Lily. They emerge through the front door about twenty minutes after Kirsten. With Rusty on a lead. I'll have to keep my distance. Dogs have an incredibly powerful sense of smell. If Rusty detects me, he'll give me away. He won't have forgotten me.

I walk several metres behind them and stop when it becomes obvious where they're heading. I've already explored the area and know there's a primary school at the bottom of the hill. Assuming Jamie will come back this way after taking Lily to school so he can drop off Rusty before going to work himself, I cross the street. I don't want Jamie to see me or Rusty to smell me. I know nothing about Jamie's work or habits – nothing about Jamie at all, in fact – and yet, I'm a little surprised when he turns into a little road next to the school and disappears. I run to catch up.

We end up in a small park, perhaps the one in the family selfie that Jamie took and posted on Instagram. The sign at the entrance clearly says that dogs are to be kept on the lead, but there's no one around and Jamie unclips the lead from Rusty's collar. To Rusty's delight, Jamie seems to magic a tennis ball out of nowhere to play fetch. I spot a bench halfway up the slope on the other side of the pond from where they're playing. As discreetly as possible, I make my way to the bench, steering well clear of Jamie and Rusty. Sitting on the bench, I take my book out of my handbag and pretend to read.

I notice my book is shaking and realise it's not just my hands that are unsteady; I'm trembling all over. I don't know why. I'm not cold. I'm angry, but that has become part of my default setting and it has nothing to do with Jamie. As far as I'm aware, he had nothing to do with Greg's death and I imagine his wife has kept him in the dark about her role in it.

I think the reason I'm shaking is because I'm so close to something that was part of the life I've lost. It feels almost tangible and at the same time completely out of reach. That's my dog playing by the pond. He's pretty much all that's left of everything that once defined home for me. So close, and yet so far.

Suddenly, my sight blurs and I no longer see the pond in front of me. It's not Jamie who is throwing the ball next to the pond; it's Greg who is throwing a stick as we walk along the South West Coast Path near our cottage. It could be any one of dozens of memories, or a fusion of several memories – Greg and I walked that path countless times together.

I'm lost in my daydream, trying not to give in to tears, when the unthinkable happens. Rusty ignores the ball Jamie has thrown and instead starts to chase a pigeon that was pecking at the ground a few metres away from him. The bird takes off and Rusty races after it, skirting around the pond. They're heading in my direction.

'Rusty! Rusty!' Jamie calls after him.

This, rather than my dog bounding up the slope, is what jolts me out of my reverie. She has kept his name. How did she know his name? Did she speak to Greg? Did he tell her our dog's name? But as Rusty gets closer, I notice he has a new collar and it comes to me. His name was on his dog tag.

The bird has long gone, but Rusty is still running towards me, his tongue lolling out of one side of his mouth. Without realising what I'm doing, I lean forwards and suddenly Rusty is in my arms, licking the tears from my cheeks, his tail going like a metronome on full speed. The next second, he rolls over on his back for me to tickle his tummy and then he jumps up again, his front paws now on my lap. He barks, overexcited, as I bury my face in his fur.

It takes all the strength I can muster to pull myself together before Jamie reaches Rusty and me. He perches on the end of the bench, as if careful not to invade my space or give me the wrong impression.

'He loves you,' Jamie says. 'He doesn't normally greet strangers like that.'

'I love dogs,' I say, ruffling Rusty's ears. My voice sounds far from familiar to me, but that won't alarm Jamie. This is the first time I've spoken to him. 'Good boy, Rusty. Down now.'

'Ah, you've met Rusty before?' Jamie says. 'That explains it.'

'Sorry? No, I . . .' I break off, wondering how to cover up my error.

'I assumed you'd bumped into my wife when she was out with the dog.'

'Oh, no. You called him. That's how I knew his name.' I wince. I've just told a lie and I hate being dishonest.

He nods, accepting my explanation. 'He's taken quite a shine to you! I'm Jamie, by the way.'

I hesitate. I'm not prepared for this. 'Rose,' I say eventually.

It's my middle name. It's the best I can do. I can't tell him my real name. Just in case. But his wife and her lover gave me fake names and I can't help comparing myself with them. I don't want to sink to their level. I've always considered myself straightforward and honest. Months ago, I wouldn't have thought myself capable of spying and lying. Perhaps you only really know yourself when you've lost everything. Or maybe losing everything transforms you into someone else.

'Do you live near here?' he asks.

'No.'

'Ah, you're lost, then. No one would come here on purpose.' He means it as a joke, I think.

'No.' I'm trying to work out what to say, fabricate a quick background story for myself, and it comes out sounding curt.

'Sorry. It's none of my business.'

'Oh, that's OK. I'm looking for a place to live round here.' With each lie I tell, it seems to get a little less difficult and a lot more convincing.

'It's a great area to live in. A ten-minute walk from the nearest Tube station, good schools, fairly quiet for London.' He stops and chuckles. 'I sound like my wife,' he explains. 'She's an estate agent. Perhaps I can put you in touch with her?'

I'd never be able to afford a house in a suburb like this and I'm sure it shows. I'm dressed scruffily – in worn jeans, a washed-out hoodie and Converse. I'm already blowing my cover. 'Thanks, but I'm only looking for somewhere to rent. Somewhere small.'

'Kirsten does rentals, too. Her agency is situated in Kensington, but she'd give you good advice and there are other branches in the neighbourhood, so she has contacts here. I could introduce you to her, if you like?'

'No,' I say too quickly, regretting it as I clock the card he has extracted from his wallet. I don't want him to introduce me to his wife, for obvious reasons, but if that's his business card rather than hers, it might have come in handy. But he slides the card back into his wallet and the wallet back into the pocket of his jeans before I can tell him I've changed my mind.

Rusty's sitting with his head on my lap, looking up at me, occasionally whining or prodding me with his paw or licking my hand as I stroke him. He sweeps the grass from side to side with his tail. I scrabble for something to say.

'It was nice meeting you, Rose,' Jamie says before I can think of anything. 'Rusty and I should get going. I promised him a nice long walk, didn't I, fella?'

I'm making a mess of this. Jamie has been friendly and chatty. I must have come over as cold and brusque. I need to keep him talking. He's my only link to Kirsten. I have to find a way of using that to my advantage.

I say the first thing that pops into my head. 'He's a fox-red Labrador,' I say, 'isn't he? I used to have a fox-red Lab.' That last sentence, at least, is truthful.

'I believe so, yes. Kirsten has been looking after him for a colleague of hers who's sick.'

So, that's the story she's concocted.

'We don't really have enough time for him during the week,' Jamie continues, 'but I try to make up for it at weekends and on days like today when I'm working from home. Ideally, we could do with a dog walker. We said we'd advertise for one, but we haven't got round to doing it.'

Without stopping to ask myself if it's a good idea or if it could be dangerous, I hear myself volunteering to walk my own dog. 'Really. It would be my pleasure,' I add.

'Well, that would be great!' Jamie stands up. Rusty's ears twitch, but he stays put. He knows it's time to go for walkies, but he's glued to me. Jamie slides his hand into his back pocket to retrieve the wallet he pulled out a moment earlier. 'Think it over and if you're sure, give me a ring or send me a text and we'll take it from there.'

I almost snatch Jamie's business card when he holds it out to me this time. I put it safely inside the zip-up pocket of my handbag. I still don't have a plan, but this feels like a step towards coming up with one. If I can gain Jamie's trust, I might be able to gain access to their home. And, to use Jamie's expression, we'll take it from there.

Chapter 28

Kirsten

Still no word from Nick. It's now been a fortnight since he dumped her. Kirsten has lost her appetite and, as a result, about eight pounds in weight. She tries not to think about him, but it's as if he has taken up residence in her mind, occupying nearly all her headspace. She has a permanent knot in her stomach that tightens with every unbidden memory that assaults her. Nick is – *was* – the love of her life and it's going to take some time to get over him.

On the Tube home, Kirsten replays some of their conversations in her head. She doesn't always recall what was said word for word, but she remembers the gist. Images of the two of them flash before her eyes at times when she least expects it, but when she deliberately tries to summon them, they won't appear. She has a sudden urge to reread some of their emails and text messages. But when he dumped her, she deleted the lot from her phone in a fit of anger. Since her mobile is synced with her computer and since she has deleted everything from the cloud, too, she has no way of getting back what she has erased. Ironically, Nick would often warn her to delete everything daily and she would pretend that she had, while secretly keeping everything so she could read some of their exchanges again from time to time.

The only messages she still has are hers, text messages that vary in length, all of them asking him for another chance. She won't reread those. They make her cringe and want to curl up in bed and never get up again.

It's probably just as well that the earlier messages between them – the loving ones, the suggestive ones, the ones where they row and then make up – are all gone. She would only get upset raking through them. She needs to stop wallowing in self-pity. She should really block Nick altogether, but she can't bring herself to do it. She resolves to focus on her family. Spending time with Jamie and Lily will help her get Nick out of her head. Not to mention Amy and Gregory Wood. She tries not to listen to the voice in her head telling her she doesn't deserve a loving husband and beautiful daughter.

Last night, she and Jamie had an argument and Jamie implied that he doesn't think she deserves them, either. He reproached her with not pulling her weight at home. As she's the main breadwinner of the family, Kirsten doesn't see why Jamie can't undertake most of the tasks at home. To be fair, he is the one who tends to their small back garden, does the shopping and makes the meals.

'You rarely cook and never clean,' he'd said. 'The only time you set foot in the garden, it's to sunbathe.'

'I do the ironing!' She didn't add that on the few occasions Jamie had ironed their clothes, he put in more creases than he smoothed out.

Jamie went on to admonish her for doing as little as possible with Lily. His words come back to her now. 'You take no interest in how she's getting on at school,' he'd said. 'You don't take her to any of her activities or to the cinema or swimming pool or anything like that.'

As she remembers their row now, a hot flush rises from Kirsten's neck and brands her cheeks. She's not sure if it's due to shame or anger. She doesn't like to admit she's wrong, but deep down she knows Jamie is right. If anything, he went easy on her. She has been a terrible mother and a terrible wife. She doesn't often cook their meals. She likes baking – biscuits, cakes and bread – at the weekends. But in the evenings, when she gets home, it's usually late and she's always tired. And she doesn't do enough with Lily. On her walk home from the Tube station, she decides to help out with making the meal this evening and with the clearing up. Then she'll put Little Lil to bed and read her a bedtime story.

But when Kirsten arrives home, there's no one there. Where are her husband and daughter? She has finished work earlier than usual, but Lily and Jamie should have got in an hour or more before her. Perhaps they've gone out for a walk. Kirsten immediately brushes off that idea. The dog's here and Jamie has found a dog walker to take Rusty out in the week. Maybe Jamie needed something to get the dinner ready. But that can't be it, either. He would have sent her a message to stop at the convenience shop on her way home.

She picks up the post from the doormat and kicks off her shoes. In the kitchen, she dumps the post on the central island and makes herself an espresso. She should really have a herbal tea or a rooibos – she's still suffering from insomnia – but she needs a pick-me-up at the end of a long day.

Holding her coffee cup in one hand, she brings up Jamie's number on her phone with the other hand and rings him, but he doesn't answer. Seconds later, her mobile pings with a text. It's from Jamie.

> At Lily's school concert, where, incidentally, you're also supposed to be.

Kirsten swears. She checks the calendar app in her phone and sees that she has noted the event for tomorrow. Lily only started learning the violin at the beginning of this school year and it sounds like someone strangling a cat when she plays. Kirsten hates the instrument, although at least Lily didn't ask to learn the drums or the trumpet. Kirsten has repeatedly asked Jamie to get Lily to practise before she comes home so she doesn't have to put up with the caterwauling. Jamie will think Kirsten has missed their daughter's performance this evening on purpose. She looks at the time on her mobile, but it's far too late to show up at the school now. They'll be home any minute. She'll have to make it up to Lily. When it comes to Lily, Kirsten's always trying to make up for her mistakes and shortcomings. If only she could get it right first time occasionally.

Kirsten prides herself on being well organised and methodical, and yet she has messed up the dates in her calendar app twice recently – not only missing Lily's concert because she saved the event on the wrong day, but also not showing up at an important appointment for work yesterday because she hadn't saved the event at all. She clearly remembers opening the app and entering the appointment, but she must have forgotten to tap on 'Add' when she'd completed the details. It's the only explanation she can come up with. It's not like her to be this unreliable. Nor is it like her to make mistakes.

Kirsten sets her phone down on the worktop and flicks absent-mindedly through the post, not expecting anything interesting and thinking she should make some dinner for when Jamie and Lily get back. There are two utility bills and a flyer for a takeaway restaurant opening in the area. And, finally, a white envelope that appears to have been hand-delivered. The words 'PRIVATE AND CONFIDENTIAL' are printed in capital letters in the top left-hand corner of the envelope. But what grabs her attention is the name of the addressee, typed in the middle of the envelope, in smaller letters and underlined.

She drops her coffee, the glass cup smashing as it hits the tiled floor and the hot liquid splashing the legs of her beige, linen trousers. She swears again. She continues to stare at the name until it smudges. She closes her eyes, as if that will make the letter go away. But she can still see the name etched on the insides of her eyelids.

Mrs Kirsten Taylor.

Taylor. This must be from Nick. No one else knows their pseudonym. But her hands shake as she rips into the envelope. She knows that's just wishful thinking, an explanation she has come up with to try to stop her world spinning and set it back on its axis. Nick wouldn't have delivered a letter to her home in person. He'd have texted or called. There's no way he'd have sent a letter with the name 'Taylor' on it to her house, where her husband could so easily have been the one to find it. She and Nick haven't used that name since they came back from Devon. The letter can't be from Nick. And it can't be good.

She extracts a piece of A4 paper. The first thing she notices is that it's typewritten. There's no sender's address at the top of the letter and no signature or name at the bottom. It appears to be anonymous. As she reads the letter, an invisible hand tightens around her throat, threatening to cut off her air supply. The walls of the kitchen start to close in around her and the floor pitches. Her breathing comes in erratic gasps and her head spins. Her back against the kitchen island, she slides to the floor, cutting her hand on a shard of broken glass as she steadies herself.

She's having a panic attack. She hasn't had one since the year she took her A levels. Her parents put a lot of pressure on her to obtain good grades and she put a lot of pressure on herself. She remembers – more or less – what the school matron told her to do and concentrates on her breathing until the room stops spinning and the ground stops lurching.

Ediye. Could this be from Nick's wife? Kirsten has been searching for an excuse – a valid one – to get in touch with Nick, but now she has one, she fervently wishes she didn't. *Be careful what you wish for*.

Rusty is fussing around her and she pushes him away, noticing only now that her hand is bleeding. She has to clean up the glass before he cuts his paw. Slowly, she gets to her feet and walks to the sink, opening the cupboard under it, where the dustpan and brush are kept. When she has swept up the broken pieces of the coffee cup, she grabs her phone from the worktop and scrolls through her contacts to Nick.

She mentally prepares a message, anticipating that he'll let his phone go to voicemail when he sees the caller ID, but he answers her call immediately.

'Hang on,' he says to her, then, to someone else, 'Excuse me for a moment. I have to take this. It's important.'

While she waits, she squeezes the phone against her ear with her shoulder and runs cold water over her free hand – her cut hand – at the sink. She watches the blood swirl down the sink. Then she turns off the tap and tears off two sheets from the roll of paper towel, using them to bandage her hand.

'Hi,' he breathes. 'I'm so glad you called. I miss you. I miss you so much. Will you forgive me? Edie had a full meltdown when she found out about us and, stupidly, I gave in to her demands. But I can't live without you! I don't know what I was thinking!'

His voice and words take away Kirsten's own voice and words. She's engulfed by an overload of emotions. She has been texting him and he has been ignoring her and she wasn't expecting this. She wasn't even expecting him to answer the phone. She's used to Nick blowing hot and cold, but this is overwhelming. She opens her mouth, but the only thing that comes out is a sob.

'I just want things between us to go back to normal,' Nick persists. 'Can I see you?'

'Yes, but, Nick . . . that's not why I'm ringing.' Her voice quavers.

'What's wrong? What's wrong, baby?'

Kirsten makes an effort to pull herself together. 'I've just received a letter. There's no stamp. I think someone pushed it through my letterbox.' She pauses as it dawns on her what this means. Whoever wrote it knows where she lives. 'Someone knows what happened in North Devon. Someone knows what we did to Gregory Wood. I'm being threatened, Nick. The letter . . . it's blackmail.'

Chapter 29

Amy

Soon we have a deal. And a routine. I arrive about ten minutes before Kirsten is due to leave for work every morning so I can make sure she does set off. I can't run the risk of encountering her if one day she happens to start later or is off sick. I wait until Jamie gets back from taking Lily to school and then I knock on the door, even though he has given me a key. He always has a coffee with me before he leaves, unless he's in a hurry. The Baileys have a state-of-the-art espresso machine that takes up most of the worktop.

We chat easily, usually small talk about trivial things – the weather, Rusty, the news. I stick as close to the truth as possible when the conversation touches more personal matters and try to keep him chatting about himself so that he doesn't get a chance to probe too much into my life. I'm getting to know him slowly, but given the little he knows about me, he's very trusting. Far too trusting. I have access to his home and he doesn't even know my real name. He'd texted to ask if I could bring proof of identity the first time I came to take out Rusty. When I showed up, I had to spin a story about losing my wallet with my ID documents in it.

He asked for my surname, I gave him my maiden name – Salter – and he added it to my mobile number in his phone. Then he made me a coffee, gave me a front door key and forgot all about the ID. Neither of us has mentioned it since.

Jamie has his back to me, making our espressos. I didn't use to drink coffee in the mornings. It's a habit I'm getting into with him. I perch on one of the high stools at the kitchen island. Rusty sits by my side, looking up at me through brown, expectant eyes. His tail swishes enthusiastically when I reach down to pat him.

'You really do have a lovely house. It's beautifully decorated,' I say, as Jamie hands me my espresso and sits on the bar stool next to mine. I look through the kitchen towards the living room. There's nothing out of place and not a cobweb or speck of dust anywhere. There are no toys in sight, either. They're all neatly stored on the shelves and in the toy box in Lily's bedroom. I know this because I've had a good nosy around the whole house. 'From what I've seen of it, anyway,' I add hastily.

Jamie shrugs. 'I mean, I can't take credit for any of it. It's my wife's house,' he says. 'She inherited it and she's lived in it pretty much all her life. She's got a natural talent for interior design. I don't get a say in any of that. Quite right, too, I have terrible taste in home décor.' He lowers his voice and says confidentially, 'Between you and me, I don't always feel completely at home. I could do with a man cave or something, somewhere I can be myself, you know, just relax and be messy.' He smiles.

I think what Jamie means is that this is very much Kirsten's house and he feels out of place in it. I can relate to what he's describing, I think, although what I feel now when I'm at home isn't quite the same. My cottage doesn't seem like home without Greg in it. It used to be our house and not just mine. I can sense both his presence and his absence in every room. All our stuff, all the memories – everything just reminds me he isn't there anymore.

'So, how's your house-hunting going, Rose?' he asks me, breaking into my thoughts.

207

'I'm renting a room,' I say. 'In Pimlico. It's temporary.'

'Are you looking for work?' he asks.

'Not at the moment, no.' He looks at me, a prompt to elaborate, and I can't leave it at that. 'I'm taking some time off work, actually. I have a few things to sort out.'

'I see.' He doesn't. 'What's your profession?'

'I'm a primary school teacher.' I *was* a primary school teacher. I'm still not sure if I'll ever go back. 'What do you do?' I ask, getting in a question before he can ask me another one.

'I'm a copywriter. Ads and websites, that sort of thing. I work part-time so I can look after Lily. What that really means is I work part-time in the office and I have to do the rest of the work at home, but at least I can spend time with my daughter.'

So far, he hasn't asked me if I have children. I brace myself, but he slides off the stool.

'I'd better get going,' he says, loading our glass cups into the dishwasher. 'Perhaps you'd like to come round for dinner one evening. I'd love you to meet Kirsten and Lily.'

I open my mouth but nothing comes out.

'You can bring someone, if you like. A friend or your partner . . .' He trails off, glancing at my wedding band. I look down at it, too, my worthless ring that's worth a fortune to me.

We've danced around the issue of my marital status a few times. He talks about his family and I don't mention mine. It's getting awkward.

'I have no one to bring and I'm not good company at the moment.'

'I think you're good company,' he says, then blushes.

'I lost my husband recently,' I say. 'I'm not really up to socialising.' I'm not sure why I'm telling him this. It's more information than I need to give, even though I'm sure he won't ask me to have dinner with him and his family again. Am I letting my guard slip? Perhaps because he has just confided in me, I feel I can share this with him.

'I'm so sorry.' He turns to me. 'How awful. Was he ill?'

'No, it was sudden. An accident.'

I watch his reaction closely, although my gut instinct tells me he knows nothing about Kirsten's weekend in North Devon. He may report our conversation to Kirsten, although somehow I get the impression that she's not the sort of person who would take an interest in their dog walker. I doubt she'll put two and two together even if he does repeat all this.

'What sort of accident?' His eyes lock into mine.

'A car accident.'

'I'm so sorry,' he says again.

'That's why I'm in London,' I continue, before he can ask me for more details. 'I have some stuff to sort out relating to his death. Then I'll go back home.'

I've already told him I'm from the south-west, although he doesn't know precisely where I live. I feel less guilty when I can tell Jamie the truth instead of giving elusive answers, half-truths or, on occasion, downright lies. I hate all the subterfuge.

'If there's anything I can do, Rose, please don't hesitate to tell me.'

'Thank you.'

When Jamie has gone, I clip on Rusty's lead and we head outside. Every day, we walk for miles in Alexandra Park. As the Baileys live in Muswell Hill, Alexandra Park is on their doorstep. Jamie takes Lily there often, apparently – she loves the playground and the pitch and putt. The two of them picnic there when the weather's good. But I haven't yet witnessed Kirsten so much as set foot in the eighty-hectare green space. It's dog-friendly and vast; offers incredible views of London and has hilly, flat and woodland paths. I'm not sure who enjoys our walks more – Rusty or me.

When I get back, I get to work. Kirsten has an iMac in her office. It's not a recent model, thankfully, so I don't need touch ID to get into it. The first day I came here to walk Rusty, I found all her passwords and codes in the back of a notebook in a desk drawer. Her computer is synced with her phone, so I can follow her from a distance. I don't want to alert her by connecting to her accounts from a device that doesn't belong to her. If I connect with one of my devices, I'll be leaving a trace as well, so I check her appointments and go through her files and apps on her computer.

So far, to my disappointment, there has been no mention of an appointment with Nicholas Hunter. She doesn't use a fake name for him – not even Mr Taylor – but the events I've found in her calendar app are for past dates. As far as I can work out, they met up frequently in the past, but don't seem to be seeing each other at the moment. The text messages seem to confirm this. Kirsten has sent a handful of texts, in which she practically begs Hunter for a second chance, but he hasn't replied to a single one of them. There are no emails at all. If she emails him, either it's not from the phone she has synced with her computer or she deletes them afterwards.

Because there hasn't been anything in the calendar app I can use, I've changed the date for a couple of events, including her daughter's school concert, which I feel guilty about now. I've also deleted two or three of her work appointments altogether, which I have fewer qualms about. It's not part of a revenge plan – for now, I have little more than a hazy, half-cooked idea in my mind – but I get a perverse sense of satisfaction out of knowing I've probably caused trouble.

I sit in Kirsten's office chair and boot up her computer. I enter the passcode and wait for the desktop screen to appear. I start, as always, by going through Kirsten's text messages. But there's nothing of any interest to me. Then I open her calendar app. Immediately, an entry for the next day grabs my attention. Kirsten has an appointment – or a date. It's abbreviated, but the message is clear. *12pm Nick. Vic Embkmt Gdns.* Kirsten is meeting up with Nicholas Hunter tomorrow in Victoria Embankment Gardens at midday. My heart races in trepidation.

My mind races, too. I'll have to invest in a better disguise than my clichéd cap and sunnies. Perhaps I should buy a wig or get my hair cut and dyed. I need to get as close to Kirsten Bailey and Nicholas Hunter as possible. It's been several months since it happened, but what they did to Greg must still be on their minds. If they discuss it, or even allude to it in a throwaway remark, I need to record it with my phone.

But this thought unravels as soon as it enters my head. What would it achieve if I had evidence of their crime? I'm no longer aiming to get justice for Greg, so even if I had signed, full confessions from both Bailey and Hunter, I'd still be sceptical about going to the police. There's no doubt in my mind that if he faced trial, Hunter would find some technicality or loophole. He'd get off altogether; he'd get away with it. And I'd be satisfied only if the pair of them got life sentences. They've taken a life. Three lives, in fact, because I lost my baby and my own life is unrecognisable to me now Greg's dead. A life sentence would be the only punishment to fit their crime.

I'll just have to play it by ear. If I keep tabs on Kirsten, something, at some point, will fall into my lap. When it does, I'll know how to use it to come up with a plan and carry it out. I close down the computer and give Rusty a big cuddle before I go.

As I pull the front door shut behind me, my mobile rings from inside my handbag. The caller ID shows that it's my father-in-law. My brow furrows as I swipe to take the call. I have Hugh's number in my phone, but I don't think he has ever called me, although we've spoken on the phone. It's always Pam who rings. It was always Pam who rang Greg, too. Instantly, I know something is wrong.

'Hugh, is everything OK?' I ask.

'Hello, Amy, dear. No, I'm afraid it isn't. It's Pam. She's had a heart attack. She's in the North Devon District Hospital.'

'Oh no! Oh God! Will she be OK?'

He doesn't reply and I think I hear a stifled sob. How much more do my parents-in-law have to go through?

'I'll get the next train home, Hugh,' I promise him. 'I'll text you when I'm on the train.'

He's still thanking me profusely when I end the call. Walking away from the house, I text Jamie to say that I can't come for

211

Rusty tomorrow. I'm terribly worried about my mother-in-law and it only dawns on me when I'm on the Tube that I won't be able to go to Victoria Embankment Gardens tomorrow at midday, either.

Chapter 30

Kirsten

Nick peruses the letter slowly, over the top of prescription glasses that Kirsten has never seen before, his arm outstretched. When did he become long-sighted? They're sitting on a bench in Victoria Embankment Gardens. Behind them stands the statue of Robert Burns; in front of them an effigy of a man on a camel, representing the Imperial Camel Corps, according to the base of the statue, and to Kirsten's left, a stinking bin. She wrinkles her nose. She deliberately averts her eyes from the letter, but she has read it so many times that she knows what it says by heart. Three sentences from it writhe around in her head. *I know what happened in Croyde. I know you killed Gregory Wood. I have proof.*

Nick chose this place as it's a short walk from his chambers, along the banks of the Thames. Kirsten shudders as she realises that a short walk in the opposite direction would take them to the spot where Gregory Wood's body washed up, on the north side of the river, between Embankment and Westminster, if she remembers correctly. Still, she's glad Nick didn't suggest meeting up at their hotel. She wants him, she really does, but she wants him to sort out the mess she's in more.

When Nick has finished reading, he lowers his arm, but says nothing, pensively stroking imaginary stubble on his clean-shaven chin with his other hand. She doesn't prompt him, but waits with bated breath for him to speak. She values his take on her predicament, his verdict.

Kirsten picks the skin around her thumbnail and, more out of habit than curiosity, she people-watches. It's a chilly and foggy autumn day, and no one is lingering, walking briskly through the gardens rather than sitting on the benches. A suited man about her age strides by, whistling and swinging his briefcase. There follows a group of silly schoolgirls, looking scruffy despite their uniforms, whispering, chuckling and eating junk food as they half-skip, half-walk through the gardens. A giggle of girls – the collective noun comes to her. How appropriate. A young mother pulls her son along by the hand; an elderly woman shuffles past with a rat-like dog on one of those ridiculous retractable leads. Is the old biddy allowed to bring her dog in here? None of the passers-by appears to have a care in the world. Kirsten envies them for that.

'So, what are we going to do?' Nick says eventually.

Kirsten turns to him, her heart sinking. She was hoping Nick would advise her on how to deal with this. If she's honest, she was hoping he'd run to her rescue. At least, he said 'we' and not 'you'. Kirsten doesn't understand why she is being blackmailed but not Nick. She was the one driving, but they were both in the car. And Nick's the one who got rid of the body. Why was the letter only addressed to 'Mrs' Taylor and not 'Mr and Mrs'? If the blackmailer knows she and Nick don't live at the same address – that they're not married – why hasn't Nick received a letter, too?

'I don't think we have a choice,' she says. 'We're – I'm – going to have to pay the blackmailer. I was thinking of going to the bank today to organise the cash withdrawal.'

'Don't do that,' Nick says.

He pauses. Is he going to offer to pay the money? Ten thousand pounds. That's what the blackmailer wants. It's a huge amount of money, although she'd have been willing to pay a lot more. It will have to come out of her secret savings account, the one where she has regularly squirrelled away large sums of money without Jamie knowing, for the day when she'll leave him for Nick.

But Nick has no intention of bailing her out with the money the blackmailer is demanding. 'You mustn't pay this,' he says. 'It's a form of coercion, akin to terrorism, and we mustn't give in to that sort of demand. The only way to deal with extortion is to ignore it completely.'

'Nick, this isn't about whether it's morally defensible to make concessions to terrorists. It's about us – *me*. You've read the letter. Basically, if I don't pay up, I'll go down. The blackmailer has evidence that will be forwarded to the police.'

'If you pay up, he'll ask for more money, Kirsten. That's the way it works. He's asking you for a piddling amount given what you earn. He knows that. He'll make you cough up a lot more, believe me.'

'How do you know what I earn?'

'I have a rough—'

'And what makes you think the blackmailer's a "he"?'

'What makes you think it isn't?'

'I thought . . . I wondered if . . . Nick, could Ediye be behind this?'

Nick falls silent again, his expression inscrutable.

'You said your wife discovered you were having an affair,' Kirsten says after a moment when he still hasn't reacted. 'She found out from the tracker she put on your Audi that you were in Devon. Is it possible she knows what happened there? Could she have been following us that day, do you think?' Kirsten's aware she's gushing, but she can't stop herself. When Nick's quiet, she always feels the urge to talk. 'I'm just wondering why I'm being blackmailed and not you. It would make sense if the blackmailer is Ediye. She doesn't work, does she? Is she short of money? Nick! Say something!'

'Sorry. I was thinking. Look, Edie knows about us, well, she knows I was cheating on her. I admitted that much to her when she confronted me. She doesn't have a clue about the accident. But it's not her, Kirsten. She'd have said something to me. And she doesn't want for money. She has joint access to all our accounts and comes from an affluent family – she has loads of money of her own. She has no financial motive. If she'd wanted to cause trouble because of our affair, she'd have found a different way.'

'But—'

'Listen, Kirsten, Edie doesn't know the meaning of the word "dishonest". She couldn't bend the truth if her life depended on it. Trust me.'

'OK.'

'Your blackmailer is an amateur. He hand-delivered a letter that your husband could have opened and he's given you a drop-off point in a public place.'

It's hardly a public place – it's someone's back garden, but Kirsten takes his point.

'He should have emailed you the demand anonymously and made you send the money to a numbered bank account,' Nick continues.

Kirsten's eyes widen. If Nick retired as a successful criminal defence lawyer, she has no doubt he could become a successful criminal.

'Look, Kirsten, get rid of this—' he hands her the letter '—and forget about it. Blackmailers are opportunists and cowards. Chances are, you'll never hear from him again.'

Kirsten's not convinced, but she nods and makes a show of ripping up the piece of A4 paper and the envelope it came in. She meant to take a screenshot of the letter with her mobile before setting off this morning in case Nick wanted to keep the original, but she forgot. No matter. She usually has a memory like a sieve, but she has read the letter so many times that she can recite what it says word for word. She gets to her feet and throws the torn pieces into the smelly bin. Nick smiles and pats her hand when she sits down again. She notices he's not wearing his wedding ring. He has never taken it off before when he's with her. It's not like they have to hide their marital status from each other. But before she can ask him about it, he leans in and kisses her passionately. Kirsten is surprised – Nick never indulges in PDA. She responds eagerly to his kiss.

'Just to be on the safe side, keep text messages between us to a minimum. And keep them vague. Or use WhatsApp if you need to get in touch. It's more secure. We don't want to give your blackmailer any more ammunition.'

Your blackmailer. That says it all really. Nick doesn't want anything to do with this.

'I'll call you, I promise,' Nick says, squeezing her hand as he stands up. 'I need to head back to chambers now.'

Kirsten watches him as he walks away from her. She so badly wanted his advice, but now he has given it, she decides not to take it. When he disappears from view, she takes her mobile out of her handbag and calls her personal banker.

Chapter 31

Amy

My train arrives in Barnstaple after visiting hours at the North Devon District Hospital. Liz picks me up from the railway station. I ring Hugh on the car journey home. Pam is stable, he informs me, but they're keeping her in for a few days to run more tests. Hugh and I will visit her together tomorrow.

I chat to Liz in the car. We discuss my mother-in-law's health, then we talk about Liz's work and her kids. After that, Liz is silent for a moment, as if deep in thought. I know what's coming next.

'So, what are you doing in London?' she asks me. 'How long do you intend to stay there?' She has asked me this once before, when I told her I was going.

'I'm trying to find out who's responsible for Greg's death,' I say. 'I don't think the police have deployed the necessary resources and I want to do everything I can to bring the culprit to justice. London seems like a good place to start, seeing as that's where Greg's body was discovered.'

It's the same answer I gave her last time. Liz isn't quite buying it. I shouldn't have mentioned London to her. I haven't told her any more than that. She knew I was going away for a few weeks. She asked me where I was going and I didn't want to lie. So I gave her a watered-down version of the truth. I so badly want to tell her the whole truth and I feel terrible about hiding things from her. But this is self-protection, survival. And if I do commit a crime further down the line, I'll be protecting my best friend, too, by keeping her in the dark.

I've made Simon promise to say as little as possible. He seems to be fond of me, perhaps even a little obsessed with me, but will that be enough incentive for him to keep the identity of Greg's killers secret? Simon is potentially my weak link. Apart from David, who has now moved away from the area, Simon is the only other person who knows we've found Hunter. Even though he swore not to tell anyone he'd identified Hunter on the television news, I don't know if I can count on him. I can't pinpoint the reason why I'm dubious, but I am. There's something about him. Something off. I try to reassure myself; I try to trust him. He's a bit creepy, but that doesn't make him untrustworthy.

'When are you coming home?' Liz says, breaking into my thoughts.

'I am home.'

'You know what I mean.'

As Liz pulls into my driveway, I ponder that question. This is my home. This is where I belong. This is the place where my friends live, where I work. *Worked.* I met Greg here. We lived in this house. We built our life here. But I think perhaps that's the problem. I feel close to my husband here, but everything reminds me of him. Good memories that have become treacherous, threatening to hold me down instead of lift me up.

This last fortnight or so in London, I've relished the anonymity of the city. No one knows me or my story. No one looks at me pityingly or avoids me because they can't think of what to say to a grieving widow. No one even knows my real name. I'm a country girl at heart. I don't feel at home in such a large city, but sometimes, even though I've never felt so lonely, I feel almost normal.

'I have no idea when I'm coming home, Liz,' I say truthfully.

The next morning, I pick up my father-in-law to drive us both into Barnstaple to visit Pam. I get out of the car and knock on the front door. It opens immediately. Hugh must have been waiting for me even though I'm bang on time. He gives me a tight hug.

'I want that woman dead,' Hugh says as I stop at a red light in Braunton. I turn sharply to look at him, misunderstanding for a split second before my brain kicks in. He's referring to Kirsten Bailey. 'Dead or behind bars,' he continues. 'The pair of them. They're responsible for Pam's heart attack. They've killed Gregory and your baby. I swear to God if they . . . if Pam . . . I'll kill them both with my own bare hands. I'll have nothing left to lose.'

My father-in-law's voice is filled with such hatred and vehemence that I'm speechless. But it's as if he has voiced my own thoughts. I reach over and squeeze his hand as it rests on the gear stick.

Pam looks pale and drawn, but she stoically assures Hugh and me there's nothing wrong with her. 'I'll be discharged within a day or two,' she says.

The doctor confirms this on his ward round. He's a young man with thick, black hair that stands to attention on his head as if he's had an electric shock. 'The test results show that both your cholesterol and blood pressure are a little high,' he says, 'so we've started you on statins and beta-blockers. This will reduce the risk of future heart attacks.'

He explains how the medication works and what doses to take. He checks Pam's pulse and blood pressure. Despite his age and appearance, the doctor inspires confidence and Hugh becomes visibly more relaxed.

'Any questions?' the doctor asks when he has finished.

'When can I go home?' Pam enquires.

'Tomorrow or the day after.'

Pam looks at Hugh with an expression that says, *I told you so*, and he smiles at her. It's an image that both amuses and saddens me. I wanted to grow old with Greg. I know we'd still have been in love at their age. Greg's parents were our role models, an example of a long-lasting, loving marriage that we aspired to emulate.

On the drive home, my mind wanders miles away, back to London. I can't help wondering what happened today in Victoria Embankment Gardens. Why did Kirsten Bailey and Nicholas Hunter meet up? What did they talk about? Did it have anything to do with Greg?

I get up at six a.m. the next day and make myself a light breakfast and a coffee. My coffee is instant and tastes nowhere near as good as the espressos Jamie makes, so I throw it down the sink and opt for a mug of tea instead. Then I pull on my swimming costume and wetsuit, grab my surfboard and head for the beach.

Two hours later, I'm still sitting on the sand, looking out to sea. My board is lying next to me, its leash Velcroed around my ankle. The sun has risen behind me. There's a light offshore wind and the surf is great: fast, five-foot waves, many of them breaking cleanly all the way to the shore. There are quite a few surfers in the water despite the early hour, one of whom – Sharky – I recognise from his goofy-footed style. I should be in the water, among them. But I can't get psyched up to get in. I've surfed alone before, of course I have, although I always preferred to go with Greg. Other than in the shallows with the kids from the *Smile and Wave* surf school in August, I haven't surfed since Greg died. Just as I haven't played the guitar. It's almost as if I've fallen off my bike and can't pluck up the courage to get back on it. I feel like I would drown if I went into the water.

'Hi there, Amy.' A man's voice. Deep.

I didn't hear anyone approach, but now I notice a shadow across the sand. Someone is standing behind me holding a surfboard

221

under his arm. Thinking it's Simon, I groan inwardly and pretend I didn't hear. I haven't seen Simon since I've been home. I thought he'd be round like a shot as soon as he got wind of my arrival. I keep expecting him to ambush me somewhere or show up at my front door. It's uncharitable of me to want to avoid him, especially as he's the one who found Hunter.

'Amy?'

The shadow with the surfboard gets larger, approaching. It can't be Simon. He doesn't surf. He does a bit of bodyboarding and gets teased for it – surfers tend to look down, literally and figuratively, on bodyboarders.

I turn my head and look up, squinting and using my hand to shield my eyes from the sun. To my relief, it's Sharky. Matt is standing behind him. They've just got out of the water, no doubt to go to work. 'Hi, Sharky. Hi, Matt.'

'Thought it was you,' says Sharky. 'We walked right past you coming out of the water, then did a double take. You going in?'

I shake my head.

'You OK?'

I shake my head again. Matt and Sharky sit on the sand either side of me.

'Anything we can do, Amy?' This from Matt.

'No. Thank you for asking, though.'

'The surf forecast is good for tomorrow,' Sharky says. 'Fancy catching some waves with us then?'

It's as if he has read my thoughts and is trying to coax me gently. 'Yes, OK. Thanks. Tom not with you or is he still in the water?'

'Tom's been laid off, Amy,' Sharky says. 'The company he worked for has been struggling, you know, ever since the pandemic. They had to restructure. Sandra's giving him a hard time while he finds a new job. He'd be in for it if he crept out to ride a few waves at the mo.'

'Oh dear. Poor Tom.'

'We'd better get going, if we're going to be on time for school,' Matt says, getting to his feet. Sharky follows suit.

I'm not sure if Matt is addressing Sharky or me. I force a laugh because his remark was meant as a joke, but it reminds me that, like Sharky and Matt, I'm a teacher. And like Tom, I'm more or less out of a job. It's only when they've left that I think about Greg's shop. I decide to ring Tom later and ask him if he'd consider managing it, reopening it. It's the beginning of October, so we're heading for the off-season right now, but there's still work to be done.

I sit on the sand for a few minutes more, feeling better for bumping into Sharky and Matt. I'll go for a surf with them tomorrow. I get to my feet, ready to go home. But after taking a few steps in the wrong direction, I turn around, and instead of walking slowly home in a dry wetsuit, I wade into the sea. I wait for the last wave of the set to break, then I lie on my board and paddle out towards the horizon.

Hi,

It took the jury only two hours to reach a unanimous verdict. A guilty verdict. I was sentenced immediately. To life imprisonment, obviously. A life sentence is mandatory when you've been convicted of murder, as everyone knows. The judge said that there was a significant degree of premeditation in the murder I'd committed and he imposed a minimum term of thirty years before I'm eligible for parole.

My legs were wobbly and I could barely stand up when the judge passed his sentence, but it came as no surprise, and afterwards I felt almost indifferent. I'll be behind bars for the rest of my life, or a big chunk of it, anyway. I can't spend the rest of my life as I'd planned, growing old with the one I love. That dream was shattered, taken away from me. And so I don't much care about my fate. In my darker moments, I wonder if I'd be better off dead. Dead or behind bars? If you had the choice, what would you choose? Maybe the Americans have a better judicial system. The death penalty seems pretty desirable from where I'm standing.

In a way, I suppose, justice has been served. There's irony in there somewhere. Humour. It's no laughing matter for me, though. I did my best to avoid getting caught, to avoid being sent to jail. And yet, here I am, in my cell, writing you another letter that I'll scrunch up and never send.

Chapter 32

Kirsten

The address Kirsten's blackmailer has given her is for a house in a residential street off Brigstock Road. Pretexting a viewing in Knightsbridge, Kirsten leaves the office, takes the Tube to Victoria and then the train to Thornton Heath. The house is within walking distance from the station. Kirsten came here two days ago to scout around, although she turned back when she got to the end of the street, not daring to go right up to the house in case she was spotted. It's highly unlikely her extortionist lives in the house itself, no matter how amateurish Nick has made them out to be, but she didn't want to take unnecessary risks.

Today, Kirsten does turn into the street. There's no off-street parking, but there are relatively few cars parked in the road – most of the residents must be at work, which is probably why Kirsten's blackmailer chose the middle of the afternoon for the drop-off.

Number 6 is a slightly rundown semi-detached house near the end of the street. There's a FOR SALE sign on display, just as it said in the letter. So far, so good. Kirsten looks all around her. She can't see anyone, but that doesn't mean no one is watching her.

The blackmailer might be hiding behind a tree or peering out of the upstairs window of one of the houses opposite. Kirsten shudders. She must stay on the alert.

Not for the first time, she wishes she'd taken a screenshot of the crook's letter with her phone before tearing it up in front of Nick, but, although her memory is not nearly as reliable as she'd like, she's fairly sure she still knows the instructions by heart. She read it so many times, it will probably be inscribed on her brain forever.

As she lifts the latch on the front gate, she notices that the lawn is unkempt, even though it's so small you could practically cut the grass with a pair of nail scissors. The paint is peeling off the windowsills and the whole house looks as if it hasn't been lived in for a while. She wonders how long it has been on the market. She'd have thought a house like this – a three-bed semi, by the looks of it, conveniently located for overground transport links to central London – would be snapped up in a matter of days, even if it did need a little work on it. Perhaps it has mould or asbestos or dry rot.

She walks up the short driveway, glancing over her shoulder. She probably looks very suspicious. She has an excuse prepared if she gets caught. She'll say she's looking for a place to buy in the area, she happened to be passing and, noticing the FOR SALE sign, she couldn't resist taking a peek at the house.

She squeezes past the dustbins at the side of the house to get to the wooden gate leading to the back garden. She pushes the gate, then pushes again, more forcefully, but it won't budge. It's supposed to be unlocked! Beads of sweat break out on Kirsten's forehead and her pulse accelerates. The gate has a standard deadlock and she scans her surroundings for somewhere a key might be hidden – in a plant pot or under an ornament. There's nothing obvious. She kicks the door hard, more in anger than in an attempt to force it open. Having come here straight from work, she's wearing her low-block heels; the leather is thin and she hurts her toes, but she barely registers the pain as the gate swings open. It wasn't locked; it was just stiff. Kirsten inhales deeply and exhales slowly.

The back garden is marginally larger but no better kept than the tiny patch of overgrown grass at the front of the house. It's secluded and unless someone is curtain-twitching in the adjoining house, Kirsten is confident no one sees her as she makes her way to the trellis at the end of the garden. She extracts the plastic bag of cash from her cavernous handbag and stuffs it into an empty hanging basket dangling precariously from the rickety trellis.

She should go, but she stays rooted to the spot, vacillating. She's tempted to take back her money at the eleventh hour. Nick's right. Her blackmailer is an amateur. Their instructions and intentions are clear, but this whole procedure is slipshod. She was anxious about coming here today, but right now she feels ridiculous. She has just crammed an old supermarket carrier bag containing a fat wad of banknotes into a hanging basket in the back garden of a shabby semi near Croydon. It's ludicrous. She should have listened to Nick and ignored the letter.

Then again, if her blackmailer is an amateur, perhaps they'll be satisfied once they get their grubby hands on the ten grand; they won't demand any further payments and that will be the end of it. She's aware her logic is flawed, but she's in no state to think anything through rationally. She wants to get out of here. Fast. She leaves the money in the basket, hurries out of the garden, closing the wooden gate behind her, and retraces her steps, breaking into a run as she turns into the road leading to the railway station.

She stops before she gets to the station. She picked out a café on her reconnaissance mission the day before yesterday. She wouldn't normally be seen dead in a place like this and the coffee is probably dreadful, but the café affords a good view of the main entrance to the railway station. She glances all around her to make sure no one is looking her way, then she dives inside. She'd contemplated bringing a change of clothes and a wig to disguise herself in the ladies', but she couldn't stoop to that. She does tie up her hair, though, using a scrunchie that she was wearing around her wrist. She doesn't want to draw attention to herself, and her hair, now

227

she dyes it strawberry blond, is her most striking feature. She orders a double espresso at the counter and takes up her position in the window seat.

She's acting on a hunch, but Kirsten thinks the blackmailer will want to retrieve the money straight away. It's unlikely they would choose a drop-off point close to their home, however inexperienced they might be. So, by Kirsten's reasoning, her extortionist may, like her, arrive by train. If that's the case, maybe, just maybe they'll walk past the café, on their way to or from the drop-off. But it seems like a lot of ifs and the longer Kirsten waits, the more disheartened she becomes.

She shreds a paper napkin into smaller and smaller pieces with shaking hands. She feels as if she's being forced to play a game of cat and mouse where she's the mouse and the dice is loaded against her. Not for the first time, she racks her brains, trying to come up with suspects. She still hasn't ruled out the possibility that Ediye wrote the letter, but Nick insists his wife has nothing to do with it. Kirsten can think of several people who might hate her, but she can't fathom how anyone could have found out what happened in North Devon that day. Could it be one of the thugs Nick roped into getting rid of Gregory Wood's body? If so, she won't recognise him even if he does walk past the café window.

It's late – nearly closing time – when she gives up. She drains her fourth coffee, which wasn't that hot to begin with and is now stone cold. Then she scoops up the pieces of napkin from the table and puts them into her cup.

As she picks up her handbag and gets to her feet, she catches sight of someone on the other side of the street. Doing a double take, she sinks back into her seat, her heart hammering in both her chest and ears. She follows him with her gaze as he walks towards the entrance to the train station. He looks familiar, but she can't place him. She resists the urge to press her face up to the window to try and see him more clearly and instead squints at him. He's gangly and dressed sloppily in torn jeans and a faded sweatshirt.

His hair – a dirty dark blond colour – is messy with thick strands dangling in front of his eyes. It badly needs a cut. He's carrying a tote bag, holding it in his arms as if it were a baby. He's got the bag with her money inside it – she's sure of it.

He's gone! He has entered the train station. She should follow him, find out where he's going. She jumps up to run after him, but her legs feel weak and she gets the feeling she should know where he's going. He hasn't seen her; she has recognised him. She can turn this around so that she has the advantage. If she can remember who the hell he is. Desperately, she fumbles around in her mind for his name. She's terrible with people's names, always has been. Her eldest brother once said – rather unfairly and nastily, in Kirsten's opinion – that it was because she simply couldn't care less about other people and didn't pay attention to what anyone else said. But, as she'd retorted at the time, lots of people have difficulty remembering names.

Does she actually know what he's called? She doesn't think so. Where has she seen him before? He doesn't look like the sort of person she'd have met through work. Way too shabby and dishevelled. *Think, Kirsten, think. What do you know about him? Where do you know him from?*

And then it comes to her. She doesn't know his name. He didn't introduce himself. But she knows who her blackmailer is. And where he's going.

Chapter 33

Amy

Dead or behind bars. My father-in-law's words echo in my ears as I get off the Tube and walk to the Baileys' house. He didn't mention it again while I was in Croyde, but I could tell he was serious. It wasn't just an impulsive, throwaway remark. He alluded to our conversation as I was saying goodbye to Pam and him, warning me to be careful.

'Whatever you do, don't do anything rash, will you?' he said. I thought he regretted what he'd said in the car until he added, 'And don't forget Pam and I will back you up in any way you need.'

He held me tightly as he spoke these words into my ear so that my mother-in-law wouldn't hear. Hugh never used to be a hugger, but since Greg died, he seems to crave physical contact, from both Pam and me, as if it somehow reinforces our presence or reassures him that she and I, at least, are still here. I strongly suspect my mother-in-law would prefer us to tell the police everything we know without further delay, but Hugh will talk her round and allow me some time. He and I are on the same page.

The idea my father-in-law raised is essentially what has been going through my head, too. I want to see both Kirsten Bailey and Nicholas Hunter locked up for life or else dead. But I haven't got a clue how to go about this. I don't think I'll ever find enough proof of what they did to Greg, and I fear that even if I do, it won't keep them in jail for the rest of their lives. They may escape a prison sentence altogether. I'm not a violent person and can't even bring myself to kill spiders, even though I'm terrified of them, but I feel murderous every time I picture either Kirsten or Nicholas. My mind sifts through possible schemes, but they're all far-fetched and fanciful and I eliminate them one after the other.

I need to be cautious – Hugh's right. This could easily backfire. If Kirsten and Nicholas catch me snooping around, they could turn the tables on me. I don't want to end up behind bars or dead myself. I have no choice but to wait for something – a sign, an event, some sort of conspiratorial or confessional message, I don't know what – that will enable me to hatch a risk-free plan. I'm hoping to find something useful today on Kirsten's computer that will point me in the right direction. I'm desperate to know what transpired in Victoria Embankment Gardens. I'm convinced it had something to do with Greg. Maybe they followed up on their conversation with text messages that I'll be able to access via Kirsten's iMac.

I'm so lost in my thoughts that I almost barge into her. Luckily for me, Kirsten Bailey seems to be ruminating over her own thoughts, staring blankly straight ahead as she strides past me, and I leap out of her way. I glance at her, over my shoulder, but she doesn't look back. Another close shave. So close I could have reached out and touched her. She has set off from home earlier than usual. I need to be a lot more cautious and keep my wits about me. I take a deep breath and resist the urge to sprint the rest of the way to put distance between her and me.

I arrive at the house in Muswell Hill only to discover another breach in the Baileys' routine. Jamie opens the door, wearing casual clothes. He's obviously not going to work today. This isn't unusual as he works from home at least one day a week. I have mixed feelings

231

about this as I enjoy chatting to him – he's really the only person I've talked to since I've come to London. But whenever he's home, I can't check out Kirsten's computer. Jamie doesn't need me when he's at home, as he can walk Rusty himself, but he seems to think I need the money. Once, he accompanied Rusty and me on our walk.

'You're home today,' I say, trying to keep the disappointment out of my voice.

'Yes,' Jamie says. Then I spot Lily, peeping out at me from behind her father's legs. 'Home with Lily,' he continues. 'There's an inset day at her school.'

'Oh.'

'Mummy was supposed to look after me,' Lily pipes up, pouting. She doesn't seem shy, even though she's still hiding behind Jamie.

'Mummy got the wrong day, sweetheart,' Jamie says, then to me, 'Usually, I'm the one who takes the day off, but Kirsten offered to look after Lily today for a change.'

'She forgot,' Lily says.

'Yes, she's mixed up her dates and events a few times recently, hasn't she?' Jamie says without even a hint of resentment in his tone.

It had slipped my mind, too. With my mother-in-law's hospitalisation, I've taken my eyes off the ball. I should have noted Lily's inset day before changing the date in Kirsten's calendar. Relief courses through me, tinged with a tiny pang of guilt. I could be standing face-to-face with Kirsten right now. But privately, I vow to stop messing around with Kirsten's appointments, especially where Lily is concerned. It was only to cause trouble while I bided my time. It's gone too far and it's not achieving anything. It's not fair on Lily or Jamie. And my tricks could end up rebounding on me. If Kirsten decides to jot down her appointments by hand instead of using the calendar in her phone, it will hamper my progress.

Jamie smiles at me, spreading his hands theatrically. 'So, here I am.'

I suppress a sigh. I'm itching to boot up Kirsten's computer and it's not going to happen today. 'Do you still want me to walk Rusty?' I ask.

'I mean, seeing as Kirsten doesn't often walk Rusty – she doesn't have much free time – I didn't cancel, but Lily and I can take out the dog, if you like. I'll still pay you for—'

'Oh no, that's fine. I'd like to walk him.'

'Coffee first?'

'Yes please.' I follow Jamie and Lily into the kitchen.

'So, you've got a day off school, have you?' I say to Lily, instinctively bending down to her. 'What have you got planned?'

'Mummy promised me we'd make some choc-chip cookies,' Lily says, climbing onto one of the bar stools. I sit on the one next to her. 'But Daddy's hopeless at baking.' She rolls her eyes. 'Are you any good?'

'I haven't made any biscuits for a while,' I say. Lily's face falls. 'But I used to enjoy baking. We could give it a shot when I get back from walking Rusty if your daddy's OK with that.'

'Can we all walk Rusty?' Lily asks.

'I was going to suggest the same thing,' Jamie says, coming over to join us, an espresso in each hand.

We drink our coffees. Lily babbles non-stop about school, her violin teacher, the vegetables she planted in the greenhouse with Jamie. She tells me about the musical of *The Lion King* that Jamie and her auntie Claire took her to see a few months ago, outlining the differences with the animated film. She summarises the plot of *The Boy at the Back of the Class* that Jamie is reading to her at bedtime, stumbling only slightly over the word 'refugee'. She informs me that her dad has one sister and her mother has three older brothers.

'They treated Mummy like a princess when she was little,' Lily says, 'but she doesn't see them much anymore, does she, Daddy?'

'No, she doesn't.' He turns to me. 'Kirsten is estranged from most of her family members. It's . . . complicated.'

'Family relationships often are,' I say, wishing, not for the first time, that my mother lived closer.

Lily's clearly a bright, rather precocious child. Listening to her chitter-chatter, I'm filled with both awe and sadness. I wonder if my child would have grown up to love the theatre and books, if my baby would have been a boy or a girl.

Jamie drains the dregs of his espresso and slides off the stool. I follow his lead. Jamie supervises Lily as she puts on her shoes and coat; I clip Rusty's lead onto his collar and grab some dog poo bags.

We take Lily to Alexandra Park and head for the playground. While Lily plays on the climbing frame and slide, Jamie and I sit on a bench. We chat inconsequentially, about the weather, Lily, Rusty, Jamie's work, both of us keeping our eyes on Lily. Jamie tells me he's taking Lily to his cottage in Folkestone not this weekend, but next weekend, at the start of the half-term holidays. Kirsten's staying at home as she's busy, but they're taking Rusty.

'He's still not really allowed on the beach in October, but we can get away with it in the evenings now the summer season is over. He loves the beach.'

'I know,' I say. Jamie gives me a sideways look. 'Labs do, don't they?' I add hastily.

As we watch, Lily climbs onto the swing. 'Daddy! Come and push me!' she calls out, even though she's managing the swinging motion expertly by herself.

I watch Jamie push Lily on the swing, maintaining a smile despite the emotions swirling through me. Kirsten has a kind, caring husband and a beautiful, bubbly daughter. She has the life I dreamed of, the life she took from me. I can't help but be envious of all she has. My loathing for her boils inside me.

My thoughts are interrupted by a chirruping next to me. Jamie has left his phone on the bench with Lily's coat. I take his mobile over to him in case it's important. He answers the call and I push Lily as he takes a few steps away, his phone pressed to his ear.

'Today's difficult . . . Can I do it from home . . .? I can't really come in . . . OK then, but I'll have to bring my daughter.'

He ends the call and forces a smile as he catches my eye. 'Work,' he says to me. 'I'm going to have to go in after all.' To Lily, he says, 'We'd better go. Daddy has to go to work for a few hours, sweetie. You're coming with me, to Daddy's office.' He tries to make it sound exciting, but Lily's not fooled.

'You said I could bake some cookies! You promised!'

'I know. I'm sorry. It's an emergency. I'll make it up to you. You can bring some toys and a book with you.'

'Do you want me to . . .?' I glance at my watch. It's not even eleven o'clock yet. 'I could look after Lily if that helps?'

'Yes! Daddy, say yes! I want to stay with Rose!'

'Are you sure?' he asks me. 'She can be very demanding.'

'Yes, of course. I used to teach kids around Lily's age. We'll be fine.'

Jamie holds out Lily's coat for her to put back on. She zips it up herself and we head back to the house. Once Jamie has left for work, Lily and I make some cookies. Fortunately, all the ingredients we needed were in the cupboard, including the chocolate chips. We get all the equipment set out and I help her read the recipe step by step. She's obviously done this before, carrying out each stage proficiently.

'Would you like to watch a film?' I suggest when we've put the biscuits in the oven and cleared up the mess.

Lily heads for the living room and picks up the remote control. Seconds later, she's lying on her side on the sofa, her head on a cushion, watching *The Secret Life of Pets 2*. Hearing the oven timer, I go to the kitchen to take the cookies out of the oven. I realise I should make some lunch for Lily and myself and go back to ask her what she'd like. But she has fallen asleep on the sofa, her thumb in her mouth.

I turn the sound right down and watch the rise and fall of her chest. I'm trying not to like this kid – I want her mother dead or behind bars and I won't be able to do that to Lily if I get too attached to her. But she's so adorable. Does Kirsten appreciate what she's got? She doesn't deserve a daughter like Lily. And Lily certainly doesn't deserve a mother like Kirsten. She deserves so much better.

I stay for a minute or two, to make absolutely sure Lily's out for the count. Then I seize my chance. I tiptoe out of the living room and head for Kirsten's study. Moments later, I'm sitting in her office chair, waiting for her laptop to boot up. I'll go through her calendar, text messages, phone log and emails.

I enter Kirsten's password and stare at the home screen as it appears. There must be something in here somewhere that I can use against Kirsten Bailey and Nicholas Hunter, something that will enable me to cause their comeuppance. Their downfall.

Chapter 34

Kirsten

Kirsten was supposed to look after Lily today – there's an inset day at the primary school – but she got her dates muddled up. Again. She's not sure why she's so scatter-brained at the moment. She hopes there's nothing seriously wrong with her. Surely she's too young for a brain tumour or dementia or the menopause. She has taken to writing down her work appointments on Post-its as a back-up. Already, there are several stuck around her desk and on her wall at the agency. She looks at them now, and swaps two of them over so they're in the right order, chronologically. She pulls another one off the wall and sticks it back on straighter. She has decided to buy a large wall calendar at some point. She'll put it up in the kitchen and use it as a back-up for her personal diary.

She looks at her watch. She has been looking at it all morning. It's nearly midday now. Her best hope of catching Nick is around lunchtime, but it's probably a bit too early. She can always leave a message, a voice message, seeing as they've decided to keep texts to a minimum. She gets up from her desk and goes outside, away from the nosy parkers who would gladly listen in if she phoned from the office.

To her surprise, he answers her call straight away.

'Can I see you?' She sounds like she's begging. She clears her throat and aims for a more forceful tone. 'I need to see you. It's urgent.'

She's worried he'll say he has too much work to do, as has often been the case – or his excuse – in the past. He likes to see her on his terms, call the shots, choose the time and place. But they've been having a sort of honeymoon period recently, since they've resumed their affair. Nick's still making an effort, still making amends for splitting up with her in the first place. He has even mooted the idea of them leaving their respective spouses. She always assumed it would take years before she felt Lily was old enough for her to leave Jamie without causing her too much damage, years before Nick got round to actually leaving his wife. But he seems to want them to be together sooner rather than later. She doesn't know how she feels about that, but Nick has only mentioned it once, in passing, so he may not mean it. She's trying not to think about it because leaving Jamie would certainly mean leaving Lily, too – Nick's hardly stepfather material and Kirsten couldn't possibly tear Lily away from Jamie.

'Let me see . . . I can spare half an hour this afternoon around two-ish, if I reschedule an appointment and you meet me near the Royal Courts of Justice. Is that any good?'

They arrange to meet at Ye Olde Cock Tavern, in Fleet Street. Kirsten arrives a few minutes before two. She reads the inscription on the blackboard easel outside: *Today's Inspirational Quote: Don't be a dick!* Apt, she supposes, given the name of the establishment. It doesn't elicit a smile. Her sense of humour seems to have abandoned her some time ago. She chooses a table for two as far away from the door as possible. Nick could bump into someone he knows so close to the courts. She orders a coffee while she waits.

Her mind wanders to Lily, home today with Jamie instead of

with her. She has messed up. Again. Kirsten should make much more of an effort with Lily – Jamie's right. But when she tries to spend quality time with her daughter, she ends up feeling like a total failure. She has always avoided doing things that she's not good at – ball sports, singing, drawing, swimming, that sort of thing – but she can't avoid being a mother. So, subconsciously, perhaps, she ends up avoiding her daughter instead.

Kirsten envies the ease with which Jamie sails through parent-hood. It's an effort for her. How long before Lily sees her mother for the fraud she is? She does love her daughter, but she can't seem to bond with her. Kirsten has a low boredom threshold and she finds most of the activities Lily likes – colouring-in, making sparkling slime or friendship bracelets, plaiting hair – utterly mind-numbing. But baking, that Kirsten can do. Well, Lily more or less does it by herself, really. Kirsten just has to supervise and handle the oven.

She toys with the idea of heading straight home after seeing Nick. That way, she'd have time to make some biscuits with Little Lil, as promised. It would be a nice surprise for Jamie, too, if she got home early, for once. It might make up for forgetting that she was supposed to look after Lily today. Kirsten had an important work appointment early this morning, followed by a meeting she couldn't miss, but she could feasibly bunk off work this afternoon. It would mean rescheduling a viewing and a valuation, though. She'll make up her mind once she's seen Nick.

She drums her fingers on the table and glances at her watch again. He'll be here soon. He's always on time. She wonders how he'll react when he knows. She'd decided against telling him she'd paid off her blackmailer. Even when she'd recognised the bastard, she'd intended to keep it to herself. She was a little afraid of what Nick would do. Or, more accurately, what he might have his henchmen do.

But this morning before she set off for work, she found another typewritten letter addressed to Mrs Taylor on her doormat. Nick was right. The blackmailer wants her to fork out more money. His presumptuousness, his insistence, after she paid up what he demanded, leaving her hard-earned cash in the garden of that ramshackle semi in Croydon, has made her livid. She no longer cares what Nick does as long as he puts a stop to this. How dare this swine try to fleece her out of more money! What Kirsten did – running over Gregory Wood – was an accident. But blackmail is different. It's malicious. Manipulative. Premeditated. This guy's a criminal. And Nick knows how to deal with criminals.

Nick arrives before her coffee does. She waits until they're both served to tell him that she coughed up the amount for the pay-off and now she has received another demand.

To his credit, he doesn't say 'I told you so'. 'How much this time?' he asks.

'Another ten grand,' she says. Nick strokes his chin, apparently deep in thought. 'Nick! I know who it is.'

'Kirsten, for the last time, it's not Edie. I—'

'No, I know. You were right. It was a man. I saw him. I waited in a café near the train station at Thornton Heath, where the drop-off was. He entered the station, carrying a tote bag. My money was inside it, I'd bet on it!'

Nick straightens and leans across the table, towards her. 'Who was it?' he whispers.

'I don't know his name. You remember that half-wit who almost drove into the back of your car?' It comes out sounding indignant, as if the other driver was the reckless one, and Kirsten winces as she catches herself.

Nick furrows his brow. 'When? Where?'

'In Devon. Just after we ran . . . into the hedge. He was driving a battered old VW.'

Nick's eyes widen. 'Him? Really?' She nods. 'The conniving little prick! But how on earth did he find you?'

'I've been thinking about that,' Kirsten says. 'I was also wondering why he came after me, but not you. I reckon he must have recognised you that day. He'd seen you on TV and he knew enough about you not to mess with you. But—'

'But he found me and I led him to you,' Nick finishes. 'And you were an easier target.'

Kirsten nods. 'Something like that, I think. Yes.'

There's a voice in Kirsten's head that she's doing her best to ignore. She can see the envelope when she closes her eyes. It was addressed to Mrs Kirsten Taylor. *How did the blackmailer know we went by the name of Taylor?* She refuses to think that one through, unable to handle what that might mean. She chooses not to remember they haven't used that name since the accident. She can't tell Nick, even though he would certainly come up with the answer. But then she comes up with one herself. Perhaps her blackmailer asked questions when he came to London and followed Nick around. Waiters, staff in their day hotel. They might have known them by that name before they changed it to Baker. Yes. That must be it! Her mind is pulling her in a different direction – there's a more plausible explanation somewhere. But she doesn't want to go there.

Nick's silent for a few seconds, too, then he says, 'OK, leave it with me. He shouldn't be too hard to find. I'll sort him out.'

'How? I don't want you to take any risks.'

'I won't. I'll send some contacts to scout around and find the owner of the rusty Volkswagen in or near Croyde.'

'Contacts? You mean cronies? Criminals?'

'Yes, Kirsten. The same cronies who helped us out when we got back from Devon. Do you have a problem with that?'

'But how can you trust them? They're thugs. Do you just take their word they'll keep quiet?'

Nick scoffs. 'No, Kirsten,' he says. 'Trust doesn't come into it. I pay them for their silence.'

Kirsten nods, unconvinced. She tried to pay the blackmailer for his silence and look how that turned out. 'Will you . . . have him . . . you know, killed?' she asks.

'Do you want me to?'

'No!' she protests fervently, but deep down she just wants Nick to sweep up the breadcrumbs they've left scattered in their wake.

He shrugs. 'Only as a last resort,' he says nonchalantly. Kirsten shudders at his coldness. 'Don't worry. I doubt it will come to that.' He flashes her a smile. 'Now, are we still on for the weekend after next?'

She welcomes the change of subject and returns his smile, albeit a little falteringly. 'Yes.'

She's been looking forward to Nick coming. He has been to her place for a coffee before, and sex, of course, but he has never spent the night there. She likes the idea of being on her home turf instead of holed up in a hotel, however luxurious. A stroke of luck that Lily insisted on taking the dog with her and Jamie on their trip to Folkestone, even though he's not allowed on the beach. If Nick knew she'd kept Rusty, he'd kill her. In a manner of speaking.

'You won't forget, will you?' He's teasing her. She's told him about her recent absent-mindedness. 'Have you set up an alert?'

'No. No need.' She has put the event into the calendar app on her phone. But even without that, there's no way she'll forget. It's Nick's birthday. They always find a way to celebrate it together. She plans to make this weekend as special as possible, to make this birthday a memorable one.

'I'll make dinner,' she says, 'and I may even bake you a birthday cake if you're good.'

'I'll bring the wine if you like. Red or white?'

'I'll let you know when I've decided what I'm cooking. No, on second thoughts, leave it to me. It's your day, your weekend.'

'Hmm. I don't like to show up empty-handed. I'll bring chocolates.'

'Fine.'

He reaches across the table and takes both of her hands in his. She has chosen a table at the back of the room in case they were spotted by someone Nick knew, but he doesn't seem to be worried about that today. She remembers his kiss in Victoria Embankment Garden, too. Glancing at his hands, she sees he hasn't put his wedding ring back on. His tie is crooked, the knot smaller than usual. Kirsten looks at Nick, a question whirring in her mind that she doesn't dare to ask. Have Ediye and Nick separated? Maybe Nick's wife walked out when she found out about the affair. But she can't probe into his marriage. It's off limits.

'Listen, I've got to get going, Kirsten,' he says, pulling an apologetic face. 'Speak soon? I'll see you before our weekend together, anyway.'

They haven't spent the whole weekend together since the May bank holiday weekend they went to North Devon. Kirsten wonders if that has crossed Nick's mind, too. She gets up and follows him out, the sun blinding her for a moment as she steps out of the dimly lit tavern and into the street. She watches Nick as he crosses the road and walks away from her. Then she heads in the other direction for the nearest Tube station.

Chapter 35

Amy

Before I can start trawling through Kirsten's laptop, my mobile buzzes in my pocket. I take it out and look at the caller ID, thinking it might be Jamie checking up on Lily. But it's my father-in-law. Hugh rings me often now, every other day at least. The calls never last long and he'll worry if I don't pick up.

'Hi, Hugh. How are you? How's Pam?' Our conversations have become perfunctory and always follow the same pattern.

'Hello, Amy dear. Pam's doing well. She sends her love.' He always tries to sound upbeat and it breaks my heart because I know he's irreparably damaged inside. We all are. 'We went for a long walk this morning, along Saunton Sands and out to Crow Point,' he continues.

They go for a long walk every morning – only the location varies. Braunton Burrows, Valley of the Rocks, Watersmeet . . . Never Croyde Bay or the South West Coast Path to Baggy Point, which would no doubt remind them too much of Greg.

'How are you getting on?'

He's not asking how I am. He never asks how I am and he never

244

answers the question when I ask how he is. He's asking for an update on my progress. I'm usually vague about this. Fine. Getting there. More news soon. That sort of thing. I tell myself – and I've told Hugh – the less they know the better. But the truth is, I find it hard now to confide in them. It's as if by deciding to go after Kirsten Bailey and Nicholas Hunter, even with Hugh's full support, I've crossed the Rubicon and left them behind on the other river bank. I've put distance between them and me, put up an invisible boundary, and I can't go back until this is over.

'Getting there,' I say. Then I lower my voice and add, 'Hugh, this will be over soon. Very soon. Trust me.'

His voice is infused with a mixture of warmth and hope as he says, 'Thank you, Amy dear. That's good to hear. Pam and I are both here for you – you know that. Whatever we can do. Whatever you need.'

Pam sometimes speaks to me when Hugh rings, but not today. When we talk, she invariably begs me not to put myself in any danger. I know she'd like me to come home and drop this; she'd prefer us to let the Major Crime Investigation Team manage this. But she wants Greg's killers punished as much as Hugh and I do.

I end the call with my father-in-law, desperate to get back to the task at hand: Kirsten's computer. First, I open her calendar app. She has added a few events since the last time I looked. Most of them appear to be work-related. But two stand out. Two events, the same weekend. From the evening of Friday 21st to the evening of Sunday 23rd. The first entry reads: *Jamie & Lil in Fkstn.* The second entry is for the same dates – the weekend of Nicholas's birthday, apparently. But I barely register it, feeling suddenly cold all over. *Fkstn.* Folkestone.

Jamie told me earlier that he and Lily – and Rusty – were going to Folkestone that weekend but it's only now that it occurs to me: Folkestone is near Dover. I received an aborted, incoming call from Dover that I assumed had something to do with Greg. Could it have been Kirsten? But how did she know my number? And then it dawns on me. My mobile number was engraved on Rusty's collar. I don't often swear, but I call Kirsten all the names I can think of, the volley of insults firing from my mouth like bullets.

It takes me several minutes to calm down. I pace the room, suppressing the urge to hurl objects at the wall or punch it. I want to scream and shout, but I mustn't wake Lily. I check on her before I continue. She's still sound asleep. I realise it's the middle of the afternoon and I haven't fed her. I should have made lunch before I turned on the television. Oh well, it can't be helped and I can't wake her just yet. I've still got work to do before Jamie gets home. I've promised Hugh that this will soon be over. I have to come up with something.

I sit down again at the computer and examine Kirsten's emails. Nothing of particular interest. Kirsten and her lover don't appear to communicate by email. Finally, I go through her text messages. Unless she has deleted them, she and Nicholas haven't exchanged many text messages recently, either. There's nothing about their meeting at Victoria Embankment Gardens. There are two messages – one from her, one from him – both succinct, both sent the day before yesterday. Kirsten: *J&L away 21st–23rd. Spend WE at mine?* He hasn't replied, but I can see from the call log that he rang her about an hour after that. And I already know from the second calendar entry for the weekend after next that he has accepted Kirsten's invitation and plans to celebrate his birthday with her.

Apart from that, the most recent text messages are about five weeks old – several desperate texts from Kirsten, begging Nicholas to reconsider and to give her a second chance. I've read through these messages before. I inferred from Kirsten's messages – and Nicholas's apparent lack of reply to any of them – that they'd split up – judging from the dates, around the time I first came to London. But I assume, given their plans to meet up in Embankment Gardens the other day, as well as their plans for the end of the month, that they're back together now.

Absent-mindedly, I open the desk drawers and rummage

through them. Everything's pretty much the same as always until I get to the bottom drawer, where I find a large, square, white envelope. The flap of the envelope is tucked in rather than sealed, so I open it. It's a birthday card – with a sexual pun on it. I know where Kirsten bought this card – I was following her when she went into the stationer's the other day. She has already written it and the words she has written inside confirm that she and Nicholas are definitely very much together.

I look again at both calendar entries and both text messages and commit everything to memory. So, Nicholas is going to spend the Friday and Saturday nights the weekend after next, here, in this house, with Kirsten, while her husband is at their cottage in Kent with their daughter. My thoughts wander. People have affairs for all sorts of reasons, and usually I don't judge, even though I couldn't imagine ever cheating on Greg. But I feel so sorry and sad for Jamie. He's a good husband and a good father.

I need to focus. There must be something I can use here. But what? And then it comes to me. I knew something would eventually fall into my lap! A germ of an idea forms in my head. And then sprouts into something resembling a plan. Leaning forwards in the chair, my elbows on the desk, I steeple my hands and rest my chin on them.

Can I really do this? I'd be committing a crime. It seems like a good idea, but it feels wrong. I'm not a dishonest person. I'm not cold-blooded and calculating. I'm not a criminal. That's not who I really am.

But then I think of Greg, of our baby that I miscarried, of my parents-in-law who lost both their sons, of Kirsten Bailey and Nicholas Hunter, who accidentally took a life, but deliberately covered their tracks. And I realise this is who I've become, who I've been made into. I consider myself to be a good person, on the whole. I try to be good, anyway. But I think that even fundamentally good people, when they're focused on revenge, can wind up doing something very bad.

247

Before I can fully organise my ideas, I hear a voice outside. Jamie's home! My pulse racing, I hastily shut down the computer and run through the hall as the front door starts to open. I reach the living room just in time. Sitting on the end of the sofa, next to Lily, I pick up a magazine from the coffee table and flick through it. Jamie materialises in the doorway. I put my finger to my lips, then point at Lily. My heart slows to a more normal rhythm. And then stops altogether. Jamie's not alone.

'Rose, let me introduce you to my wife, Kirsten.' He looks over his shoulder.

And suddenly she's there, standing right behind him.

'Pleased to meet you, Rose,' she says.

It's an automatic response. She hasn't recognised me. For a split second, I think I might get away with this. Perhaps the game's not up after all. Then, almost in slow motion, her eyes widen and her mouth forms a shocked 'O' as the colour drains from her face.

She knows who I am.

Chapter 36

Kirsten

It only takes Kirsten a split second. *Rose?* She's not usually good at situating people out of context and she has only met her once, for a minute or two at most. But Kirsten has scrolled through this woman's posts on social media and looked at her photo in online newspapers so many times over the past few months that she'd know her anywhere.

Amy Wood.

Kirsten gapes at her. She can feel her mouth opening and closing like a goldfish. She can't register the fact that she's staring at the widow of the man she ran over and killed. She can't believe this woman is in her home.

She wants to scream at Amy Wood to get the fuck out of her house. But she can't do that in front of Jamie and Lily, who has woken up and is running towards Kirsten with outstretched arms.

'Mummy's come home early,' Jamie says. It sounds to Kirsten as if he's underwater. Or as if she is. 'Isn't that a lovely surprise?'

'I'd better get going,' Kirsten hears Amy mumble. 'I'm running late.'

Kirsten bends down to Lily, but turns her head, glaring at Amy who darts past her into the hall. Through the doorway, Kirsten sees Amy shove her feet into her trainers and make a hasty exit. Jamie closes the front door behind her, then kicks off his own shoes. He comes back into the living room.

Kirsten struggles to regain her composure and her voice sounds strangled as she says, 'It was good of Rose to look after Lily, wasn't it?' Without waiting for Jamie's response, she turns to her daughter. 'Did you have a good time, Little Lil?'

'Yes. We made choc-chip cookies. Would you like one?'

The very thought of eating something makes Kirsten feel like retching. 'Not just now. Perhaps after dinner.' Kirsten notices Lily's smile fade.

'I'll have one with you, sweetie,' Jamie says to Lily, throwing Kirsten a worried look.

She summons up a grateful smile. She can always count on her husband to come to her rescue. She watches as Lily takes Jamie's hand and he allows himself to be led to the kitchen.

'Are you all right?' Jamie calls to Kirsten, over his shoulder. 'You look a bit peaky.'

'I'm fine,' she says. 'Be down in a minute.'

Kirsten scuttles upstairs and sits on the bed. Her breaths are coming too fast and ragged. She tries to breathe in deeply and breathe out through her nose. Should she be exhaling through her mouth instead? She tries that, too. Eventually, she manages to pull herself together. More or less. Her heart is still racing and she feels too dizzy to stand up, but she's starting to think more coherently.

What was Amy Wood doing in her house? Is she spying on her? What does she know? How did she find out? Kirsten tries to tell herself that it shouldn't come as a complete surprise to her that Amy Wood has found her. She should have known when she received the first blackmail letter, addressed to Mrs Taylor. The idiot in the VW and the widow must know each other. Perhaps

250

they're in cahoots. Or maybe the blackmailer told Amy Wood he knew who she and Nick really were. He may even have made her pay for the information.

But what does Amy Wood want? Is she trying to inveigle her way into Jamie's life? Lily's? But why? An explanation comes to Kirsten. Maybe the widow is hunting for a piece of evidence, something that will prove what Kirsten and Nick did to Gregory Wood, so that she can get justice for her husband. Well, she won't find anything. There is no evidence against Nick and her. Nick has seen to that. At best, Amy Wood could go to the police with the cock-and-bull story of a half-wit who saw Nick's Audi after it had been driven into the hedge in the pouring rain. They'd stick to their story: they'd swerved to avoid a sheep. This maniac's narrative doesn't hold water. His testimony wouldn't hold up in court. Even Kirsten realises that. He saw nothing. His eyewitness account would prove nothing.

She wants to text Nick, even though he has warned her to avoid sending text messages. She'll ring him instead. She wants him to reassure her some more. But she has left her phone downstairs. She's about to go and fetch it, but thinks better of it. Kirsten doesn't expect Amy will be back straight away – she imagines Amy must have been just as shocked by their encounter as she was herself – so she's confident she has a little time.

She will bring Nick up to speed, but not yet. No need to ruin his birthday – for him or for her. She needs to know what Nick has done about that wanker in the Volkswagen. If he has had him beaten up, or . . . worse . . . bumped him off, then she absolutely can't tell him about Amy Wood using false pretences to get inside the house. Kirsten doesn't like the woman – she didn't think much of her before with her laid-back lifestyle, questionable sense of fashion and unsightly tattoo, and she hates her now. But she and Nick have caused Amy Wood enough trouble and pain.

She does have to come up with a way of making sure that woman doesn't come anywhere near her or her husband or her daughter ever again, though. She mulls it over for a few minutes, then gets to her feet and walks over on slightly shaky legs to her dressing table. She takes one of the most expensive necklaces she owns out of her jewellery box and hides it in her washbag in the en-suite bathroom. Then she pastes on a bright smile and heads downstairs to join Jamie and Lily in the kitchen. Lily tries again to persuade Kirsten to eat a choc-chip cookie, holding it out to Kirsten in one of her grubby hands. This time, Kirsten accepts the biscuit and takes a small bite.

'Mmm, that's delicious, Little Lil,' she says.

As soon as Lily looks the other way, Kirsten discreetly slips the rest of the biscuit to the dog. He'll appreciate it far more than she will.

She waits until bedtime before she brings it up. 'Darling, have you seen my diamond necklace?' she asks Jamie as she takes off her earrings and tidies them into the jewellery box. 'You know, the one on the gold chain you bought me from Cartier when Lily was born?'

'No, I haven't. Have you mislaid it?' Jamie's already in bed, sitting up with an open book in front of him. But Kirsten knows he hasn't read so much as a paragraph. She can sense his eyes riveted on her as she parades around the bedroom wearing only skimpy underwear.

'Yes. It's strange. I haven't worn it recently. It's not in my jewellery box. I can't think where it can have got to.'

'I'm sure it will turn up.'

'You're probably right. I'm getting scatter-brained lately, what with mixing up dates and things,' Kirsten says. 'I thought the emergency cash I keep in my desk drawer had gone missing, too, the other day. I must have spent it on something. I just can't remember when or on what. Most unlike me.'

She turns to him and catches him furrow his brow and glance downwards, as if in thought. She smiles, knowing she has planted a seed of doubt in his mind. She's confident she has done enough.

She's confident he'll make sure that bloody woman is evicted from their lives and home. After all, it's Jamie's role to protect his family and he takes that task seriously.

But Jamie doesn't like to upset the apple cart, as he admits himself – his words. Kirsten calls it weak-balled, although not to Jamie's face, obviously. So, in case he needs a nudge, she has a treat in store for him. Jamie is always more malleable for a day or two after he has had good sex. She slinks towards him, wiggling her hips, all her movements exaggerated for Jamie's benefit. They haven't made love for weeks – he knows better than to pressure her after a long day at work – but it's about time, really.

She pulls back the covers, closes Jamie's book and puts it on the nightstand, then straddles him, unhooking her bra and pressing her body against his. She can sense he won't need much encouragement.

She spends the weekend with Jamie and Lily, striving to play the part of loving wife and mother, a role she finds exhausting but that she pulls off quite well for a change. She even walks the dog with them. She'll have to walk Rusty more often if, as she hopes, Jamie fires the dog walker. She'd better show willing.

'Rose has had to go back home for a while,' Jamie says on the Sunday evening. 'She sent me a text message.'

They were talking about Lily's violin – two of the strings have snapped, which is strange, so they need to take her instrument to a luthier – and Kirsten is momentarily thrown by the abrupt change of subject. 'Oh. Is she OK? Where does she live?' Kirsten has several more questions on the tip of her tongue. *What do you know about her? Did you even ask her for ID? Has she got a key to our home? Why did you let her in?* But she holds them back.

'She hasn't been well. Some time ago, she mentioned her mother-in-law wasn't well, either, so maybe that's why she's gone home, I don't know. She lives somewhere in the West Country, I believe.'

Just as Kirsten suspected. Jamie knows very little about Amy Wood. It's just as well, really, but she can't believe her husband let a complete stranger into their home and left their daughter in her care without doing some sort of preliminary background check.

'She's a widow,' Jamie says.

She's sitting on the bar stool and Jamie has his back to her as he washes up the saucepans and utensils, so he doesn't see her stiffen.

'What?' Kirsten splutters. How much did Amy Wood tell Jamie?

'Her husband was killed in a car accident. Not long ago. I mean, she didn't go into any detail, but I think she feels a bit lost.'

Kirsten should feel relieved – Jamie knows nothing – but she has a sinking feeling in her stomach. She can read between the lines; she can read her husband. Jamie thinks 'Rose' is going through a hard time, so he's reluctant to accuse her of stealing his wife's necklace and money. Classic Jamie. Always the good Samaritan.

But Amy will hardly dare to show her face around here any time soon, will she? Not after Kirsten caught her in this very house. Kirsten remembers the look on Amy's face. Eyes and mouth wide open, the blood draining from her face. An expression of pure shock. Whatever Amy was up to, running into Kirsten wasn't part of her plan.

Jamie grabs the tea towel and a saucepan and turns to face her. 'I've been thinking, I need to sound her out about the necklace. I'll talk to her about it, OK? I didn't check out her . . . credentials and stuff, so I should probably do that, too.'

'Do you really think she could have stolen . . .?' Kirsten feigns surprise, raising her eyebrows, and deliberately trails off.

'I don't know. Can you have a good look for it before I bandy about accusations?'

'Of course. I can't imagine I'd have put it anywhere else, but I'll definitely double-check. Do you know when she intends to come back?'

'No.'

'Well, keep me posted.'

These past few days, since the afternoon she came home and saw that woman in *her* house with *her* daughter, Kirsten has been looking over her shoulder, feeling jumpy and anxious. But if Amy has gone back to Devon to look after her late husband's mother, then that's her out of the picture for a while. And when she gets back, Jamie can make sure she stays well away from them. Depending on what Nick has done to the fool who made the mistake of black-mailing her, Kirsten will probably have told Nick about Amy Wood by then, too. He won't think twice about sending in the cavalry if that turns out to be necessary.

So, she needn't worry. She mustn't allow herself to get too smug, but she can breathe. She's safe.

For now.

Chapter 37

Amy

My plan has been foiled before it was even fully formed. I can't believe my bad luck, but I suppose it had to happen. I've had so many near misses I was bound to find myself face to face with Kirsten Bailey at some point.

The rest of our encounter is a daze. It was over in a matter of minutes, maybe even seconds. I got out of the house as quickly as possible. I don't know what I said to Jamie; I don't think I said anything to Kirsten. She eyeballed me, clearly as shocked to see me as I was to see her.

I texted Jamie the next day to say I wasn't feeling well. He texted me back immediately, thanking me again for looking after Lily and telling me to get well soon. I sent another text the day after that, saying that I was needed at home for a while and he wrote back, saying he hoped everything was all right, to let him know if there was anything he could do and that he was looking forward to seeing me again soon. I hope he'll relay my message to Kirsten so that she believes I'm in Croyde and not in London. Hopefully, she'll lower her guard if she doesn't perceive me as an immediate threat.

I feel terrible about lying to Jamie again, but I find his replies to my text messages reassuring. Kirsten can't have said anything to him about me if he's still expecting me back at some point. What would she say? What would I do if I were in her shoes? She certainly can't tell him the truth. She could make something up, though. She has no qualms about lying to him when it comes to her affair with Nicholas. She could just as easily concoct a story about me and insist that Jamie must put an end to our arrangement. I realise this would make me sad – I've come to think of Jamie as a friend and, although I tried not to become attached to her, I adore Lily.

Kirsten may not have said anything to Jamie about me, but she has probably told Nicholas she has seen me, that I have infiltrated her home. Why wouldn't she tell him? Unlike Jamie, Nicholas knows who I really am. And he knows who Kirsten really is. He was there, with her, when she ran over Greg. If they share that secret, she can tell him anything.

I'm utterly terrified by the idea that Nicholas knows I'm in London, snooping around. That man has a rep for getting the most hardened criminals off the hook. He must have some very grateful clients from whom he can call in a few favours. What if he knows people – murderers he has successfully defended – who would kill for him? Should I be in fear of my life?

For the two days following my encounter with Kirsten, I barely leave the tiny room I'm renting, even though it feels claustrophobic and airless. When I go out for food, I look over my shoulder all the time, imagining I'm being followed, unable to shake the sense that I'm in danger.

But by the weekend, I've persuaded myself I'm being paranoid. I don't know Nicholas or much about him. He's probably nowhere near as influential or evil as I've built him up to be in my mind. And he can't possibly know where to find me. There's no reason for me not to go ahead with my plan. It's not perfect – it's not even complete – and it relies heavily on opportunity and luck.

It may need to be revised at the last minute, but I hope to put it into action next weekend, when Jamie and Lily are in Folkestone and Kirsten and Nicholas are at her home in Muswell Hill.

I have one week to find out as much as I can about what Kirsten has got lined up for Nicholas's birthday weekend. I need to trail her as much as possible before then and rake through the house when no one is home to gather any information that might help me. I set out from my cramped room to do just that. I'm striding towards the Tube station, my head down, trying to look inconspicuous, when my mobile rings from inside my handbag, startling me. I stop, in the middle of the street, and get the phone out of my bag, groaning as I see the caller ID.

Tempted to ignore the call, I let the phone ring until it almost goes to voicemail. But then I answer, thinking it might be important.

'Hi, Simon,' I say with as much enthusiasm as I can summon up.

Simon dispenses with formalities. 'Amy, are you on your own?' he asks. The urgency in his tone unnerves me.

I look around me. I don't think anyone is following me. But that's not what Simon means, of course.

'Can you talk?'

'Yes. Why?'

'You're in danger. You're dealing with some very dodgy people. Take my word for it. You need to drop what you're doing and come home,' he gushes. 'Now!'

I feel the hairs on the back of my neck prickle and I whirl round again to double-check there's no one observing me. I've just convinced myself I'm not in danger and I don't want Simon to scare me off now. He has a tendency to exaggerate, I remember that from school. Our form tutor said he was 'melodramatic' and 'OTT'.

'Simon, how do you know who I'm dealing with or what I'm doing? What do you mean, "dodgy"?'

'They're unscrupulous people, the "Taylors". Killers.'

I think of how Kirsten Bailey and Nicholas Hunter ran over Greg and the lengths they went to in order to cover their tracks.

I can't argue with Simon's assessment. They are unscrupulous killers. But what I don't get is how Simon seems to know what I'm doing. I barely know myself. *You're in danger. You need to drop what you're doing.* Why should I take his word for it? What does he mean by that?

'Simon, I think I've missed an episode. Can you fill me in?'

'I know you've gone after them. The fancy-pants lawyer and his floozy.'

'Well, I confided in you before I left Croyde,' I say, hoping Simon's still onside. I hope he has kept that to himself. If he tells anyone else, it will ruin everything.

'I know you've been hanging out in front of her house.'

I shudder, looking over my shoulder yet again. Is Simon the one I should be looking out for rather than Nicholas or one of his buddies? 'Have you been following me? How do you know this?'

Simon ignores my question. 'If you can find her, I can, too!'

He's on the defensive and I'm not getting anywhere. 'Simon, what makes you think I'm in danger?'

'The bigwig lawyer . . . he threatened to kill me.'

'What? When? Why?'

'Well, *he* didn't. Probably not used to doing his own dirty work. He sent a couple of goons down here to intimidate me. Just now. They waved their knives around—'

'Knives? They were armed? Have you been to the police, Simon?'

'—and said they'd kill me if . . .' Simon breaks off, as if he has said too much. 'No! I'm not going to report it.'

'If what? If what, Simon?'

'If I didn't . . . back off.'

I try to read between the lines. What isn't Simon telling me? Why on earth would anyone wave a knife around and threaten to kill him? Why won't he go to the police?

My silence seems to prompt him and I hear him sigh. 'Amy, I wasn't going to tell you this, but, like you said, you confided in me, so I'll share this with you. In confidence.'

It's my turn to sigh at his longwinded preamble.

'I sent a letter to Kirsten Bailey, asking for a . . . donation . . . a small amount of money . . . to, you know . . . in exchange—'

'You blackmailed her?'

Simon doesn't answer. I picture him, nodding, but when he stays silent, I pull the phone away from my ear to make sure we haven't been cut off.

'Let me get this straight. You asked Bailey for money to keep quiet and Hunter sent in his pals to warn you off. Is that about the gist of it?'

'Yes,' Simon admits. He sounds sheepish.

My mind reels. What has Simon done? Will this wreck everything? But I scratch that thought. As Simon says, I confided in him – not that I had much choice – and he has confided in me. He knows my secret, and now I know his, he's more likely to keep mine.

'Simon, listen to me,' I say sternly. 'Keep all this to yourself and stay away. I'm coming home very soon. Don't mess with these people.' I want to add, *This has nothing to do with you*, but I bite my tongue. I can't afford to get Simon's back up.

'OK,' he says. 'Be careful, Amy. Don't underestimate them. You need to watch out.'

'So do you, Simon,' I say, ending the call. I don't intend it to, but it sounds like a threat.

Chapter 38

Amy

The countdown has begun. Time is flying by. Only one day to go. Tomorrow evening Jamie and Lily leave for Folkestone, taking Rusty with them, and Nicholas arrives to spend the weekend with Kirsten in her home in Muswell Hill.

I've spent my time this week following Kirsten around outside, or else inside her house, going through her things. She and Nicholas don't appear to be texting each other much. I can't find any emails between them, either. Perhaps they're worried about someone sifting through their stuff. Someone like me. Or Simon. I can see they've FaceTimed and called each other quite a lot recently, but I have no way of knowing what they discussed.

Kirsten's at work and I'm in her house, sitting in her office chair, when I notice I have a missed call from Jamie. He rang me yesterday, too, and we chatted for ages, about everything and nothing. But I got the impression he had something on his mind, something he'd rung to tell me, something he couldn't bring himself to say.

I decide to finish what I'm doing before calling him back. I've found a baby monitor in its box in Lily's room and I want to read through the instructions carefully and try it out. Perhaps I can use it to listen in on Kirsten and Nicholas's conversations this weekend. I need to plug it in somewhere they won't find it, in a room – other than the bedroom – that they're likely to spend time in. I find a socket in the living room behind the sideboard. I test the baby monitor before boxing it up again for now and tidying it away where I found it.

Then I head back to Kirsten's study, sit back down in her chair and ring Jamie. He answers straight away. This time, after enquiring about my mother-in-law's health and asking if I know when I might be coming back to London, he gets to the point.

'Rose, I've been trying to ask you something,' he begins, 'but the last thing I want to do is upset you.'

'Oh-*kay*,' I say, drawing out the two syllables, both a prompt for him to just come out with it and a promise to try not to take what he says badly. I hear him take a deep breath. I swivel from side to side in Kirsten's chair, without disturbing Rusty, who is sprawled across my feet.

'I want to be clear, Rose, I'm not accusing you of anything, but Kirsten has misplaced an expensive gold and diamond necklace . . .'

He pauses. He doesn't really need to say any more. I've got it. Kirsten has hidden a piece of her jewellery and either blamed me outright or implied that I may have stolen it. How clever of her.

'Neither my wife nor I believe you have anything to do with the necklace going missing. Kirsten would be the first to admit she's been particularly scatty recently and has no doubt mislaid it herself. But just to set Kirsten's mind at rest and to get me out of the doghouse . . .'

Jamie pauses again. I'm sure he's rehearsed what he wants to say in his head, and he's drafted a speech that's as tactful as possible, but he's making a hash of getting the words out. I want to help him. *This is the bit where you ask me for the key back and say thank you and goodbye.*

'. . . I wonder if you would mind bringing some ID when you come back,' he continues eventually when I say nothing. 'You will

262

come back, won't you? Rusty misses you—' I glance down at Rusty, guilt slicing through me like a knife '—and so do Lily and I. But if you could bring your driving licence or something – anything. You see, I left Lily with you that day and I didn't think twice about it because I've got to know you and trust you and knew Lily would be in good hands. But from my wife's point of view, I mean, I left her daughter with a stranger. I'm sorry. I should have—'

'It's no problem, Jamie,' I say. 'I've got my passport here at home.' I picture myself in my cottage in Croyde, where I'm supposed to be, sitting not on Kirsten's office chair in her spacious study, but on my own chair in the tiny room that was once a pantry and is now an office, opening the desk drawer where Greg and I keep our passports. Our expired passports. Mine is in the name of Amy Wood, not Rose Salter. 'I'll bring it with me when I come back, along with a bill or something so you have my home address. That's no problem.'

'Thank you for being so understanding.' I hear the relief in his voice. It makes me feel slightly better for lying to him. *Again*.

I find the necklace half an hour later in Kirsten's washbag in the en-suite bathroom. I hold it in my hands for a moment, wondering what to do with it. I don't want Jamie to think badly of me, although this strikes me as ironic, even hypocritical, given that I've been lying to him since the day we met. I'd like him to know with certainty that I didn't steal this.

I expect Kirsten usually keeps it in her jewellery box in the master bedroom, but if I put it in there, Jamie might believe that I had indeed stolen it and then, following our phone conversation, let myself into the house to put it back where I'd found it. Worse than that, Kirsten will know I've been inside her house while no one was at home and I'm hoping she believes I'm miles away, in North Devon. There's nothing for it but to leave the necklace in the washbag.

I wonder what to do about the ID Jamie has asked me for. I could ask Reverend Rob if he can make me up a fake bill or something. After all, making fake ID used to be part of his skill set, as Greg and he would sometimes joke, along with forging letters from schoolmates' parents. The document wouldn't have to be that convincing. I could have a black and white photocopy made to hide any imperfections.

But I rule out the idea. I've already asked Rob for a favour. I cringe as I think of the suggestive birthday card I sent him a week ago, identical to the one Kirsten bought for Nicholas that I found in her desk drawer. Plus, Rob's a man of the cloth now, to use the phrase he himself uses, and although he said he'd do anything to help, I'd be asking him – again – to do something dishonest.

Hopefully I won't need the fake ID. It should all be over after this weekend and, although my heart sinks at the thought, I suppose that will mean the end of my friendship with Jamie, too.

I'm jolted out of my thoughts by the sound of the front door closing downstairs. I freeze. I hear Kirsten's voice as she greets Rusty in the hallway and this spurs me into motion. She has finished work very early! I dive under the bed and lie still, trying to slow down my breathing and my heartbeat. But she doesn't come upstairs. I can make out the sound of the coffee machine. Minutes later, I hear her tell Rusty she'll be back in a few minutes and then the front door slams behind her.

I race down the stairs and peer through the frosted glass of the aluminium door. I can't see anything. I go through to the living room and look through the window. Kirsten has disappeared. She's on foot – the car is still parked in front of the house. Like many Londoners, Kirsten doesn't use the car that often. She's no eco-warrior, though. I don't think Kirsten actually likes driving, but perhaps that's recent. Maybe she has avoided driving as much as possible since she drove into my husband.

I dash back into the hallway and then I'm outside, sprinting to the end of the cul-de-sac. I spot her walking down the hill, an empty hessian tote bag in each hand. I know where she's going. There's a Tesco's at the bottom of the hill, just past Lily's school. I saw Kirsten's shopping list earlier – about a dozen items, written

264

in neat handwriting on a piece of paper, folded and hidden in a drawer in the kitchen among flyers for local take-away restaurants.

Kirsten and Jamie have a pad on the kitchen worktop, where they jot down what they've run out of or what they need from the supermarket. Jamie usually does the shopping. He goes in the car. Kirsten occasionally picks up things they've forgotten from the corner shop on her way home. I've gathered all this from observing their routine.

But this isn't part of their routine. This isn't the weekly shop for the family. This is for Kirsten's weekend with Nicholas. I know exactly what she plans to buy and more or less what I have to do.

Keeping a safe distance behind her, I follow her. I remember her glancing over her shoulder when I followed her a few times before, much as I've been doing lately, as if sensing someone was behind her. But today, she doesn't check once.

Outside the supermarket, I hesitate. This will be tricky. If she sees me, it's game over. There's something I need to buy, but I don't have to go into the supermarket at the same time as her. I can come back later. Or go elsewhere. But it would be better if I could pull this off now. I've had my hair cut short, apart from some strands around my face to hide behind. But it's not much of a disguise. Taking a deep breath, I walk towards the automatic doors.

I grab a basket and put a few random things and the one item I actually need into it. I remember Greg telling me about the super-market game he and his brother Will used to play when they were little and Pam took them shopping with her while Hugh was at work. To begin with, when Pam wasn't looking, they'd add things to her trolley – sweets and cakes, mainly. She found it funny when she discovered the items at checkout and always went ahead and bought them anyway. Then Will and Greg progressed to the next level of their game and discreetly put groceries into other shoppers' trolleys. Greg told me this story once when we discovered a packet of cuttlefish bones for budgies and a packet of incontinence pads in our trolley one day. I assumed someone had put their shopping in the wrong trolley, but Greg thought it might have been kids, messing around, as he and his brother had done.

I have a back-up plan. If it comes to it, I can buy what I need myself. But, ideally, it would be perfect if Kirsten could buy it for me. It should blend in with most of the other stuff on her shopping list. She may not notice an extra item at checkout. If she does notice it and doesn't buy it, this will all have been for nothing.

I find Kirsten in the baking section. I walked down this aisle just a few seconds ago. This is very risky indeed. Perhaps I should abort this mission and play it safe. I remind myself there's a much easier way. But I decide to continue now I've come this far. I keep an eye on her, keeping well away from her at the same time. My heart skips a beat as I notice she doesn't have a trolley. She has a basket. That makes sense. She walked here and will have to carry home everything she buys. But it will be harder to slip the packet into a basket than a trolley without her noticing me – or it.

Then I get lucky. She sets down her basket. She's scanning the shelves, looking for something. She turns and scours the shelves opposite. *Now!* I walk briskly down the aisle, holding my basket like a shield. Bending as I pass Kirsten, I put the item inside her shopping basket. I manage to push it down the side so it's hidden by her groceries. I smell her perfume as I straighten up. I'm close, too close. I could reach across the aisle and tap her on the shoulder or she could turn round and . . . I've done it! I've reached the end of the aisle. I exhale. I don't dare look back.

As I head up the next aisle, I abandon my own basket. I resist the overwhelming urge to run towards the exit. Just before I step outside, I see them. Volunteers, all wearing pink T-shirts, putting people's groceries into shopping bags. I can hardly believe my good luck. My heart does a little somersault. Outside the supermarket, I'm accosted by a woman about my age, dressed in the same pink T-shirt as the baggers, waving a money collection box in my face.

'For breast cancer research,' she says.

I keep a few coins in my pocket for buskers at Tube stations, so I pull out what I've got and, with shaking hands, I feed the coins through the slot of the money box. It's not much. Fifty pence in total. I've probably got more change in my purse, but I need to get out of here.

My heart plummets as the realisation hits me. I don't have my purse on me. It's in my handbag. Which I've left at Kirsten's house. How can I have been so stupid? I'm usually so careful.

I sprint up the hill. Unlike Kirsten, I haven't been wearing any perfume or using scented toiletries and I've been careful to leave everything in its place so she can't tell I've been in her house. I can't believe I forgot my bag! But I left in such a hurry. I try to calm myself down. Kirsten hasn't seen it – it's in her study and she didn't go in there, she went into the kitchen to make herself an espresso.

Rusty greets me as if he hasn't seen me for several weeks instead of just a few minutes. I jump as the front door slams behind me. I'd deliberately left it open for a quick getaway, but it has swung closed. I go into the office and grab my bag from the floor by the desk. As I straighten up, I happen to glance out of the window. A car has pulled up and Kirsten is unfolding herself from it, a shopping bag over each arm. For a second or two I'm rooted to the spot, terrified I'm about to be caught. I watch as she lifts a hand and one of the bags in an awkward wave goodbye or thanks to the neighbour who has apparently given her a lift home.

I look around me frantically, but there's nowhere to run. 'Out, Rusty!' The dog has followed me into the study and I'm scared he'll give me away. He obeys and rushes to greet Kirsten as I flatten myself against the wall behind the open study door.

She goes into the kitchen and I strain my ears. Seconds later, I hear a door shut. Not the kitchen door. It was closer, louder. I think it must have been the toilet door in the hallway. I peep out. Rusty is sitting in front of the closed toilet door.

I'm about to dash out of the front door, but then I have an idea. I creep through the hallway, past the toilet and into the kitchen.

267

The shopping bags are on the central island with the groceries still in them. I rummage around in one bag, but I can't find it. Quick! I have to hurry up! I find my packet in the second bag and take it out. The receipt is in there, too, and I shove it into the pocket of my jeans. I pat Rusty on the head on my way out.

I pull the front door shut behind me just as the toilet flushes. As I turn into the main road, I allow myself a small smile. I've carried out the first part of my plan.

Chapter 39

Kirsten

Kirsten has skived off work quite a bit at the agency lately and she has overheard her colleagues bitching behind her back about having to take up the slack. She'll have to start pulling her weight again soon. But she so badly wants everything to be perfect for this weekend. This evening in particular, as it's Nick's birthday today. So, in the end, she takes the day off. Kirsten has told Jamie that she has viewings on the Saturday – her excuse to get out of the Folkestone trip – and that she's taking the Friday off in lieu.

She hoovers downstairs, as usual picking up enough dog hairs to make a rug, and cleans the kitchen. She did the upstairs yesterday – cleaned the loos and bathrooms; dusted and hoovered the bedrooms. Ideally, Kirsten would prefer to pay someone else to do this sort of work, dirty work. She has got through a string of cleaning ladies – or whatever the politically correct term for them is – but she can't seem to find one who will do the job properly. The first cleaner she employed drank their scotch, vodka and Pernod; the second knocked over a full bucket of water on the beige carpet in the hall; they had a cleaner who never did the toilets and one who cleaned the toilets with the dishcloth.

Since Kirsten let the last cleaner go, Jamie has done the housework. He'll be impressed that she has cleaned the place for once. Everything is looking spick and span. She'll make up the bed in the guest room later – she knows her moral compass is askew, but even she draws the line at having sex with her lover in the marital bed.

Marital bed. Nine years she has been married to Jamie. They met at a mutual friend's thirtieth and hit it off straight away. They slept together that very night. The sex was better the following morning when they'd sobered up. Cue a whirlwind romance that morphed into a serious, long-term relationship. He desperately wanted children; she wanted to concentrate on her career first. Then Lily came along. Lily was a toddler when Kirsten met Nicholas. Jamie thought it was a good time to try for another baby. He still wants another baby. But although Kirsten loves Lily and doesn't regret having her, she doesn't want any more kids. With Jamie or Nicholas. She's somewhat lacking in maternal instinct.

Nick has been talking more and more about getting divorced – Nick from his wife and Kirsten from her husband. She didn't take him seriously when he first brought it up, but he insists he wants to marry her. It's all or nothing with Nick. He's like a dog with a bone when he sets his mind on something. She has promised to think about it and she's supposed to give him her answer this weekend. It feels like an ultimatum. Will he break up with her again if she refuses to leave Jamie? *And* Lily, because Jamie will want primary custody and Kirsten won't contest it. Kirsten tells herself that Lily will be better off without her. She doesn't know if she's trying to convince herself of this or if she's already convinced, but she has to face facts. Jamie's a terrific father and she's a terrible mother. She was never cut out to be one.

Anyway, Kirsten has made up her mind. She can't live without Nick. Their break-up made her realise this. She smiles to herself as she thinks about the birthday card she has bought him. It has a rude joke on the front, but inside, she's serious. She has written: *For better, for worse; for richer, for poorer.* Her answer.

Kirsten's thoughts are disturbed by a dull noise. It came from upstairs. How strange. The dog is here, in the kitchen, by her side. He doesn't go upstairs anyway. There are no windows open in the bedrooms. Then two familiar voices call out and Kirsten realises the thud must have been Jamie opening the front door. Lily rushes into the kitchen and nearly bowls her over, wrapping her little arms around Kirsten's waist and squeezing her tight.

'Hello, Little Lil,' Kirsten says, smiling at Jamie as Rusty pounces on him. She winces, noticing neither of them have taken off their shoes. She has just done the housework! She's about to scold Jamie as he walks into the kitchen to fetch some snacks for the drive. But she refrains from comment. 'Got time for a coffee?' she asks him instead.

'No,' he replies, to her relief. 'Got to get going if we're going to beat the traffic.' He turns to Lily. 'Upstairs, sweetie. Quickly. Get changed out of your uniform and back down here fast.'

'Take your shoes off first,' Kirsten adds.

Kirsten follows Jamie and Lily into the hall, where Lily takes off her shoes and scampers up the stairs on all fours and Jamie picks up the suitcase he left by the front door this morning. Kirsten watches her husband walk away from her, down the driveway, to load the case – and the dog – into the car. A minute later, she's locked into a hug with both Jamie and Lily. She wants to hold on to this moment, she wants to press pause while she and her husband and her daughter are all here, still together. At the same time, she can't wait for Jamie and Lily to leave and Nick to arrive.

'Drive carefully,' she says to Jamie. Advice she should have taken herself a few months ago, she thinks darkly. She stands on the door-step and waves them off, then steps back inside and closes the door.

After making up the bed in the guest room upstairs, she comes down to the kitchen to make Nick's cake. She turns on the oven to preheat. It seems strangely quiet all of a sudden now that Jamie,

Lily and Rusty have gone, so she streams a playlist from her phone through the Bluetooth speaker. Singing along to The Kooks, 'Forgive & Forget', she opens her recipe book and gets out all the ingredients and equipment.

Kirsten is good at baking and it doesn't take her long. She has made this cake before. It's a simple sponge cake with the zest of half a lemon in the cake and lemon icing on top. Nick loves citrus fruit. She divides the mixture between the two tins and puts them in the oven.

She sets the timer and looks at the clock on the oven door. She has got about an hour before Nick arrives. She told him she'd take care of the wine, but she had enough shopping to lug back up the hill the other day, so she didn't buy any. If she'd known that, in the end, the busybody from next door would give her a lift, she'd have bought the wine there and then. She needs to pop out to Tesco's and get some now. It won't do to down the best bottles from her husband's wine rack with her lover. She wouldn't really have any scruples about doing that, but Jamie wasn't impressed when he noticed how many of his bottles she'd managed to work her way through the week she was at home on sick leave. She can't pilfer any more of them. If she leaves now, she'll be back before the cake is ready. She'll clear up in the kitchen when she gets home.

The supermarket is quite busy – she supposes that's only to be expected on a Friday evening, not that she would know. She hardly ever does the shopping other than picking up bits and pieces from the local convenience shop. She waits impatiently at the checkout, clutching a bottle of red in one hand and a bottle of white in the other, hoping someone will offer to let her jump the queue. But no one does. The baggers in their oversized candy-floss-pink T-shirts aren't here today, so at least she won't have to cough up her loose change.

The timer is bleeping when she steps inside the house. She kicks off her shoes in the hall and rushes into the kitchen to take the cake out of the oven. She selects a sharp knife from the wooden

272

block on the worktop and inserts it into the centre of the cake, first in one tin then the other. It comes out clean both times, so she turns the two halves out onto the cooling rack and switches off the oven. She'll have to wait until the cake cools before she can ice it and put candles on top. She pops the bottle of white wine she has just bought into the fridge and opens the bottle of red, which she leaves on the worktop.

She made a huge jambalaya last weekend. Jamie was pleasantly surprised that she'd made dinner for them all. It didn't occur to him that the trouble she'd gone to was really for someone else. She takes the other half of that meal out of the freezer now. All she has to do is heat it up and make some saffron rice. She's just finishing the washing up when Nick arrives. Perfect timing.

Nick has brought a box of chocolates and a chilled bottle of something bubbly. She gets out a couple of champagne flutes and prepares some nibbles – green olives, Iberian ham, Manchego cheese – and they take everything through to the living room. Once she has taken a seat next to Nick on the sofa, she feels a draught on the back of her neck. She must have left the window open when she aired the room earlier. She should probably pull the curtains, too. She doubts there will be anyone around, but you never know.

She knows Nick will be trying to work out how to press her for an answer to his marriage proposal, if you can call it that when they're both already married – to other people. So she hands him his birthday card straight away.

'Thank you so much for the present, by the way,' he says, opening the envelope. 'I received the email today. What a thoughtful gift!'

Nick's always saying he'd like to know more about wine, so she has signed him up for an online masterclass with some renowned wine buff she'd never heard of. She's a little worried that she might be encouraging him to drink more than he already does, but she couldn't think of a better present. She observes him as he reads the card. He chuckles at the crude joke, then reads the message inside. Is it her imagination or does he tear up?

'For better, for worse; for richer, for poorer,' he reads aloud. 'Is this a yes?'

'Yes,' she whispers. She's about to take a sip – or a gulp – of her prosecco or champagne or whatever it is, but he wraps her in his arms and smothers her with kisses.

'So we're really doing this, getting divorced and getting married?'

'Yes,' she says again. Kirsten is doing her best not to pay any attention to the nagging suspicion that has corkscrewed its way into her mind, that if Ediye has left Nick, this might have been the catalyst to his proposal. She doesn't want to go there; she doesn't want to know.

'When will you tell your husband?' Nick never refers to Jamie by name.

'Soon,' she says. 'I've decided to give Jamie primary custody of Lily.'

'That might be for the best,' he remarks into her ear.

She stiffens briefly, wondering what he means by that, but she lets it go. She doesn't want anything to spoil this evening, this weekend. She unwinds herself from his embrace, gets to her feet. Nick follows her into the kitchen, bottle of bubbly in one hand and flutes in the other with the birthday card between his fingers.

'I'll just put this in my bag so I don't forget it or leave it lying around,' he says, setting down the champagne and glasses and waving the card at her.

He makes the rice while she ices the cake. They eat the meal in the kitchen, sitting on the bar stools. They've finished the bottle of fizz and Nick has poured them each a glass of red from the bottle she'd left breathing on the worktop. She knows far less about wine than Nick, not that he knows a lot, but she does know you're supposed to uncork the red half an hour or so before you drink it. That's what Jamie does when they have guests, anyway. Other than that, she hasn't got a clue. She bought the most expensive bottles she could find in the supermarket and they're French, so they should be good.

'This is delicious,' Nick says, glass in hand and with his mouth full. He looks into her eyes, an expression of adulation on his face. He has morphed from a dog with a bone into a faithful puppy now he has got what he wants.

'The wine or the food?'

'Both. It's all wonderful. Thank you.'

She smiles. She tries to imagine what it will be like waking up next to him every day, watching him get ready for work, knotting his tie for him. They've been together for over five years, they've been to Michelin-starred restaurants and stayed in posh hotels, but what she craves with him is domesticity. She wants to do normal, everyday stuff with him – lounge around on the sofa in front of Netflix, sit next to him in bed reading a book, heat up ready-made meals or order take-outs, even do the shopping with him – why not? She hates the idea of hurting Jamie and Lily, but this is what she wants. This is who she wants to be with.

They pack the dirty crockery and cutlery into the dishwasher. Kirsten hands Nick two small plates and a large knife.

'Take these through,' she says, nodding towards the door to the living room, 'and wait for me in there. Turn off the lights.'

'Ooh,' he says, raising his eyebrows suggestively.

'Keep your clothes on,' she says to his back as he exits the kitchen. 'For now.'

She lights the candles and sings 'Happy Birthday' as she carries the cake in. She walks slowly, resisting a sudden urge to giggle. She's drunk quite a lot and is tipsy. There are five candles on the cake, one for every year they've been together, and Nick blows them all out in one go.

'I hope you made a wish,' she says.

'It's already come true. It came true this evening.'

Kirsten can't help thinking of Lily's last birthday. She baked her a pink unicorn cake and Lily invited her four best friends – all spoilt brats – whose mothers duly admired Kirsten's handiwork. She'd had a brief insight into what it would be like to be a good mother. She'd felt like an imposter. The kids were high on sugar all afternoon and Kirsten was glad when it was over. Lily is eight in a few weeks' time and Kirsten will have to do it all again. Probably.

Nick removes the candles and cuts the cake. Kirsten bites into her slice. It's not her best effort – it doesn't taste quite right. Not enough sugar, perhaps. But it tastes pretty good and it looked good with the icing and candles.

It doesn't happen until he's almost polished off the whole slice. He drops the plate to the floor and Kirsten doesn't notice at first. She bends across him to pick up the plate and the remaining bite of the cake. It's only as she sets down the plate on the coffee table that she realises he's choking. He must have swallowed it down the wrong way. She leaps to her feet to help him up. The Heimlich manoeuvre. She knows what it's called, although her only notion of how to actually do it comes from a vaguely recalled first-aid course and films. But Nick can't stand up, not even with her help. He clutches his throat, wheezing. His eyes, wide open in panic, fix on hers. His face has gone puce and it looks like it has swollen up.

'In . . . je . . .' he manages. She gets it from his mime as he injects himself in the thigh with an imaginary needle.

She knows what's happening now. Suddenly she is stone-cold sober. He's having a severe allergic reaction. Anaphylaxis. Kirsten knows what to do because Nick has told her. She leaves him gasping for air on the sofa and dashes into the hallway. She opens his duffle bag and tips out the contents onto the floor. She rummages through his clothes, but she can't find his EpiPen. She picks up the bag again. It must be in an inside pocket. There are no inside pockets. His coat is hanging in the cupboard under the stars. She checks for the injection in his jacket. Then she runs back to Nick.

'Where is it? Your EpiPen? It's not in your bag.' She shouts. He just about manages to nod. 'No, Nick, I promise you. It's not in the bag.'

She needs to call an ambulance. Where's her phone? She must have left it in the kitchen. Or in her handbag. Where the fuck's her handbag? She races from room to room, then remembers it's in the living room, next to the sofa.

Nick's crazed eyes fill with tears. He reaches out one arm to her as she snatches her phone from her bag. She rushes to sit next to him, holding him, cradling his head in her lap in one hand, fumbling with her mobile with the other. He convulses, once, then he's still. He's no longer gasping for breath.

He's no longer breathing.

'Nick! Nick! Stay with me, Nick!' She feels for a pulse in his neck. She's not sure if she'd find it even if there was one. Still, she tries, desperate to feel evidence of his heartbeat in his neck. 'Nooooooo! Please, no! Nick! Don't leave me!'

Carotid. This word also came to her last time she fumbled around in vain for a pulse. But Gregory Wood was dead.

And Nick's dead now, too.

Chapter 40

Amy

Is Nicholas Hunter really dead? If so, this is murder. I'm having trouble getting my head round that thought. I need to get out of here, but I can't move. My nerves are shot to pieces and my legs have gone to sleep and I can't seem to get the message from my brain to my limbs. I've been lying under Lily's bed, or sitting on the floor behind it, for hours. It was the safest hiding place I could think of. Kirsten was in when I got here this morning – she had clearly taken the day off work, probably to get things ready for her weekend with Nicholas – and I had to slip into the house when I was fairly sure she was in the shower and the coast was clear.

I'm surprised I haven't been discovered. There have been a few narrow escapes. I thought I'd had it when I reached into the cupboard to take out Lily's baby monitor and knocked several toys to the floor at the same time. The carpet dulled the noise, but still. If Kirsten did hear anything from downstairs, she was distracted by Jamie and Lily arriving home. I'd just finished replacing the toys on the shelf, one by one, when Lily thundered up the stairs. I managed to dive back under her bed only a second or two before she erupted into her bedroom to change out of her uniform. Her skirt and blouse are still lying on the floor. I could see her small feet as she came towards the bed. I was terrified she would look under it and find me.

I'm still clenching the receiver to the baby monitor. I turned down the volume when Kirsten started wailing. It was as if she was screaming in my ears. I've eavesdropped on Kirsten and Nicholas's conversation all evening, at least when they were in the living room, where I plugged in the transmitter. I heard every word as clearly as if I was sitting on the sofa between them. It was just as I thought. Kirsten intended to leave Jamie, and Nicholas was going to leave his wife. Knowing this has eased my conscience a little. There have been times when I've felt so guilt-ridden, thinking about Lily, that I didn't know if I could go through with my plan.

But after listening to them discuss this so callously, I'm more convinced than ever that Lily deserves so much better. Everything is calmer now. The noise of Kirsten's sobbing drifts to me from downstairs, but I can barely hear her over the noise of the blood rushing through my ears. I turn off the baby monitor and put it back inside its box.

I've known since I saw the calendar entry that day that Kirsten planned to make a birthday cake this evening. Under *Jamie & Lil in Fkstn*, she'd noted for the Friday – today: *N's b'day. WE at mine. Make cake.* There was also a cake emoji. I knew which recipe she'd chosen – she'd used the flap of the recipe book to mark the page. So, that was her plan. And mine sprang from hers.

I thought about what I knew about Nicholas Hunter QC. Not much, really. Most of what I did know I'd gleaned from his Instagram posts. He was married, he cheated on his wife with Kirsten who sold him his house about five years ago. He liked expensive restaurants and tropical holidays, wine and champagne. He had a reputation for getting his clients off, against all odds, even when they'd allegedly committed the most heinous crimes. He got driven around in a Mercedes by his chauffeur and he had – or at least used to have – an Audi A8. None of this was very helpful. But there was one detail I knew about Hunter that was useful.

He was allergic to tree nuts.

Given the fuss Hunter made in The Thatch, making David write down a list of tree nuts to check with the chef that the food couldn't possibly have been contaminated, I'd have said he was *deathly* allergic. And, judging from the sobbing, now rising from downstairs in a crescendo, that has turned out to be the case.

So, my plan was simple. All I had to do was sprinkle ground almonds over Kirsten's finished cake. I thought I'd only get a short window to do this, when Kirsten was distracted or in another room or something. But when Kirsten popped out earlier, I raced downstairs, clutching in one hand the packet of ground almonds – the one I'd slipped into Kirsten's basket at the supermarket and taken out of her shopping bag together with the receipt – and in the other hand the transmitter of the baby monitor.

In the kitchen, I took the cake out of the oven and divided the ground almonds between the two tins, mixing the ingredient in carefully with a wooden spoon that I then washed up and put back in the pot. A slightly amended – and better – version of my plan. I always knew I would have to play it by ear, revise my plan as I went along and rely on a bit of good luck. I put the cake tins back in the oven.

In the living room, I plugged the transmitter of the baby monitor into the socket behind the sideboard. I had no idea how long Kirsten would be gone, so when I'd finished, I ran back upstairs and took up my hiding place again.

I can hardly believe my plan has worked. But my work here isn't done. Not yet. I must get out of this room. Now! What I have left to do is tricky. Dangerous. This is make or break. I could easily blow my cover, even if I'm very careful. I get to my feet. My legs wobble as I walk over to the cupboard. I'm not sure if it's because they're cramped from sitting on the floor or if it's because I'm petrified. I put the box with the baby monitor receiver back in the cupboard, careful not to knock any toys to the floor this time. The transmitter is still plugged into a socket in the living room. I'll have to leave it there. Hopefully, if anyone finds it later and wonders what it's doing there, they'll assume Lily was playing with it at some point.

I open Lily's bedroom door slowly, peeping out, all my senses on high alert. I creep down the stairs. I'm so tempted to sprint out of here, but I need to be cautious and meticulous. When I tiptoed down earlier to take the EpiPen, I zipped Nicholas's overnight bag back up. The contents have been tipped out since then and are strewn across the floor at the bottom of the stairs. I slip the EpiPen under Nicholas's clothes.

With shaking hands, I slide the card Kirsten wrote to Nicholas out of the envelope and push mine into it. The front of my card – with its poor sexual pun – is identical. But Reverend Rob has written a slightly different message inside, imitating Kirsten's neat handwriting faultlessly from the screenshot I sent him. I doubt Kirsten would appreciate it, but I've stuck to the wedding vow theme. It reads: *Till Death Do Us Part.* I couldn't resist. And I'm hoping it might make Nicholas's death look like premeditated murder. Which, of course, it is.

Next comes the really risky bit. I make my way stealthily into the kitchen. To do this, I have to walk along the hallway, past the door to the living room, which is open. If Kirsten looks up, she'll catch sight of me. I steal a glance at her as I sneak past. She's cradling Nicholas's head and rocking, still sobbing. Is she going to ring the emergency services?

There's also a communicating door between the living room and the kitchen, but luckily for me, that one has been left ajar rather than wide open. I push on the pedal of the dustbin with my foot and drop the supermarket receipt and empty packet of ground almonds in. I'd really like to leave them in a more obvious place – on the worktop, for example – but Kirsten seems rather OCD about her showroom home and it would be out of character for her to leave rubbish lying around. This will have to do. I scan the room, run through a mental checklist. Have I forgotten anything? I don't think so.

Kirsten still hasn't rung the emergency services. What is she waiting for? She should have called an ambulance. Did she hesitate like this when she ran over Greg? If she and Hunter had called the emergency services in time, could Greg have been saved? Is she thinking back to that day, asking herself what to do with Nicholas's body, as she asked herself what to do with Greg's? Is she thinking of covering this up, too?

I'll have to make the call myself, but I can't do it from my own mobile. Have the Baileys got a landline? In Kirsten's office, maybe? Surely I'd have noticed if there was a phone in her office. Perhaps in the master bedroom, but that will mean walking back in front of the open door to the living room. Can I pull it off? I only need to sound a bit like her. She'll be distressed, which will explain it if she doesn't sound quite like herself on the recording afterwards.

But as I'm clutching at this straw, Kirsten's posh, nasal voice drifts towards me from the next room. 'Ambulance, please.' I inhale deeply and exhale. I step into the hallway, where I can hear her more clearly. Kirsten stumbles over her name and address and I realise her wavering was probably due to shock. She has just lost the man she loves, after all. I know how that feels.

'My . . . my . . . my ex-lover is dead,' she says. She sounds distraught and panicked.

I wonder why she called him her ex-lover. She could have said 'friend' or 'boyfriend'. I suppose she couldn't find the right word, if there is one, in the heat of the moment. Who is he to her? A future fiancé? He's only an *ex*-lover because he's dead.

'Nicholas Hunter. His name is . . . *was* Nicholas Hunter . . . I don't know . . . anana . . . an ana . . . phyl . . . an allergic reaction, maybe?'

I don't linger any longer. I slip out, into the night and stride to the end of the road before breaking into a run. Although I can't catch my breath and it seems as if the air that I do snatch lacks oxygen, I keep running.

I've almost reached the underground station at Wood Green when I hear the sirens. Moments later, an ambulance tears by, followed closely by a police car, heading in the opposite direction to me, towards the place I've just come from.

Hi,

Looking back, I can't pinpoint the exact moment I realised I'd been set up. Did I already know when you lay dying in my arms, your terrified eyes fixed on mine? Or did it only hit me later, when the police found the evidence she'd planted?

What tortures me is whether you knew I'd been framed. Did it cross your mind, as you fought to take your last breath, that I might be responsible for your death? Did you doubt me, even for a fleeting instant? Would you have believed me capable of murder? Of your murder?

If you were still alive, I would have left Jamie and you would have left Ediye and we'd be living our dream by now. Spending the rest of our lives together in my childhood home, my forever home in coveted Muswell Hill.

Instead, I'll be spending the rest of my life, or at least a sizeable chunk of it, languishing in a six-by-nine-foot cell in His Majesty's Prison Sevenhams Park. Condemned for a crime I didn't commit. Ingenious, when you think about it. Devious. Amy Wood executed her plan – executed being the operative word – to perfection. I've gone down, not for accidentally causing the death of her husband, but for deliberately taking my lover's life. Your life. Oh, the irony! She got us, both of us. One of us dead; the other jailed for life.

I hate her with a vengeance, not that I'll ever be able to wreak revenge now I'm cooped up in here. But, sometimes – and you're the only person I'd ever admit this to – I find myself thinking about her with grudging admiration. I underestimated her and she outwitted me. I used to think she and I had absolutely nothing in common. But I understand her better now. I get where she was coming from. You see, like her – because of her – I've lost the man I planned to grow old with, the man I love. I know better than anyone exactly how she feels.

Epilogue

Amy

Jamie hasn't seen Kirsten since her arrest. It was too much for him to process, the fact that she'd allegedly murdered her lover and the discovery that she'd had a lover in the first place. He's still struggling to digest her betrayal. He wouldn't set foot in the courtroom. But I attended the trial. I was there nearly every day. Jamie doesn't know I went, but Kirsten spotted me sitting in the public gallery. If looks could kill. I'm sure she knew even before she saw me that I was behind this, that I was the one who murdered Nicholas and framed her. The only way she could have pointed the finger at me for killing her lover would have been to admit that she was responsible for killing my husband. How else would she have explained my motive? But she had no proof against me for my crime, just as I'd had no proof against her for hers.

The jury reached a unanimous verdict this morning after deliberating for only two hours. Guilty. I'm not sure who was more shocked when the foreperson read it out: Kirsten or me. The evidence against her seemed largely circumstantial. The empty packet of ground nuts and the supermarket receipt; old text messages with Kirsten pleading with Nicholas not to break up with her; a neighbour who also heard Kirsten scream 'Don't leave me' through the open living-room window; a 999 call in which Kirsten referred to the victim as her *ex*-lover; a birthday card with the words *Till Death Do Us Part*.

As Nicholas Hunter QC once said in an interview I watched on YouTube, the prosecution's job is to tell a story and convince the jury that the story is true. The defence has to find plot holes in that narrative and cast doubt in the jurors' minds as to its veracity. Those were more or less the words he said. The tale the prosecution spun was about a woman who killed her lover after he'd discarded her, luring him to her marital home on his birthday for old time's sake and deliberately and cold-bloodedly feeding him something she knew he was lethally allergic to. It was about a woman scorned who decided that if she couldn't have him, no one could. The jury seemed to swallow the story.

I don't think Kirsten's counsel did a great job of refuting it. Her barrister had a great reputation, apparently, but I didn't find him very convincing. Evidently the jury didn't, either. As I watch Kirsten being led away in handcuffs, I wonder if the same thing is going through her mind as mine: how deeply ironic it is that the one person who could have got her off is the person she killed?

Electronic devices and cameras aren't allowed in the Central Criminal Court building and there are no lockers, so I've got into the habit of leaving my mobile in the care of a barista in the café just down the road. The first thing I do when I retrieve my phone is ring my parents-in-law to tell them Kirsten has been found guilty and sentenced to life imprisonment with a recommended minimum term of thirty years. It's finally over. It has been a whole year, almost to the day, since Greg disappeared. Pam cries. Hugh thanks me for calling. They both want to know when I'm coming home.

'Soon,' I promise.

I really should get back to Croyde, move back into my cottage, even though it doesn't feel like home anymore. Not without Greg.

Pam and Hugh are my family, and they and my friends – my tribe – are in North Devon. Plus, my stepfather's money is running out. I've sold the holiday flat in Woolacombe for a good price – Kirsten would be impressed – and Greg's surf shop has been making a good profit since Tom reopened it, but even so, I'll need to get a paid job myself before too long. I'm planning to teach again from September. With Liz's help and support, I know I can do it. I can rebuild my life, reconstruct myself.

I head for St Paul's Tube station and take the Central Line to Holborn, then the Piccadilly Line to Wood Green. From there, it's a short walk. Door to door it takes me just over half an hour. From the Old Bailey to the Baileys'. (If the birthday card is anything to go by, Kirsten liked puns and word play. I wonder if she'd like that one.) For the past few months, I've been living here, in Kirsten's house in Muswell Hill with Jamie, Lily and Rusty. Jamie persuaded me that there was no point in me paying rent for a cramped place in Pimlico when he had an empty guest room.

I wasn't sure it was a good idea. But I felt awful about what I'd done to Jamie and Lily and wanted to make up for that by keeping Jamie company and helping out with Lily. The arrangement has worked well for us. I volunteer for a few hours a day at Lily's school, assisting the pupils with their reading and that sort of thing. I look after Lily while Jamie's at work and, of course, I still get to walk Rusty every day. And I think Jamie and I both feel less lonely.

Initially, I decided to stay on in London until the trial was over. But although I feel homesick and a little displaced, I've become attached to Jamie and Lily, and I can't bear the thought of leaving them . . . and Rusty. I'm also not up to facing Greg's ghost just yet.

So I think I'll stay here, just a little longer, in Kirsten's house, with her husband and daughter. Sometimes it feels as if Kirsten took my life as I knew it away from me and now I'm living hers. But I don't intend to live her life the way she did and one day soon I'll get on with my own. I know it's time to move on, but I'm not quite ready to go home just yet.

A Letter from Diane Jeffrey

Thank you so much for choosing to read my book. I hope you enjoyed it as much as I enjoyed writing it! If you did and would like to be the first to know about my new releases, you can follow me on Twitter, Facebook, Instagram or my website below.

It takes me just over a year to write each book – once I actually start writing. Before that, there's usually a few months where I just let the initial idea percolate until it has formed into something I start to get enthusiastic about. For my dog, Cookie, this is the best bit, as she gets to go on lots of very long plot walks. But for me, this is the hardest phase, as it sometimes takes a while for the initial idea to come (and when it does, it's usually the middle of the night, when I'm never quite sure how coherent my thoughts are or if I'll even remember them in the morning). Even after six published novels, when I think I have the beginning of a plan, I'm always doubtful I can turn it into an 80,000-word novel.

I'm often asked where I get my ideas from. (Obviously, having a warped mind helps!) Occasionally, I'm inspired by something that happened in real life. This was the case for *The Guilty Mother*, where the premise for my novel sprang from a news story that had stayed with me for years about several women who had been victims of miscarriages of justice. *The Silent Friend* was also something I felt I had to write after a very traumatic incident shook the whole of France and indeed the whole world. For both *The Couple at Causeway Cottage*, which is set on the remote island of Rathlin, off the Northern Irish coast, and *He Will Find You*, for which the backdrop is the Lake District, the setting was strong in my mind long before the plot came to me. For this book, Kirsten and Amy formed in my mind before anything else. I wanted to create two completely different female characters who would end up playing a sort of cat-and-mouse game to the bitter end. I wrote pages on their personalities, appearance, likes and dislikes, education and expressions before I sat down at my computer to draft the first chapter.

This novel, largely thanks to the characters of Kirsten and Amy, has been my favourite book to write. I believe (and my agent and editor both agree with me) that it's my best book so far. I hope you think so, too.

If you enjoyed this book, I'd be very grateful if you'd consider leaving a review. It doesn't need to be long and it will be greatly appreciated. The more reviews a book has, the more visible it becomes, so reviews are vital for an author. They also enable potential readers to decide if they would enjoy that book. And, obviously, positive reviews make authors feel as if the hard work was worth it!

Many thanks,

Diane

xxx

https://www.instagram.com/dianefjeffrey/
https://twitter.com/dianefjeffrey
https://facebook.com/dianejeffreyauthor
https://www.dianejeffrey.com

The Guilty Mother

She says she's innocent.

DO YOU BELIEVE HER?

2013

Melissa Slade had it all: beauty, money, a successful husband and beautiful twin babies. But, in the blink of an eye, her perfect life became a nightmare – when she found herself on trial for the murder of her little girls.

PRESENT DAY

Jonathan Hunt covered the original Slade Babies case for the local newspaper. Now that new evidence has come to light, Jon's boss wants him back on the story to uncover the truth.

With Melissa's appeal date looming, time is running out. And, as Jon gets drawn deeper into a case he'd wanted to forget, he starts to question Melissa's guilt.

Is Melissa manipulating Jon or telling him the truth? Is she a murderer, or the victim of a miscarriage of justice?

And if Melissa Slade is innocent, what really happened to Ellie and Amber Slade?

The Couple at Causeway Cottage

New start. Old secrets.

Kat and Mark move to an island off the Northern Irish coast for a new beginning. Far away from their frantic life in London, it's the perfect place to bring up the family they're longing to start.

But as soon as they arrive, cracks begin to appear in their marriage. Mark is still texting his ex-wife. Kat is lying about a new friendship. And one of them is keeping an explosive secret about the past.

The couple in Causeway Cottage are hiding something – and the truth can be deadly . . .

Those Who Lie

Emily Klein doesn't know she has killed her husband until the day of his funeral.

At first, signs point to a tragic accident. Yet, as Emily pieces together the events leading up to the accident and her own memory loss, she begins to suspect that her husband's death may have been the result of more than a terrible twist of fate . . .

But the accident is only the beginning. Because while Emily's physical scars will heal, the trauma of the accident has awakened old ghosts. She hears strange sounds, catches things that can't possibly be there in the corner of her eye . . . Before long, everywhere she looks, she seems to see her husband.

Emily doesn't know who to believe or who she can turn to. And suddenly, she finds herself asking the most dangerous question of all:

Can she really trust herself?

Read on for an extract of
The Couple at Causeway Cottage

THE
COUPLE
AT
CAUSEWAY
COTTAGE

NEW START.
OLD SECRETS.

DIANE JEFFREY

Chapter 1

It's only when I'm on the ferry, minutes before arriving, that it hits me how isolated I will be. Standing on the deck, using my hand to shield my eyes from the sun, I glimpse the island for the first time. The cliffs, imposing and impressive, even from a distance, then the port, a speck bobbing in and out of view, becoming bigger and more distinct as we approach. Until now, I've only seen images of Rathlin from googling it: a map of a small island shaped like a boomerang or an upside-down sock, pictures of its two churches and its white seafront cottages as well as – and this was the clincher when Mark tried to talk me into moving here – numerous photos of seals and birds.

When I announced I was going to live on a tiny island I'd never been to before, everyone was astonished. I still can't believe it myself. But new home, new start. The decision wasn't as rash as it sounds. As I explained to my friends, my dad was from Northern Ireland, so it feels a bit like going back to my roots. And it's familiar territory for Mark. He grew up eight miles away in Ballycastle, where he recently secured a place for his mother in a nursing home. It was the best thing to do – the only thing to do, but he's riddled with guilt. An only child who has lost his father, Mark is very close to his mum. I can certainly relate to that. It's only natural he should also want to be closer to her geographically, especially as she's so ill.

At the time, it felt like the right decision for me, too. The right move. For several reasons. I mentally tick them off on my fingers as I try to curb the uneasiness swelling inside me. Thumb: I grew up in Devon and I miss the ocean. Index: I was desperate to escape the frantic rhythm of London. Middle finger: I've always wanted to be an outdoor photographer – wildlife or landscapes. Rathlin will provide the perfect playground for me to pursue this goal. Ring finger: with its tight-knit community and tiny primary school, Rathlin Island strikes me as an ideal place to bring up our children when they come along. Little finger: the smallest digit on my hand, but an important consideration nonetheless – both Mark and I needed to get away from his ex-wife.

But enumerating all the advantages of this move does nothing to allay my agitation. I'm out of sync with the calm sea.

'Mark, show me the photos of our house again,' I say.

'You'll see it with your own eyes in a few minutes.' He hands me his mobile, an amused look on his face, clearly mistaking my jitteriness for excitement.

The estate agent showed Mark around the house while he was over three months ago visiting his mother, who has dementia. He took lots of photos and I've swiped through them on his phone so many times I can visualise in detail the place I'll call home from now on. But I had to make do with a virtual visit of the three-bedroom detached cottage we've bought. It doesn't have a garden, but neither of us is green-fingered, and with it being so close to the beach, that didn't bother us.

We'd initially been looking for a house on the mainland, but when Causeway Cottage went up for sale, our plans changed. Mark has always had this romantic notion about living on an island and this was the chance of a lifetime. It was the only suitable place for sale on Rathlin – the others were new builds, social housing – so we had to snap it up quickly. I was terrified we'd be gazumped – a word I didn't even know before Mark made a verbal offer on the house – and delighted when all the paperwork was finally signed and Causeway Cottage was officially ours.

But it feels disconcerting now, moving into a house I've only ever seen in photos. Is it because I don't like the idea of living in a house where someone died? I shudder, then berate myself for being morbid. I'm on my way to a beautiful island, where I'll be living the dream. It's not like I'm being ferried across the River Styx.

I give Mark back his mobile. He smiles at me, his turquoise eyes blazing in the sun. A rictus stretches across my face as I force myself to smile back.

'The finish line's in sight,' Mark says, as we make our way to the car, which is laden to the hilt with our mattress strapped to the roof rack. His Northern Irish accent is already more pronounced, even though he hasn't talked to anyone except me since we left London.

As Mark starts up the car and drives slowly off *The Spirit of Rathlin* and onto the island itself, I sigh with relief. We travelled for nearly fourteen hours yesterday – getting up at six a.m. and driving from London to Liverpool to take the ferry to Belfast, driving north from there as far as the coastal town of Ballycastle, where we stayed overnight at the house my mother-in-law lived in until very recently. Our crossing this morning – from Ballycastle Harbour to Rathlin – was mercifully short. The first boat of the day and the last leg of the journey.

Causeway Cottage is barely a minute's drive from the harbour, halfway up a steep hill. I throw off my seatbelt and leap out of the car before Mark can even turn off the engine. Standing at the front gate, I take it in. Now I'm here, I can finally get a feel for the place. The house is quaint and perfectly symmetrical. Red roses climb up the pure white walls on both sides of the front door and, for a second, I picture the cottage as a child might draw it, like a face, the flowers depicting red lips curling upwards as if the house is smiling at me. Or maybe it's laughing at me. The upstairs windows are eyes, their sills thick lines, pencilled with black kohl. I wonder what they see when they look down at me.

'It needs a bit of work on the façade and on the roof,' Mark says, materialising beside me, 'but other than that, the property's in pretty good shape.' I wonder if he's repeating the estate agent's words. 'So, what do you think?'

'It's beautiful. Like a cottage in a fairy tale.' I turn to look at him, but instead my gaze is drawn to the old, stone building behind him. 'I hadn't realised the cottage was so close to the church.'

'We don't have to go,' he says jokingly. 'Apparently there's no bell-ringing, so we can still have a lie-in on Sundays.'

'I was thinking more of the graveyard.' My imagination fills in what I can't make out, even with my neck craned: tombstones, scattered across the hillside, overlooking the sea and exposed to the elements. Frosty fingers walk down my spine as I wonder if the previous owner of our cottage is buried there.

'The estate agent assured me our new neighbours are only noisy one night a year.'

Mark's jovial mood is infectious. 'Let me guess,' I say, playing along. 'Hallowe'en.'

Mark chuckles. 'You got it.'

I laugh, too.

'That church doesn't actually have a graveyard,' Mark adds. 'The island's only burial ground is at the other one.' As he says that, I remember reading it online.

Mark whisks me up into his arms and carries me up the path to the front door. 'I didn't think this through,' he says, setting me down to fish the key out of his jeans pocket. Then he opens the front door, picks me up again and carries me over the threshold, the two of us giggling like newly-weds.

The first thing I notice is the smell. A stale odour only partially masked by disinfectant and bleach. It's because it has been shut up for a few weeks, I tell myself. I walk through to the living room, past what I know from Mark is a working fireplace, and fling open the windows to let in the sea air.

'Wow,' I breathe. The village sprawls below us and, beyond that, the sea stretches to the horizon.

'The views are even better from upstairs.' Mark grabs my hand and leads me upstairs to the front bedroom – the master bedroom.

A cool breeze wafts in through the window when Mark opens it and I shiver.

'Cold?' Mark asks.

'Not really. I was wondering which room the last owner died in. It wasn't in here, was it?'

'I don't know, Kat. I didn't think to ask.' He combs his fingers through his wavy, salt and pepper hair. 'He was an old man. He died peacefully in his sleep.'

'It probably was in our bedroom, then.'

'Does it matter? I don't think the house is haunted.'

I'm being ridiculous. The house doesn't feel creepy. It's smaller than it looked in the photos, but it's massive compared to the flat we were renting in Hammersmith.

We spend the next half an hour or so walking around the house, upstairs and downstairs, opening cupboards and doors and planning where our furniture will go when it arrives. The removals van won't make it as far as the island – we'll unload everything at my mother-in-law's house, then we'll decide what to keep and bring over on the ferry and what to get rid of or replace.

Mark's mother had a lot of stuff in her house – she's a bit of a hoarder – but Mark cleared out most of it when he was offered a place for her in the care home. She insisted Mark should sell her house, and anything in it that would fetch some money, to cover the fees. The house wouldn't have suited us, not permanently. It's a very small bungalow with no sea views. On top of that, it's on a busy road. So we didn't see ourselves living there. We'd intended to stay there temporarily and take our time finding our dream home. But when Causeway Cottage came onto the market, everything happened more quickly than we'd anticipated and now we're about to become islanders.

Secretly, I was relieved we wouldn't be living in Ballycastle itself. As my mind wanders to the fortnight I spent there the summer I turned fifteen, Mark provides a welcome interruption to a painful memory and snaps me back to the present.

'Shall we do some unpacking?' he says. 'Then we can go for a pub lunch.'

*

McCuaig's Bar is on the seafront. Sitting outside at the wooden picnic table, I tuck into my scampi ravenously, enjoying the squawking of the seagulls. I take a sip of Mark's beer. I'd love a glass of wine, but I've resolved to cut back on drinking. When I stopped taking the pill a few months ago, we hadn't discussed moving to Northern Ireland. I suppose, with the stress and upheaval of the move, it's just as well I didn't get pregnant before now, and there was little chance of it happening with Mark away so often for work. But now would be the perfect time for me to get pregnant and I know too much alcohol could affect my fertility.

I finish my meal and put down my knife and fork. Feeling the sun warm my face, I close my eyes and tip back my head. Then I open them and look around me. At the table next to ours, two tourists are chatting animatedly, their backpacks on the ground by their feet. At another table, a man is sitting by himself, but there's an empty plate and pint glass opposite him. He's wearing a checked shirt with his sleeves rolled up and he's holding a hamburger with paint-stained hands.

Mark drains his beer. 'I think I'll have another one,' he says. 'Sure you don't want a drink?'

'I shouldn't.'

'I don't suppose one will hurt,' Mark says. 'We should be celebrating!'

'Go on, then,' I say, cursing myself for being so weak-willed. 'I'll have a glass of white wine.'

Mark gets up to fetch our drinks from the bar. He clambers over the wooden bench and walks straight into a man carrying a pint of lager in each hand.

'I'm so sorry,' Mark says. 'That was terribly clumsy of me.'

'Don't worry, mate. No harm done.' His voice is deep and sonorous. He's at least six foot two and towers over Mark, even though my husband isn't short.

'I've spilt beer all down your T-shirt.' Mark is clearly mortified.

'It's no big deal. It was dirty anyway. These are work clothes.'

As Mark continues to apologise profusely and insists on replacing the pints, the stranger glances my way briefly, although I don't think he takes me in. When he turns back to Mark, his expression has changed, as if he's struggling not to lose his temper. Perhaps because of Mark's fussing, he's more annoyed now than when Mark collided with him. I watch, mesmerised, as a red flush spreads from his neck to his cheeks and a vein in his forehead bulges. I would find the transformation amusing if it wasn't so dramatic. But he looks as though he might punch Mark if his hands were free. Instead, he clenches his jaw and glares at him.

As Mark scuttles inside, the man makes his way over to his table. Taking his seat opposite the guy in the checked shirt, he looks so calm and collected I wonder if I imagined his change in demeanour. I sneak a glance at him over my shoulder. He has a large, slightly hooked nose. Huge biceps. His fair hair is unkempt and a little too long, framing his suntanned face. If not exactly handsome, he's certainly attractive.

Mark comes back, carrying a tray with four glasses on it. He puts the tray down on our table and takes the pints over to the two men, apologising again.

'His face is familiar,' Mark says when he has sat down. 'I'm sure I know him from somewhere.'

I turn to look at the man again, but he's staring our way and, catching his eye, I whip my head back to face Mark.

'I've never seen him before in my life,' I say. 'Maybe you went to school together.'

'Maybe.' Mark sounds dubitative. 'I think I knew him when I was younger, but I don't think it was at school.'

'It's hard to place people out of context sometimes. Hey, maybe he's a celebrity and you've seen him on TV.'

Mark isn't listening to me. His eyebrows pinch together into a frown. 'I'm pretty sure I didn't like him.'

'What makes you say that?'

Mark shrugs.

'Oh well,' I say brightly, 'with a bit of luck, you won't bump into him again.'

I hadn't intended it as a pun, but Mark laughs wryly. 'If I do, next time I'll make sure not to knock beer down his front.' But then his face clouds over. He leans towards me and lowers his voice. 'I've got this strange feeling about him. Sort of gut instinct. Like he's bad news. I can't quite put my finger on it.'

I remember the thunderous look that came over the man earlier, when I thought he wanted to hit Mark. Perhaps I didn't misread his expression after all.

Acknowledgements

I think I spend nearly as much time writing the acknowledgements as I do writing some of the chapters in my book! I still haven't found a way to make the acknowledgements look less like a list and sound as grateful as I feel.

Writing a novel can sometimes be a solitary experience, but publishing that novel is a team effort and I'm indebted to many people for getting my sixth psychological thriller out into the world. First and foremost, a massive thank you to my brilliant editor, Abigail Fenton, for your insightful feedback and magical powers. I love working with you! I'd also like to thank the fantastic team at HQ, in particular Audrey Linton, Anna Sikorska and Helena Newton. Thank you, Sam Copeland, agent extraordinaire, for your phone calls and pep talks and for championing my books. I think you manage me pretty well! My thanks, also, to the hardworking team at RCW, particularly Honor Spreckley and Tristan Kendrick.

As always, I'm immensely grateful to my parents, Caroline and Ken Maud, for your invaluable feedback, support and enthusiasm. Thank you, too, to my aunts, uncles and cousins in England, Northern Ireland and Australia for reading my books and for your praise and encouragement.

Above all, I'd like to thank my husband, Florent, and our amazing children – Benjamin, Amélie and Elise – for putting up with me and believing in me. Amélie, thank you for your beautiful drawing of the ocean wave for the section break (I believe this is called a 'dinkus', a word I absolutely love!). Elise, thank you for going running with me and for letting me run my 'novel' ideas by you while we jog! Anyone who knows me knows that my family is my world.

Heartfelt thanks to my writing buddy, Louise Mangos, author of *The Beaten Track*, for your friendship, help and advice at every stage of the writing process.

One of the pieces of advice often dished out to writers is to write about what you know. It's not advice that I heed as I fear that otherwise my books would be very boring! I often write about things I know little or nothing about. Fortunately, I have friends whose knowledge can help fill the gaps in mine. Thank you to Neil Lancaster, author of the DS Max Craigie series, for helping me out with police procedure; thank you to Imran Mahmood, author of *All I Said Was True*, and Lia Middleton, author of *Your Word or Mine*, for patiently answering my questions about legal proceedings, wigs, gowns and so on; thank you to my former swimming and surf life-saving teammate in North Devon, Keith Gammon, for clueing me in with vital information about the local area. Everything has changed since I left home.

Any mistakes are mine.

A big thank you to Barbara Enticknap for supporting the charity Young Lives vs Cancer by bidding to have the name of your nephew, David Jacob, in this novel. Your donation was incredibly generous and I hope you like the character I have chosen for you!

Heartfelt thanks to two lovely ladies whose support for my books has been overwhelming: Monica Carter-Burns, whom I know through West Buckland School and who has advertised my novels in numerous editions of *The Buckland Brief*, and Mary O'Driscoll, who allowed me to host a book launch for my last book at the Manor House on Rathlin Island and ended up buying most of the books herself! I'm very grateful to both of you.

Finally, many thanks to everyone who has bought / borrowed / blogged about / read / recommended / reviewed / raved about my books. I'm astounded that I have readers as far afield as Sri Lanka and New Zealand!

HUGE thanks to YOU for reading this book. I hope you enjoyed it and if you did, perhaps you would consider leaving an online review, choosing it for your book club or recommending it to a friend.

THANK YOU!

xxx

Dear Reader,

We hope you enjoyed reading this book. If you did, we'd be so appreciative if you left a review. It really helps us and the author to bring more books like this to you.

Here at HQ Digital we are dedicated to publishing fiction that will keep you turning the pages into the early hours. Don't want to miss a thing? To find out more about our books, promotions, discover exclusive content and enter competitions you can keep in touch in the following ways:

JOIN OUR COMMUNITY:

Sign up to our new email newsletter:
http://smarturl.it/SignUpHQ

Read our new blog www.hqstories.co.uk

🐦 https://twitter.com/HQStories

f www.facebook.com/HQStories

BUDDING WRITER?

We're also looking for authors to join the HQ Digital family!
Find out more here:

https://www.hqstories.co.uk/want-to-write-for-us/

Thanks for reading, from the HQ Digital team

ONE PLACE. MANY STORIES